BEYOND WHAT IS GIVEN

BEYOND WHAT IS GIVEN

REBECCA

#1 *NEW YORK TIMES* BESTSELLING AUTHOR

YARROS

Copyright © 2015 by Rebecca Yarros. All rights reserved, including the
right to reproduce, distribute, or transmit in any form or by any means. For
information regarding subsidiary rights, please contact the Publisher.

Entangled Publishing, LLC
644 Shrewsbury Commons Ave., STE 181
Shrewsbury, PA 17361
rights@entangledpublishing.com

Amara is an imprint of Entangled Publishing, LLC.

Visit our website at www.entangledpublishing.com.

Edited by Karen Grove
Cover design by Bree Archer
Cover images by vvvita/Getty Images
Interior design by Toni Kerr

ISBN 978-1-64937-568-1
Ebook ISBN 978-1-63375-392-1

Manufactured in the United States of America

First Edition December 2023

10 9 8 7 6 5 4 3 2

To Brody, my wild one.
You are the icing on my cupcake and my quiet
snuffle at the end of the day.
Our most precious treasure from Fort Rucker isn't
a pair of silver aviation wings,
it's you—our little gray-eyed wonder.

At Entangled, we want our readers to be well-informed. If you would like to know if this book contains any elements that might be of concern for you, please check the back of the book for details.

CHAPTER ONE

Sam

What exactly was the protocol for leaving tampons in a guy's bathroom? A guy's freakishly neat bathroom, at that? Well, it was half mine now, so the pristine state wasn't going to last for long.

I opened and shut the cabinet door a few times, but the pink box stuck out like...well, a bright freaking pink box. Maybe I should have gotten a different box to put them in? *Are you seriously debating tampon placement?* I let the door stay shut and backed away from the cabinet slowly, like I'd planted evidence or something.

My makeup bag rested on the left side of the sink, but my lotions and army of haircare products I'd need to tame my unruly curls in the southern humidity consumed more than my allotted counter space and one of the newly emptied drawers. Yeah, it practically screamed *girl* in here.

Screw it, I lived here now, too, and so did my tampons...for all of twelve hours. I walked down the hall to my room, careful to tiptoe past my new roommate's door, and made it through mine, directly across from it. Just because I was up at six forty-five a.m. didn't mean he needed to be, and a rude wake-up wasn't the first impression I wanted to make.

"Time to get up!" Ember sang before she swung into my room, one hand behind her back. Best friend or not, she looked way too happy for this early, glowing from the Alabama sun and things I didn't want to know about with her boyfriend, Josh. The boyfriend I now quasi-lived with, along with his best friend, Jagger, and the other guy, whose name I could never remember. Three boys. One girl. Well, there were awkward situations and there was *me*. Ember glanced around at the half-unpacked boxes. "Whoa. Did you sleep at all?"

"A few hours." *Barely at all.* "You're going to wake those guys if you're not quiet."

"Please. Grayson got home sometime last night and all three of them went running a half hour ago. Why do you think I'm already so perky?" Her smile gave far more information than I wanted.

Grayson. That's right. "They left already? They must be part ninja, because I didn't hear a thing. And as for you two, ugh. I swear. Ridiculous." *And enviable.*

She laughed in response and handed me the bag she'd kept behind her back. "Welcome to Alabama!"

"You live in Tennessee."

"Hey, as a part-time Alabamian…or whatever, I'm allowed to say welcome. Now take your present." She shook the silver gift bag.

I took it, tossing the crimson tissue paper onto a discarded pile of boxes, then holding up the maroon V-neck tee that spelled out TROY across the chest. A smile erupted on my face. "It's perfect, and I love it!" It had been so long since I'd felt happy that I almost didn't recognize the emotion.

"New start. New school. New shirt." She grinned and pulled me into a hug. "I know you don't start summer classes for another few weeks, but it seemed like a good day to give that to you."

I gave her a squeeze before I let go. "Thank you. Seriously. If it wasn't for you telling me to apply to Troy, or for Jagger offering to let me live here, or Josh helping me pack all that furniture…"

"That's what we're here for. Oh! I almost forgot." She pulled a piece of paper from her pajama pants pocket. "Wi-Fi password. I know you have a Skype date with your mom. You ready for coffee?"

"Hell, yes. Is that even a question?"

"Never," she answered, already headed down the hallway.

The apple reflected in my dresser mirror as I fired up my laptop. I connected to the Wi-Fi. "Flyboys. Of course," I muttered with a laugh, and signed into Skype three minutes early.

She was already on.

The computer rang and I answered, Mom's face coming into focus a few seconds later. She looked tired as she unzipped her multicam top and hung it over the back of her chair, leaving her in a tan T-shirt.

"Samantha, baby. How are you?" she asked with a wan smile. Her walls in Afghanistan were bare except for a framed picture of my high-school graduation.

"I'm good." I propped my laptop against the dresser. "Halfway unpacked. How are you?"

"Long day here, but holding up just— What on earth are you wearing?"

I glanced down and back up at her. "Um…pajamas?" I had outfits that made these boxers and tank top look downright prudish.

"You cannot wear pajamas like that now that you live with men. Go buy some proper pajamas."

"Or I could skip right to a bundling bag or a chastity belt, Mom."

She gave me the *look*. "Don't get smart. I'm only suggesting that you show a little less skin and a little more common sense."

"Yes, ma'am," I answered in song.

"Samantha."

I sighed. "I'll go today, Mom, but your whole theory is hugely antiquated."

"Just make me feel better, okay? I'm already not too keen on the boy roommates, or you shipping off to the middle of nowhere Alabama to go to college."

"Well, this college said yes, unlike the other twenty I've applied to." My fingers stroked across the silver lettering on my new shirt.

"And whose fault is that?" she barked.

My eyes snapped to hers. "You don't think I know? I'm doing everything I can to make up for what happened. I got into a *real* college like you demanded, I'm on my own, and I'm looking for a job today. I can't go back and change last year." *I would if I could.* Regret was a nauseating constant in my life. "If I pull good grades, I might have a chance of getting back into Colorado for spring term." *If I can face them.*

Her hands covered her face as she sighed. "I'm sorry. I hate you going through this when I'm not there."

"I don't need you to save me, Mom. I only need you to cut me a little slack." An inch would be nice. Just once.

"Maybe I gave you too much slack to start with." A knock sounded at her door. "Come in," she answered, immediately straightening in her chair. I'd learned a long time ago that she was really two women, my mom and—

"Colonel Fitzgerald?" A nondescript head popped through her door.

Yup, *her*, Colonel Fitzgerald, my mother's alter-ego.

"Captain, I'm talking to my daughter, can this wait?" Her tone implied so.

"No, ma'am, I'm sorry, but it can't."

"Then I'll be right there."

My shoulders dropped a little bit.

She turned back to me with her I'm-sorry-Sam smile. "Samantha, I'm—"

"Sorry," I completed with a forced smile. "I know, Mom. Duty calls. Same time tomorrow? Maybe you want to chat about my class options?"

"That should work, baby. I'm so proud of you for pulling yourself back up. I have to go."

"Bye." I waved and clicked the little red button that ended our conversation. She drove me nuts, but it had always been just the two of us. She'd put herself through hell raising me while climbing ranks in the military, always looking up to Marcelite Harris, the first Black woman Major General. I had the distinct feeling she'd top her as the first Lieutenant General.

As long as I didn't stand in her way.

My email *dinged*, updating from the last twenty-four hours I'd been offline. I passed over sale alerts and a couple personal items before I saw one with How Was Your Move as the subject line from Apoole@gmail.com. I clicked in curiosity and gasped.

IT DOESN'T MATTER WHAT STATE YOU MOVE TO. YOU'RE STILL A WHORE.

I deleted the email and slammed the screen to close the laptop, my pulse leaping. How far did I have to go to get away? You'd think after the last nineteen times this happened, I'd stop opening unknown emails. I'd even created a new email address, but then they started showing up in that one, too.

I brushed it off, or at least tried to. New day. New start. New School. Like Ember said. Would she feel the same way if she'd known what I'd done? I hadn't even told my mother, just glazed it all over as bad grades and moved on. Some things were too ugly to let out into the light.

The hardwood floor was cool beneath my feet as I headed down the stairs to the kitchen. The morning looked nice and cool through the sliding glass door, but I'd already learned that there wasn't much cool about southern Alabama in May. It was already hot, and about to get hotter.

There was no sign of coffee, or Ember, but there was a note: *Looks like the guys are out of coffee, go figure. I'll grab some and come right back. I hope you had a good convo with your mom.*

As if on cue, my head started to pound, like it knew I'd denied it the caffeine it was sorely addicted to. I rubbed my temples and opened the cabinets slowly, taking stock of where everything was.

It was as neat as my bathroom had been before I moved in, everything in precise, spotless order. I couldn't remember Josh or Jagger ever being this clean. I opened the second top cabinet after the sink and glimpsed the coffee cups, and two shelves higher, a box of K-cups.

"Sweet salvation," I muttered, reaching on tiptoes but barely grazing the bottom of the shelf. Crap. I couldn't reach it. I dragged a chair across the tile and braced the back against the cabinets. Why the hell did they go all the way to the ceiling? Who were they expecting to put away the dishes? LeBron James?

Okay, this wasn't too high. I could do this. One knee at a time, I kneeled up onto the granite and reached with my fingers but still couldn't touch the coffee. I moved the drainer, where a few cups were drying, and gingerly stood up on the counter, grasping the center support of the cabinets so hard that the edges of the wood left imprints on my skin.

Keeping my death grip on the cabinet with one hand, I reached with the other until I had hold of the box. "Got it!" *Ha! Take that, LeBron.*

"What the hell do you think you're doing?"

I jumped, but maintained my balance. *Good girl.* "Reaching for the coffee, what does it look like?" He stood to the side of me, dripping sweat, his massive, bare arms crossed over his even bigger chest. Holy shit. What did this guy do? Bench cows before breakfast and then eat them? By the time my eyes dragged themselves up the cut lines of his shiny muscles to his face, I was lightheaded. Breathing might have helped.

His jaw was cut and as strong as the rest of him, and those lips…well, if they weren't pursed together like he'd tasted something sour, I'm sure I would have been just as enthralled. His nose was as straight as the stick up his ass, but it was his eyes... They were narrowed in suspicion, and the slate gray color cut straight through me. I'd never seen eyes that color before, that hypnotizing, or that serious.

He waved his hand in front of his face and shook his head. Crap. He'd been talking while I was ogling. "I'm going to crush his skull, I swear. Look, I don't know who you are, but I know you don't belong here."

"What?" I stepped back toward the dish drainer.

"Which one is it? Because they *both* have girlfriends. Great girls who don't deserve the shit storm you just dumped on them, so *which one is it?*"

The veins in his huge neck stood out.

"I have no clue what you're talking about." He was hot, but maybe a touch unstable?

"Jagger or Josh? Which one brought you home with them?"

My eyebrows puckered. "Both, I guess?" Something was way off.

"You're sleeping with both of them?" His voice echoed off the tile and ricocheted through my heart.

My head snapped back like he'd struck me. "What the hell gave you that idea?" I hugged the coffee to my chest in case the word *whore* had been tattooed across my boobs or something.

"You're barely dressed in my kitchen at seven in the morning." *My kitchen*, the eyes...this had to be Grayson. Holy hell, couldn't Josh have any ugly friends? My skin tingled where his eyes raked over my flesh, but he squeezed his eyes shut and took a deep breath. "You could at least put on some clothes. People live here."

Blood heated my face. Thank God my complexion didn't show the blush easily. "Yeah. People like me!" My chest tightened.

"What—"

"Why do you jump to the conclusion that I'm sleeping with them? Because I'm a girl in your kitchen on a Sunday morning? Let me tell you something, I don't care how hot you think you are—" I shook my finger and let go of the cabinet in the process, taking another step away from him. "You don't get to make assumptions about me!"

"Hey, Grayson—" Jagger called out, and I turned to look as he walked into the kitchen.

I squawked as my foot slipped in a puddle of water and I pitched forward. My knee slammed into the granite, and my balance shifted over the side of the counter...and into Grayson. He caught me without complaint, rolling me into his chest with one arm tucked securely under my knees and the other behind my back. We locked eyes, and something in me shifted from hot and angry to hot and...not so angry. *No. Don't you dare.*

He arched one dark, perfect eyebrow.

"What?" I fired out of self-preservation. "I'm not going to say thank you, if that's what you're waiting for. Not when you all but called me a whore."

"I did not use that word!" His mouth dropped open. Yep. I was right. Those lips were full, soft, and way too close to mine.

Jagger laughed. "Well, I'm glad you two are getting acquainted."

"What are you talking about?" Grayson fired back, his voice vibrating through my body.

"He'd like to know what the hell I'm doing in your house and which one of you I'm sleeping with," I growled.

Jagger bit into an apple and swallowed, then let out an impossibly impish grin. "Sleeping with? Holy shit. No. Grayson, meet Sam, our new roommate."

Thank God my feet were ready, because Grayson all but dropped me.

"Sam is a guy," he said slowly.

"I most certainly am not." He steadied me, his hands on my hips, and then nearly ran behind the breakfast table like he needed to fend me off with a chair. What. The. Hell.

"Obviously," he replied, those silver eyes huge like I'd scared him.

"Why are you so surprised?" I blew an errant curl out of my eyes. *Oh God.* What if he didn't want me here? Would Jagger let me stay?

"You never said Sam was a girl," he accused Jagger.

Jagger chewed another bite. "Dude, Sam has always been a girl. You said you were cool with this."

Grayson flipped out his phone and flicked through screens. "No. Let me read these. *'Hey man, is it cool if our friend Sam takes the other bedroom? We're old friends from Colorado, and Josh is cool with it.'*"

I took my prized K-cups to the machine. If I was putting up with this bullshit, I was sure as hell going to need coffee. "Yep, I'm Sam, short for *Samantha*, a.k.a. the friend from Colorado."

"And you're a girl."

I tilted my head and smirked. "Apparently."

"You're not sleeping with either of them."

"Nope."

"And I just…" He squeezed those amazing eyes shut and took a breath before opening them again. "Samantha, I'm incredibly sorry for what I implied."

Oh, look, he can apolo—

"But if you could put some clothes on, that'd be great."

So much for him removing the stick from his ass. He nodded his head, pursed those beautiful lips, and retreated toward the front door, muttering something about the gym.

"What the hell is his deal?"

Jagger's grin was a step past shit-eating to downright comical. "No clue, but that's the most worked up I've ever seen the guy, and I've lived with him for almost a year. Way to go, Sam."

"That's not a compliment." I spooned sugar into my steaming cup of coffee. "I really need to pick up honey, and please tell me you have creamer."

"Ember lives here every other weekend," he replied, moving past me to the fridge, then handed me a bottle of Amaretto creamer.

"Thank God for little things."

"Sweet and blonde," he commented with a wink. "Just like I like my women. Oh, a letter came for you yesterday. I left it on the entry table. Make yourself at home, and welcome to Alabama, Sam."

He patted me on the back and left me sipping my coffee as I headed toward the front door. Sure enough, a letter addressed to Samantha Fitzgerald from Troy University sat on the polished wood.

I balanced my cup as I opened the letter, hissing as the skin of my thumb split. I popped it into my mouth and set my coffee down, opening the letter with my empty hand. The sweetest pressure settled in my chest as I unfolded it. This was my fresh start. This was my hope.

"Dear Ms. Fitzgerald," I started to read along. Then stopped. *No. No. No.*

How? They'd admitted me. They'd promised me a clean slate, that my grades from last semester wouldn't matter. They would start me on academic probation and then let up when I did well this first semester.

"Sam?" Ember asked, balancing two cups of coffee as she stood in front of me. I hadn't even registered her coming in. "Are you okay?"

Failure stung like a bitch. Oh wait, that was my thumb. "Shit." I squeezed the skin, opening the paper cut, and almost laughed when I saw it wasn't bleeding. Anything that hurt that badly should at least give you something to show for it.

Kind of like the last two and a half years I'd wasted in college.

My voice didn't shake, or hold any tone. It was as numb as I was. "Upon further review of your transcript, we regret to inform you that we cannot accept you into Troy University."

It doesn't matter what state you move to. You're still a whore.

CHAPTER TWO

Sam

"Sam? Let me in." Ember knocked for the hundredth time.

"Go away," I answered, my head tucked between my knees as I leaned back against my bed. *Breathe in. Breathe out. This will pass. It has to.*

"That's so not going to happen," she called through my bedroom door. "Let me in."

Let her in? To what? The absolute mess I'd made of my life? Another school rejection. Another chance...lost. God, what if it was my *last* chance? What if this was it? No college was going to accept me, not when my records came with that giant black mark. Every carefully constructed plan, dream...gone. Again.

And maybe I deserved it for what I'd done.

My stomach rolled and saliva pooled in my mouth.

I bolted to my feet and threw open the door, tripping past Ember as I raced to the bathroom. The bath mat cushioned my knees as I fell and curled over the toilet in time to bring up what little coffee I'd managed to drink.

Ember pulled a curl from my face as I dry-heaved, the pain nothing compared to the shredding my heart was taking.

"Here," she whispered, handing me a cup of water as I flushed the toilet.

I swished and spit, keeping my eyes on the cup.

"Is this why you've lost weight?" she asked as we sat on the bathroom floor, leaned back against the tub.

"I haven't—" She cut me off with a glare. "It's been hard lately," I finished.

"You've been my closest friend since we were thirteen, Sam. I want to help." She reached for my hand and squeezed my fingers.

The irony was almost funny. I hadn't even told my best friend, and here she was, desperately trying to help me. But if she knew? No. Ember would never understand. She planned out every minute detail of her life and controlled every situation she found herself in. Ember was a fixer.

I was a wrecker, in more ways than one.

I slid another brick into the wall I'd been building between us and forced a smile. "Nothing you can do, Ember, really. I have to figure this out for myself."

"What are you going to do? Do you want to come back to Nashville? You can stay with me until your mom comes home."

Fuck my life, what was I going to tell Mom? My stomach turned over, and I breathed through the need to heave, reminding my body that it had just done that, thank you very much.

She'd lecture. She'd judge. She'd be disappointed. And if she really knew? She'd say, "I told you so." And she'd be right.

To hell with that.

"No. I'm staying," I said with more conviction than I felt. "I'm staying right here." *Are you convincing Ember or yourself?*

"Okay?" She tilted her head to the side.

"I'll get a job, work through the summer, and keep applying to schools." *And keep opening rejection letters.*

"Okay."

"There's a ton of places I can apply to for a job down here, and maybe with a solid work reference, I'll have a better chance at getting back into a good school." The more I spoke, the faster my words came, like my brain was vomiting because my stomach couldn't.

"Okay." She nodded her head slowly.

"Right. That sounds like a plan. Work. Apply to schools. Get in. Get my life back."

"Okay…"

"Will you stop saying *okay*?" I snapped. "It's not okay. It's shit, but it's the best I can do, and it's not like I didn't do this to myself, right?" Staying here? Was I nuts? *You will not go back to Mom with your tail between your legs.*

Ember sighed. "People flun—" Her eyes widened. "Shit. I mean, people leave college all the time. It's not the end of the world."

I rolled my eyes. "Flunk. You can say it. I flunked out of college. Flunk-a-fucking-roo, there went two and a half years of my life down the toilet." My head fell back, knocking the glass of the sliding shower door.

Silence stretched between us, more uncomfortable than the tile floor currently making my ass numb.

"You can talk to me about it, Sam. Holding it in isn't doing you any good."

The last tether holding me to my civility, my reason, snapped. "No, I can't. Because you weren't *there.* You left. You were my best friend, and you got into Boulder for Riley, and you left. And that was okay, because I was happy for you, and I wanted to stay in the Springs. But then you quit returning calls, and I know it wasn't on purpose, you got…busy. You can't tell me you didn't feel that distance."

She looked down at her hands. "I'm so sorry. I got caught up in Boulder. I didn't mean for us to grow apart. It just happened."

"I know. It happens to a lot of high-school friends, I just never thought it would happen to us. And then your dad died…" My words failed.

"And you took me in and put me back together, no questions asked."

I shook my head. "That wasn't what I meant...no. You are my best friend, and the closest thing I have to a sister. Hell, you were my sister that year I lived with you during Mom's last deployment. Of course I was there for you when your world fell apart. I wasn't going to let you go through that alone. When you're around, we skip over what we've missed, and go back to being us, but you left again. You got into Vanderbilt, and I'm so proud of you, but you weren't *there*, you didn't see..." I took a deep breath. "Things happened. I did bad things." My throat closed. "I made stupid choices, and this is all on me."

"Do you want to talk about it?" She extended the olive branch.

"I'd rather shower." I flashed the fake smile and burned her tree to the ground. "After all, a girl's got to look her best to nail a job, right?"

Her gaze dropped to the floor as she stood. "Absolutely. I'll jump online and see who's looking."

Ember, the fixer. "No, girl. You never get to see Josh. Go spend time with him. I'll be out in a little while."

"You sure?"

"Absolutely."

She squeezed my hand and left me to my shower. I held in the tears until I stood naked under the scalding hot spray. Then I let them loose, sobs racking my body as the water all but burned my skin.

It didn't matter how long I scrubbed, I couldn't get clean enough to get him off me or out of my life.

I gave myself those moments and let it all in, absorbing the shittiness of the situation and making peace with what I'd lost. "The only constant is change." That's what Mom always said, usually followed by, "Now embrace the suck. There's work to do."

But maybe the work could start tomorrow, because all I wanted to do today was forget.

CHAPTER THREE

GRAYSON

Sam was a girl. *Samantha.*

Check that. Not a girl—a woman, and damn it, not only was she beautiful, but I *noticed.* Not noticed like Paisley or Ember, but in the way where my body woke up and paid attention.

She'd climbed up onto the counter, her incredible ass nearly peeking out of those tiny pajama shorts, all curves and warm gold-brown skin. The door slid home behind me as I got out of the shower.

My hands gripped the counter and I took a good, long look in the mirror. "Get a grip. She's your roommate." *Don't lie. She's a woman. A woman you're attracted to.*

It wasn't the first time I'd been attracted to another girl who wasn't Grace, but it was the first time I'd had to physically restrain myself from doing something about it. *Avoid her.* I could do that. Hell, I'd made it to lunchtime without seeing her, so this couldn't be too hard.

Then I looked down.

Boom. I'd gone back to living with four sisters. Sam's rainbow of girl stuff took over half my sink. Shit. *Our* sink. Okay, maybe *avoid* wasn't really going to work as a strategy. But I wasn't fifteen, and hell, I'd been with Grace then anyway. It wasn't like I actually liked this girl, I could get over an annoying chemical attraction.

I'd have to treat her like she was one of my sisters. Yeah. A sister. I could do that. But none of my sisters looked like *that*.

The door swung open. "Oh, I'm sorry!" she squeaked, her arms full of bottles. How much more bathroom stuff did she have? Her eyes sparked, impossibly green, wait, hazel, nope, definitely green, as she skimmed over my body, and given the way her lips parted, she liked what she saw.

My jaw clenched as I ripped my eyes off the line where her short bathrobe met her thighs. This towel was about to— *Sister. Think sister.* "Knocking is something we should probably make a habit of."

She blinked rapidly, her eyes rimmed red—*why hadn't I noticed that before?*—and backed out of the bathroom. "You're right. So right." She shut the door behind her, and I heard a thud in the general area her head would have been.

Damn. I hoped I wasn't the one to put the tears in her eyes. We were off to a fan-fucking-tastic start.

I didn't need to shave on a Sunday, so I could get dressed and get out of here...except that I hadn't brought a change of clothes in with me. I let out a huge breath and counted the ceiling tiles until my body was under control. Looked like Samantha wasn't the only one who needed to adjust.

The hallway was mercifully empty, and I made it to my room without seeing her, or having to justify that I was now the one who needed to put clothes on.

Clothes, Powerade, and a ham sandwich later, I settled in at the kitchen table with my Apache Helicopter 5&9 flashcards, mentally quizzing myself over fuel pressure limitations.

"You know we don't even start the Apache course until next month, right?" Jagger asked, reaching for a drink from the fridge.

"I heard there's a test on the first day, and if you fail, you're out." I flipped the next card over.

"I'll say again—a month."

"Yeah, well, not all of us have a photographic memory to depend on. Some of us actually have to work for it."

He slapped his hand across his chest. "You wound me. Besides, last time I checked, you were the one who graduated top of our class during Primary."

"I wasn't distracted by a girl." *Shit.* I closed my eyes and tried to rewind time thirty seconds. My foot lived in my damn mouth today. The problem with always being honest was it bordered on insulting. I was working on it. I counted to three and looked up to see him waiting with a smirk. "Not that Paisley isn't worth it."

He laughed. "I'd have failed flight school if it meant keeping Paisley. Come to think about it, you'd better study your ass off. I'm taking you down." He drew out the last word like a movie villain.

I flipped another card. "Challenge accepted." I'd take him down in the air. Jagger might beat me academically, but I could outfly a fucking bird. It was a good thing my instincts and reflexes were rock solid, because I had to fight tooth and nail to keep academics up, which was fine with me. Things that came easy were seldom worth it.

Besides, if the army found out why it was so hard for me... well, they wouldn't let me so much as finger the throttle on an Apache.

The cards flipped by along with the minute hand, then the hour hand. The door opened and shut a few times, but I kept my eyes locked on the cards until the house was empty and my cell phone rang out with Pat Greene. My scheduled four-hour study session was over.

I silenced the alarm, closed up the cards, and slipped them back into the little box I kept in the cabinet above the coffee mugs. My eyes trailed upward to the extra boxes of coffee, and my chest tightened in a heartbeat of panic, envisioning Samantha slipping on the counter. I quickly switched my study box with the coffee, bringing it to her level. Another adjustment.

My phone rang. I checked the caller ID, and my stomach dropped.

"Miranda?" I answered.

"Hey, Gray." Her soft Outer Banks drawl pulled me into North Carolina like she'd physically tugged.

"Everything okay?"

"Absolutely. I wanted to call you with the baby news. We're having a girl!"

"That's great, Miranda. Your family must be thrilled." Grace would be over the moon for a niece.

"Everyone is pretty excited. Are you going to stop in when you're home for your birthday?"

I opened my mouth but wouldn't lie, and didn't have the heart to tell her the truth. An awkward silence fell between us.

"Gray, we still think of you as family."

I tried to swallow past the knot in my throat. "I know. Same here." I also knew I didn't deserve it.

"We're hoping to bank her cord blood, for the stem cells."

I scrubbed the surface of the counter, taking out a stain like I could do the same with the last five years. "Yeah, I've heard that's a thing now."

Call waiting *beeped*, and my shoulders softened. "Hey, Miranda, that's Mom. I have to go. Congrats on the girl, and I'll catch you later, okay?"

"I'll give Grace your best."

"Tell her I'll see her soon." Two weeks.

I clicked over, hitting "speaker," and rested the phone on the counter as I took ingredients out for dinner.

"Well, I thought you might stand me up," Mom answered, her accent drawing out the final word.

"I'm three minutes late, Mom. That's hardly being stood up. Besides, when have I ever stood you up to cook Sunday dinner?"

"Never. That's why you're my favorite son."

That almost made me smile. "I'm your only son."

"Well, that secures your position in my heart."

"Is that Gray?" Mia asked in the background.

"It is," Mom answered.

"Hey, Mia," I said as I started to trim the chicken.

"Dustin Marley asked me to prom!" she squeaked.

"Dustin Marley is like five years old, and so are you, for that matter," I answered, wondering if I'd need to bury the body of a teenage boy in a couple weeks when I went home. Eighteen-year-old girls shouldn't be going to prom. Ever.

"Oh, whatever. I'm off to go dress shopping with Parker. I miss you, Gray!"

"Tell Parker nothing above the knee," I replied. "She may be twenty-one, but you're not."

Mom burst into laughter. "He's right. Your sister has horrid taste, Mia. Text me a picture before you so much as think of buying a dress."

"Yes, Mama," she sang as her voice faded.

"She's eighteen." I sighed, filleting the chicken.

"Tell me about it. Your father's been fending the boys off for years, and you know she's his baby. He's been polishing the shotgun since she told him. I'm mixing bread crumbs, where are you at?"

"Finishing the last fillet. I didn't get them thin enough last time."

"Take your time, no one likes dry chicken. I was thinking maybe we'd try coq au vin next week?"

I washed my hands, thinking over the dish. "That takes a little longer, but I think it's doable. Or maybe we could make brownies?"

"You're not getting that recipe out of me, Grayson Masters."

"It was worth the try." Those brownies were epic.

"Keep trying. Maybe when you're in for your birthday we could make them for a party—"

"No," I snapped, and she sucked in her breath. *Shit.* "I'm sorry, Mom, but you know how I feel about that."

Oil sizzled in the background. She'd started browning her breaded fillets. I turned up the heat on the stove, not far behind.

"I know, Grayson. I just thought it's been five years, maybe something had changed."

"It hasn't," I answered, careful to keep my tone soft.

The sounds of frying chicken popped between us. "Well, in that case, I'll fill you in on the gossip."

She launched into the latest news, or what she qualified as news. In Nags Head, North Carolina, everything in the off-season counted as news, but it was slimmer pickings once the tourists arrived. I listened, rapt, 814 miles away while she worked in a kitchen that would fit in half of this one but served just as many people.

"How are things down South?"

I placed the browned fillets in the baking dish and spooned marinara over them, finishing up dinner while I filled Mom in on the random duties I was assigned to right now, but was careful to leave out anything flight-school related.

"Did you hear that Miranda is having a girl?" she asked.

My hand froze momentarily. "She called."

"Tess sure has her heart set on those stem cells."

"She's Grace's mom, of course she's going to hope. I also know there's not one clinical trial that she'll qualify for."

I pictured the soft narrowing of her eyes, knowing that she'd pushed me into territory she couldn't follow. She changed subjects. "So when will we get you for more than a weekend?"

"I think over the Fourth of July, but don't hold me to it." *Do not mention my birthday.*

"You should bring a couple of your friends home with you," she suggested as I covered the dish.

"I'll think about it." And I would. For about thirty seconds.

"Walker!" Jagger yelled, flinging the front door open with a phone to his ear.

"He's not here," I answered. "Hey, Mom, I have to go." Hot air from the oven blasted my face as I slid the baking dish in and set the timer for an hour. "Same time next week?"

"Coq au vin," she answered, and an ache hit my chest when I pictured her smile.

"It's a date."

"Fuck!" Jagger answered, hanging up his phone after I did the same. Good thing—Mom wouldn't let him in the front door with that mouth. "Were you talking to him?"

"No, my mom."

He raised his eyebrows. "Huh. I figured you hatched out of a rock or something."

"Very funny." It wasn't his fault. I let them in as far as they needed for their sakes, not mine, and no further. "What do you need Walker for?"

"He's not answering his phone." He tried one more time, nodding his head absentmindedly to the beat of Josh's ringback. "Still not there. Can you drive a stick shift?"

I arched an eyebrow. "What do you think?"

"Yeah, well, I need you to drive Sam's car home." He glanced over my shoulder at the timer on the oven. "We have more than enough time before your precious cuisine burns."

"Where is Sam's car, and why can't she drive it?"

He sighed. "Oscars." He named the local flight-school bar. "And she passed driving standard two hours ago."

CHAPTER FOUR

SAM

I felt alive. And drunk.

Whatever, it was awesome, and a hell of a lot better than crying into my pillow over stuff I couldn't change. No matter what I did, my life was now defined by one stupid mistake.

A mistake that had felt like the first rational decision I'd ever made—and burned me worse than half the stupid shit I'd ever pulled.

"Can I buy you a shot?" a half-attractive guy asked, coming into my field of blurred vision and checking out my girls. There was a way hotter guy behind him, but he wasn't looking my way, and truthfully, I wasn't interested in anything but drinking.

"Yes!" I gave him my hundred-mega-watt grin, pushing every dark thought far enough back that I could drown it with alcohol. "Tequila?"

The bartender lifted her eyebrow at me, and I mirrored the expression. *What?* Ember had left for Nashville a couple hours ago after not even having a single drink with me, and I didn't need another babysitter. The bartender shook her head and slid the shot across the bar with salt and lime. I slammed it back, savoring the burn and anticipating the numb that would quickly follow.

I was so sick of feeling. Hoping. Trying.

"So what's your story? You a local? Because I haven't seen

anything nearly as hot as you are around here."

I took in his crew cut, arrogant grin, and West Point ring on his left hand. "Nope, Lieutenant, I'm a transplant, and entirely out of your league. But thank you for the shot." Crap. I think that came out more slurred than intended.

"Is there anyone we can call for you?" the hot one asked, tearing his eyes off the football game playing on the big screen.

"Do I look like a baby who needs a sitter?" I spat back, my head feeling blissfully detached from my body.

"Hell no," the mediocre one answered. "Not with those curves."

The hot one glared at the mediocre one. "You look like you might need a ride home."

"Well, I don't. Thank you." Home. Like I even had one of those. No, just a collection of different houses Mom moved us to at duty stations. But I did have Jagger's house. Shit. Did I bring my house key? I hadn't attached it to my key ring. Jagger was going to be pissed if I lost it on the first day.

"Bateman?" Hot one asked. Shit, I'd spoken aloud.

"You know him?"

A strange smile flirted across his face. "You could definitely say that." He nodded to the bartender and then stepped outside.

Another shot and a cut-off warning later, the jukebox cranked, and "Pour Some Sugar on Me" raced through my veins. Dancing. Yes, dancing would be awesome. My fingers dug into the bar as I hoisted myself onto the barstool.

"Holy shit." The guy muttered. I was past caring that my miniskirt probably didn't cover my ass at this angle. "Need a hand?" He reached up and helped me step onto the bar.

The bartender rolled her eyes, and I almost missed the nod she exchanged with the hot one as he walked back in, but it was there. Whatever.

I moved my body to the beat, letting it rule my movements and leaving everything else behind for a song, then two. My top drifted above my waistline as I raised my arms.

"Okay, Coyote Ugly, it's time to get down." Jagger's voice made me giggle, and I looked down to see his half-amused face.

"What? It's not like I haven't seen you drunk on the bar a few times."

"Which is why I'm not giving you shit, Sam." He shook his head. "But I can't say the same for Grayson."

I stiffened like he'd tossed cold water over me. Grayson stood a few feet away, his thumbs tucked into his pockets and his face unreadable. I refused to be embarrassed…right?

"Let's go," Grayson snapped.

A sly smile spread across my face. "If you want me to go, come up here and get me." There was no chance an uptight jerkface like him was going to do that. A muscle in his jaw ticked a second before he climbed up onto the barstool and then consumed the bar. He was huge. "Will this thing even support you?"

"Now."

I moved back, but before I could take a step, he pulled me up against him and into his arms. "We're not repeating this morning." He jumped off the bar with me in his arms, barely jarring me as he landed on his feet.

"How King Kong of you."

"I wasn't the one climbing up there in the first place." His grip tightened on me as he strode out the door into the evening air. "Thanks for calling us, Carter," he tossed to the hot one. Well, next to Grayson, he was a pale second.

I bet everyone was a pale second against Grayson.

Jagger walked out behind us, my purse in hand, which he handed to Grayson. "What? Like I can't handle my own purse?" I giggled.

"You're not getting near your keys," Grayson growled.

"I never said I was driving," I argued, trying to wiggle against his iron grip. He glared down at me, his lips impossibly close.

His mouth opened like he wanted to say something, but thought better of it and snapped it shut. He unlocked my car, still carrying me, and then dumped me into my front passenger seat.

"She's not usually like this," Jagger said as Grayson shut my door. "You got her?"

I opened it back up in time to hear Grayson say, "Yeah, I didn't think you'd want her puking in the truck."

"Amen."

"Stop talking like I'm not right here."

"Trust me, we're well aware that you're here, princess," Grayson snapped, promptly shutting the door in my face again.

He slid behind my wheel, cursing my height while the seat took precious seconds to move back to accommodate him.

"Maybe my car doesn't like you, either," I slurred.

His eyes cut toward me, and he shook his head but snapped his mouth shut as he turned the key.

"So stern." I gave my best uptight-guy impression but blew it when I descended into snickering.

"God help me," he muttered, putting my little Cabriolet into first gear and taking us out of the parking lot.

I let my head loll back against the seat and watched the muscle in his jaw tick. Everything about him, from his eyes to the cut of his jawline, was so severe. "You're not going to give me crap?"

"Not my job to judge," he replied, his eyes never wavering from the road.

"Not my circus, not my monkeys, that's what my mom says," I said louder than I intended, my finger poking him in the shoulder. Crud, when had my hand gotten over there? I pulled it back to my lap. If I sat perfectly still, maybe he wouldn't realize how truly drunk I was.

"Something like that." His dismissal, that flat tone, scraped me like no amount of lecturing could have.

"Anyone ever told you it's not good manners to be rude to your new roommate?"

He parked in the driveway behind Jagger's Defender and glared over at me. "Anyone ever told you it's not good manners to be dancing drunk on a bar on a Sunday afternoon?" As soon as the words were out of his mouth, his shoulders dropped and he closed his eyes. "Crap, Samantha, I didn't mean—"

I forced my door open and stumbled out, barely catching myself on the frame. "So much for not judging," I fired back, slamming the door and entering the toddler-esque phase of drunkenness. I scowled away his offered arm and made it into the house, nearly tripping on the doorstep.

"Don't!" I snapped when Grayson reached for me. "I'm not helpless."

I'm pretty sure his sigh was heard in Florida as he dropped my purse on the entry table. Wait, he had my purse?

I gripped the back of the couch and took deep breaths as my head buzzed. "Here." Jagger forced a bottle of water into my hand.

"I'm fine," I argued.

"Sam, I said I wouldn't give you shit, but fine isn't exactly drunk at five p.m. on a Sunday unless it's the Superbowl. What is going on?"

I swallowed past my numb tongue and glanced over to where Grayson stood, his arms across his chest again like a damn statue. As if on cue, the oven began to beep, and he walked past me into the kitchen. "Wow, this house smells amazing." I wanted to lick the air now that I noticed.

"Grayson cooks. Focus, Sam."

"Knock, knock," Paisley drawled as she came in through the front door. "You ready to head out to dinner?"

"Hey, Little Bird." Jagger smiled, which lit up his face like a freaking Christmas tree. Paisley wrapped her arms around his waist, and he kissed her. Love radiated from them. That was all I had wanted. Love. A chance to belong to someone—my someone. She'd had heart surgery two months ago, her scars were still pink, but it wouldn't surprise me if Jagger popped the question soon.

"You guys are so cute I may vomit." The room turned slightly. "Or maybe that's the tequila."

"I'm not letting this go, Sam. What's going on with you?" Jagger reached over and opened the bottle of water I still clutched in my hand, and I took two long pulls.

"I got kicked out of college."

"Right, which is why you're here…"

I rolled my eyes at him. A year ago, I'd never have guessed that Jagger Bateman would have his life more together than me. "Not just Colorado. I got kicked out of Troy."

"But you haven't even had a class yet." He dug a little deeper.

I laughed, the sound as hollow and empty as I felt. "Yeah. How special am I?"

"They can't do that."

"They withdrew their acceptance, Jagger. It's done." I looked up at the ceiling fan like it was going to spin me away into my dream life, or at least away from here. "What am I going to do?" My eyes burned.

"Oh, Sam," Paisley whispered.

"I moved down here—completely inconvenienced you and Josh and…" I motioned to the kitchen, where Grayson watched my meltdown quietly. "…him. Took this last chance, hundreds of miles away from home. Hell, not that I have a home, right? She's gone so damn much, and it's not like we stay in one place long enough to mark up a height chart on a freaking doorframe or anything. What the hell am I doing here? I have no job, no school, no family, and no direction." My fingers bit into the plastic, distorting the bottle as a tear slipped down my cheek. "What am I going to do?"

The question hung in the air, devouring any other thought

that could come to mind as seconds ticked on the wall clock.

"You're going to eat," Grayson answered from the kitchen, the sound of clattering dishes breaking the silence as he put plates on the large, bar-height, square table. "We all are."

"Uh, we have this family thing to—" Jagger started, glancing down at Paisley.

"*This* family thing is happening now," Grayson finished.

"What did I miss?" Josh asked, toweling off his hair as he walked into the living room and glanced from Grayson to Jagger.

"We're eating dinner. Now," Grayson ordered. "Sunday night. Family dinner. No excuse."

Josh's eyebrows hit the ceiling. "Uh. Okay? Since when do we—"

"Since now."

We shuffled into the kitchen, and Grayson heaped my plate with chicken and pasta, then sat me down at the table next to him. Once everyone was seated, I reached for my fork and nearly knocked over my water. Grayson caught my glass and moved it far enough from my plate that it wouldn't happen again. "Thanks," I muttered, then concentrated on cutting my chicken. My knife slipped twice before Grayson sighed.

He stole my plate and cut my dinner into bite-size pieces, sliding it back without a word. I side-eyed him, but his face gave no indication of what he was thinking.

Conversation struck up between the guys, punctuated by a laugh or answer from Paisley, like everything was normal. They didn't give me a chance to feel embarrassed, either by my outburst or my drunkenness, just drew me in as I relaxed and sobered up. *Wow.* That chicken was good. *Okay, maybe still a little drunk.*

"I'm sorry for everything," I said to Grayson as he cleared my plate after dinner, the other three having left. "I'm not normally so..."

"Drunk?" he supplied, keeping his wide back to me as he loaded my plate in the dishwasher.

My cheeks burned. "Yeah. I know I'm a giant inconvenience. Hell of a first impression, right?" He stilled, took a few breaths, and I stood as he turned toward me. His face was unreadable, which I was beginning to think might be the status quo. "I'm going to head to bed and hope today was all a nightmare. Thank you, seriously."

"Samantha," he called as I was passing the half wall that divided the kitchen from the living room.

"Yeah?"

"You're not an inconvenience. Maybe a pain in the ass, but you're not an inconvenience. And if there's something I've learned from living here, it's that Josh and Jagger make you family. We're a dysfunctional one, but family nonetheless, and now you are, too."

His eyes locked on to mine, and I forgot to breathe. Intensity poured off him, holding me captive, and I was torn between longing to get closer to whatever fire fueled him, and my sense of self-preservation warning me from the burn. Not that it mattered what I was thinking. He was talking about family, and my mind was skipping to things most definitely not PG, and way inappropriate. *Do not make an ass out of yourself any more than you already have.* He dropped his gaze, breaking the moment, and I sucked in a breath.

There was definitely more to him than I initially thought.

"Get to bed, so you can get up early and pull your shit together, Sam. We all make mistakes, but I'm not pulling you off another bar."

Never mind. He was still an ass.

CHAPTER FIVE

GRAYSON

Tacos? The scent hit me as I walked in the door from the gym on Monday night, and my mouth watered. With Jagger and Josh on a different detail, both working late, it had to be Samantha cooking. Alicia Keys playing on the iPod confirmed the thought. It had been a week since Sam moved in with us, and despite nearly constant contact while I was home, I'd managed to control my reaction to her. I dropped my gym bag on the floor and rounded the corner into the kitchen to tell her I was here.

Damn.

She swayed with the slow beat, stirring the meat sizzling in the pan, and a new hunger took precedence over my stomach. Her khaki shorts—if they could be called that—hugged her ass perfectly, and the white tank top only made her skin look warmer, more kissable.

But something was different... *Her hair.* It didn't rest against the tops of her breasts anymore. She'd cut it clear to her chin in a sleek bob that Mia would have called "edgy."

The most ludicrous vision played itself out in my mind—how easy it would be to slide up behind her, brush her hair away from her cheek, and run my lips along the delicate line of her neck. I shook my head to clear it. "Hey," I muttered, hoping not to scare her.

She jumped anyway.

"Ooh! Grayson!" She turned, revealing a fitted apron that read *Kiss the cook,* which was longer than her sorry excuse for shorts. "You're home!"

The words struck something in me, cracked open a piece of me that I thought I'd fortified a little thicker than that. But she looked like a better meal than the one on the stove, she was happy to see me, and she...she cooked for me. I was defenseless against that combo. "Yeah." I cleared my throat. "You cooked?"

"Apparently." She pointed the spatula up at the cabinet. "Grab the plates, we're about ready to eat."

"I always cook." *Wrong thing to say, you moron.*

She arched an eyebrow. "Are you complaining?"

I shook my head. Why couldn't she do something foolish? It was a hell of a lot easier to keep her at arm's length when she was drunk on a bar. Well, until I'd pulled her into the very arms I was trying to shove her away with. But she'd been ready to topple over, guys ogling right up that tiny skirt, and it was either get her down or start swinging punches.

So naturally I'd climbed up onto the bar like any other rational roommate. *Right, because Jagger was climbing up there, too. Roommate, my ass.*

"Good. Then get the plates."

"I should shower first." I was still soaked in sweat from the gym. Where the hell was this self-consciousness coming from?

Her eyes raked down my frame with a healthy amount of appreciation. "Well, you have about five minutes before dinner starts getting cold."

Maybe it had to do with me cranking the water temperature all the way to frigid, but I showered even faster than I did at home where I fought for shower time with four sisters. I made it back a minute after Sam's deadline.

She pulled the shells from the oven as I took down two dishes, keeping my eyes on the cabinet and not the curves of her ass. Holy shit. Eight days with this woman and I was turning into a sex-starved perv. *Sister. Treat her like a sister.*

Yeah, only problem was I'd never wanted to jump one of my sisters. This attraction had to wear off, right? Sam tucked her hair behind her ear.

"Your hair looks nice," I said carefully.

She fingered the ends of the strands. "Yeah? I found the only place in Enterprise with an opening. I just…"

"Needed a change?" I supplied.

She raised her eyebrows.

"My mother," I explained. "She told me if a woman cuts her hair that much, she's looking for a compliment or a change. I figured you didn't really need a compliment."

"I'm going job hunting again in the morning. They all want a college degree, so I haven't found anything yet, but I haven't given up. This guy I know told me to get my shit together, so I'll find something. Anything." She smiled, and my heart fucking stopped. Dead. Right there in the kitchen.

I remembered to breathe, sucking in air slowly, and gripped the plates. That pounding in my chest, I'd only felt it with one other woman in my life. Well, make that two, now.

"Only two?"

"What?" Was she reading my mind? Was I that obvious?

"You only took down two plates," she said, motioning to my hands.

"Walker and Bateman are on late shift." And we were alone.

"Doing what? You guys don't even start your next classes for a couple weeks."

"We still have to work. They're rounding up SERE students running through the woods so they can get tortured." Her eyebrows shot up, and I shrugged. "Practice. Just practice." Survive Escape Resist Evade training had sucked. I didn't envy the students getting rounded up.

I barely suppressed a groan as she bent over into the fridge, pulling out two hard ciders. Couldn't she *not* bend over? "Then shall we?"

I shook my head, taking the cider she offered and slipping it back into the fridge.

"That's right, you don't drink," she said, filling her tacos.

"I drink," I countered, heat rushing up my arms where our skin touched at the stove. "I just have rules about it."

She took the seat diagonal from me. "Rules. For drinking."

I bit into a taco instead of answering her, groaning at the taste. "Wow."

"Yeah, my mom likes Mexican food. It's the only thing I do well, so don't get used to it. Now about these rules?" She looked at me expectantly. Were it Walker or Bateman, I would have simply ignored the question, but there were circles under her green-rimmed hazel eyes, and something lurked in them that looked like loneliness. I was all too acquainted with what a bitch loneliness could be.

"I don't drink outside the house. Ever. Not if there's the slightest chance I'll need to drive anywhere. I don't drink if there's no one else sober. And I don't drink if I know I'm in a situation that requires me to be in complete control of myself." I downed two more tacos and avoided her eyes.

"Do you have to control everything?"

"Yes."

She leaned back in her chair, sipping on her cider. "Care to elaborate?"

"No." I'd already told her more about myself than I'd ever told Walker or Bateman. I waited for the crushing guilt that usually pulverized what was left of my heart whenever I let someone close. After all, I was having dinner alone with a woman I was attracted to, shouldn't that trigger the betrayal clause of my conscience? But none came. Odd.

She raised a single eyebrow and chased a drop of cider off her lip with her tongue. I shoved another taco in my mouth to keep it busy. "I'm trying to understand you..."

"Good luck." *Not today.*

"I've got some of the pieces already figured out."

"Oh?" *This should be interesting.*

"Right now I'm leaning toward narcissistic control freak, but the jury's still out."

I choked on my food and started sputtering. She calmly handed me my drink, and I swallowed the lodged pieces of my temper. "Narcissistic?"

"No one spends three hours a day at the gym for their health. Do you get off watching yourself in the mirror?"

"Do you get off dancing on bars for strangers?"

Her bottle slammed onto the table, and I bit my tongue so hard it almost bled. *Shit, that came out all wrong.* Why the hell couldn't I control my mouth around this girl? I lifted for the same reason she drank—to silence the demons.

"Let's adjust that first thought. Narcissistic control-freakish asshole"—she pushed back from table—"who is now doing the dishes."

I fought every urge I had to apologize, to go after her. I had no business screwing up that girl's life more than it already was, and there was no room for her in mine.

It was better this way.

I repeated that in my head over and over while I cleaned up dinner.

"When are you going to let me ink you, Masters?" Matt asked as he worked on one of Jagger's hundred or so tattoos a week later. Two weeks of living with Samantha. Two weeks of being home as little as possible, and hence another trip to the tattoo parlor.

It didn't stop my mind from wandering to her, and how

sad she seemed. It was worse every day, and she wasn't talking about it. As much as I wanted to keep the hell away from her, someone was going to have to get her to talk before she broke herself.

A girl not talking about her issues is a definite clue that it's worse than she's letting on. Constance's sisterly advice ran through my head.

"Not happening," I answered, flipping through my 5&9's and stretching my legs out from the plastic chair. "I'm just here to babysit."

"Chicks dig it," Jagger answered with a cocky grin.

"Not too concerned." I flipped another card and looked at oil pressure limitations.

"Guys dig it, too," Matt offered.

"Definitely not concerned," I answered.

"You owe me $50," Jagger whispered loudly to Matt.

I looked up at them over the cards, told Jagger with my look exactly what I thought about that idea, and went back to studying. I had to blink a few times at the jumble of words, so I closed my eyes. Time to break.

"Finished for today," Matt told Jagger as he sprayed one of Jagger's pieces down and wrapped him in saran wrap like leftovers.

He settled his bill, and we headed back home. "So how is sharing a bathroom with Sam?" he asked with a sideways look at me.

"Fine." I was not going there with him.

"Her incredible amount of hair stuff isn't driving your OCD nuts?"

"I don't have OCD." I liked things neat. Orderly. In their place. Go figure, I was panting after the one woman who wouldn't let me keep things that way. She left stuff everywhere.

"Right. Well, I'm glad you're getting along."

"I grew up sharing a bathroom with four sisters. I think I

can handle some hair crap on the counter." What I couldn't handle? The way the bathroom smelled like her after a shower, all vanilla and caramel. I got a raging hard-on just walking in.

"She rattles you."

I ignored him and stared out of the window, watching the outskirts of Dothan fly by as we reached the edge of the small city. If I couldn't come to grips with the effect Sam had on me, I sure as hell wasn't using it as bonding time with Jagger.

"I don't mean to pry—"

"Then don't."

"She's been through a lot lately." His hands tightened on the wheel.

"Yeah, and she needs someone to get her back on her feet, not coddle her. She's stronger than you give her credit for."

"And you're her person?"

"I'm not anyone's person. But I do know what it is to mess up your life." I couldn't go back and fix mine. I was too far gone, my path concrete. But Sam's? Maybe I could help with that, even earn a few karma points.

"Want to talk about—"

"No." I looked back out the window as we stopped at the red light and—"You have to be *fucking* kidding me." My hands morphed into fists, and I sucked my breath in through my teeth.

"Wow. I think I've heard you swear like...twice?" Jagger jerked his gaze to me, then back to the road as the light turned green.

"Pull the car over. Now."

"At the strip club? Dude, I'm not sure now is the time—"

"Now!"

He swerved across the open lane and into the dirt parking lot in front of the small, ridiculously pink building. "Okay, well, you're on your own, because Paisley will fucking kill... *Holy shit.*"

"Yeah."

He pulled into an empty spot. Right next to a bright yellow cabriolet with Colorado plates.

"What the hell do you think Sam is doing here?"

I'm going job hunting... "Nothing good. Go home. I got this."

My feet hit the ground before Jagger killed the ignition. The Alabama heat matched my temper, both overrunning my senses. I swallowed back the immediate urge to rip the building to shreds and remembered that I didn't have all the facts...yet.

I opened the door, and the bouncer stood, eyeing me up before stepping back. We both knew I could have destroyed him if I wanted to. "ID?" he asked.

I handed mine over, and he scrutinized it, reading over my name several times while I did the same to his club. A skinny blonde was up on stage, wearing a cowboy hat and not much else, gyrating to a Kid Rock song while a few leering scumbags drooled.

"Here you go," the bouncer handed my ID back and tried to size me up.

My eyes adjusted to the dim lighting as I swept the club, spotting her sitting at the bar. Her skirt rode high on her thigh, and the guy she was talking to had definitely noticed.

"What experience do you have?" he asked, not noticing my approach.

"I took a year of pole classes back in Colorado, but only for exercise," she answered, fingering a white piece of paper...an application. *Fuck that.* "I'd be a quick study at the bar, too."

"Very nice," the manager drawled, his eyes lingering on Sam's cleavage, where her shirt was unbuttoned. "Let me give this a once-over and see what I can do." He reached across to take her application, and she leaned back before he could brush up against her. He shot her a sick smile, then headed back behind the stage.

Something dark twisted in my stomach and threatened to

erupt. Sam turned in her seat, offering me her profile as she watched the girl on stage. Her strong, sure facade slipped, and her swollen eyes turned dim. She looked like I'd felt the morning after...*yeah, not going there.*

I slid onto the barstool next to her, and her shoulders dropped. "What do you want, Grayson?"

"To get you out of here."

"I'm on an interview." Her spine straightened.

"This is your dream job?" What the hell was she thinking?

She threw me a look that clearly said I was an idiot. What? Like I was the one about to audition as a stripper?

"You know what I realized the last couple weeks? I have no money. My savings account can cover one last month of my cell phone bill. I have no job to make money. No college degree to get the job. Even the jobs that don't need a degree? All full. I've spent three weeks searching out every job in Enterprise, Daleville, and Dothan. No one is hiring. I'm not going to freeload off of you guys while I figure out what the hell to do."

"So this is what you want to do in the meantime? Work here?"

Her gaze hit the floor. "It's the last thing I want. But these girls make a lot of money, and it beats the alternative of moving back in with my mother."

"Well, as much as I'd love to see what that pole class taught you, this is not where you belong, Sam." *Shit. That is not what I meant to say.* Not the first part, at least. The girl on stage hooked her leg around the pole and spun.

She raised her eyebrow and smirked, sending a jolt of electricity through me that settled in my dick. I shifted my weight. "Well, there's no one here harping on me to put on more clothes." She toyed with the buttons on her blouse.

It would have been hot as hell, if she was doing it out of genuine interest in me. But she was proving a point, and I knew it. "Samantha."

She flicked a button open, enough to glimpse the lacy white

material of her bra, but I kept my eyes locked on hers. "What's wrong? Don't think I have what it takes? Just because you're immovable doesn't mean I can't turn on at least one of those guys." She nodded her head toward the guys hovering at the stage.

Immovable? Good thing she didn't have a clue.

"You could turn on a statue, Samantha, and I'm not immovable, no matter how much I wish otherwise." *Shut the hell up before you say something else that's going to get you in trouble.*

Her lips parted and her eyes widened slightly, enough to see her defenses slide down a little. "Why do you do that? Call me Samantha?"

The music shifted to *Porn Star Dancing*, and the manager whistled at Sam like she was a Labrador retriever. My fist clenched. Sam looked from me to him and back again, clearly torn.

"I call you Samantha to remind myself that you're not just a roommate but a woman, and to make sure I don't jump to the wrong conclusions about you like the first time we met." *When I assumed you were sleeping with my roommates.* "Don't do this."

Her eyes flickered, showing the uncertainty, the doubt. "You don't control me," she whispered.

"I'm not naive enough to think that any force in this world could control you, Samantha. But I will remind you that in the last three weeks I have caught you off the kitchen counter and pulled you off a bar. That stage doesn't scare me." *If she got anywhere close to it, I'd burn the damn thing to the ground without a second thought.*

She pulled her bottom lip into her mouth. "God, why is this so important to you?"

Because the thought of you taking your clothes off for money makes me want to rip every man in here to shreds for making it possible. "Because you're in freefall, Sam. You can't see it because you're the one in mid-air. But you're spiraling in the wrong direction."

The manager waved his hands at Sam.

"I have to go."

She hopped off the barstool, raised her chin, and headed for the stage. She didn't make it two steps before I swung her over my shoulder. My fingers spread on the warm, bare skin of the back of her thighs to keep her still, and I tugged her skirt down to cover more of it. Then I grabbed her purse and headed for the door. "Grayson!"

"Hey, you can't—" The bouncer stood in front of the door.

I glared at him, letting all of my fury show that a place like this even existed, and he stepped back. I pushed open the door and squinted as the dying sun hit me in the face.

"Fucking put me down, Grayson!" Sam shouted. She braced her hands on my back, trying to get upright.

Her waist was tiny in my hands as I lowered her to my eye level. She was furious, her lips pursed and her eyes on fire. I breathed a sigh of relief. I'd take the fire over the defeat I'd seen in there any day.

"What the hell do you think you're doing?" she shouted in my face, uncaring that we were inches apart.

The girl didn't back down, I'd give her that much. Now if she'd realize that I didn't, either.

"Well?"

"Catching you."

CHAPTER SIX

"What the hell are we doing here?" I asked as we pulled up in front of Anytime Fitness. He hadn't even trusted me to drive, and I'd gotten perverse satisfaction at his grunt when he tried to fold himself behind the wheel again. "And what's the point of a twenty-four-hour gym? Who honestly works out at three o'clock in the morning?"

"I do." He killed the engine.

"Because you aspire to vampirism? Or maybe you can't get enough of those bulging muscles in your dreams, so you need to see them in the mirror for yourself?"

"Sometimes I can't sleep. I end up here."

"And why are we here now?"

"You need a job. Maggie is hiring." He got out and walked around to my side, then opened my door. "And I know she needs some help with her books, and you're good with math."

"How would you know that?"

"Ember." He made no apologies for prying into my life, just waited for me to get out.

I made a mental note to give my best friend a call. "And someone I've never met is going to hire me because you say so?" I asked as I reluctantly climbed out.

"Actually, you've already met her," he answered, opening the glass door to the gym.

The air conditioning was heavenly. "What? When? I know every application I've put in."

"Hi, Flyboy!" a smiley red-headed girl in an Anytime Fitness polo called out, pushing her glasses up her nose.

"Hey, Avery. This is Samantha. Is your mom around?"

I gave the girl a small wave, which she returned. "She's in the back. I'll grab her." She ran off in jeans that were easily two sizes too big for her frame.

Grayson leaned over the counter and brought an application back with a pen. "I spend a lot of time here," he explained with a shrug. "Now fill it out."

"How do I know her?"

He fidgeted with the pen attached to the sign-in sheet. "She owns Oscars, too."

Oh, shit. Oscars, where I'd given my impromptu Coyote Ugly impression. "The bar?"

"Yeah, she was tending the bar the day you...visited."

This was not happening. There had to be hidden cameras somewhere. "Oh, hell no. She's going to take one look at me and laugh, and that's not something I can take right now."

He took a deep breath. "You are so frustrating. You'll take your clothes off for a room full of men, but you won't ask Maggie to hire you?"

"I don't expect you to understand." Like he'd ever made a mistake in his life, let alone left a trail of them in his wake.

He turned, leaning one elbow on the counter, dangerously invading my space, and my head. "Understand what? That your skin is a lot easier to expose than your pride?"

I sucked in my breath and tore my eyes away from the gray ones that were currently cutting through my defenses. "Yes."

"Then I understand just fine, and I'm telling you they're equally important. Now fill out the application, Samantha."

"She's going to throw me out," I whispered, looking up at him.

Grayson arched an eyebrow. "Not everyone judges people on a first impression."

"You did."

"Something I'm still paying for when it comes to you."

"There's...people here." I counted at least fifteen people working out in the immediate vicinity who would all bear witness to my humiliation.

"Are you going to let them stop you?"

I weighed my options as Maggie walked toward us with her daughter. I couldn't get by without a phone or gas money, and at least this would keep my clothes on. *Head high. Let's do this.* "Something you might not know about me, Grayson? I don't let anyone stop me."

"Something *you* might not know, Sam? I was depending on it." The corner of his mouth lifted into what I could almost define as a smirk, but that might mean a smile was possible.

"Here she comes," Grayson said into my ear, his lips barely brushing my skin. Chills raced down my neck. "Hold on." He walked through the line of treadmills to meet Maggie halfway. At least two spandex-clad girls eye-fucked him, but he didn't seem to notice, and not in the way a cocky guy would ignore it, but more like...he didn't see.

What was a guy like him doing single? Sure, he still had a stick up his ass, but there was more to him than the wall he used to keep people out.

Maggie smiled when she saw Grayson and met him near the entrance to the locker room. Her gaze jerked toward me, and I gave a half wave. Nausea rolled through me, but I fought the urgent need to puke. I'd made my bed, I was strong enough to lie in it.

Maggie made her way to me and cocked her head to the side. "If it isn't my personal show-stopper. Grayson tells me you need a job."

I swallowed, my throat suddenly dry. "Yes, ma'am. I'm

so sorry for how I behaved. I promise that's not my normal"—
anymore—"and it won't happen again. Ever."

"Well, you got Grayson here up on the bar, so I have to give
you credit there."

"Yes, ma'am." Another time he'd saved me from being an
idiot.

She sized me up. "You're a math girl?"

I nodded. "That's my major. I'm only a junior, but I'm a fast
learner and a hard worker."

She clucked her tongue and glanced from Grayson to me.
"Well, Grayson vouches for you. I need some part-time help
behind the front desk. Mostly secretarial duties, mail, schedules,
phones, supply orders. Are you up for that?"

Wait. What? "Really? You're going to let me work here?"

She laughed, showing perfectly straight teeth. "Darlin',
you're not the first girl to dance on my bar, and chances are you
won't be my last." She glanced down at my button-up. "We're
pretty informal around here, so why don't you grab a shirt off
my desk, and my daughter will show you the ropes? Take her
back, would you, Grayson?"

"Yes, ma'am." He put pressure on my lower back and guided
me toward the door past the locker rooms. The office was
neat, and I easily spotted the stack of shirts. "Here," he said,
thrusting a white polo shirt with Anytime Fitness embroidered
on the front.

"She sure knows you pretty well," I questioned, taking the
shirt and pulling it on over my blouse.

"Like I said, I'm here a lot."

I glanced over the huge muscles of his arm as he curved the
brim of his baseball cap. "I can see that."

He shook his head and walked me back out to the desk.
"I'm going to lift a little while you train up. Avery, take care of
her." He abandoned me for the locker room.

"Hi there, Sam." She smiled, revealing a set of sparkly

braces. "Ready to get started?"

"Sure," I said, and we began with the computer system. There were four managers, three receptionists, five trainers, and Avery, who filled in behind the desk when she wasn't at school.

"Mom doesn't want me at the bar, of course, so I'm here."

"It's cool that she owns two businesses," I said as I familiarized myself with the mail system.

"She got the bar in the divorce, but she's trying to sell it. This is pretty much our place, now." She reached into her bag, pulling out a heavy math book.

"Aren't you on vacation?" I asked.

"One more week and it's finals. Junior year algebra three is kicking my butt."

"Want some help? I used to tutor high-school math back in Colorado."

"You wouldn't mind?"

"Not in the least," I answered with an easy smile.

"Nice to see you again," a vaguely familiar guy said as he signed in, a bag slung across his shoulder. He flashed me a smile. He was good-looking, but my usual hot-guy response must have been broken, because he didn't so much as stir my interest.

"Welcome back," I said with a polite smile, trying to remember where I'd seen him before.

He laughed. "You don't remember me. It's okay. I'm Will. I'm the one who called Jagger a few weeks ago."

Ugh. The hot one from the bar. Because I wasn't embarrassed enough already today. "Nice to meet a friend of Jagger's. Well, officially meet since I'm guessing you didn't exactly get my best side last time."

His grin was contagious. "Well, if you'd ever like to show me your best side—"

"No chance, Carter. Not happening." Grayson said as he walked over, dressed in shorts and a loose tank. My heart jumped and my breath caught at the possessive glance that swept over me before glaring at Will. Maybe I wasn't broken; I was simply having a hard time comparing guys to Grayson. Shit. That was inconvenient.

"Whoa, you marking territory, Masters?" Will teased.

"She's my new roommate, so hands and eyes off, or I'll explain the many different ways in which you really are second-choice Carter." The muscle in Grayson's jaw flexed.

"You're an asshole." Carter tipped his hat. "Ma'am, you have my most sincere sympathy at your living situation." He turned back to Grayson. "We still on for Memorial day?"

Grayson smacked his back. "You bet. Barbecue starts at two, but I'm missing out. I'll be home."

"Ah, yes, the mysterious trips. We'll catch you when you're back." Will nodded and headed to the locker room.

"He's an acquired taste," Grayson explained.

"Yes, you are," I responded, tossing him a flirtatious smile and digging into the algebra book with Avery. Crap. I'd just flirted. With my roommate. I needed to watch that. I also needed to not ogle him lifting weights between learning my job and helping Avery out.

Epic fail.

He got me a job. Thank God. Such a simple thing, but simply knowing it made breathing easier, like I'd been under water for so long that coming up had me drunk on oxygen and possibilities.

He took me home a couple hours later.

"Thank you," I told him as we walked up the stairs to our bedrooms. Josh and Jagger were both on the main floor, which gave us the entire second story of the split level.

"You're welcome. You'll be on your own next weekend, since I'll be going home." He gave me a nod and headed into his room.

"Why do you go home so often?" I asked, curiosity getting

the better of me. "Will wasn't the first person to say something about it."

He turned, hand on his doorknob. "What's the pool up to?" He countered with that half smirk that was sexy as hell. *Oh, so inconvenient.*

"No pool, just wondering."

He studied me for a moment, making me wait so long that I figured he was going to blow me off. The intensity he wore so easily was exhausting to be around, draining me mentally because I couldn't stop wondering what he was thinking.

"Everyone is accountable for something, Samantha. Me included."

He shut the door on me and the topic.

The sirens woke me, piercing through the haze of sleep better than any latte could have. My legs didn't get the *we're awake* memo and buckled under me as I stumbled from the bed.

The clock flashed 1:37 a.m. Wednesday morning. Wait. Thursday morning. Whatever. With the late shifts I'd been pulling at the gym for almost a week now, I'd only been asleep an hour.

"What the hell?" I called out, peeking between the mini blinds. A few neighbors stood on their porches, all wrapped in robes or pajamas.

"Grayson?" I yelled, tripping into the hallway. His door was open, the bed as messy as I figured I'd ever see it, but he wasn't in it.

I raced down the stairs, shouting "Guys?" before I remembered that Jagger and Josh were out of town for a few days on a detail. Holy shit, that siren was loud. Like being bombed at Pearl Harbor loud, or tornado in Kansas loud. *Shit. Tornado.*

There was no way. Right? We were in southeast Alabama, not the Midwest. Did we have a shelter? That close call while we were stationed at Fort Leavenworth was bad enough, but we'd had a shelter.

I adjusted the girls inside my shelf-bra, those things never were enough support, and then swung open the front door. Humidity, thick and heavy, hit me in the face, almost as if I could drink the air. Wind gusted, whipping branches of the lilac tree against the porch railing.

The siren blasted from the electric post four houses down. "What's going on?" I yelled toward our neighbors.

"Tornado warning," Grayson answered from behind me, his voice low and raspy from sleep. He reached around me, showing me his cell phone alert.

Tornado Warning, Coffee County, AL until 3:30 a.m. Seek shelter immediately.

"Where are we? Kansas? This is so not right." A knot formed in my stomach. There were very few things that scared me, but tornadoes were on that list. They made me small, insignificant, and powerless to my own fate. I'd had enough of that lately, thank you very much.

"'Tis the season, and warning means they're not kidding. One's been spotted in Elba, not far from here. Now get inside, get some clothes on, and meet me in the bathroom." He pulled me back gently by my elbows until we were inside, and then shut the door.

"But we're in the south, and not like...Tennessee south. Like Deep South." I turned around, my hand brushing the skin of his chest...his bare chest, and damn, but he was warm, and cut, and smelled better than chocolate. His hair was sleep-mussed, but his face was still set in stern lines. Did he even relax when he slept?

"Yeah, and you live in a town where a tornado destroyed the

high school and killed some of those teenagers a decade ago, so get your ass in the bathroom. The weather doesn't care if we're in Oklahoma or Oz."

"Okay." All thoughts of naked Grayson fled as I bolted up the stairs to my bedroom.

"And put on some clothes!" he called out.

I threw a sweatshirt over my head, unplugged my phone from its charger, grabbed my iPad, and skipped back down the stairs to the bathroom. "Grayson?"

"The little bathroom."

I moved quickly down the hall to the powder room, where I found him pulling a shirt over his head. His sweatpants hung low enough on his hips to see that V of his muscles that was probably illegal in a dozen states...or should have been. Those hours he spent every day at the gym seriously carved the guy. "Being invited to the bathroom by a guy is definitely a first."

He raised an eyebrow before he shook his head. "No windows in here, and it backs up to the kitchen, so it's the safest place to wait it out." His eyes glanced down at my very bare legs. "You and I have different definitions of clothes."

"Not the time, Grayson."

"Right. Stay here." He left.

"So, we'll hang out in the bathroom for"—I checked my phone—"another couple hours. Good call," I muttered to myself. The siren stopped, but if it was like Kansas, on a timer, it would be back while we were still under warning. I set the iPad on the counter and cued up the weather app. We were entirely surrounded by red on the Doppler. The knot in my stomach tightened.

Grayson walked back in, his arms full of his comforter, a couple bottles of water, and my shoes. "Just in case," he said, dropping them to the floor.

The bathroom wasn't big to start with, but with Grayson closing the door behind him, well, it may as well have been a porta-potty for how small it felt. He sat on the floor and leaned his head against the wall, closing his eyes. Where was I supposed to sit? On the toilet? Because that wouldn't have been awkward or anything. Grayson occupied almost every spare inch of space in the room.

"Get comfortable, Samantha. We're going to be here for a while."

How could he be so calm? Oh, right, because the man had zero emotions. Maybe if I was a robot like he was, I wouldn't be on the verge of using the toilet to vomit in. But then I'd be left sitting on a vomit-splattered toilet. Ugh.

He cracked open his eyes and held out an arm. "Let's go."

I swallowed. Being that close to him felt more dangerous than anything going on outside. "Samantha, I'm not going to bite you."

"Well, you don't exactly like me."

He let out an exasperated sigh. "I don't understand you. I like you just fine. Now sit down."

If the distant way he'd treated me since I got to Alabama was him liking me, I'd hate to see how he treated someone he didn't like.

I lowered myself slowly and slid into the space he left under his arm. He reached with his other arm and brought the comforter over us. God, it smelled like him. I physically restrained myself from burying my nose in the fabric. "So now we wait?"

"Yep."

I swallowed and tried to ignore how easily I fit against him, but every sense was taken over by Grayson. The strength in his arms, how indestructible he felt next to me. Did he have to smell so good? For someone who spent that much time worshipping his body in the gym, shouldn't he smell a touch…well…smelly?

Of course not. He had to torture me by smelling like the ocean, with a hint of cedar like the body wash I secretly sniffed when I showered. *Don't think about it. Think about anything else. Anything.*

"So you're headed back home tomorrow?" I asked.

"Yep."

"You're such a conversationalist."

"It's two in the morning, Samantha."

"Well, it's not like I'm going to sleep on the bathroom floor," I pouted. Not that his warmth wasn't relaxing me, because I hated to admit that it was, tornado warning and all.

He sighed. "Yes, I'm going home tomorrow."

I'd shoved a car jack into the tiniest crack in his wall, and I twisted it a little. "Where are you from?"

"Nags Head, North Carolina."

"The Outer Banks?"

"That's the one."

"Do you like it there?"

He sighed, but it was the short kind I was beginning to understand meant he was about to let me into his world a tiny bit. "I love it. My father builds sailboats, the racing kind, and he's pretty certain I'll come back to stay, but I just… Sometimes I need the space."

"I've always wanted to go there. My mom spent a summer there in college and loved it. I was born right before she graduated UNC that spring after." My stomach turned sour again thinking about her. "I still haven't told her about Troy."

"Scared she'll lose it?" His arm flexed around me, pulling me closer.

"No." I shook my head slightly, unintentionally burrowing into his shoulder. "I wanted to prove to her that I could do this on my own. That I didn't need her approval, or disapproval, rather. That's why I'm staying here. All she sees is this giant screw-up, and I love her, but she wants to fix me. This Troy thing proves that I'm a step beyond fixing."

His chest rose and fell a few times in the silence. "There

are broken people in the world, Samantha. But you're not one of them. Dinged-up maybe, but not broken, and definitely not beyond repair."

A small, empty laugh burst free. "If you only knew, you wouldn't say that. You would shove me outside and let the tornado spin me away."

He pulled back enough to look down at me. The turbulence in his eyes was enough to suck my breath away. "I don't abandon people."

It was there in my throat, the secret I'd been holding in for too long, suffocating me in its need to be heard, to quit festering inside my body. But what would he think if he knew? Guys like Grayson didn't sleep with the wrong people, let alone have their lives ruined by them. Grayson's choices were so calculated, so deliberate, I doubted he'd ever so much as been late for a class.

"Samantha?" His eyes softened, revealing the give in him, and it cracked my own defenses.

"Have you ever made a mistake, Grayson? And I don't mean the kind that costs you an apology. I mean one that destroys you? Where you lie awake at night, unable to sleep, because you're terrified of what's going to happen the next day, and the one after that? Where you'd give anything, and I do mean *anything* to go back and make a different choice? Where you're sick all the time at the thought of what you've done? Because I have. I've crumbled my entire future, shredded any hope of finishing college, and killed off who I used to be. And I don't...I don't know how to come back from something like that."

"You don't."

I jerked back, but he held me immobile against him.

"Stop, and listen to me. I'm not going to belittle you by saying nothing is that bad, because some things are. Things happen that change who we are, and what we're capable of. So you're not going to 'come back' from that any more than you're going to erase whatever you did. You have to decide if you're going to try to keep patching yourself up or if you're going to tear down and rebuild."

"I don't know how to do that."

"You wade through the pain, and the guilt, and the excuses you make to yourself. Stop drowning in alcohol to numb the fear, and suck up the bitter taste of accountability. You move on with who you are now. It's not easy. If you think you screwed up that badly, then maybe you did, but you also have to leave room for the chance that you didn't. Have you talked about it?"

I shook my head. There were two of us who knew the whole truth, and that circle was big enough. "I'm not sure I'm ready to let go of everyone's vision of who I am. It's so much prettier than the truth."

"Not even Ember?"

"Definitely not think-through-everything-twice Ember. She wouldn't understand, and I'm not sure I could handle her reaction."

He swallowed and broke our stare like it had become too much because we both knew the truth—it had. "That's the hardest part, letting someone see who you really are—scars and all. I'm..." He cleared his throat. "You need to trust someone enough to tell them the truth. Make peace with it before it eats you alive. I listen really well if you don't have anyone else."

I scrambled to throw up a wall between us. It was safer when he was hurling snotty comments at me. That, I knew how to handle. But this Grayson? The one holding me carefully, keeping me warm while the storm raged outside, offering to help carry the crippling weight destroying me? I didn't know what the hell to do with that one.

"Why would you even offer? Everything you know about me is a mess. I drink too much, wear too little clothing, dance on bars, and impose on everyone around me because I can't get my shit together."

"You can get your shit together, you've just chosen not to

up until now. You took that first step with Maggie. I'm offering because I've made that kind of mistake, Sam, the one you don't come back from. I look at you, and I see what I went through. It's too late for me." He took a deep breath. "But you? You're going to spring back, so yeah, I'm offering."

"As friends?" I held my breath, needing to hear it. The push and pull, the attraction, it was all there on my side, but I wasn't sure about his, and I wasn't about to make an ass out of myself. We were roommates, and this could get complicated really quickly.

Our eyes locked, and heat skimmed down my limbs, leaving chills in its wake. "We're both adults—"

"Well, trying to be," I joked.

His lips quirked up at the corners. *Almost a smile.* "Right. I'm not going to say that I'm not incredibly attracted to you. I don't lie. Ever. Plus, I'd have to be dead not to realize the way you affect me. But I'm also not in any position to act on it, and let's be honest—you're not, either. But I think we can stop picking each other apart and be friends."

"Friends that are incredibly attracted to each other?"

He inhaled sharply, like my attraction to him had been some secret. *Yeah right.* I'm pretty sure my body threw out "screw me now" signals the minute he walked into a room, even when I was angry with him. Hell, perversely, especially when I was angry with him.

The siren wailed again, and I jumped, despite the exhaustion pummeling me.

"An hour to go," I muttered, looking at my iPad.

"Relax and try to get some sleep."

"Like there's a chance of that." But he tucked the comforter up to my chin and drew me closer, so my head rested on his chest.

"Just try. Some of us have to get up for work in the morning." His tone was light and teasing, so I didn't jump his case about giving me shit.

I yawned, feeling my body betray me and start to shut down like he'd flipped some magic Sam-sleep button. "I'm glad we can be friends." Sleep slurred my words.

"Me, too."

Sleep claimed me quickly, my body and emotions both run into the ground with exhaustion. His heartbeat filled my head and kept the nightmares at bay, but not the weird dreams. No, because I dreamed he kissed my forehead and lingered.

CHAPTER SEVEN

GRAYSON

My heart pounded time with the ticking on my watch. Thirty-seven questions to go, and thirteen minutes to do them in.

Stop thinking about time and concentrate on the questions.

I took a deep breath and pushed it out slowly while I read the next question.

If it becomes apparent that TGT will exceed _____°C (701) or _____°C (701C) before NG idle speed (_____% ____ _____) is attained.

I read it twice, slowing down and willing the question to make sense and the answer to come to mind. I made it through Primary, I could do this. 869, 851, 63, or more. I filled in the answers and moved on, taking only as much time as physically necessary to fill out the blanks. *You're not moving fast enough.*

My grip on the pen was almost painful, and my throat closed with every minute that ticked by, until my quick math told me there was no way I'd finish in time.

Fuck! The timer blared on my cell phone, and I silenced it with a quick swipe. I slammed the edge of my fist onto the wooden table, and my phone fell over from where I'd had it balanced against my coffee cup. Sixty-seven questions answered. Thirteen more to go. Those thirteen meant the difference between flying the Apache and getting kicked out of flight school in ten days on the first day of Apache training.

I set the timer to zero and hit start, then went back to the questions. I stuck to method, reading each question twice, making sure I understood what it really said and not just what my brain translated, and then answered.

"Hey, you okay? I heard something that sounded suspiciously like a temper tantrum." Jagger checked in as he opened the door to the tiny private office where I was working.

"Yep. Studying." This was all so *easy* for him and his photographic memory. If I didn't really care about the guy I'd fucking hate him.

"We still have two weeks until the course starts. You know that, right? You don't have to hide in the janitor's closet to take practice tests."

"Ten days. A mop bucket does not make it a janitor's closet. And yes, I do."

"Stop harassing Masters," Josh called from the hallway. "He's got more work ethic in his finger than you have in your whole body, Jagger."

Jagger smirked. "True story. Half day, you up for lunch?"

I looked at the time on my phone. 11:30. Shit, I'd been in here for two hours already on three different tests. "Yeah, give me a couple minutes."

"Mind if I tag along?" Second-choice Carter called out. He'd been our class leader through Primary, and as much of a West Point douche bag as he'd been, he ended up giving his Apache slot to Jagger, so I couldn't hate him, either. As long as he kept a healthy distance from Sam, we'd keep the arrangement.

I was getting really sick of having to like people lately.

"Sure," Jagger answered with a fake smile. Given the fact that the dude was Paisley's ex, he handled it pretty well. Her grace was rubbing off on him.

"Right. Lunch settled. If we only have a half day today, then

I'm studying. Get out," I said, turning the timer back on and settling into the rest of the test.

"Always a pleasure chatting, Grayson." Jagger laughed and shut the door.

Seventeen minutes later, I finished with a 93% score. I was getting faster, but not fast enough. I was seventeen minutes and seven percent away from getting my ass kicked out of flight school.

I rethought lunch. Maybe I needed to skip today, grab something from the chow hall, and get back in here for another test. I could easily sneak in another few rounds at failing my future before I caught my flight home. Yeah. That was a way better plan than sitting with the guys and getting nothing accomplished. Or the gym. I could definitely use that release. No lunch, it was settled.

"Hey, let's go, Einstein. Sam said she'd meet us there, and I'm not keeping that little hurricane waiting."

Hurricane? At least you saw those coming. Sam was more like a squall, coming out of nowhere and knocking you on your ass. On second thought, lunch sounded great. My brain was close to shut-down from the workout I'd put it through, and unless I could fit in a few hours at the gym, I could use lunch to refocus.

Liar. You want to see her.

I crumpled up that thought with the last three tests I'd taken and tossed it into the trash can.

We all filed into our cars and headed off-post toward the restaurant. The temperature in my F150 was enough to cook an egg, not that I was going to experiment. I was used to Southern summers, but not in full, long-sleeved uniform, and not without the ocean breeze. Pretty sure I could pull some *Wizard of Oz* shit, because I was fucking melting today. We pulled up to Firehouse, and I was the first through the door. My eyes searched for her before I even realized I was doing it, but we must have beaten her there.

I flexed my jaw and attempted to relax. It wasn't like I wasn't going to see her at home. I lived with the damn girl, but my brain craved more. Four damn weeks, and if I wasn't with her, I was thinking about her, wondering what she was doing and what ridiculous prank she was pulling. It was getting more than a little out of hand. What trouble was she going to get into this weekend while I was gone?

It was my turn up to the counter, and when I heard Jagger on the phone with Sam, saying back her order to get it right, I placed it, putting it on my tab. Apparently having her as a roommate meant I needed to either curb my irrational infatuation or make a new line-item on the budget that read "For misogynistic displays of illogical possession."

We took the booth nearest the door, and the guys started talking about their plans for the Fourth of July. I heard them, but their voices took a backseat to the white noise in my head. Failing three tests. One more week.

Flying home tonight so I could spend the weekend at home. Again.

"Not sure. I have to check with Paisley," Jagger said, "and I'll answer for Josh and say that he's headed to Nashville."

"Ha." Josh threw a fry at Jagger's head. "Not like you're not just as whipped."

"Ouch, yet true," Jagger answered.

The bell sounded as the door opened, and my head whipped toward it as a few soldiers walked in. I bit into my chicken-parm hoagie like it would fill the pit that was slowly growing in my stomach.

"Little anxious over there?" Jagger asked, smirking like an asshole.

I didn't bother answering, sending a death glare across the booth. The bell sounded again, and this time Sam swept in, dressed in a flowy skirt that ended right above her knees and a strappy top that left her collarbone bare. I swallowed, my food suddenly a lot thicker. Or maybe that was my tongue.

"Hi!" She grinned and waved, skipping over to our table. "Scooch over." She nudged my shoulder, and I slid toward Carter, more than happy to be the barrier between them.

"You look happy," Josh said.

"Friday payday! So I picked up some groceries and swung by the library to ask Paisley if they need any volunteers. Oh, is that mine?" She raised her eyebrows at me, and I slid her sandwich toward her. "Thank you!"

"Sam, you didn't have to grocery shop," Jagger said, a French fry hanging out of his mouth. How he got by dating the Commanding General's daughter with those manners, I'd never know.

"I wanted to. But I wish I'd been warned that they didn't stock peppermint-mocha coffee creamer down here. I would have stocked up in Nashville." She took a bite of her food and moaned. "Ohmygodsogood," she mumbled through her chewing.

I'd never really thought a girl eating was hot, but damn. *Stop it. You're going home today.* "Do you want my muffin, too?" I motioned to the banana walnut one I'd added to my tray.

"Thanks, but I'm allergic to nuts. I'll stick with this masterpiece," she said to her sandwich. "So, are you flying straight into Nags Head?" she asked, her eyes on me.

Jagger dropped his fry. "Nags Head?"

Sam nodded, her eyebrows knitting together. "Yeah. It's where he's from. Right, Grayson?"

Their stares burned holes through my uniform, but I nodded anyway. "Yep."

Jagger leaned forward on his elbows. "What else do you know?"

She looked up at me for permission, her eyes wide, inquisitive. They broke me down like nothing else could, and I gave her a short nod.

"His father builds racing sailboats, and his mother believes in old-fashioned manners," she stated, then sipped sweet tea through her straw. *Those lips.*

"I didn't tell you that last part," I said softly.

"I've lived with you for the last four weeks. You didn't have to." She tipped her chin and smiled up at me.

Her lips demanded all of my attention, and I tightened every muscle in my body to keep from kissing her. Her face would fit perfectly between my hands, her skin would be soft under my fingers, and her mouth would be sweet and warm until it was hot and demanding. I wanted her needy, her hips in my hands, my name a gasp on her lips. *Snap the fuck out of it.*

I blinked and fought to picture Grace's face. The way her brown eyes softened after I kissed her, the gentle touch of her hands all seemed so far away. Too long ago. Grace was my moon, my constant, but Sam...she shone like the sun, fiery, a little temperamental, and she was burning away the darkness I'd lived in for so long.

Problem was, I didn't deserve sunlight.

"Shit, that's why you have the degree in Marine engineering?" Jagger asked.

"Yeah." I sat up straight and shoved food into my mouth.

"Huh," Jagger said with a shit-eating grin that I wanted to punch off his face. "So who's up for the Outer Banks over the Fourth of July?"

"I wish," Josh answered.

"I'm game...if you're inviting me," Carter replied. "I mean, are you?"

"No," I answered, and he scoffed. "No one is inviting anyone."

The conversation died swiftly and turned to the sounds of chewing while they looked at one another with the whole "fucking Grayson" look I'd become accustomed to.

"Well, I'm up for it. Grouchy-pants-Grayson, you don't have

to visit or anything. You stay on your side, and we'll stay on ours." Sam broke the tension with a giggle, nudging me with her shoulder.

I shook my head and sighed. "There are no words for you, Samantha."

She shrugged, then stole one of my French fries with a grin. "You're going to miss me this weekend."

Damn it, she was right.

The smell of the ocean hit me the moment they opened the airplane door. *Home.* I descended the steps out of the aircraft, the warm breeze washing over me better than any welcome-home banner could have.

I waited on the tarmac until my carry-on made its appearance and then walked into the tiny airport I'd seen far too much of this last year.

"Gray!" Mia shrieked, racing past the small crowd to fly into my arms in a skinny tangle of dark curls.

"Hey, Mia." She weighed next to nothing as I leaned back, bringing her feet off the ground. "You need a cheeseburger, little sis."

"Ugh. Shut up. My prom dress barely fit as it was!" She let go and led me through the living-room-size waiting room to where Parker leaned against the doorframe.

"Welcome home, Gray," she said with a Parker-like half smile that didn't quite reach her eyes. She was an older version of Mia, but she'd clipped her curls to pixie-length and wore her skirts about four inches higher.

"Did you draw the short straw, Parker?"

She snorted. "Dad is busy with *The Alibi*, and Mom is pulling double duty on the accounting books. Besides, I'm not sure you'd make it anywhere alive if we let Mia drive you."

I nearly blanched. "No. Mia will not be driving."

"I'm not that bad," she protested, but climbed into the back of Parker's Jeep Liberty.

I folded myself into the front seat and slid it back. "Is your boyfriend a shrimp or something?"

She rolled her eyes at me. "No boyfriend."

"Maybe that's why you're so incredibly pleasant." I raised my eyebrows at her, and she flipped me off.

Mia burst into giggles as we left the parking lot, pulling out onto 64 and heading off Roanoke Island. The traffic backed up once we crossed the bridge into Nags Head, and Parker cursed, "Fucking tourists."

"Watch your mouth around Mia."

"I'm eighteen, Gray. It's not like I haven't heard the word 'fuck,' or even said it a few times. Fuck. Fuck. Fuck. See?" Mia stuck her tongue out. That girl was going to give a guy a run for his money one day. *She'd love Sam.*

I shut that thought down pronto. There was never going to be a reason for Mia to meet Sam.

"Well, you still act thirteen, so let's hold off on the swearing. Especially around Mom. Unless you'd like to put on a show, in which case, I want to be there." I rolled down the window and took a deep breath of the ocean air. This, I missed. Everything else? Not so much.

"It's not like I have a death wish." Mia laughed, poking me in the shoulder as I took my phone off airplane mode.

A text came through.

Unknown: *Hey, where do you keep the cumin?*

My eyebrows hit the roof.

Grayson: *Who is this?*

Unknown: *Oh, come on. Like Josh or Jagger even know what cumin is?*

A corner of my mouth lifted. Samantha. I entered her as the contact on the number, whispering her name as I spelled it out on the keyboard.

Grayson: *What have you done with my kitchen?*

Samantha: *Wrecked it. There's batter dripping from the light fixture.*

I full-on snorted.

Grayson: *Top shelf to the left of where we used to keep the coffee. Please be careful when you get it down. I'm not there to catch you this time.*

My hands itched, remembering all too well the feel of her curves in my arms when she'd fallen, the way her gaze had dropped to my lips. Damn. Even a thousand miles away, I felt tethered to her by an attraction that only burned hotter the more time we spent together...the longer we lived together. Knowing Sam existed would be enough, but living with her heightened everything, like reverse immersion therapy or something.

Samantha: *Then stop putting things where I can't reach them.*

"Smartass," I muttered.

"Holy shit, is that..." Parker's head whipped back to the road. "Is that a smile?"

"What's different about you? You almost seem...happy?" Mia added in.

Happy? Everything in me locked down, like I'd been caught stealing, or worse...cheating. Sam's face flashed through my mind, the way she'd fit perfectly against me on the bathroom floor, the softness of her skin setting fire to mine, and the scent of vanilla. That was ludicrous. Yes, I had...something for Sam, but it could hardly be considered cheating, right? I rolled up the window and focused on blinking brake lights as we crawled through the Memorial Day influx of tourists. "Nothing's different."

"Who's Samantha?" Mia prodded, digging in.

"No one you need to worry about, imp. Just one of my roommates." I regretted the words the moment they were out of my mouth.

"You live with a girl? Is she pretty? Nice?" Mia leaned forward so her head was between mine and Parker's.

My jaw flexed as I gritted my teeth. "Yes, yes, and yes."

"Does that mean—"

"It means nothing, Mia. She's just a roommate." *Keep telling yourself that.*

Parker shot me a sideways look but didn't poke. "You want to go home and grab your car?"

I nodded, itching to feel the wheel of my 66 ½ Mustang under my fingers. Mia filled the silence with details of her senior prom last weekend, from the dress to the corsage to the bullshit I didn't care about but pretended to because she was my baby sister.

We pulled into the driveway as the sun started to set behind the house. "Thanks for the ride, Parker." I grabbed my bag and tossed it into the passenger seat of my car, noting that it hadn't been locked.

"Have you been driving my car?" I asked as Mia swung around one of the support stilts that raised our house off the sand.

"Headed to see Grace?" she asked, dodging.

"Uh huh. You wreck it, I wreck you. I don't care how cute you are." I raised my eyebrows. Yeah, she was definitely not getting near Sam. Those two could rule the world.

"Have fun!" She blew a kiss at me and flounced up the stairs. Something told me I was going to be killing off a few boys at UNC next year. "She'll be happy to see you!" she called back over her shoulder before I started the ignition. She purred to life.

Gravel crunched under the tires as I pulled out of the driveway. Happy? Of all the things Grace was…happy to see me wasn't going to be one of them. I let go of that dream years ago. Or at least tried to, but no matter how dead my hopes were, there was one impossible-to-kill kernel of faith that burned brighter than the darkness. It was that faith that kept me coming home to her.

But even that flame was fading, and I hated myself for it.

I fiddled with the radio, switching between the local stations as traffic moved at a snail's pace until I reached Grace's. Parking, I took a deep breath and curved the brim of my hat before heading in.

"Grayson!" Her mom greeted me at the door, her blond hair perfectly styled, leaning up to hug me. "We've sure missed you. I know your visit is just what she needs."

"How is she?" I asked, more out of habit than anything.

"She misses you, I can tell. She always perks up when you're here. Parker's been by a bunch, but it's not the same."

Parker has been here? "Yes, ma'am, well, if you don't mind, I'd love to see her."

"Of course! Why don't you head on up?"

I took the familiar stairs two at a time, a thousand memories of my childhood assaulting me. How could they not? I'd basically grown up in this house with my best friend. Grace, me...and Owen. *Asshole.*

I knocked on Grace's bedroom door and pushed it open.

She sat, half reclined in bed, watching something on television, her blonde hair draped around her shoulders, and my chest tightened. She was still pretty, but that beauty that had always shone through had dimmed. I imagined her smile, how she'd turn to me with her eyes lit up, arms outstretched, but that wasn't going to happen. Her bed depressed under my weight as I sat next to her and brushed my lips across the smooth skin of her forehead, inhaling her lavender shampoo's scent. Her brown eyes were open, but she didn't so much as look my way.

"Hey baby, I'm home."

CHAPTER EIGHT

SAM

"It's not as bad as it sounds, Mom." I forced a smile for her benefit. Because seriously, what was she going to do from Afghanistan? Hug me?

"Oh really?" Her voice sounded shrill even from six-thousand miles away. She ran her hands over her face and sighed. I saw exhaustion clearly cut into her features, from the weight she'd lost in her face to the circles under her eyes.

There was no way in hell I was going to add to the stress she was under, no matter how many of my buttons she pushed.

"Really. It's not like Jagger is charging me rent—"

"No. I've told you before you're not going to let some guy take care of you financially. I expect you to stand on your own, Sam."

"And I will. I am. I actually got a job last week at a gym—"

"You *what*?" she whispered in her I'm-going-to-kill-you-when-I-get-my-hands-on-you voice.

Air whistled through my teeth as I sucked it in slowly to maintain control. Mom was the perfect officer, steadfast, loyal, smart. But all those qualities that propelled her forward in her uniform sometimes came at a cost, and right now it was compassion in my general direction. "It's a good job, Mom, mostly admin. It's not my life's ambition or anything, but it will hold me over and pay bills while I find my feet."

"Find them. Now. Because whatever you're doing is completely unacceptable. You've been kicked out of college, can't seem to find another one to accept you, and now you're shacked up with three men. I honestly don't know how this all happened in the last six months. I didn't bust my ass raising you alone to have you do...whatever it is you're doing!"

Six months, is that all it had been? Six months since she found out I'd been expelled, anyway. I'd let everything just... slip away. Over what? A pretty smile? Sex?

My control snapped. "You don't think I know the knee-deep crap I'm in right now? I don't need you to lay it out like I don't know. I'm here, and you're not. You never are." I was on my own.

"That's not fair." She rubbed her temples.

"Haven't you ever made a mistake, Mom? Because that whole math-major thing tells me that you were pregnant at my age, right? Did you bounce back from that? No. How do I know that? The only memory I have of my father is his back as he walked away. My already-*married* father. Right?"

Her mouth hung open long enough for me to suck in my breath reflexively. *Shit.* It had been four years since I'd thrown that out there, the same length of time as the affair that had decimated my family, but only wounded his marriage. "Mom. I'm so sorry. I never meant... I'm so sorry. I know what you did for me, what you've been through for me." How could I judge her? After what I'd done? *Taboo relationships. Guess the apple didn't fall far from that tree, eh?*

She closed her mouth slowly, taking a deep breath. "I've done everything I can to make up for you not having him in your life."

"I know. He already had a family and didn't want me, or you, and it's his loss. I just... Mom, I need you to remember what it was like to be my age and maybe cut me a little slack. I'm underwater. I know that. You know that. So you can ease up on me until I start treading water, or you can drown me."

Silence dominated as we stared back at each other, six thousand miles apart in more than distance. Finally, her shoulders dropped a fraction.

"I love you, baby. I know I'm hard on you. I'm just stuck here, and I can command this entire brigade, but I can't seem to keep a grip on my own daughter. You're slipping away so quickly. As soon as I get home, I want you to move back in with me. We'll figure this mess out together. Just another month."

I shook my head. "No, Mom. Then I'd be dependent on you instead of these guys. I have to do this on my own, and you have to let me. Please. I have a plan, just...have a little faith in me. I'll find a way to get back into Colorado." I couldn't do it—move home like I needed to lick my wounds.

"You're at least coming up to see me, right?"

"I wouldn't miss it."

She sighed. "Okay. We're getting busy here tearing down, so it will be a few days before I can get some time. Just...try to stay out of trouble, okay?"

"So don't apply for jobs at strip clubs?"

Her eyes flew wide. "Don't even joke about that, Samantha."

Thank you, Grayson.

We hung up, and I scurried through my closet, discarding the wrong outfits into a pile on my bed. I wanted...*yes!* I slid into my favorite pair of shorts, the ones that hugged my ass and made my legs look longer. I paired them with a black tank top and a light green button-down.

I checked my phone. Four fifteen p.m. I had to hurry or I was going to be late.

I skipped down the steps, waving at the guys, including Will, who were camped out on the sofa watching baseball and enjoying the last day of their long weekend for Memorial Day. *Grayson will be home tonight!*

A rush ran through me, singing in my veins and making my

skin tingle. *Down girl, he said friends.* Maybe he was up for the whole friends-with-benefits thing? Because the more time I spent around him, the harder it was not to crawl up his body and attack his face with mine. *I bet he's strong enough that we could actually have sex while standing. No wall. Nada. Just him and me and those arms...*

"Earth to Sam!" Josh called out.

"Yeah?" I asked, snagging my keys off the hall table. Holy shit, I needed to get laid. Wait, that's right. I didn't have sex anymore. That's what got me here.

"Are you headed to work? We were thinking about dinner and didn't know if you wanted to order from Mellow Mushroom."

"Pizza? Again? What do you guys usually do when Grayson isn't here?" I located my purse in the hall closet.

"It's Tuesday. We order pizza. Same as Saturday," Jagger answered.

"And Thursday," Josh added.

"I miss living with Ember," I muttered, but Josh heard me and grinned. "Order whatever you want. I'll grab something on the way home. I have to run an errand before work, so I'll catch you later?"

They waved me off, and I ran out the door. "Fuck!" I shrieked as my black leather seats scalded the backs of my thighs. Could it be any hotter? I checked the dash. Ninety-seven degrees. In May. What the hell was July going to look like? I rolled down all the windows and blasted the air conditioner.

My heart pounded for the ten minutes it took me to drive past Walmart and pull into the parking lot. It kept pounding the other five minutes it took me to get the courage up to actually get out of the car, and didn't stop when I opened the doors to the admissions office at Enterprise State Community College.

"Welcome, may I help you?" a young brunette drawled sweetly.

"I have an appointment with Mrs. Traper?" My fingers flexed

on my purse. I should have filled out the application online and left it at that. At least rejection didn't actually laugh in my face.

Suck up the bitter taste of accountability. Grayson's voice rang in my ears, and I raised my chin. I could do this.

"Yes, ma'am," the girl answered, pointing down the small hallway. "She's waiting for you, second door on the left."

"Thank you," I replied, and then walked the plank toward her office.

"Come in," Mrs. Traper called to me as I peeked inside her office. She looked mid-forties, with short blond hair and a kind smile. She stood and shook my clammy hand, motioning to the seat in front of her. "What can I do for you, Ms. Fitzgerald?"

"I'd like to apply." I sat, reaching into the folder I brought with me and handing her the application I'd printed and filled out. The pleather squeaked under my shorts.

She took it from me, glancing through it with a perplexed smile. "You didn't need to make an appointment to apply. We'd be happy to look at it and let you know."

"I thought I might have a better chance in person."

She raised her eyebrows. "We're a community college, darlin', not the Ivy League."

I swallowed. "Yes, ma'am. But this is important to me." It was a step, one I desperately needed.

She raised her glasses from the necklace they hung from and slipped them on, delving into my application. "You're coming to us from the University of Colorado?"

"Yes, ma'am."

"Hmm. You had a 3.9 GPA until this last semester, and then it appears you failed all four of your classes?" She looked up, her eyes boring into mine. My breathing accelerated, and I concentrated on slowing it down.

"Yes, ma'am."

"Can you explain for me?"

My mouth opened and shut a few times before I made the

words come out. "I stopped going to classes in December. I didn't turn in any of the work or take any of the finals."

"Well, that would do it. I don't see why you couldn't take some classes here until you're ready to head back to a bigger university. I assume that's your goal, right? Your bachelors in"—she checked my application—"mathematics?"

I nodded. Not that Colorado would ever take me back until I faced the disciplinary board. "I'd like to take a few classes to boost my GPA and give me some concrete to stand on. Right now it feels like it's all quicksand."

She nodded, her eyes searching me like she knew I hadn't told her the whole truth. How could I? I hadn't told anyone. "So we'll fetch your transcript from CU and get you enrolled, sound okay?"

I sucked in my breath. "Is there any chance we can do this without my transcript?"

She took her glasses down and folded her hands on the desk. "What would your transcripts tell me, Samantha?"

Nausea turned my stomach over, but I breathed through it. "It would come with a disciplinary report."

"And what would that say?" Her features stayed relaxed and open, calming me.

"It would say that I struck my ethics professor." In the face. In broad daylight. In the middle of the quad with at least thirty witnesses if not more. And it felt great.

Her eyes widened, but that was her only reaction. "And why would you have done that?"

My chest tightened, my secret simultaneously clawing up my throat to be free and clinging to the mess it had made in my soul. I closed my eyes and centered myself.

"Samantha?"

"Because I found out that I wasn't the only girl he was sleeping with." There. It was out. The crushing weight lifted off my heart, and I took a deep, clear breath, then another. I felt lighter than I had since December, and cleaner, despite the dirt I'd laid bare to a perfect stranger. As my eyes opened, I found her staring back at me, the same kind concern shining out of her eyes as had been there before I told her. "Of course none of *that* is in the report. Just that I hit him."

"I see." She thumbed through the pages of my application again, and I awaited her verdict. At least this time my cards were on the table. There was no giant ax waiting to land in my back while I wasn't looking. I might be facing the guillotine, but I was looking at it head-on. "You used to tutor math?"

I licked my suddenly dry lips. "Yes, ma'am."

"The high school is looking for tutors, if you'd like some volunteer work under your belt..." *She's rejecting me, telling me I haven't paid for my sin yet. I'm screwed.* "...while you take your classes here. We start next week, so be sure to grab a course catalog at the front desk. I'll get you put in the system, and you can enroll online."

My mouth dropped open. "You...you're going to let me in?"

She nodded. "Everyone makes mistakes, Ms. Fitzgerald. Not everyone has the integrity to admit them as you did. Just pay Charlotte your application fee on your way out, and I'll take care of the rest."

I took in sweet, gulping breaths and laughed. "Thank you! Thank you so much!" I couldn't contain my smile, or the tears that pricked in my eyes. Relief. Light, floating relief was all I could feel.

She smiled. "This is why I'm here."

I batted away the silly tears and stood to shake her hand. "I swear I won't make you regret it." Grayson had been right. Accountability tasted bitter, but I was putting one foot in front of the other, gaining distance from the person I didn't want to be. I was almost out of her office when she called me back.

"Samantha?"

I pivoted. *Don't take it back. Please, don't take it back.* "Yes?"

"Would you do it again?" she asked, her head cocked to the side but her eyes soft.

"Sleep with him?" I pictured Harrison, his smile, his hands, the way he'd made me feel like I was special, something worth risking his job over, and then the fallout. "No. Never."

She nodded. "I'm glad to hear it. One mistake doesn't define your life."

She was right. He'd taken everything from me, and I'd stood there and let him, then run away when it had all fallen to pieces in front of me. Nothing had happened to him. He was still teaching, his record unblemished.

My handprint had vanished from his face as if it had never happened, but my academic career had been executed.

"But I'd sure hit him again. Only harder."

I swear I saw her smile as I left.

CHAPTER NINE

GRAYSON

I parked my truck in the farthest spot from the door, hoping to avoid some asshole opening a door into it. I'd been back at Fort Rucker for all of forty-five minutes, long enough to drop my bag at the house and empty the contents into the washing machine.

But now I was here because after four days of being surrounded by family, friends...and Grace, I still couldn't get Sam out of my head. It shouldn't have happened. My life here at Rucker never followed me home, the same as my world there stayed separate. It was the only way I could survive, locking the shit away so I could focus on my future. But she followed me there and didn't even know it.

The gym was fairly empty for a Tuesday night, only the regulars at the free weights and a couple local girls at the stair climber. Speaking of which...

"Hey, Grayson," Marjorie drawled as she swayed past me, her eyes running up my torso, a bottle of water in her hand as she headed for Carter, who was lifting in the corner. He was courting trouble there.

I nodded to her and immediately searched the gym until Sam sailed through the office door, a clipboard in hand. Her shirt molded to her frame, and her shorts were definitely made by someone who was out to torture me. I wanted to peel them down. With my teeth. Then I'd lick back up her thighs—

Damn. It was supposed to be better now that I'd seen Grace, remembered my responsibilities, but my brain ran away the minute Sam stepped into my sight. Something was changing in me that I couldn't stop, like a cracked dam ready to explode and eviscerate everything that lay beneath it. Four days away from her and I was ready to crawl out of my skin to see her smile or hear her laugh. The parts of me that were waking up to her, craving Sam's sunshine in the darkness were way overpowering the saner parts of my brain screaming for distance.

My trip hadn't built up my defenses, it had taken a chisel to the mortar.

Sam handed a towel to one of the local guys and gave him a sweet smile as she tucked a strand of hair behind her ear. My stomach clenched as the guy reached out and touched her arm, and I took a step toward them.

Sam retreated from his touch, still smiling, and it turned into stadium-worthy bright when she saw me. "Grayson!"

She ran the ten feet or so that separated us and flew into my arms. I caught her easily, pulling her against me while her feet dangled off the floor. She hugged me, her grip strong as her vanilla scent overwhelmed me with an unearned sense of peace. Home.

"Ooh, I'm so sorry." She tried to pull back. "I just jumped right on you!"

I held her tighter, my hand splaying wide along the small ridges of her spine. "I don't mind." She melted, resting her cheek along my neck. "How's my kitchen?"

"I burned it to the ground. I missed you!" She laughed, pulling back to beam that gorgeous smile at me. "And guess what?"

"Guessing with you can be dangerous." I raised an eyebrow and tightened my grip around her back to keep from gazing any farther south.

"ESCC let me in! I went and talked to the guidance officer, and they're letting me take classes. I know not all of them will transfer once I get back to the university level…" Her mouth fell a little, like a child who'd been told their artwork wasn't nice enough to hang on the fridge.

"That's great, Sam. In fact, I think it's amazing." She'd faced her demons head-on and came out victorious.

"Hey, Masters, you maybe want to put her down? Or were you thinking of benching her?" Carter called out with a laugh.

Sam pressed her lips together and dropped her eyes. "Naw," I called back. "I could, though, as small as you are." I whispered the last part to her.

Her eyes flew back to mine, wide and impossibly green, and I let her slide down my body, for once taking in every nuance of the way she fit against me, the press of her breasts against my chest to the way her fingers sparked my nerve endings to life as they trailed absently down my chest. Awareness sizzled between us. I'd flipped a switch from friends-only to whatever it was I was flirting with, and she knew it.

I wasn't sure I was even sorry.

"I came by to tell you I was home. You get back to work; I'll work out until you're ready to head home."

"You don't have to walk me out." Her lips curved up, and her eyes darted back and forth between mine, like she was trying to figure out what was going on.

Good luck figuring it out, because damn if I know.

"I know."

She narrowed her eyes and shook her head with a perplexed smile. "Did you hit your head while you were home?"

"Nope. Now get back to work before you get in trouble."

"Uh huh." Sam left to head back to work, and I changed, then took up the station next to where Carter had set up.

"Water," Sam said as she set the bottle next to the bench. She gave me a shy smile and skipped back to the desk.

I unabashedly watched her walk away.

"What's the deal there?" Carter asked.

I turned my attention back to the weights, anxious to lose myself in the burn. "No deal, just watching out for her."

"Or just plain watching her."

My eyes shot up to his in clear warning.

"Hey, I'm not judging. Sam is gorgeous, and funny, and... damn." He took a long drink while he watched her lean across the counter to clean it.

"What the hell would you know about Sam?" My fingers dug into the dumbbells.

He raised an eyebrow. "Feeling touchy? I spent some time with her at the barbecue while you were home doing...whatever it is you do when you go home. She's a firecracker."

My veins ran thick with something hot that tasted a lot like a jealousy I had no right to. "No. Just... No, Carter."

The West Point prick had the nerve to grin at me. "Oh, this is going to be fun. You scared you'll be second choice this time?"

"She is not a game." I leveled him with a glare, and he leaned back.

"Relax. I have no intentions of fighting over a girl ever again." He sighed. "Ever." He took another drink and eyed Sam. "Besides, she's the first person I've seen get under your skin in the year I've known you, Masters, and that's saying something." He looked back at me and waited for a response.

"We're not having a moment, Carter. This"—I motioned between us—"is not happening."

He shook his head and laughed. "Someone needs to warn her what an asshole you really are."

Grace's face sprang to mind, not like I'd seen her this weekend but before *it* happened. Her smiles, laughs, the way she'd slide over in the Mustang to lay her head on my shoulder. Then...after. The way she'd looked through me when I'd held her...when she'd stopped seeing me.

I took a deep breath and let the pain sweep across me, scalding a well-beaten path. I'd learned long ago that pushing it away only made it come back with a vengeance. Then I glanced over to where Sam leaned over a book with Avery and laughed at something. "Yeah, someone really should warn her."

If I were half the man I should have been, I would have.

"Welcome to the AH-64 course. I'm Mr. Wolfton, and I'll be your academics instructor."

The Wednesday morning light streamed through the windows, reflecting off the shiny surface of the tablet in front of me as the other pilots filed in. There were thirty of us in this class. Statistically speaking, that many of us wouldn't graduate.

"First rule in my class is to turn off your cell phones. I hear it go off, and you owe two dozen donuts the next morning. No exceptions, because it's rude to distract your classmates"—he smiled, his graying eyebrows shooting up—"and because I really like donuts. You'll all note that you have tablets in front of you that will serve as your pubs."

"Hey, Masters," Jagger whispered next to me.

I slid my eyes sideways at him.

"This"—he pointed to the power switch—"turns it on. You know, in case you wanted to have a prayer of beating me for top of the class." He finished with a cocky grin.

"Funny, I remember kicking your ass in Primary," I remarked without taking my eyes off the instructor.

Jagger laughed under his breath. "It's a new ballgame."

I swallowed. I needed to be top of the Order of Merit List for two reasons. The first was to get top choice of duty stations after we graduated. Fort Bragg was only five hours away from home. I could make the drive every weekend instead of the once or twice I made it home a month right now. What the hell was I going to do if I got stuck all the way across the country, somewhere like Lewis, or worse, Korea?

But what was my life going to look like if I succeeded and wound up at Bragg?

A sour taste filled my mouth. I washed it away with the Powerade I'd brought to class and tuned back in to the instructor. I wrote down the dates he listed, trying hard not to think about the second reason I needed to graduate at the top of the OML— so no one would look too closely at me.

But I could do this. I just had to study my ass off and use the gym to keep my brain focused. No distractions. No extras. I made it through Primary, and I could make it through the Apache course as long as I worked twice as hard as every other pilot here.

"As you know, on Friday you'll take your first 5&9 test. If you don't pass, it will also be your last." He leveled us all with the I'm-not-fucking-around glare. "You. Will. Pass."

"Good thing Gandalf isn't teaching," Jagger muttered. "You shall *not* pass!"

"Shut up, or trade seats," I answered. "Unless you're going to let me borrow that uncanny memory of yours."

He raised his eyebrows at me. "Someone's moody."

The instructor made it easy to ignore him.

"Once your academics are over this week, and your 5&9 test is perfect, you'll head to the flight line on Monday to meet your instructor pilots."

He walked us through our tablets and the general course requirements. Now death-by-Powerpoint was handheld, but it cut down on the amount of writing I needed to do, so I was all for it. My brain fumbled a few times, but I fought through it.

By two p.m. I felt like mush, trying to store the incredible amount of information that had been dumped on me.

"We're going to end our day early here"—*Thank God*—"but there's one last thing." *Fuck*. "Turn to the man next to you and introduce yourself."

I turned to Jagger, who had his hand thrust forward. "Nice to meet you, I'm Jagger Bateman."

"Very funny." I shook his hand.

"Everyone acquainted?" Mr. Wolfton asked. We all mumbled our assent, even though we hadn't looked around much. "Good. You just met your stick buddy for the rest of the class."

"Sweet!" Jagger fist-pumped.

Fuck. My. Life. If there was one person I'd look like shit next to academically, it was Mr. Photographic Memory. I could outfly him with my eyes shut, I wasn't blind to that, but I couldn't compete with him on any written exam.

"You don't look nearly as enthused as you should be." Jagger grinned.

"Yay," I responded with jazz hands.

"Hey, this is way better than getting paired with Carter. That guy would knock his fucking West Point ring on the damn cyclic if he could."

"I'll give you that one," I answered. Carter was growing on me, but that didn't mean I wanted the guy as my stick buddy. It had been bad enough having him as my class leader when we had the same date-of-rank.

This was a solid plan. Study. Fly. Work out. Focus.

"Come on up and write down your stick buddies on this list so I can get a record, and then you'll be dismissed. See you bright and early tomorrow."

The class rumbled to life, packing up for the day and shuffling to form a line at his desk.

"You cool with this stick buddy thing?" Jagger asked from behind me. "I don't want it awkward at home."

"Don't worry, dear," I answered. "I'll still put out."

"Holy shit, did you just make a joke?" Jagger looked at his watch, which cost more than my car, not that he'd flaunt it. "Let's mark the moment in time where it was discovered that

Grayson Masters has a sense of humor."

I shook my head at him. "The stick buddy thing is good. You'll push me."

"You mean pull your ass."

"You're a cocky prick for someone who landed ninth in the class." The line shifted forward.

"Yeah, well, Paisley's heart is in tip-top shape, so I think we'll avoid that situation in the future."

"Oh, you have excuses." Only two guys in front of us and we'd be to the desk. "But seriously. I need to nail this, Jagger. I can't afford to fail anything, or to be distracted. Just studying, flying, and gym time."

"What about lasagna? You wouldn't take that away, would you?"

A corner of my mouth lifted. "Food is life."

"And Sam?" He lowered his voice.

My head swung around to look at him. All the joking was gone from his eyes, leaving a serious big-brother face I recognized only because of Mia and Parker.

"What about Sam?" My muscles tensed even though my heart jumped. Damn, I reacted to her name like a prissy rom-com movie. I checked my stomach. Thank God those weren't butterflies. Just hunger pangs.

He snorted. "Don't think I don't recognize the way you guys look at each other. You two could probably power the fucking house from the electrical vibe you put out the minute you're in the same room."

"Next?" Mr. Wolfton called, sparing me from responding to a question that I didn't have the answer to.

"Second Lieutenants Grayson Masters and Jagger Bateman."

"So much better than Carter," Jagger whispered behind me.

He scribbled our names down on the running list and then looked up with a smile. "Ah, Lieutenant Masters. I have here that you graduated from the Citadel."

My forehead puckered. "Yes, sir. I did." *In the top one percent of my class, thank you.*

"Good. I've been informed that you're the class leader."

No. No. No. Hell, no. "Sir?"

He handed me a manila folder. "Here's the class roster. Split them into platoons and get me back the phone roster by tomorrow."

My hand froze on the folder.

"Is there a problem?" he asked, his eyebrows raised in question. Jagger elbowed me in the back.

Hell, yes, there's a problem. I didn't have time for this. "No, sir. No problem. Thank you for the opportunity."

I took the folder and met Jagger outside. The heat blasted us in the face as we put our covers on and headed for my truck. "What are you thinking?" Jagger asked, climbing into the passenger side as I cranked the ignition and then the air.

"Now I miss Carter."

He laughed. "Yeah, well, the guy has his uses."

I put the truck into drive and headed for home, my mind fumbling to grasp the concept of taking on the extra duties of class leader and still keep my grades up.

"Don't stress. You're not going to fail."

"Am I that transparent?" My grip tightened on the wheel.

"You're stressed."

We turned into Enterprise. "Yeah, well, this isn't as easy for me. That doesn't mean I won't work twice as hard to get it."

"We'll study, starting tonight. Whenever I'm free, I'll help." He laid out a detailed study plan as we pulled into our neighborhood, still going on about the merits of taping flash cards to the cabinets as I parked in the driveway next to Sam's cabriolet. "We'll minimize your distractions and get you into second place."

"Second place, my ass," I joked with him. If Jagger was on his A game, I'd be lucky to come in second.

I opened the door, and before I could close it, I caught the scent of vanilla...home. "Come here." Sam raced up behind me, her eyes wide as she grabbed my hand in her tiny one and pulled me into the kitchen.

"What the hell?" I asked. "Are you okay? Is your mom okay? Do you need me to kill someone?" The questions fired out of my mouth as I thought them, my filter dropped with my bag in the entry hall.

"What? I'm fine, it's not me."

"Then what?" I cupped her face in my hands to steady her and so I could feel her racing pulse beneath my fingers.

"She got here like an hour ago and just started inspecting things, and going through your room, and kind of put me through the Spanish Inquisition. I really don't think my sex life should be up for discussion." She talked so quickly that I had to concentrate to make out the words. "And not that I mind sharing my clothes, but—"

"Who did?"

"Your sister!" she whispered loudly.

"My..." *Holy shit.* "Which one?"

"How many do you have?" Sam's eyebrows shot toward the ceiling.

"Four. Now which one, Sam?" Not that they weren't all pains in my ass, but if it was—

"Gray! I love what you've done with your room! I dropped my bag there, I hope you don't mind, and oh, my heavens, aren't you just the tastiest thing I've ever seen?"

Oh, hell no.

I turned slowly, keeping Sam protected behind my back as my sister raked her eyes up and down Jagger.

Josh walked through the front door. "God, I want off this detail. Why the hell can't I start my classes the same time you guys do?" He rounded the corner to the kitchen, holding his uniform top in his hand, and my sister's eyes bugged out. "Well, hello there…" He looked at the rest of us for an introduction.

"Oh my God, are all the army guys this hot? You could seriously sell tickets to this show."

"Tell me about it," Sam muttered, stepping around me.

"Grayson?" Jagger asked, thoroughly enjoying himself.

My jaw ticked a few times as I fought for control. My life was about to crash on all fronts. There was no controlling this one. Parker, Constance, hell, even Joey, I could have handled. But not her. "Josh, Jagger. Meet Mia, my baby sister. Hands off, or I kill you while you sleep."

Jagger started laughing hysterically. "Well, so much for no distractions."

CHAPTER TEN

"What are you doing here, Mia?" I cornered her in the kitchen while Jagger fired up the grill.

"I wanted to see you," she pouted.

"I just saw you less than a week ago. Now cut the crap."

She bounced back on her heels to sneak a look out the window. "Why didn't you say that your roommates are gorgeous?"

"Because I'm a guy, Mia. Now stay on topic. Why—how are you here?" She might only have been five foot two, but she could destroy the small amount of peace I'd managed to attain here.

"I took a flight? I told Mom I wanted to see you, and she thought it was good that someone was finally checking up on you." She picked up Sam's coffee mug, which still wore her shade of sparkly lip gloss. "Plus, I wanted to meet her."

"Meet who? Sam?" I took the mug out of her hand and put it back on the counter. It was empty, which told me Sam would be back soon.

"The girl who made you smile." She grinned like she'd caught on to some elusive secret.

"Mia… This is my life. Not some kind of matchmaking game. I wasn't lying at home; Sam is just a roommate."

"I know you better than that."

"You can't say anything about home, Mia. Or Grace, because—"

"Relax, Gray. I'm not here to dish out your secrets. Why you keep it secret is beyond me, but if you need to compartmentalize, I get it."

Sam waltzed into the room and came to an abrupt halt, her gaze flickering between me and Mia. "Oh, I can come back."

I lifted up the empty coffee cup. "No, you can't. You'll drop dead on the floor or something if you don't get a fix. You're not bothering us, I promise."

Sam bit her lower lip, and damn, I wanted to suck it out, then caress the little indentation from her teeth with my tongue. Shit. "If you're sure?"

"Yes, I'm sure." *About both.*

She gave Mia, who was unabashedly taking in every detail of Sam, a shy smile and loaded a K-cup. While it was brewing, she passed me on the way to the fridge. "Ugh. I forgot I was out of creamer."

"Look behind the milk," I suggested.

Her squeal was well worth the extra effort it had taken. "How the hell?" She turned with wide eyes, presenting her bottle of peppermint-mocha creamer. "Did you do this?"

Her eyes were lit up like a kid at Christmas, and her smile could have sailed a thousand ships, easy. "It was nothing." Just a matter of checking a suitcase full of gel packs and praying TSA didn't think I was out of my mind.

She jumped at me, and I swung my arm around her back as she noisily kissed my cheek. "Thank you! I will ration it, I swear."

I scoffed. "That bottle will last you about three days at the rate you inhale your coffee."

She landed back on her feet and grinned. "Well, it will be a glorious three days."

A corner of my mouth twitched upward, disobeying my order to keep a straight face. "A glorious eighteen days."

Her eyebrows shot up as the Kuerig hissed at completion. "Huh?"

"Check the freezer." I gripped the counter behind me,

ignoring Mia's eyes boring holes into me. "Behind the second bottle of tequila."

Sam's mouth dropped for a millisecond before she opened the freezer door to see the five other bottles I'd stored there yesterday. "No way!" She jumped, bouncing on her tiptoes. She shut the freezer door and spun, this time directing her smile at Mia. "Your brother"—she pointed at me, like there was any other guy who could have been mistaken for Mia's brother—"is a god among men."

"So I've heard," Mia answered, her smile nearly consuming her little face.

Sam passed me on the way back to her coffee and squeezed my bicep. "Thank you," she whispered, sneaking a look up at me before she turned her attention to her coffee.

"Sam, will you bring me a clean plate?" Jagger called out as he slid the glass door open a fraction.

"Right on it!" she answered, and took her coffee and a plate back outside.

Mia started laughing, snorting in between gasps.

I leaned back against the counter and crossed my arms. "What is so funny?"

"Just a roommate!" She leaned over, holding her stomach. "Oh, you have it so bad, big brother."

"Just a roommate," I reiterated, but she headed into the backyard, her laughter louder than before.

Whatever. She could think what she wanted. Yes, I was ridiculously attracted to Sam, who the hell wouldn't be? But having it bad? Not in the least.

I opened the freezer and pulled out one of the bottles of creamer, taking note of the manufacturer. Maybe if I ordered a case, they could just have it delivered.

Wait. Was I seriously contemplating this?

"Damn," I muttered, shoving the bottle back in the freezer.

Bad, indeed.

...

"Please? Come on, Gray," Mia cajoled from the Fort Rucker pool. Thank God she had on a one-piece. I would have hated to kill any of the new privates for hitting on my sister. It would have interfered with my class ranking, no doubt. "I've been here for three days, and all you do is study! What the heck could be so difficult?"

I flipped another 5&9 card. I was halfway through the stack, and then I'd take another test. As of this morning, I was only three questions short of completing the timed test, and was killing it with one-hundred percent accuracy. Two days to go.

Two more days of Mia investigating every part of my life before we both flew home to Nags Head.

"You're not supposed to be here, Mia," I reminded her and flipped another card.

"You're not supposed to be here, Mia," she mocked me in the way little sisters do and climbed out of the pool. "At least Sam is on her way."

That got my eyes off the cards. "You invited Sam?"

"She said she'd head over after she finished her tutoring session at the summer school." Mia wrapped herself in a towel and wrung the water out of her hair.

"She's getting tutored? That doesn't sound right. Besides, her classes don't start until next week." Monday, in fact. Nine a.m. chemistry, if I remembered her schedule correctly. She'd taped it on the fridge with an adorable, goofy grin.

"No, she's doing the tutoring. She's got mad math skills."

"And a big heart."

She cracked a grin at me, squinting in the harsh afternoon light. "I thought you were studying?"

I dropped my gaze to the flashcards. Tutoring. Sam may have made some huge mistakes, but the way she'd stopped the spiral and started digging herself out meant a hell of a lot more to me than what got her there. Whatever it was.

That was the measure of a person to me. Not the shit they pulled, but the way they recovered from it, like when Jagger had taken the blame for us with that damn polar bear statue. The hardest thing I'd ever done was to march into that office, lay my shit bare, and risk everything I'd fought so hard for, but he wasn't going to fall on my sword.

"What is that?" Mia pointed to my flashcards. Shit.

I moved to throw them into my bag, but she caught them with those freakish, catlike reflexes of hers. She opened to a random card, and I cringed. "Fuel pressure limitations on..."

Her inhaled breath may as well have been the shot heard 'round the world.

"Are you..." Her eyes flew to mine, and I lowered my sunglasses, my chest instantly tight.

"Am I?" I challenged her.

"Dad is going to kill you." She narrowed her eyes in my direction.

"I quit seeking Dad's approval years ago." I held out my hand and waited, though every nerve ending itched to rip the study guide from her fingers. Tension coiled beneath my skin. "You're eighteen now, Mia. Legally an adult and headed to UNC in a couple months. Are you really going to tell me that your life is going to be about what Mom and Dad want?"

She sighed, then gave me the cards back. "You can't lie to them."

I didn't blink. "I never have."

"*This* is a lie of omission." She folded her arms under her chest.

"*This* has always been the plan." I stood, tired of feeling like Mia had the moral and physical higher ground.

"The plan...changed." Her voice dropped.

"No, everyone wanted the plan to change." *Because they*

don't have something to prove like I do. She shook her head at me, but I cut her off before she got a word out. "Do you really want to go there? Constance, Joey, hell, even Parker have all given me their godlike opinion. Are you ready to throw your hat in that ring?" She flinched. Fuck. I'd never taken that tone with Mia. How the hell was I going to make her understand? "This is all I have." Even my throat was tight, and it took effort to force out every word. "This is it. I'm here working my butt off, and when I'm not, I'm back in Nags Head with Grace. Forgive me, if I want just *one* thing for myself."

Her face fell. "Gray..."

"I'm not asking for your approval, or your understanding. I'll tell them after graduation. He'll need me to prove myself."

She got that stubborn look on her face, the one she'd had since she was two, scrunching her nose. "Fine."

"That's why you're my favorite sister," I said and turned around to grab my flash cards.

"Yeah, well that's not hard to do looking at the rest of them."

A skinny jackass whistled as he passed by us, lowering his sunglasses and scoping Mia out like a piece of steak, or worse—a piece of ass.

I pivoted toward the pool, tripping him with my foot in the process. He shrieked and fell into the pool. I stepped in front of Mia, taking the splash. He sputtered to the surface, and I crouched down to pool level as he swam to the side.

"Dude!" the kid called out, wiping the water out of his eyes.

"That's my baby sister. Would you like another look?" I dropped my voice and narrowed my eyes.

"N-n-no," he sputtered.

"Gray, come on, you're scaring the guy. He probably thinks you're about to go all Hulk on him." Mia tapped my shoulder, which was still tense.

I grunted but offered my hand to the guy and pulled him out of the pool easily. His street clothes dripped enough water to fill the baby pool.

"Hey, Sam!" Mia waved her arm above her head.

My eyes latched onto Sam before the rest of me even registered that Mia had spoken.

From beneath the wide brim of a straw hat and huge sunglasses, Sam gave off a megawatt grin that could have tanned my soul. Her florescent orange wrap perfectly complemented her skin. The tension in my chest instantly dissipated, like she'd pulled the thread on an old sweater, slowly unraveling me, dissolving not only the strain but my defenses as well.

"Hey, guys!" She came over to us and claimed the chair closest to Mia.

Well, that sucked. Wait. It was for the best. Damn, I couldn't even decide where I wanted her to sit. I waved. Lamest wave in the history of man.

"How was your tutoring session?" Mia asked.

"Long," Sam answered, dropping her hat to her chair with her glasses, and then stretching her arms toward the sun. At six p.m. the temp should have started dropping from its ninety-nine-degree high, but damn if mine wasn't spiking.

Get a fucking grip on yourself.

"Want to swim?" Mia asked, dropping her towel.

"Sure!" Sam nodded enthusiastically. She untied the belt around her waist and let her wrap fall to the chair.

Holy. Fucking. Shit. Fuck. Shit. Fuuuck.

Her suit was made up of a halter top and boy shorts. It left the toned muscles of her stomach bare to the sunlight and hugged her ass. Her breasts rose high and her nipples stood out against the fabric.

My mouth watered at the thought of peeling the tiny scrap of fabric away and taking a taste.

"What's with the disapproving look? Are you going to tell me to put on more clothes again, Grayson? Because last time I checked, we are at a pool, and I technically have on more clothes than you do." She motioned to my bare chest.

I looked disapproving? Hell, I'd take it. It was a lot better than horny like the kid I'd tripped into the pool...who was still standing just to the side of me. I glared at him, but his eyes were focused on someone else. Samantha.

"It's hot as hell out here," Mia commented.

"Language," I snapped out of habit.

She raised her eyebrows at me. "I don't see Mom. Hell. Hell. Hell."

"You're going to be the death of me, Mia." I sat back on my chair and reached for my cards to keep from reaching for Sam, but the chair put me at eye line with her ass, so I stood back up. "Go swim."

"I'd love to get in," Sam said and touched her toe to the water.

"I'd love to get in, too," the skinny kid remarked with a whistle, his eyes wide as he blatantly appreciated Sam a little too much.

My arm was out before I could stop it, my open palm connecting with his chest and sending him back into the pool.

"Grayson, what the hell?" Sam asked, racing to the edge of the pool.

He spit water out as he surfaced. "What, is she your sister, too?"

When he'd checked out Mia, it had annoyed me, but putting his sights on Sam sent cold rage through my veins, locking my muscles. "Fucking far from it."

"Gray! Language!" Mia mocked me.

I didn't bother to turn around, just kept my glare locked on skinny-no-mannered-asshole until he got the point.

Stop cat-calling my girls.

Shit. I blinked. When had I started to think of Sam as one of my girls? *The moment you caught her off the counter.*

"Oh my God, do you need a hand?" Sam leaned over the

water with her hand extended.

The guy looked at her like she'd grown three heads, then swam to the opposite side of the pool before getting out. *Good plan.*

"Cave man, much?" Sam glared up at me.

"He was…" I lost all words.

"Checking me out? Hitting on me? Maybe thinking of asking me out?" She crossed her arms, which only raised her breasts. *Get your mind out of her fucking pants.* "Grayson, I'm single. Did it ever occur to you that maybe I would like to be asked out?"

"You want someone like that? Someone who just wants you because of your body?" *Your very tight, very fuckable body.*

She rubbed her fingers into her temples. "No, but that's not your call to make, hothead. It's mine."

I caught Mia laughing like a loon over Sam's shoulder and glared harder. Sam's expression changed, her features schooled with a sugar-sweet smile. "In fact, I think you should cool off!"

She looped her leg around mine, hitting her heel in the pit behind my knee, and my leg buckled. "Sam!" I pitched toward the pool and knew impact was coming, but I wasn't going down solo. I pulled her to me as we tumbled into the pool.

My feet hit the bottom and I pushed off, bringing us to the air. Sam coughed and looped her arms around my neck. We were deep enough that I could touch, but she couldn't. "I can't believe you did that," I said, my mouth slightly agape.

She grinned, biting her lower lip. "I can't believe you took me with you."

"Good reflexes." God, she felt good against me, her curves slippery, but I carefully kept my hands on her waist. My gaze dropped to her lips, and I swallowed. Hard.

Her fingers sent little electric shocks as she absentmindedly stroked the back of my neck. I looked back to her eyes and caught my breath. Her grin faded, and her eyes widened, waiting for something I wasn't sure I was even able to give.

Fuck, she looked kissable.

The dynamic between us shifted like the world had tilted on its axis. We were strapped into a roller coaster, awaiting the inevitable, but not knowing when the first drop was coming.

Sam had gone from a "never" to a "not yet" in the five weeks I'd been living with her. What would she be in another month or two?

Everything, a little voice whispered in my head.

We stayed there, locked onto each other, both tasting the shift between us until water hit me in the back of the head.

"So this is where you guys are hanging out," Josh said, leaning over the edge of the pool.

Sam let her hands fall away from my neck, looking anywhere but at me.

"Hey, Samantha," I whispered.

She jerked her eyes back to mine and raised those perfect eyebrows.

I hoisted her out of the water and tossed her into the deep end of the pool. She landed with a splash and more than one curse word while I stifled the urge to laugh.

"There's something different about you here. You're lighter, somehow...not...I don't know...normal Gray." Mia glanced to Sam, who had swum over to talk to Josh. "She's good for you."

He dunked Sam playfully, and she came up with a gasp.

Ice crawled through my veins, and suddenly it wasn't the pool I was standing in, but the channel. And that wasn't Sam laughing, it was Grace screaming. Then silence. So much silence.

"Gray?" Mia touched my arm, and I jerked. "You okay?"

I nodded and shut the past out, studying the way Sam lifted her hair away from her face. Her smile, so warm that it brought the deadest parts of me to life. She was infuriating, captivating, confusing, and worth every second. Our lines were blurring, and for every inch I backed away, she pulled me twice as close without even realizing it. Being around her was more addictive than the caffeine she survived on, and I was constantly jonesing for a hit...of her.

"I mean it," Mia added. "She's good for you."

"Yeah, well, I'm not good for her."

Problem was, I wasn't sure it was a good enough reason to stay away from her anymore.

CHAPTER ELEVEN

"Bye!" God, where was that damn hang-up button? Mom's face disappeared from the screen, and I rested my forehead on the laptop for a moment. She'd been utterly disappointed in my choice to enroll in a "beneath me" community college, but she said she'd pay for it, which was more than I could have ever hoped for.

I clicked open my email and weeded through the mess until I got to a name I didn't recognize. PlayOne@yahoo.com. My fingers tapped absently above the keys. *Get over your shit.*

Right. I opened the email and my stomach dropped.

HOW DID YOU LIKE YOUR LATEST REJECTION? ONCE A WHORE, ALWAYS A WHORE. TOO BAD YOU CAN'T SLEEP WITH THEM TO LET YOU IN. JUST. STOP. TRYING.

Shaking hand and all, I closed it.

It was what I deserved, right? My penance for my sin. *One hundred Our Fathers and thirty-two harassing emails.*

It didn't matter anyway, right? I had a fresh start on Monday and time to rebuild myself. *Yeah, until you apply at another school...or finally face it at Colorado.*

Oh, I was totally pulling a Scarlet O'Hara on that one—I'd think about it tomorrow. Or never. Whatever.

But this, I could stop now. I might deserve it, but if I was going to move past it, I couldn't have it thrown in my face every time I checked my email. I adjusted my settings and only let in known email addresses to my inbox...and Victoria's Secret. I could never have enough Vickie's. Or chocolate.

One click at a time, I took back this aspect of my life.

This definitely called for brownies.

I skipped down the stairs and almost ran smack into Grayson as he was coming up. "Hey!" Did that come out as breathless as I felt? The guy usually sucked the oxygen right out of my lungs the minute he entered the room, but in an ACU flight suit? Holy shit. For someone who'd never even wanted near a soldier...well, I wanted to be *very* near Grayson. Like within a breath. A touch. Under him. Over him. Pinned between his yards of muscle and the wall.

"Hey yourself." His eyes lit up like he knew exactly what I was thinking.

"Good day?" I forced out.

"Great day. I passed my 5&9 test." His eyes danced, and I found myself grinning like a lovesick dork, but I couldn't help it. He looked happier than I'd ever seen.

"Oh yes, this is definitely a brownie kind of day. I'm going to get your kitchen so dirty." My nose scrunched while I tried to pull off the innuendo.

He didn't so much as flinch, just kept that intense Grayson-stare. "I have to leave in about an hour. Our flight to Nags Head is tonight."

My shoulders stayed straight, instead of slumping the way I felt, like a balloon that had been popped. He'd just been there last weekend. "Well, Ember is on her way, so I guess that leaves more for us." I pushed a smile out.

"Save me one. I'll be home Sunday."

I nodded, and he tucked a strand of hair behind my ear, once again depriving me of oxygen. Somehow he felt lighter... easier after passing that test.

We did the awkward both step to the left, both step to the right, before finding our way around each other, and I headed for the kitchen and pulled out a box of brownie mix. Eggs. Water. Oil. Easy.

So what, he was leaving for a couple days. He went home like twice a month, it wasn't like this should have been such a shock, or even an issue. Hell, he wasn't even mine to have an issue about. I had a crush, a ridiculous, inconvenient crush on my incredibly sexy roommate. That's all there was to it.

Twelve-year-olds get crushes, not you.

I cracked the egg and poured the ingredients over the mixture after I warmed up the oven, then turned the mixer on low. My fingernails tapped out a steady rhythm on the top of it as the powder turned into deliciousness, but my brain just wouldn't quit.

I wasn't even staying here. This was a pit stop in the road to educational and...well, moral recovery. Grayson wasn't staying here, either. He'd graduate flight school in December and no doubt ask to be assigned somewhere close to home.

Except that he'd just called Alabama "home." He'd gone from calling it "here," to *home*. Besides, if anything even happened between us, we'd only have six months together...not that anything was happening. *Yet.*

My hand slipped and knocked the lever on the side of the mixer.

"Fuck!" I shrieked as the mixer whirred a shrill pitch and batter exploded, hitting the walls, the cabinets, my face... everything. I sputtered as some landed in my mouth, and slammed my hand against the lever to turn it off.

This was going to be a bitch to clean up.

"Are you okay?" Grayson ran in, hair damp from the shower. His eyes widened as he took in the state of his precious kitchen. "You weren't kidding about the mess."

"Oh this?" I smiled. "It's a new aeration technique. I totally meant to do this." My awesome excuse died as a glob of brownie mix fell off the tip of my nose.

"Is that so?" he asked, walking over to me slowly, consuming my vision. My breath hitched as he swiped his finger across my cheek, and then licked the brownie mix off the digit. *Holy hot.* "Hmm... I think there's something to be said for this method. Maybe a little more air in the batter?"

My mouth popped open. "Are you making fun of me?"

He smirked, which must have had a direct link to my panties, because they unanimously voted to drop. Now. There was sexy, and there was Grayson's tongue sweeping across his lower lip, which was a step beyond hedonistic. His eyes took on a mischievous glint but kept the same signature intensity that held me captive, unable to look anywhere else as he lowered his face toward mine. What...what was he doing?

Do you even care? Nope. Not one bit.

"Maybe another taste to be sure?" he asked, his voice low as his lips skimmed across my jawline. "Mmm. Definitely more." Shivers coursed down my body. *Holy shit.* His mouth was actually on me, and I was awake.

He flipped the switch on the mixer and chocolate flew.

"You did not!" I let my knees buckle so I slipped to the floor, leaving Grayson to be splattered by the flying confection.

"I most certainly did!" He lifted me up like I weighed nothing, and batter smacked the back of my tank top. "Man, you're slippery." He mock-dropped me.

I yelped, locking my ankles around his waist and my hands around his neck. He turned off the mixer and chuckled low in his throat. "You can laugh?" I asked, yanking my head back to look at him.

"I have been known to on occasion," he answered, that absurd, wildly sexy smirk in play despite the chocolate on his cheeks and forehead. How the hell could someone look so hot while literally dripping brownie batter?

"I like it," I admitted.

His smirk disappeared, and his grip tightened on my bare thighs as his gaze dropped to my lips. They parted as if he'd freaking asked them to. We weren't just stepping out of the friend-zone here, we were on a damn missile into let-me-jump-you-ville.

"I do, too," he whispered.

His lips moved toward mine, and I threw up my last defense, placing my finger over his lips before I was lost to all things Grayson. "Wait. Don't you think—"

He supported all of my weight with one of his arms and gently pulled my fingers an inch away. "That's the problem. When you're near, I don't think. I can't." He sucked my middle finger into his mouth and swirled his tongue around it, licking it clean. My entire body clenched, and my breath *whooshed* from my lungs as he did the same with my pointer finger, then let it slip free. "I'm so damn tired of trying to."

He cupped the back of my neck with the hand that wasn't cradling my ass, and brought my mouth to his in a consuming kiss. I responded instantly, opening to him as he swept inside with sure strokes of his tongue. He tasted like chocolate, and sin...and sex. Really good sex.

He growled, his hand fisting my hair to hold me to him. I sure as hell wasn't going anywhere, not if I could get another sound like that out of him. Heat radiated from his skin to my hands as I stroked his neck to wind my fingers around the back of his head. I arched into him, pressing my breasts into his chest as our tongues rubbed and danced, setting fire to every nerve ending in my body. There was nothing else in the world for me, just the feel of Grayson under my hands, the taste of him filling me. He eclipsed everything else until kissing him was my existence.

He moved backward until he settled onto one of the tall dining room chairs and held me in his lap. My feet slipped from his waist to brace myself on the chair's supports. I rolled my hips over him, and he hissed as I brushed against his erection.

Holy shit. He was hard. Already. For me.

I broke the kiss, pausing a breath away from his lips as we both took gasping breaths. "Grayson," I whispered.

"More." His eyes shone nearly silver and cut through any protest I might have managed, if I'd been thinking logically enough to even contemplate stopping.

His answer sent a spiral of pure lust streaking through my body, and I whimpered as he pulled me back to him, using his tongue and lips to caress every inch of my mouth, then biting my lower lip gently. I clung to whatever shred of sanity I had left, but it fled when he ran kisses down my neck, sucking at little patches of skin and then licking to soothe the burn. I shamelessly rocked against him, then ran my fingers down the carved muscles of his back. There wasn't a spare ounce of fat on him. He was perfectly cut, honed, and strong enough to do whatever I asked him to.

The thought sent another surge of heat through my stomach, pooling lower.

A low rumble started in his chest as he gripped my ass, his hands squeezing and shaping me with the perfect amount of pressure. "Samantha."

My name sounded like a prayer on his lips, like I was something worthy of worship. Worthy of him. "Say it again."

His eyes turned hazy, and one hand drifted up my back to tighten in my hair. "Samantha." He dragged out the syllables until it sounded like a personal request to climb him like a freaking tree and use him as my personal playground.

He tugged, arching my neck, and I gasped as he set his mouth to it, kissing lower to my collarbone. The muscles in his arms bulged as he lifted me higher, running his tongue just under the neckline of my tank top. Could he hear my heart pounding? Beating out a rhythm that was demanding—

"Hey, are you ready to head to the airpor—Oh. OH!" Mia exclaimed.

My head jerked down, slamming my chin into the top of Grayson's head and rattling my mouth. To his credit, he didn't drop me. *This is so not happening.* Heat fled from my stomach and lodged in my face. What were we? Sixteen and getting caught making out in his parents' basement?

"Knocking, Mia." He growled against my skin, lowering me until I was sitting in his lap again.

"It's a kitchen, Gray."

He rested his forehead against mine, eyes closed, and took a deep breath. Then he leveled a look on his sister that had her backing up. She got the point. Or I think she did. I couldn't exactly see out of my peripheral vision, and there was no way I was going to glance in her direction. Not when she'd just caught me dry-humping her brother.

"I'll just...um...make sure I got everything out of your room? Right." She practically ran.

Grayson turned to stone beneath me and slowly turned his gaze to mine. "Grayson? What does this mean?" *Oh great, ask him the ultimate girl question. Good job, Sam.* "Not that it has to mean anything, right? I mean, we're both adults..."

"Stop, please, Sam." His hands were strong but gentle on my waist as he lifted me off him, waiting until I was steady to release me.

He stood slowly, then put the dining room table between us, just like he had the first morning we met. Did he need to protect himself from me? Wait. He kissed *me* first. My fingers skimmed across my swollen lips.

He swallowed, examining the table. "I don't know what it means, and I know if I try to figure it out this second I'm going to end up saying something we'll both regret, one way or another."

"What the hell does that mean?" It was suddenly hard to

swallow the lump in my throat. "That you shouldn't have kissed me?" My jumping-Grayson high was quickly plummeting to a he-regrets-me low. *You should be used to it. Sam, the quick-fix-regret-later gal.*

"I don't…" He shook his head. "I don't know. I never act on impulse. I just… God, I don't know. I have to go, our flight is in a couple hours."

I nodded, locking my jaw, trying to trade the ache in my heart for anger. "Yeah. You should go." *Do not cry. Don't do it.*

He came around the table, and I kept my eyes trained on a large splatter of brownie batter on his shirt. "Samantha."

I shook my head. "Just go."

He tilted my chin up, and my rage died. His eyes said everything he didn't, or couldn't, and were filled with a kind of pain I couldn't fathom but illogically needed to soothe immediately. His cheeks scratched my palms with his five o'clock shadow as I cupped them and forced a smile. "Hey. It doesn't have to mean anything. I'm a big girl."

"I have to go."

"You always have to go," I whispered, and immediately regretted opening my mouth when his eyes closed. "Grayson, go. It's okay. We can talk, or not talk, when you get back. I'll be here."

He opened his eyes and held me captive with a single longing look. "You'll be here."

"I'll be here. I promise. But you do have to do one thing first." I wrinkled my nose.

"Oh?" That smirk came back out to play, and I just about sang the "Hallelujah Chorus."

"Take another shower. You're covered in brownie mix."

He looked down as if he'd forgotten he wore the sticky mess and sighed. "Right. Okay." He paused, glancing at my lips, which still hummed from his kiss. His fingers covered mine, and he leaned into my palm. "I have to go."

I raised my eyebrows. "Yes, you do."

He nodded, then turned and pressed a kiss into the palm of my hand. Then he left me standing in a brownie-splattered kitchen.

"I think you're good for him, for whatever my opinion matters," Mia said, looking over the half wall at the mess we'd created.

"I'm not sure I'm good for myself, let alone Grayson." I wet the kitchen sponge and headed to the counter. "But your opinion means a ton, Mia. I'm so sorry you walked in on that. Slightly mortified, actually."

"I just graduated high school. Trust me, I've seen worse. Just not with Grayson. It's nice to see him happy." I raised my eyebrows at her, and she grinned. "Well, as happy as he gets, I guess. Oh! I almost forgot my phone charger!" She raced up the stairs.

Ellie Goulding blared out of Mia's phone on the counter. "Mia!" I called out. "Your phone!" She didn't answer.

I peeked at the caller ID. Parker. Grayson's other little sister. "Mia!" I yelled a little louder. I debated for about five seconds before swiping the phone on.

"Hi, Parker, this is Sam. Mia ran upstairs for just a second, but she'll be right back." I kept my voice chipper. Wait, was that a scoff on the other end?

"Sam, as in Samantha. Of course."

That tone was anything but friendly. "Did you want to hang on?"

"No need, if you can just pass a message to my sister and brother for me?" Her voice changed to syrupy sweet, and my spidey-senses tingled.

"Absolutely."

"Tell Grayson that they've transferred Grace to OBH for a bad kidney infection. Her parents made sure to get the room with the pullout couch for him, since, you know, he barely leaves her side when he's here. He's such a good boyfriend, don't you think?"

Boyfriend. My stomach lurched. *No. Not again.* The counter took the brunt of my weight as I leaned over on my elbows. "Yeah, he's something else."

"Well, it was nice to meet you, Sam. Tell Mia and Gray I'll pick them up at the airport?"

"Absolutely." My voice didn't shake, which was hard to believe when the rest of me trembled. *Breathe. Just breathe.*

"Bye now!" She hung up without waiting for me to respond, and left me staring at the phone when Mia walked in.

"Sam? You okay? Is that my phone?" Her forehead puckered.

"Parker called. Something's wrong with Grace's kidneys, and they just transferred her to OBH. But there's a pullout couch so Grayson can stay with his girlfriend." That sounded normal, right? Maybe a touch flat, but at least I wasn't screaming...just internally.

"Oh man, that's the last thing she needs." Mia rubbed her hands over her face.

"So he has a girlfriend?" I asked, my voice cracking on the last word.

She stilled, then slid her hand down her face. Truth sang out from her eyes, no matter how she tried to hide it. "Grace... Grace is really complicated. Like amazingly, soap-opera-worthy complicated, and it's just not my place. I promised him." She whispered the last part, a plea in her brown eyes to understand.

Oh, I understood all right. *You're so incredibly stupid. Well, at least you didn't fuck this one, right?* "You guys need to get going or you'll miss your plane."

She skirted around the wall into the kitchen and took my hand, which was suddenly freezing. "You need to let him explain. Don't jump to conclusions. Don't be that girl who freaks out over a miscommunication. Just give him a chance."

"Name one reason why I should," I asked.

"Because he's alive around you. You're the first reason I've seen him smile in almost five years. Seeing him here...with you, it's like having him back again. You don't see it, but I do. That's why I came here. The minute he said your name in the car, it was like...a light clicked on. I had to know you. Please, give him a chance to explain."

What was there to explain about a girlfriend back in North Carolina? Of course that's why he went home as often as possible. How stupid could I have been? I took my hand back and gripped the kitchen counter.

What the hell was wrong with me? Was I only attracted to guys who were already taken?

"Mia?" Grayson called, barreling down the steps. "You ready? We have to go now or we'll miss our flight."

He rounded the corner and shook his head as he looked at the kitchen. "Sam, I'm so sorry to leave you with this mess."

I laughed, snorting as I sucked in air, and then continuing like a hyena. "The kitchen? That's your idea of a mess?"

His mouth dropped open a fraction. The mouth I'd had against mine just a few minutes ago. "Samantha?" He moved to touch me, and I jerked back.

"She knows about Grace," Mia offered quietly.

He swung toward her like he'd been slapped. "You?"

"Parker," she whispered.

"Fuck." He seethed.

It only made me laugh harder, nearly hysterical. "Oh, now you swear."

"Sam, it's really complicated." He stepped forward, but I retreated until my back was against the chocolate-covered counter.

My laughter died. "Do you have a girlfriend in North Carolina, Grayson?"

A muscle in his jaw ticked, and his hands flexed. "That's not a simple question, and it takes a hell of a lot more than five minutes to answer."

"We're going to miss our flight," Mia said quietly.

Why was I drawn to cheating bastards? *Like mother, like daughter.* "Take my car and go, Mia. I'm not coming home this weekend."

"Go, Grayson." My fingers dug into the counter, brownie mix sliding into the crevices of my fingers. My hands remembered all too well the feel of Harrison's face as I slapped him in the quad, the satisfying sound of retribution and anger. But where I tried to draw up anger here, there was only sadness. "You are the last person I want to see right now, so just go."

He shook his head. "No. I'm not leaving you until you understand."

"You're going to miss your flight." *Don't come any closer, please.*

"I don't care. Mia, take my car and go. I'll get it from the airport tomorrow."

"You have to go. Now. Because your girlfriend there is in the hospital with kidney problems, and the girl you just kissed here doesn't want anything to do with you." My knees started to shake, and my stomach roiled. How the hell did he have the nerve to look like I'd just snapped his heart in two?

He raked his hands over his hair, and I could almost see the devil and the angel on his shoulder, determining his choice. He sighed and closed his eyes, and I knew North Carolina and... Grace had won—as she should have. He reached out slowly, like I was going to bite him, and cupped my face. I flinched away, but he followed me. "This conversation isn't over. I'll explain as soon as I'm back, and you're going to listen."

"Planes don't wait for anyone."

"Sam," he whispered.

"Go."

He searched my eyes with an intensity that made it impossible to look away. Then he nodded once. "I'll call you when I get there."

I didn't answer, just like I planned to do with his phone calls. He could shove them where the sun didn't shine.

He walked out of the kitchen, taking Mia with him. A few moments later I heard the front door open and shut, then Grayson's truck pull out of the driveway. My knees gave out, and I slid down to the floor, wincing when the cabinet handles dug into my skin. I wrapped my arms around my knees and tucked into the smallest ball possible.

I wasn't sure how long I sat there, but my butt was numb by the time Ember opened the front door. "Yoo-hoo!"

"I'm in the kitchen," I called out, my voice inflectionless.

She walked in and dropped her purse on the counter as she surveyed the damage. "Well, this is one way to redecorate."

"I made such an epic mess!" I sobbed uncontrollably, my entire body shaking from the force of emotion I couldn't contain. No matter how hard I tried, I just couldn't get my feet under me, couldn't seem to unbury myself from the crap I just kept heaping on.

Ember sank to the floor, wrapping her arm around me and pulling my head to her shoulder. "We'll clean it up, Sam. No matter what it is."

I cried in the arms of my best friend until my tears ran dry. For the part of me that died the minute I found out the truth about Harrison. For getting kicked out of school. For every rejection letter. For every one of my mother's expectations that I'd failed.

For losing Grayson, when he'd only been mine for the duration of a kiss.

I told her everything as the tears fell to a trickle, from Harrison to Grayson, and she didn't speak, only listened until I'd verbally vomited everything...everything but the emails. "He's my roommate, Ember. I'm such an idiot."

She rested her head against mine. "You see the best in

everyone, Sam, you always have. You have the biggest heart of anyone I've ever met."

"And how selfish does it make me that for the smallest of seconds, when I found out about her, I didn't care? I just wanted to keep feeling the way I do around him."

"That just makes you human."

I had to be stronger than my mistakes if I was ever going to stop the epic fuck-up train I'd somehow boarded this last year. I sent Ember out to dinner with Josh and scoured the kitchen, top-to-bottom, and then I rearranged everything, just to piss Grayson off.

And when he called...I didn't answer.

CHAPTER TWELVE

GRAYSON

"I come bearing gifts." Miranda smiled as she waddled into Grace's hospital room, a cooler bag over her shoulder. Her blond hair was pulled back into a ponytail, highlighting the heart-shaped face she shared with Grace.

"You're not supposed to be carrying anything." I took the warm bag.

"Yeah, well I figured you could use some good home cookin'." She made her way to the chair at Grace's bedside and deflated into it. "God, I feel the size of a house."

"You're beautiful."

She raised an eyebrow and ignored me. "Nothing new?"

I shook my head. "She's on antibiotics, so now we wait for the infection to clear."

"How have you been?" she asked, motioning to the bag. "Eat while you talk."

I unpacked hot biscuits and gravy. "A lot better now. Thank you, Miranda."

"Life in Alabama?"

Sam's face flashed across my mind. Damn it. Why wouldn't she answer my phone calls? I had to explain. She had to understand.

"Gray?"

I blinked. "Busy."

"Mom says you're still here once a month, if not more."

I nodded. "I get back as often as I can, and it's never really enough."

"I...appreciate that. She does, too." She sighed. "But you have a life to lead, Gray. You can't just...waste away here with her. I know you want to. I know you would have died in her place. But you didn't, and you deserve a life that doesn't revolve around"—she motioned to the hospital room—"around all of this."

My appetite died a swift death. "It's exactly what I deserve."

She tilted her head to the side and rubbed her hand over her stomach. "You didn't do this to her, Gray. I know no matter how many times I say that, you're still not going to believe me, but you didn't do this."

My gaze darted to Grace, her eyes still closed peacefully as her chest rose and fell with even breaths. It was easier while she slept, where I could pretend that she'd wake up and we'd have the same fight about me going off to the Citadel while she had opted for UNC. When she was awake...well, there was no pretending.

An alarm beeped on Miranda's phone and she sighed as she silenced it. "Well, that's my signal to get upstairs to OB. Time for the weekly poke-n-prod. This little gal is just about ready to make her jailbreak."

I offered my arm and pulled her to standing. "Thanks, Gray. I'm awful with balance lately."

"No problem."

"We're still really hopeful for her cord blood," she said as she neared the door. "I've read a ton of research on stem cells, and if she's a match, there's a chance the University of Texas—"

"That's great, Miranda. I'm really happy for you and James. Your daughter is one lucky kiddo to get you two as parents." I had to cut her off. Hope was something I couldn't afford anymore. Not after five years.

She tilted her head, so Grace-like, and paused before a small smile peeked through. "I meant what I said, Gray. You've grown into a good man. None of this is your fault. None of it."

She left for her appointment, and I turned my attention to Grace, pulling my chair closer so I could hold her hand while she slept. Her fingers were so slender, long to match the rest of her dancer's body. Well, the body that had once danced.

It didn't matter what anyone else said. I knew the truth.

I'd done this to her.

S am still wasn't answering my calls. I gripped my cell phone so tight I thought it might crack and rested my forehead against the wall in the hospital hallway. I was ripping in two, half of me here with Grace, where I was obligated to be, and the other at Fort Rucker, where I needed to be.

I touched the icon next to Josh's name, and it started to ring.

"Man, I have no clue what the hell you were thinking, but you've had me cock-blocked all weekend."

"How is she?" Damn, was that my voice or a frog?

"My girlfriend? She hasn't had nearly enough sex due to the insane ice-cream mope-fest your girlfriend is putting her through. Or wait, are you in North Carolina with your other girlfriend? Does kissing the hell out of your roommate make her your girlfriend? I'm all sorts of confused." His voice was about as subtle as a razor blade.

What the hell was Sam? My girlfriend? My friend? My roommate? Fuck. I wanted her, that much was pretty self-evident by the raging hard-on I got the minute we breathed the same air. But it wasn't just sexual. I admired her strength, her courage, the way she stood up after she got knocked down. Hell, I even liked the way she had an impetuous streak...as long as she kept her ass off the bar. But saying she was my girlfriend was a commitment, and how could I make that kind of statement when I was still committed to Grace?

"Masters?"

"Yeah."

"Is it true? Do you have a girlfriend there?" His voice dropped just beneath hostile.

Shouldn't there have been an audible boom, or something else to signify my worlds crashing together? Shit. I needed advice.

"Have you ever kept something from Ember? Something you knew wasn't deliberately to hurt her, but could just...wreck everything?" I had officially turned into one of those drunk frat boys at one a.m. telling everyone he loved them.

Josh went quiet for a breath. "Yeah. I have. Jagger has, too, and we both almost lost the women we love because of it. All I can say is learn from us and don't wait until it's almost too late. We both fucked that one up. Whatever's going on, you have to put your cards on the table with Sam. She's been through too much shit for you to pile yours on, too. Lay it all out, and then let her decide if she wants to put up with your ass."

"It's just...really complicated." And that didn't begin to cover the half of it.

"It always is, otherwise we wouldn't keep it from them, right? Besides, weren't you the one dishing out the same advice to Jagger not too long ago?"

"Yeah, well, it's a hell of a lot harder to get perspective when you're in the middle of it."

Josh laughed. "Yeah, the view is a hell of a lot clearer from that really tall horse you like to ride."

I scoffed. "Kiss my ass." A nurse waived to me, signaling that they'd finished running this round of tests. "I have to go, but I'll be home around five."

"Sounds good. Sam works this afternoon, so don't be surprised if she's not here when you get back."

"Thanks for the heads-up." At least he was still looking out for me. Hopefully they weren't waiting with pitchforks and torches when I got back. I'd done some serious damage to Sam, and she'd been their friend a hell of a lot longer than I had. We hung up, and I headed back into Grace's room. I only had another hour or so before I had to leave for the airport.

She was sitting up now, staring toward the television screen where she watched *One Tree Hill* for the tenth time.

"Hey." I kissed her forehead, and she blinked. I'd gotten used to that being the only response I'd get. "How about we do some reading? You usually like that."

I pulled out the new copy of *The Odyssey* I'd just ordered. It had shown up on the syllabus for Sam's fall class, and I could use a brush-up on my Greek poetry. It was the hardest to read for me, and the best practice.

I made it through the first page without issue, watching Grace to see if she'd react, or even acknowledge that I was still there with her. I flipped the page and started again, but paused when my brain didn't want to cooperate.

"You'd think this would get easier after all these years, right?" I asked Grace. "But here we are. I'm still reading to you like we're seven, and you're still listening to me without judgment." Except she didn't climb into my lap anymore.

I got back to the pages and began to read aloud.

"'Oh for shame, how the mortals put the blame on us gods, for they say evils come from us, but it is they, rather, who by their own recklessness win sorrow beyond what is given...'" My voice trailed off.

It was my recklessness that brought us here.

"God, I'm so sorry, baby." I closed the book and laid my cheek against the back of her warm hand, wishing the other would come over to run her fingers through my hair like she used to. Wishing she'd offer the advice only a best friend could. "I'm sorry for everything that's brought us here and for what I have to tell you now."

I sat up and took the empty place on her bed, so I could look into her eyes, even if she wouldn't look back at me. "I know you can hear me, and I wish... God, I wish so many things. But I would kill for you to speak to me, Grace."

Her skin was soft beneath my fingers as I picked up her hand and placed it against my heart. "I've met someone, Gracie, and I don't know what it means. I don't. She's not you," I whispered, and then laughed softly. "She's hard where you're soft, and she's stubborn where you're so peaceful. She's all fire, and sass, and part hurricane, I'm pretty sure. But she does something to me, makes me see the world again. She's so hurt, and she's struggling to repair this wreck she's made of her life, and I think I can help her.

"I crossed a line with her that I'm not sure I should have, and I kissed her. I'm so sorry. But I don't know where the line is anymore. It's so blurred when it comes to her, and you, and everything that was between us...is between us? I don't know anymore. I don't know anything except what I feel when I'm around her. And she...she makes me feel alive in a way I haven't been since I lost you. She makes me feel like I'm flying my helicopter. Free. Like I'm standing on the edge of something I can barely control, and it could be the most amazing ride of my life, or I could burn one into the ground."

I squeezed her hand as my voice broke. "God, Grace. Tell me what to do. You've been my best friend since we could walk, the only woman I thought I'd ever keep around for the rest of my life, so tell me what to do, and I'll do it."

I searched the big brown eyes I'd grown up loving—the ones that had cried when she'd skinned her knee riding my first bike, or gone hazy with passion when we'd lost our virginities our junior year. Now they stared through me, like she couldn't bear to hear what I was saying.

I waited for words that never came. She wasn't going to

absolve me of this sin any more than she was going to scream at me for betraying her. I would get the same silent treatment I always did, no matter how many days I stayed at her bedside. The same silent treatment I deserved.

"Hey, you ready?" Mia asked as she knocked gently on the door.

I pulled the raw edges of my nerves back together and kissed Grace's forehead, receiving just the blink, as usual. "I'll see you in a few weeks, baby."

While I gathered my things, Mia said hi to Grace in hushed tones I couldn't quite make out.

She held in her excitement until we reached the elevator to the ground floor. "You're coming home for your birthday?" Mia asked with a huge grin, pulsing a few times on her tiptoes.

"I'm coming for the Fourth of July with...my friends."

"Ooh! Sam? Is Sam coming?"

"I don't know, Mia."

"Man, you're grouchy. Not enough hospital gym time or something?" she mocked and pressed the button. "Just explain it to her. Sam will be okay."

I sighed. I'd actually worked out a ton while I was here. It was becoming increasingly hard to be around Grace, and the gym was the one place I could work my body and my brain to exhaustion.

The elevator doors opened, revealing Parker lounged in one of the waiting room chairs. Damn, I'd managed not to see her the whole trip since Mom had picked us up at the airport.

"Parker." My jaw flexed.

"Gray." She flashed me a sunny smile. "How's our girl today?"

"On an IV drip." I passed her, not waiting for her to get out of her seat as I headed for the parking lot.

She raced after us, her flip-flops louder than rotor blades as she ran. "Wait up!" She clicked the "unlock" on her car, and

I held out my hands for the keys. "Oh, there's no way you're driving my car, Gray."

"Well, I'm sure as hell not giving you an ounce more control over any aspect of my life, Parker. So give me the keys, or I'll call a damn cab."

"Language!" Mia shouted from the backseat.

Parker glared, but there was zero chance I was backing down on this one. "You wouldn't pull this shit with Constance or Joey."

My older sisters were easily the most logical of the four. "Yeah, well, neither of them would have taken my love life into their own hands and wrecked an innocent woman because they didn't approve." Joey and Connie would both love Sam, I was sure of it.

"Your love life is here, Gray. In case you forgot, Grace needs you."

Apparently Parker was not going to be on Team Sam.

I inhaled through my nose and exhaled through my mouth, counting to ten. "Give me the damn keys."

"Lang—"

"Oh, shut up, Mia!" Parker yelled.

"Don't talk to her like that. She didn't do this, you did. You stuck your nose where it didn't belong, and you hurt Sam. You hurt *me*."

Her eyes widened. "You care about this other girl?"

"Yes."

Her shoulders drooped, and she dropped the keys into my hand before walking around to the passenger side and climbing in. I adjusted the seat for my height and cranked the engine.

Parker didn't speak until we were crossing the bridge to Roanoke Island, and I wasn't complaining.

"Grace needs you."

She sounded like a broken record. I shook my head. "Yeah, well maybe I need Sam. Did that ever occur to you?"

"No. It's always been you and Grace. G-squared, the it-couple of First Flight High School. You have to give her some time—"

I hit the brakes a little too hard at the red light. "Does this look like high school, Parker? Does it?"

"No," she mumbled.

"I've given her five years!" *And it still wasn't long enough.* "Do you think this is easy for me?" I pulled into the tiny airport and parked while Parker seethed.

"Parker, Sam is really amazing. And Gray is like...happy around her." Mia tried, God bless her, but I silenced her with a look in the rearview. I didn't need her involved in my love life, either. Life would have been a hell of a lot easier with four brothers.

"So you're giving up on her? Are you too good now?" Parker fired back, crossing her arms over her chest. "Mr. Top-of-my-class at the Citadel, big bad Army Lieutenant? Funny, I didn't realize they let people in too stupid to *read*."

Mia sucked in her breath. "Parker."

I snorted. "Yeah, well, let me know when you decide to see if there's life beyond the OBX, Parker. At least I wasn't too scared to leave." My feet hit the pavement. Then I dropped her keys in the empty seat, and Mia handed over my backpack.

"I love you, Mia," I said, squeezing her hand.

"I love you, Gray, and I think you need to get back to Alabama and fight for Sam, because she's phenomenal."

"Yeah, she is," I agreed, then turned to where Parker sulked. Why was she so hung up on this? "Parker, I love you, no matter what. But grow up and worry more about your life than mine."

I shut the door on whatever protest she was going to make and made my way inside. Mia was right. Sam was phenomenal, but was she going to stay once I explained everything to her?

I wandered into the tiny gift shop while I waited for my flight and passed a Kitty Hawk deck of cards. Josh was right, too, I needed to lay my shit out in front of her and let her decide. As terrified as I was of letting her see that I was nowhere good enough for her, she deserved the truth.

I bought the cards.

The gym was busy as I walked in at four thirty p.m. I'd driven like a bat out of hell to get here before her shift ended. At least here, she couldn't run away from me.

Her eyes were puffy and had dark circles under them as she leaned over a math book with Avery. Shit. I'd been the reason she'd been crying. Like she didn't have enough going on already. I leaned on the counter and waited for her to notice.

"What do you want, Grayson?" she asked, her voice tired.

"I'm not good for you."

"So you keep saying." She smiled as a high-school boy signed in.

"That's my cue to leave," Avery drawled, and practically ran.

"Sam." I fiddled with the card in my hand.

"What could you possibly want that couldn't wait?"

"You." She sucked in her breath, and I forged ahead. "You once asked me what you did to get past the mistakes. The stuff that keeps you up at night and leaves you nauseous in the morning?"

She nodded her head. "Yeah, well, I'm not exactly an angel, right? Is she? Your Grace? Is she as perfect as you no doubt need her to be? Because, honestly, I don't see you with an imperfect person. You're too good for that, or I thought you were. All this time I've thought I was the one too damaged for you, and yet you're the one kissing me while she's waiting for you."

"Can't you stop talking for a second?"

Her mouth snapped shut.

"Thank you. I told you that I understood that kind of mistake, like the one you're running from, and yes, you ran five states away from it, don't argue. I understood that choice because I've done something that I still can't recover from." The wariness in her eyes killed me. I wanted the trust back, the ease between us. I would forsake kissing her for the rest of my life if I could get the trust back. *Yeah, you know what she tastes like now, so try and keep your hands off her, you liar.*

"What could you have possibly done that's so bad?" she scoffed, and turned to dismiss me.

I grabbed her wrist, careful not to bruise her skin, and put the ace of spades into her palm, face up. "I'm responsible for what happened to Grace. I killed the woman I loved."

CHAPTER THIRTEEN

SAM

Seriously? He gave me a fucking card, declared himself a murderer, and then walked away? I pulled the e-brake in the driveway and tried to compose myself. He couldn't have really meant it. They didn't let murderers into the army, and he'd clearly been going to visit someone.

And I'd bet my life that Grayson wasn't any kind of murderer.

I opened the door and put my keys next to his in the dish on the entry table, and then hung my purse in the hall closet. The house smelled like...steak? "Grayson?"

"Kitchen," he called out. Of course he was.

"Hey," I said softly from across the half wall.

He pulled sweet potatoes out of the oven and then turned toward me. "Hey."

"Um. What are you cooking?"

"Sunday family dinner," he answered with a raised eyebrow like he hadn't dropped a bombshell on me an hour and a half ago. "Wash up, it's on the table in five."

"Where are Josh and Jagger?"

"They made themselves scarce," he responded with a shake of his head, like it hadn't been his decision. "Are you scared to be alone with me now?"

I shook my head. "Of course not. I saw two plates."

He exhaled and closed his eyes in obvious relief. "Right."

"I'll be right back," I said, then ran upstairs. I changed out of my work clothes, throwing on cargo capris and a soft, fitted tee. "Don't freak out. You can do this." Great, I was seriously pep-talking myself in the mirror.

"You ready?" Grayson asked, holding out my chair as I came back into the dining room.

I took a seat, and he took his on the corner next to mine. He laid out green beans, sweet potatoes heaped with marshmallows, and a succulent steak. My stomach growled, reminding me that I hadn't given it a decent meal that wasn't out of a processed bag since Friday. "Thank you for cooking dinner."

"Well, it's Sunday. It was a little harder since nothing is quite where I left it," he said with a half smirk that still sent a jolt through my core. My body apparently didn't care that he had a girlfriend...or had killed her.

"I rearranged. Want a beer?" I asked, hopping up to get to the fridge. I did. Or a shot of tequila, whatever would help me through what was going to happen next.

"Nope. Not tonight."

"Well, I'm having one." *Or fourteen. Whatever.* I popped the top and took my seat, digging into my food as he was.

We ate in silence, both looking up at each other at intervals, and neither of us brave enough to say the first word. But it had to be spoken, right? You didn't just declare yourself a murderer and then...ignore it.

An entire steak and a beer later, I pulled the ace of spades from my pocket and put it on the table before him. "Explain."

He stood, took a deck of cards out of the cargo pocket on his shorts, and sat back down. "Diamonds or hearts?"

"I'm sorry?"

"Diamonds or hearts? Pick a suit." He had them separated before him.

"Hearts." Because he'd stuck a knife in mine and then turned it. Hell, I think he was sitting in the actual chair where I'd basically ridden him like a prized pony.

"Fitting," he muttered, handing me the stack and then clearing our dishes to the sink. The bare wood of the table was instantly very intimidating.

I had a feeling we were about to cover it with his secrets.

"What are we doing?" I asked, my pulse skipping.

He consumed his chair again, curling the brim of his Citadel baseball hat and leaning forward on his elbows. "I watched Jagger nearly fuck up everything he had because he was too stubborn to tell Paisley the truth from the get-go."

"Right. I remember."

"You and I...whatever we are, or could be...*that* won't be us. I'm going to tell you every bad, ugly thing about me. You're going to tell me every bad, ugly thing about you, and then we'll decide what to do about this incredible pull between us."

I licked my bottom lip. "Oh, you think there's a pull between us? I thought we were just friends."

His gray eyes sliced through me, cutting me all the way to my soul. "Samantha, if we weren't about to discuss our deepest secrets, I'd lay you across the table, strip those sexy little capris off your ass, and bury my tongue between your thighs. God knows I've thought about it enough. How's that for *friends*. Really, it's more a force of nature, but I'll settle for you admitting that there's a pull."

My mouth was suddenly dry. I was never going to look at this table the same way again. "There's a pull," I admitted softly.

"Good, now that we have that established." He took a deep breath. "Grace and I grew up together in Nags Head. Well, Owen, Grace, and I did. It was always the three of us, but she was my best friend and I was hers, and one day that flipped, and we fell in love. We've been together since we were fifteen."

I wanted to throw in a smart-ass quip about how perfect that they were high-school sweethearts, but it would be a defense mechanism, and if he was stripping his defenses for me, I owed him the same courtesy, even if it hurt like a bitch. "Okay."

"The summer of my senior year, we had a huge party at the beach. Everyone was there, and everyone was drunk. I'd had a couple beers, but I made sure to stop a few hours before I knew we needed to leave. I wasn't reckless enough to chance anything with Grace, you know?"

His eyes darted between mine, begging for understanding, but he hadn't told me anything I needed to understand yet. I nodded. "Right."

"Owen got a brand new truck for graduation. This amazing Chevy, and he wouldn't let anyone wear dirty boots inside the cab, let alone drive her. And it got late, and Grace needed to get home. I told Owen to leave it at the beach and we'd get it in the morning, but he wouldn't hear of it." His eyes dropped to the table, and he took a shaky breath. Grayson took off his hat and rubbed at his forehead, like the memories were physically painful. "I should have fought him harder. I should have stolen the keys, or hog-tied him and put him in the car, but I didn't. I shook my head and said, 'suit yourself.' Can you believe that shit? Suit yourself." He swallowed and then brought his eyes back to mine. "I killed Grace with those two words."

My stomach rolled. He deserved a happy story. Even if he'd kissed me when he belonged to her, I wanted to hear that they woke up the next morning and laughed about how drunk they'd gotten.

"Grace and I took off for home. I drove her car, since mine was in the shop, and we got into a fight about colleges. I'd been accepted to UNC like her, and I wanted to go there, but she was pushing the Citadel. She knew I'd been accepted there, too, and how badly I wanted to go."

His knee started to bounce with nervous energy. "We were stopped at a light before the bridge, and when it turned green, Owen passed us driving way too fast in that goddamned truck. He cut off the oncoming traffic before jumping back into our lane, but he overcompensated."

His eyes went vague, and I knew he wasn't with me anymore. He was there, on that bridge, with Grace in the car...and I didn't want to know. But I had to.

"He slammed into the guardrail, and I swerved. I mean, I couldn't hit him head-on, right? We'd both be killed. Grace's little car wouldn't stand a chance. So I swerved, and we went through the rail, into the channel. She screamed, and we hit so hard. *So hard.* The airbags deployed, but my head cracked against the window, and I don't remember anything for another couple minutes. When I came to, we had already sunk, and landed on our side. Funny, I used to think cars always landed on their tires, right? They don't—not when there's uneven terrain to land on. The water was what woke me. It was already up to my shoulder. Grace...she was under it. Unconscious."

I held my breath like it was me underwater, and reached out to hold his hand. "Grayson."

He ran over my whispered plea. "She had one of those seat-belt cutter things, thank God. She was always so paranoid about that stuff. I cut myself free, then cut her free, but she wasn't breathing, and the car was filling with water faster than I could think. I held her as tight as I could, and I used the glass breaker to destroy the window. God, it was cold. The pressure pushed us back into the car, and it was dark. So dark.

"I got us out and made it to the surface, but she still wasn't breathing. I swam us to the nearest support pillar and tried to hoist her onto it, but I didn't have any leverage swimming, and mouth-to-mouth wasn't working in the water.

"By the time I got her onto the base of the pillar, my fingers were bleeding from scraping the concrete, and she was blue. I pulled myself up on top of her and did compressions...and I prayed. I prayed so hard." His hand squeezed mine, but I knew he was still there pressing on her chest.

"She finally sputtered out the water on reflex, but wouldn't breathe on her own, so I did it for her until help came."

"How long were you down there?" I asked softly, unable to imagine what that must have done to him.

"Probably about a half hour until they got the boats out to get us. They'd sent the ambulances to the bridge, but we couldn't get back up there. They took us to the hospital, and I fought when they tried to take her where I couldn't go, so they sedated me."

"Oh, Grayson." How much worse could this get?

"Days, then weeks passed, and she got strong enough to come off the ventilator, but her brain swelling had already caused the damage." He looked up at me, a shell of the man I usually knew. "She's comatose. She's been in a persistent vegetative coma for almost five years. She sleeps. She wakes, but she's not...there. I killed her. I didn't take his keys. I shouldn't have swerved that wide. If I hadn't passed out, I would have gotten us out before we sank. Before she drowned."

"This was not your fault. You did not kill her, Grayson. You were in the wrong place, at the wrong time, but you are not responsible for what Owen did."

"He told the police that we'd been racing, that other than his alcohol level, I was just as at fault as he was. I was never charged, but I'm pretty sure most people believe him, even my own father."

Silence stretched while I put it together. "You go home to sit by her bedside."

He nodded. "Yes. She has no chance for recovery according to the docs, but I know she's still in there, locked away."

I reached over and stroked my hand down his face, cupping his cheek. He leaned into it. "And you've been faithful to her, haven't you? That's why you freaked after we kissed."

"There's been no one else. I don't let anyone in, because I don't know how to anymore. I haven't wanted to. What's the point of loving someone if it hurts that much? Every second has been spent studying, exhausting myself at the gym, or home with her. There's never been someone that I was willing to betray her for. And I know it's not...betrayal. I've been through the counseling, I've made peace with the fact that she's gone in all except heartbeat. But I can't forget that last kiss, and there's never been a woman I was willing to replace it with." He stroked his thumb over my lower lip. "Until you."

My lips parted, and my heart stopped, then pounded a furious beat.

"You moved in and infuriated me because you took down every single one of my defenses before I had a chance to fortify myself against you. I never stood a chance, especially not with us living together."

I leaned away from his touch and dropped my hand. He couldn't do that, put me up on the pedestal Grace stood on—not when I was anything but worthy.

"Samantha?" He leaned forward.

"We can't do this...be together." I shook my head, hating the words as they slipped free, and fanned out my suit of hearts. I had way more sins than thirteen cards, and his only fault wasn't even a transgression. It was a horrific accident, something he'd had no control over, where mine were conscious choices. Bad choices.

"Because of Grace?"

I grabbed his hand and placed my ace of hearts in it. "Because I'm no good for you. Because I'm not a good person. I'm selfish, and spoiled, and entitled, and make horrible decisions that hurt people."

"Sam—"

"You want every bad and ugly thing? Do you want to know why I got kicked out of college, Grayson?"

"Yes, but you need to know that it doesn't matter. Not to me. It won't change how I feel about you."

"Well, it matters to me. I got kicked out over a guy. My entire collegiate career, gone. *Poof.* But he was nice, and showed interest in me when I was all alone. Ember had left for Vanderbilt. My mom had moved to Kentucky, and I was on my own, really on my own for the first time, and it wasn't...freeing like I thought it would be. I was so lonely. So I took summer classes to fill the time, and I met Harrison. He was everything I thought I was supposed to want. Stable, educated...worldly, I guess. He made me feel like the luckiest girl when I was with him. Fall came, and..." I swallowed. What was he going to think of me when he found out? Would he label me a whore? Say I deserved the emails that popped into my inbox?

Grayson squeezed my fingers gently, and the card pressed into my skin. "You don't have to, if it's too much. I'm not doing this to hurt you, or to find an excuse to walk away, and if you're not ready, we can do this slowly."

Of course he was giving me an out. Being supportive. Pulling me off bars and out of strip clubs. He was everything I needed, and nothing I deserved. "Stop being so nice!"

His brows drew closer together, hurt streaking through his eyes. "What—"

"He was my professor, Grayson. I slept with my professor, and it wasn't a one-time thing. We were together for months." Four months, thirteen days, if I had been counting. Which I had.

"Okay." His thumb stroked over mine, and I focused on that small movement to get me through the rest.

"It wasn't just...sex. I loved him, or what I thought was him. I didn't ask questions when he was busy. I never wondered why he was so against spending the night at my house. I mean, come on. He was a twenty-eight-year-old ethics professor, and I was a twenty-one-year-old student. Of course he couldn't spend the night with me. He was risking his job by being with me. I couldn't ask more of him when he'd already given me so much." A sour laugh slipped free. "You have to know where this is going, right? I'm the only naive one who didn't see it coming."

His eyes weren't judgmental once I found the courage to meet them. But of course they weren't. The closer I got to Grayson, the more I understood that he wasn't aloof because he felt superior. He was aloof because it kept him alive.

"You weren't the only one," he whispered.

I shook my head. "It seemed so romantic. So...forbidden. I kept thinking that he must have really loved me if he was willing to risk so much. But then I slipped into his office one day with this sexy little note to sneak into his pocket, and I found it—his wedding ring." It had been cool in my palm, that tiny circle that flat-lined my heart.

Grayson's deep inhale was the only sign that he'd heard me.

"Guess the apple didn't fall far from the tree, huh?" I forced a fake smile.

He tipped my chin to pin down my gaze. "Your mother?"

"I hated her for years, because I couldn't have my dad. He was already someone else's husband. Someone else's father, and after yanking us around for four years, he chose them. Funny how I turned out just like her after I swore I'd never make her mistake. Does that earn me another card? Maybe the jack or something?"

He leaned forward, pressing his lips firmly to my forehead. "This is not your fault. You didn't know he was married. You are not responsible for his sin. He, and he alone is."

The pit in my stomach widened, threatening to suck me in. "You don't understand. There was this moment, when I held his wedding ring in my hand...I thought—just for a second—about simply putting it back and not saying anything. I'd been so happy, and I didn't want it to end. I wanted him to choose me. I'd finally realized why Mom had stayed all those years, waiting for a man who would never keep his promise, and I hated myself for being weak enough—selfish enough—to even contemplate the same."

"But you ended it."

"Sure, before Harrison could. Before he could make the promises that he'd leave his wife, or say that I was his world, only to eventually walk away."

"Like your father."

I nodded, unable to really voice what Grayson knew.

"I wigged out in the middle of the quad when he came running after me, and slapped him so hard he wore my handprint on his face to his next class."

A corner of his mouth tilted up. "I bet you did."

"Another professor saw it and reported it. Harrison didn't... press charges, but I didn't exactly show up for the disciplinary hearing, either." I shook my head and dropped my gaze. "His family is an institution there. His mother is on the board, and his sister works there, too. No one was going to believe me, and even if they did, I still struck a professor."

"Classes?" He ran his hands down my arms, warming my chilled skin, until he clasped my hands in his.

How long until he saw me for what I really was and pulled away? "I quit going. I tried...once. I made it all the way to the parking lot, but when I saw the other students, I couldn't do it. By then there was a video posted online someone had taken. Harrison had it removed, mostly for his dignity, but everyone saw that I hit him. I couldn't sit in his class, hell, any class where the teacher had been *warned* about me. That was November. December I missed finals, and my expulsion letter came before Christmas."

"You were scared."

"Terrified." Paralyzed with it and unable to say how much until this moment. "Telling my mother meant she'd know, but I haven't told her the whole truth. I can't stand the thought of her looking at me any differently, or seeing her bad choices echoed in me."

"You are not the villain here."

"Being a villain and being guilty are two different things. I still could have ripped apart that marriage. Maybe it's my mother's karma biting me in the ass, or maybe it's because I'm incredibly selfish, but I will screw this up somehow if we try."

"Let me make that call." His chair squeaked against the hardwood as he pushed back from the table, but he didn't drop my hands. Instead, he tugged, pulling me to my feet and then into his lap. His strong arms surrounded me, and my head fit perfectly against his neck. "I'm so sorry for what happened."

"What?" I asked. "Why on earth would you be sorry? You've been through hell. I'm an adulterer. There's nothing for you to be sorry about. If anything, you should be tossing me off your lap and heading for the nearest exit, not pulling me closer." He did just that, one of his hands dwarfing the side of my face as he stroked my cheek with his thumb. "I don't even know what we're thinking. You only have six months before you graduate."

"Yes, and we'll handle that when it comes." He gently lifted my face. "Samantha, take the chance. No matter what's happening between us, whether we're friends—or more—whatever we decide, I will be here for you. I will not abandon you, no matter what you've done, or what you do. If you can still trust me, take a chance on me, and I'll prove it."

"Why? I slept with my professor, dance on bars, and apply at strip clubs. I'm not the kind of girl you need." I wasn't Grace and never would be.

"Well, you're the only girl I want."

My heart cracked, flayed open in front of him...for him. But could I do this for only six months? Could I try? Trust? Hold him far enough away to salvage whatever he didn't take of my heart when it was over? But could I forgive myself if I didn't take the gamble? Let him walk away?

No.

I took the three of hearts and put it face up on the table. "I only sleep on the left side of the bed."

He cocked an eyebrow.

"That's a selfish fact," I warned. "Not an invitation."

"I'd sleep on the floor to get closer to you."

I was so fucked.

CHAPTER FOURTEEN

Grayson

I executed the roll-on landing with precision and tensed my hand to keep from fist-pumping. Fucking perfect.

I taxied and parked us, then started the shut-down.

"Good flight," Mr. Stewmon, my instructor pilot said as we walked off the flight line. Stewmon was a retired CW5, pushing fifty with a stocky build, and wouldn't hesitate to kick my ass if I screwed up.

He was more than a little terrifying and quizzed us mercilessly during debriefs.

"Did I kick your ass? I did, didn't I?" Jagger asked with a cocky grin once we were headed toward the car.

"No." Stewmon answered as he came up behind us. "You didn't. Study up and have a nice night, lieutenants." He waved his dismissal.

"So what's up with you and Sam?" Jagger asked once we were headed home.

Shit. We hadn't exactly labeled "us" in the last two weeks.

"Man, you can try to ignore the question, but I'm still going to ask it until you answer." Why was he always grinning?

He stayed silent, even as we rolled out of the gate, but his eyes stayed on me. I knew Jagger. He'd wait me out. Prying, cocky friend that he was.

"I'm not sure," I finally answered.

"Is she sure?"

"What? Did she say something? What did she tell you?" Holy shit. I'd gone back to junior high. "Never mind."

He had the nerve to laugh. "No. But it's not like we haven't noticed you guys sneaking out on Friday nights. And the way you two orbit around each other? You're definitely something."

I swallowed. Orbit. That was the word for it. She was the Earth, full of life, raging rivers, erupting volcanoes, mysterious oceans, and breathtaking views. I was a satellite in her orbit, witnessing from a distance while she bloomed.

Damn, I loved to watch her shine.

"She's doing great, isn't she? Nailing her classes, holding down a job, helping Avery out with her summer school." She'd seemed lighter, like laying her cards on that table had physically unburdened her.

"She is," Jagger agreed. "I think you bring out the best in each other."

"I'm not sure I have a best."

"Okay, then she makes you less statue, more human."

"Ha, ha." I debated, then went for it. "We're...exploring the possibility of an 'us.' Slowly."

"What's holding you back?" Jagger asked as we crossed the Enterprise line.

I glanced at him sideways and back to the road.

"Oh, come on. You watched me break down when I almost lost Paisley, and you pretty much held me together. I'm not going to judge."

I nearly snorted. "No one is as harsh on me as I am. You don't scare me."

"Yeah, well *you* scare everyone. Well, everyone but Sam, but she's fucking fearless."

The corners of my mouth lifted. "She is." Fearless, passionate, strong, tender...and mine, if I would just reach for her instead of dancing around what we now knew we both wanted. I was running out of reasons not to.

"So about that Fourth-of-July trip we were talking about," he said while looking anywhere but at me. "I may have rented a beach house in Nags Head for the weekend."

"Right."

"You're cool with it?"

"I'm not thrilled, but I'm not ready to kill you over it." I was a little nauseous about my parents finding out exactly what I'd been up to, though. "I'd really like you guys to not mention what we're doing here though, and not ask why."

"I know you like to keep shit separate. Come hang when you can, and when you can't, just be…you know…you. We're not going to be pissed."

"Who is this we?" I asked.

He cleared his throat. "Josh and Ember are going to Colorado to see her family, so it's you, me, Paisley, Sam, Morgan, Carter—"

I hit the brakes a little too hard at the red light just to toss him against his seat belt. "You invited Carter?" I nearly growled as I took off at the green light.

"Morgan insisted. Said he was lonely or some bullshit. So now I get to vacation with my girlfriend's ex. It's glorious." He rubbed his hand over the back of his neck. "He's really not all that bad."

Okay, that earned a half smile. "He's growing on me. Josh?"

Jagger laughed and shook his head. "Hell no. Those two glare at each other more than high-school girls."

We pulled into the driveway, and I nearly bolted to the door when I saw Sam's car. *Relax, it's only been ten hours.* I tossed my keys as I walked in the door and Jagger sang out, "Honey, we're home!"

"Oh!" she squeaked from the kitchen, but I didn't see her as I looked over the half wall. "You guys are early!"

"It's after five," I answered, coming around the wall to

see—*Holy shit*. The floor was covered in water, as was Sam with her bare legs extended from beneath the kitchen sink. All the cleaning crap that was normally kept under the sink lay scattered around her.

"Samantha." I gripped her warm calves and pulled gently, dislodging her from the cabinet. She grimaced and then gave me a really fucking cute smile as she waved a wrench.

"Grayson."

"What the hell happened?" Jagger asked, leaning over the wall.

I raised an eyebrow at Sam as I pulled her to her feet. Her soaked red tank top clung to her skin, and I pried my eyes away from her hardened nipples before I decided to suck on them. *Get a grip, you're not there yet.*

I held out my hand, and she wrinkled her nose but put the wrench into it. "Samantha?" I asked again, loving the way her name sounded.

She reached in her back pocket and then handed me a very wet four of hearts card.

"I tend to get in over my head before I ask for help." She blinked up at me.

I took her card and pocketed it. "Apparently."

Jagger burst into laughter. "She is all yours."

She grinned shamelessly up at me. "I kind of am," she admitted.

"I know." My voice dropped, and I stood there like an idiot for another minute, a breath away from her, standing in a giant puddle of water, craving her mouth. "What happened?"

"I...uh...lost my ring." She licked her lips.

"So you ripped apart the kitchen sink."

She nodded enthusiastically. "Seemed the most logical path to getting it back."

"Right." I unzipped my uniform top and hung it on the back of the dining room chair before taking Sam's place under the kitchen sink. "Only a few more turns and you would have had it," I said as I finished removing the U-bend. "What's the story with the ring?"

She took the pipe out of my hands and dumped the contents into a bowl. "Thank you." She sighed, taking the sapphire ring out of the mucky leftovers. "It was my grandmother's. Mom gave it to me when I turned sixteen. My grandparents are dead, so it's the only link I really have left."

"I'd rip the sink apart for that, too," I answered, putting it back together. As I washed my hands, Sam hopped onto the counter and swung her feet.

"You know I could have done that if you'd explained how. You didn't have to get gunked up or take over all man-style."

I grimaced, reached into my pocket, and handed her the eight of spades. "I overstep boundaries to fix problems the women in my life can probably handle themselves. Maybe it's from growing up with four sisters, or maybe I'm overprotective."

"That's hardly a sin," she said with a grin, "but I'll take it." She hopped to the floor and tugged her shorts down so they covered her to mid-thigh. "So, Friday date night?" she asked.

My fingers tightened on the counter. "I know we usually go out on Friday..."

"Are you canceling on me?" She shot me a look so full of sass that I almost kissed it off her.

"Hell no. I was thinking we'd keep it low-key tonight? Jagger is headed to Paisley's, and Josh—"

"Is out!" Josh called as he passed by the kitchen. "I can make it to Nashville by ten if I leave now, so I'll catch you later!"

"Right," I finished.

Sam swayed toward me. "Are you trying to get me alone? Maybe score a little make-out session?"

My stomach muscles tightened as she ran her fingers down the lines of my abs. "Sam, we're not fifteen, and if all I wanted was a make-out, I'd carry you upstairs and shut my bedroom door."

"That's a date-night I could get behind. Or I could set the timer for seven minutes and pull you into the closet." Her eyes sparkled.

"Dinner, movie, closet. Gotcha."

She laughed, brushed her lips across mine, and skipped off to the shower. It took all my willpower not to follow her in.

"I like this," she said a couple hours later, her head in my lap as we pretended to watch whatever chick flick she'd chosen.

"Me, too." I skimmed her cheekbone with my thumb.

"You know what would make this room perfect?"

If you were naked. "What?"

"A window seat. I mean, it's almost my perfect house. Hardwood in the kitchen, granite counters, porch swing out front, a big backyard... It's almost there."

"And the window seat would make it perfect?"

"A window seat and a view of the front range." She smiled wistfully.

"You want to live in Colorado?" My stomach plummeted.

"It's the only place that's ever really felt like home. I still have this hope that I can get back in. Even if I have to face him, it would be worth it."

"You can. Are you excited to see your mom?"

She nodded. "It'll be nice to spend a few days with her. Definitely worth making up my classwork for. Her homecoming is still on schedule, so this time tomorrow night, I'll have her."

"And this time Thursday I'll pick you up in the Outer Banks," I promised.

"That, I can't wait for." She cupped my cheek. "Look, just because I'm there, don't think you have to..." Her gaze fell away. "I mean, I don't expect to bake brownies with your mom or anything."

"One, if you bake brownies with my mom, please get her recipe. She's irrationally stingy with it. Second, Samantha, I'm not hiding you. In fact, my parents want all of you to come over for dinner when we get there. You're a part of my life, and I want them to know you."

A small family gathering was exactly perfect to introduce her to our madness.

"I'll wear a longer skirt," she promised.

"Just be you, Sam. That's all I need."

She sat up on my lap and kissed me softly, sweetly. "I'm going to miss you."

I captured her hand with mine and pressed a kiss to her palm, savoring her indrawn breath. "Same here. Have I ever told you what beautiful hands you have?" Everything was beautiful on her, fingers included.

"You'll like them better once they're on you," she promised, her eyes darkening.

"Anytime you want, Samantha." Sex wasn't something we'd really discussed, and our hands had stayed strictly above clothes, although I wasn't sure how much longer I could keep my hands off her skin without going out of control.

"Soon," she whispered.

"Soon."

"Hey, you should be at the airport," I lectured Sam, balancing my phone on my shoulder so I could check my watch.

"We're pulling into the airport," she said.

"Good. I just got here to help Jagger unload."

"I'm glad you got out early today."

"Me, too." We'd all been able to catch an earlier flight, which gave me a couple hours to kill before I got my hands on Sam.

Almost six days without touching her was killing me.

"Don't be a dick!" Morgan yelled at Carter as he held the tiny strings of her swimsuit high above his head.

"Wear something that covers more than two percent of your body!"

"Or maybe not..."

Sam laughed. "I can hear them from here."

Comfortable silence passed while I heard the doors opening and shutting. "I'll see you in a couple hours?"

"Yeah..." She drew out the word.

"What's wrong?"

"Hold on a sec." She put the phone down while she said good-bye to her mom, and then picked it up again. "Sorry. She's not one for good-byes, so I try to give her an excuse to not look all emotionally unavailable."

"I'm happy to be your excuse. What's really bothering you?"

She sighed, and I pictured her lower lip between her teeth. "I was at her welcome-home ceremony, and there was this woman there, balancing a little girl on her hip."

"Okay."

"It could just be that homecomings are emotional. Especially for me since Ember's dad died? It's probably stupid." There was a rustling of paper. "Roanoke," she told the attendant. "Thank you so much."

"So you were emotional?" I kept at her because if I didn't, she wasn't going to offer up the truth.

"Yeah. This mom was maybe a year or two older than I am, but she'd held herself together through a deployment with a kid, and I was lucky to have not ended up a stripper."

"I'm listening."

"How freaking long is this line? Security sucks." I heard flights called through her speaker while she debated, so I waited. "She was the kind of woman you'll need. Someone who can handle her own crap and shoulder yours, too. Someone who isn't a giant pain in the ass."

"You're not a pain in my ass. In fact, you have a very nice ass."

"Focus, Grayson. It just hit me. You're in the army. That means deployments, and PCS moves, and temporary duty assignments, and all the shit that comes with it."

I clamped down on the panic that was clawing its way up my throat. "Does that bother you?" I waited. "Sam?"

"That's the thing. It's everything I've sworn up and down that I don't want in my life. There's never been a big enough pro to outweigh the cons of that lifestyle for me." *Fuck.* "But even when I'm looking at all the cons, it still doesn't stop me from wanting you, from choosing you. What does that even mean?"

That we're done dancing around this. That I'm yours as much as you are mine. Fuck, why couldn't she be here for this conversation? My hands itched to touch her, assure her.

"Just get here, Sam."

"So we can beat this subject to death?"

"So I can kiss the hell out of you." My voice dropped an octave.

"That may be worth standing in this line."

Two hours, and then I had four days to introduce her to my family, my home, and maybe make her realize that I was the only pro she'd ever need on that list. "Oh, it will be, I promise."

CHAPTER FIFTEEN

GRAYSON

"What do you have in here, an elephant?" I asked Sam as I carried her suitcase up to the third floor of the rented beach house.

"Oh, come on. Like you don't have the muscles to carry a few pairs of shoes?" she teased, tossing back a flirty grin. The white, wide-brimmed sunhat just about did me in. Or maybe it was the flirty, pale green sundress, or seeing her here in the Outer Banks.

"Few pairs. Right."

I followed into her bedroom, set her suitcase down at the foot of the king-size bed, and cursed the fact that I'd promised my mother I'd sleep at home. That mattress was going to swallow Sam's tiny frame whole if I didn't hold down one side. *Stop making excuses and admit that you'd kill to sleep next to her.*

I glanced around the room. It was a typical OBX rental, decorated in soft blues and whites. "And remind me why you had to have the room farthest away from everyone?" I asked, turning to see her open the wide French doors that led to a private balcony overlooking the Atlantic. The ocean breeze blew her hat toward the bed.

That impish grin made an appearance again. "It has the best view."

She brushed her hair from her face as we stepped out onto the deck, easily fifty feet in the air. She didn't look down, only rested her hands on the polished wood of the banister and looked out at the waves. "It's beautiful here."

"Yeah. Beautiful," I said, my eyes locked to the delicate lines of her face.

Sam caught me staring and smiled, then trailed her fingers along the railing as she closed the distance between us. My hands cradled her head, and I brought my lips to hers, kissing her gently, trying to show her without words how much it meant to me that she was here. I struggled to keep myself in check. With Sam, one taste was never enough.

Our lips lingered a breath apart until she made the next move, grabbing fistfuls of my shirt and arching up on her tiptoes. Her curves crashed against me, and I took her mouth without hesitation, sweeping inside to taste her. She rubbed her tongue along mine. *Damn.* She felt so right in my arms.

Her whimper frayed what little restraint I had left, and the kiss spiraled as I sank deeper into her, losing myself along the way. I let go of her face, only to slide my hands up the backs of her thighs. Her skin was hot and softer than silk. "Samantha," I whispered against her mouth.

"Touch me," she pleaded. "Just...touch me, Grayson."

We were crossing the line, and I couldn't bring myself to give a fuck. I let her thighs slide through my hands until I palmed the perfect globes of her ass—*holy shit*—by her bare skin. My thumbs grazed upward, feeling the tiny, easily breakable straps of her thong, and I groaned as I lifted her higher against me so she could feel my raging hard-on against her stomach. She brushed her palms along my cheeks, trusting me to carry her full weight, and kissed me with abandon.

I lost my common sense to the feel of her under my hands, the sweet slide of her tongue with mine, the press of her breasts against my chest as she arched to get even closer. Blood pounded in my ears, keeping rhythm with the crashing waves beneath us. She wound one hand around the back of my neck, licked along my lips, and I sucked her tongue into my mouth. She stroked the roof of my mouth and ran the sensitive ridge behind my teeth. *Fuck. Just like that.*

Her sweet little moan snapped the last of my control. I pivoted her slight weight into a bridal carry and made my way to her bed, laying her in the center without so much as breaking our kiss.

Careful to keep my weight on my elbows, I licked and sucked my way down her neck, inhaling the scent of vanilla that was becoming home to me. I pressed my lips along her collarbone and nudged the spaghetti straps of her sundress down her arms.

My eyes locked onto hers as I pulled her dress down, looking for the slightest hint that she didn't want this. Instead, she arched her back to make it easier and exposed the nude lace of her strapless bra. "Please?"

Damn. This gorgeous, brilliant woman was actually asking me to put my hands on her. My mouth watered as I tugged her bra down just enough for her breasts to spring free, and my breath caught. Everything about her, from her pebbled nipples to the way she filled my hands was perfect.

Her gasp filled the silence as I swirled my tongue around one nipple, her nails biting into my scalp as she held me to her. *Make her do that again. Now.* I switched breasts and repeated the treatment, savoring her reaction. "Oh my God, that feels incredible," she whispered.

"You're incredible," I told her, blowing lightly across her wet skin. She jumped and I immediately warmed her again with my mouth. Her legs parted, and she brought her knees up, settling me right...fucking...there.

Damn. A couple tugs of fabric and I could be inside her. Just the thought had me painfully hard. I thrust my hips against her once, matching with a pull at her breast and she moaned. "Again."

Yes, ma'am. This time the moan was torn from my throat. I felt her heat through my board shorts and counted to ten to keep control as I thrust against her in a gentle rhythm.

Then my thoughts ceased as she pulled me into her kiss. Nothing existed in the world outside Samantha and my craving to be absolutely everything she needed. One of her hands took mine and placed it on her thigh, then slid it up under her dress.

My fingers grazed the lacy scrap of underwear. "Fuck, I can feel how wet you are."

"I want you," she said without embarrassment.

I plunged my tongue into her welcoming mouth, as I slipped my finger under the lace just grazing—

"Hey, you two! We're going to be late!" Jagger's voice echoed up the stairs through the open door.

"Damn it. Fucking Jagger. Fucking family dinner." The only thing I fucking wanted was already under me.

I rested my forehead against hers and tried to calm my breathing, but she was looking up at me, those green eyes hazed with lust, and then she had the nerve to *giggle.*

"What's so funny?"

"I've never heard you swear so much. Ever." She grinned, like our little predicament was funny, so I slowly slid my fingers from underneath her panties, catching her gasp as her giggle died. "Grayson," she whispered as she closed her eyes.

"Screw staying with my parents. I say we stay here. In this bed. The whole weekend." The pillow collapsed under the weight of my arms as I caged her in.

"And tell your mother that you missed your family dinner because…"

Well, if that didn't kill my hard-on. "Right. My mother."

"Grayson? Sam? Jagger says we need to get going," Paisley called up. "I am most certainly *not* saying that, Jagger Bateman," she hissed.

"Put your dick back in your pants and let's go!" Jagger yelled.

"I'm starving."

Sam snorted, and I rolled my eyes. "I wish my dick had made it out of my pants," I mumbled. Sam full-out laughed, and it was the sweetest sound I'd heard. "I'm desperate for you, Samantha."

"Well, I hardly think your mom should meet my girls." She dropped her eyes to her beautiful breasts, still bare. And if I gazed there much longer...we wouldn't be leaving. "So maybe we should put them away?"

"If you insist." My tongue ran across my lower lip, still tasting her.

"I fucking insist! Let's go!" Jagger sounded closer this time.

I rolled to the side, blocking her from view in case he decided to come in, while she tucked herself away and pulled the straps to her sundress back up.

"Shall we?" I stood and held out my hand.

"We shall." She put her hand in mine, and I walked her into the lion's den.

"Why don't you stay with us?" Paisley asked me as I carried my bag out of the back of the Yukon Jagger rented. My parents hadn't come out of the house and ambushed my friends, so we had a chance at this not being a total disaster.

"You guys are a little tight on bedroom space," I answered, looking at my parents' much smaller house and thinking the same thing about theirs.

Morgan, Paisley's best friend, raked her hand over her dark brown hair. "Are you sure I'm not intruding?"

"You're never an intrusion, Morgan, and we're happy to have you along. Carter, on the other hand..." I raised my eyebrows.

"Fuck off," he answered, climbing out of the backseat.

"He like...teases people now?" Morgan whispered to Paisley.

"Who said I was teasing?" I kept my face as still as possible, and Morgan glanced between me and Will, no doubt trying to figure out if I was kidding this time.

Yes, and no.

Sam wound her arms around my back, immediately calming my introduce-her-to-my-parents nerves. "You can always sleep next to me."

I pulled her under my shoulder and kissed her forehead. "I will take that under consideration." Yeah, only after we decided on having sex. There was no way I'd be able to keep my hands off her fuckable little body if she slept next to me. I was already perma-hard whenever I smelled her, let alone touched her.

"Gray!" Mia bounded out of the house and skipped down the long staircase and didn't stop until she had her arms around my neck. "We need to talk," she whispered in my ear.

I nodded, setting her down. "Okay. Morgan, this is my baby sister, Mia. Carter, stay the hell away."

He rolled his eyes at me while Mia hugged Sam. "I'm so glad you're here!"

"Me, too, and the house is gorgeous!"

"Dad built it when Connie was born," Mia explained, as I started to lead them up the steps that would take us to the first level. Everything was stilted to accommodate the times the island was more water than land. "Gray, I seriously need to talk to you," she said, coming up next to me.

"Right now?" I asked as we made it to the porch. She tugged on my sleeve.

"Before you get—"

"Grayson!" Mom came through the sliding glass door and hugged me, her dark curls coming to just beneath my shoulders.

"Hey, Mom."

She turned my face left and right, inspecting for damage as usual. "Well, you're no worse for wear. Your father is closing the shop, but he'll be here soon. Introduce me to your friends."

Sam stepped onto the porch, and my heart swelled like a damn girl. I guess I appreciated what I had, too. She hung back, worrying her lip between her teeth.

I pointed to each of them in turn. "This is Carter, Morgan, Jagger, and Paisley." Then I held out my hand and raised an eyebrow at Sam. *Take the challenge, Sam.*

She swallowed, straightened her shoulders, and raised her chin enough to remind me she'd been raised in social circles a hell of a lot higher than mine. Then she smiled and took my hand. I reeled her in until she was securely tucked beneath my arm. "And, Mom, this is my Samantha."

Sam's wide eyes flew to mine at the same time Mom's assessed her quickly and smiled. "I'm so happy to meet you, Samantha." She pulled Sam into a hug and held it until Sam visibly relaxed, and then she let her go. "We're so glad you're here."

Sam tucked a strand of hair behind her ear and gave a shy smile that told me she was still on her toes. "Oh, you can call me Sam, and I'm thrilled he asked." Then she turned that smile on me, and it became genuine.

"Well, now that we're all acquainted, let's get inside. Supper is about ready." Mom ushered the crowd in.

"Gray, now?" Mia asked, her eyebrows furrowed.

"Mia, what's wrong?"

"Mia, get inside and help your sisters." Mom ordered in the I-said-now voice.

"Yes, ma'am," she mumbled, but did as she was told.

"Whoa," Sam whispered as we entered the living room. It was vaulted to the third floor and boasted huge canvases of Dad's boats in full sail. "You built these?"

"Not all." I pointed to the one furthest left. "That was before me, but the one over here is the one we built my junior year in high school."

"That's amazing," Paisley remarked.

"What the hell are you doing flying helicopters?" Jagger asked. "These are seriously badass."

I cringed, and checked to make sure Mom hadn't heard. She'd already found her way to the kitchen. "Can we keep the helicopter stuff a little more quiet?"

I got what-the-hell looks tossed my way, but they didn't have time to ask before Mom came back over. "We're all set up out back."

What? "Out back? On the deck?" It faced the channel, with a nice view, but were we all going to fit on the deck?

"Aren't you hungry?" she asked, not really answering.

"Yes, ma'am," Carter replied, somehow manifesting the southern drawl he'd beaten out of himself at West Point.

Mom led the way, and I held Sam back, kissing her just because I could. "Welcome to my home."

She glanced around. "I like it. It feels...solid, sturdy." Anyone else might have taken that as weird, but I understood what she was saying. She'd never had a home for more than two years, so to Sam, solid was golden. She unleashed an impish grin. "Do I get to see baby pictures?"

"Hell no." I glanced down the hall and made sure everyone had followed Mom out onto the deck, and then I kissed Sam again, gently sucking on her lower lip.

"Your mom is going to catch us."

"Let her."

She laughed, making my house feel more like home than it had in the last five years, and kissed me enthusiastically with a smacking sound. "Stop avoiding your family and feed me."

I nodded, resigned myself to the chaos of the evening, and walked with her down the hall, pulling her past the pictures that lined the hallway with a promise that she could examine them later. Later like *never*. I'd been scrawny until a few years ago, and I knew she was attracted to *this* body. I'd keep that.

Mom opened the sliding door to the back deck with a huge

smile and bright eyes. "It's about time, Gray. We have a little surprise for you."

My stomach clenched. *They wouldn't. They know better.*

I held Sam's hand while she stepped over the barrier, but the deck was empty. *I will fucking kill them.* Mom pointed to the edge of the banister, and I just...knew.

"What a gorgeous view," Sam said, looking over the water as the sunset turned it an array of colors. Then she looked down. "Whoa."

"Surprise!" the crowd yelled from beneath us. There had to have been seventy people, all crowded onto the patio and the pool deck, hell, even the walkway to the beach. I swallowed and held Sam's hand in a death grip, using her to ground me in the present. "Happy Birthday!" they shouted in unison.

Every muscle in my body tensed, and my stomach contents turned over, threatening to make an encore appearance.

Sam looked up at me, her eyes wide and a little hurt. "It's your birthday?"

I let go of her hand and stretched out my fingers. I couldn't hurt her. I had to keep in complete control. Space. I needed space. Then I turned to my mother, whose mouth had drooped slightly, understanding that her plan had failed.

I gave a swift shake of my head and walked back in the house before I devastated her feelings by saying something thoughtless.

"Gray," she called after me.

I didn't look back.

CHAPTER SIXTEEN

SAM

The moment Grayson disappeared, his mother stepped to the banister and raised her arms. "Thank you! Let's get this party started!"

She sounded joyful, but the small tremble to her jaw told me otherwise.

Something had gone terribly wrong. I searched for Jagger in the crowd, and when I found him with one arm around Paisley, he raised his hand in the what-gives position. I shrugged in answer, but I wasn't going to stand there like a clueless idiot when Grayson was obviously in pain.

Over a birthday?

Music blared to life through the speakers around the pool, and people started mingling and heading for the bar that had been set up near the beach. Nearer the water I could see a volleyball net. His parents had gone all out for him. It was a phenomenal beach party.

The summer of my senior year, we had a huge party at the beach.

His words sliced through my memory, and I gasped. Mia charged up the steps and I finally understood why she'd been trying to get his attention on the front porch. She'd been trying to warn him.

I turned to his mom. "He wasn't ready." It was half excuse,

half accusation, but I let it hang there between us for a few seconds until Mia reached us.

"Sam," she started.

"Where is his room?" I interrupted. As much as I adored Mia, I wasn't in the mood for anything she had to say.

"Up the stairs to the third floor. It's the one on the left," his mom answered, her voice low and a little defeated.

I squeezed her hand. "He'll be okay." Not that I had any right to make a promise like that. Were people ever okay after they went through what Grayson did?

I walked inside the house and found the stairs, following them to the second floor and then taking the spiral staircase to the third until I located his door. I knocked once and opened without waiting for an invitation I knew I wasn't going to get.

He sat on the queen-size bed, his back to me as he stared out at the water. Every line on his body was tense, sharp, as if he might explode at any second.

The bed sank under my weight as I sat next to him, but he didn't speak, or even look at me, so I simply waited. Gone was the teasing demeanor he'd grown into over the last few months. This was the Grayson I'd met in the kitchen—aloof, hard, and cold.

But I could be warm enough for both of us. I reached out my hand, letting it rest between us without touching him, and waited. Sixty-seven breaths later, he slid his hand over mine and wove our fingers together. Relief streaked through me, and I squeezed his fingers gently.

"It was your birthday party five years ago."

He nodded.

"I'm so sorry." I scooted toward him until our hips touched, and then I rested my head on his shoulder. "How old are you?"

"Twenty-three last Friday. I figured we'd be safe coming tonight." He cleared his throat. "For a math major, I figured you could add better than that."

At least he was trying to tease me. That was something, right?

"Maybe I just wanted to hear your voice."

He turned his head and kissed my hairline. "It worked."

"Friday as in the night we stayed in?"

"Being with you was the closest to a celebration as I've wanted to be. You made it perfect, and you didn't even know."

But I wish I'd known. I would have baked him a cake, or bought him one. But maybe he'd known that.

I let the minutes pass without speaking, content to just be there. This wasn't about words, or even comfort, but simple presence, and I could give him that.

Without moving my head from his shoulder, I surveyed his room. The walls were dark navy with white trim and covered in sailing pictures, but they weren't like the ones downstairs, professional and staged. These were candid shots of Grayson sailing, beautifully intense as he handled a boat. They were taken close up, by someone who obviously knew the value of the moment, watching him firmly grow into developing the control he was so known for now.

I knew without asking that Grace had taken them.

I reached over to his nightstand, where a picture sat framed of a gorgeous blonde. Her smile was effortless, her hair blowing in the wind with the full sail behind her. She radiated warmth, kindness from her brown eyes, and the way she looked at the photographer...it was love. For Grayson.

"What was she like...before?" I asked, my voice soft.

He took the picture from my hands and stroked his thumb over the line of her cheek. "Kind, slow to temper, completely selfless. She was pretty perfect as best friends go."

The opposite of me. How could I even compete with that?

He reached across and put the picture back on his nightstand.

An uncomfortable chill crawled up my spine. *You're trespassing.* Like this Grayson belonged to Grace, and I had no right to kiss him or hold his hand.

Would he always be haunted by her ghost like this? Would he ever be able to celebrate a birthday with happiness? Or would it always be a date he avoided, tucked away? Did I even have the right to question it?

"We should probably head down," he said, his eyes still locked on her picture.

"We can do whatever you want," I offered. If he wanted to leave, I'd steal the keys from Jagger and strand the rest of them here.

"No, they went to a lot of trouble for this. I can't hurt Mom's feelings."

He stood, stiff and guarded. He'd blocked me out, thrown up the walls he was so well-known for, and it *hurt*. But this wasn't about me.

"Okay," I answered, then followed him downstairs.

He never let go of my hand, even when we descended the porch steps to where the party was in full swing. "Do you know all these people?" I asked before we hit the crowd.

"Yes. Some family, mostly friends of family, or friends from high school. Everyone is home for the holiday weekend." Tension rolled off him, reminding me of the waves that struck the beach.

"Gray!" Mia called out from the bar area, and Grayson led us over. He acknowledged everyone we passed with a nod, but his fake smile looked more like a closed-lip grimace.

We found Mia next to three other women, who by their similar looks must have been Grayson's sisters. "I'm so sorry!" Mia said as she hugged him. He looped an arm around her waist briefly.

"It's okay," he replied. *But it's not.*

"I had no clue what they were planning until this afternoon, I swear."

"Let it go, Mia." He gently pulled me forward, then looked

left to right as he introduced us. "Sam, you know Mia. This is Joey, Connie, and Parker, my other three sisters."

I flashed a nervous smile. Joey was older by a few years with a tomboy look and a quick grin. Connie was the oldest and resembled Grayson's mother the closest. She smiled back at me with the same warmth, and then smacked Parker in the arm lightly. That didn't stop Grayson's younger sister from glaring daggers into me.

I guess we're not going to be friends.

"It's so nice to meet you," Connie said, stepping forward and embracing me.

"Mia won't shut up about you," Parker snapped.

"Or Grayson," Joey shot a sideways look at Parker.

He tensed.

"I'm so happy to meet you all," I said, proud that my voice didn't shake. "It's really beautiful here." A greeting and a compliment. Mom would be proud.

"Yeah, well, it's nicer when the *dingbatters* leave," Parker said with a pointed look my direction.

"Parker," Grayson warned in a soft growl. "She means tourists, and she won't say it again."

My cheeks heated, and I bit down on my tongue. Parker wasn't some girl to annihilate with a sharp retort, no matter how much I wanted to. She was Grayson's sister.

"Don't be a bitch," Joey snapped, and I internally fist-pumped.

"Whatever." Parker turned a sugar-sweet smile on her brother. "I'm going tomorrow morning to visit with Grace, want to come with? Or are you staying there tonight?"

Ouch. That wasn't supposed to hurt, right?

He sucked in his breath, and my teeth nearly drew blood on my tongue. That's what she was after—my blood. But she couldn't have his.

I reached over and stroked his arm under the cuff of his

rolled-up shirt and squeezed the hand that held mine. "I certainly don't mind."

His eyes snapped to mine, and he held my gaze while we communicated wordlessly. I kept mine open and honest as much as possible and gave him a soft smile, hoping he couldn't hear the way my heart was ripping at the thought of sharing him with someone else. *Don't be selfish.* This had to be torture for him, splitting himself between Grace and me—between Fort Rucker Grayson, whom I was falling for, and Outer Banks Gray, who belonged to someone else entirely. "It's okay," I whispered. "Just pretend I'm not here."

His eyes flew wide.

"Sounds good to me," Parker snapped before walking off.

I counted to five as I released my breath. "I mean, just spend your time like you normally would. I'll be fine. More than fine. Do what you need to. It's not like I don't live with you...in the roommate sense, of course." *Stop word-vomiting already.*

Mia cleared her throat.

"Can I get you a drink?" Joey offered, motioning to the bartender.

Tequila sounded perfect right about now.

"Sure. I'll have a—" I said.

"No!" Grayson shouted at the same time.

"—Coke." I blinked at his outburst. "I wasn't going to drink, Grayson," I whispered the last to him, but it didn't take the panic out of his eyes. "It's okay."

They were all staring. Holy. Fucking. Awkward.

"Sam! You have to see this view!" Paisley slid behind me and grasped my dangling hand. "Thought I'd stop the hemorrhage," she whispered in my ear.

"Absolutely," I said to Paisley. Grayson was still staring at me, utterly unreadable, like a stranger. Like he hadn't had his tongue in my mouth and his hand inside my panties an hour ago. "It was really nice to meet you," I repeated like a freaking parrot as I took my Coke, and then let Paisley pull me down to the beach.

"You okay?" she asked as we crossed the wooden walkway to the beach.

"I'm so glad I was an only child." I stopped dead in my tracks. "Holy shit. Paisley, I'm so sorry. I wasn't thinking." Could I stick my foot in my mouth any more?

She shrugged. "Peyton had her moments of being a pain in the rear." She nodded to where Jagger, Will, and Morgan had commandeered the volleyball net. "Let's forget about... everything."

That was something I could go for.

We played as the sun set behind us, the colors dancing pink off the channel. Even Paisley jumped in for a few minutes, much to Jagger's disapproval. She'd had her heart surgery three months ago, but he still hovered.

I felt his eyes on me before I saw him, as though the intensity he radiated traveled the thirty feet that separated us. He leaned against the wood railing of the walkway, looking over at me with walls up and locked away.

I picked up my sandals from where I'd left them and climbed the steps to where he stood, leaning my back on the railing so I could see him. "Hey."

"Hey." His eyes darted toward mine before wandering back to the channel. Every line in his body was rigid, tense, and utterly breathtaking. The shiver that caught me by surprise wasn't just because of the falling temperature.

I rested my hand on his forearm and winced when he pulled it away.

"People are starting to leave," he muttered.

"Okay," I answered. "Would you like us to head out?" *Say no.*

His jaw flexed, and he threw a look back over his shoulder when his name was called from the party. "Maybe that would be best. You guys can't be having fun at this thing."

He was sending us away. Because we didn't belong in this part of his life. *I* didn't belong.

I ignored the deep, dull ache in my chest and slipped my strappy sandals onto my feet and then folded my arms, rubbing my skin. "Okay, I'll get everyone." My legs felt shaky, or maybe the ground beneath me was simply moving.

"Is he okay?" Jagger asked while we walked the bridge back to the party that was swiftly dying.

"I don't know how to answer that," I said as we passed the bar and I spotted Grayson talking to Joey. "It's like he's an entirely different person here, and it's more than the party. I get being pissed over the party, but the rest of him...he's not Grayson, you know?"

Jagger nodded and threw an arm around my shoulders. "Sam, you're one of the most genuine people I know. The good, the bad, you put it out there with no regrets and no apologies. But some of us...we're not that easy. Sometimes we're one person with our families and another once we're out from under them."

I watched as people said their good-byes to Grayson. He was stiff, formal, with a tight, closed-lip half smile. He was ten steps beyond the guy I'd met when I moved in.

"But which one is the real Grayson?" I asked.

Jagger glanced back to where Paisley walked between Morgan and Will. "In my experience, limited as it may be, he probably doesn't know."

"He always seems so steady."

"Sometimes steady is just stuck, Sam."

"Look at you, all wise," I joked, elbowing him in the side.

"Yeah, well, the love of a good woman will do that for you." He stopped us at the edge of the patio and turned to face me with his hands on my shoulders. "Grayson is a lot more grounded than I am and, oddly enough, a hell of a lot more damaged. But, Sam, I've never seen him as happy as he is around you. As relaxed. Don't forget that."

"You guys ready?" Paisley asked, slipping her arm around Jagger's waist.

"Yeah," I answered, shivering slightly when Grayson's eyes met mine over the couple he was talking to. The older woman touched his arm, and he covered his hand over hers and turned his attention back to her.

"Why don't you tell Grayson we're leaving, and we'll meet you in the car?" Will suggested.

I agreed, and they filed out, all stopping to thank Grayson's mother for having them. Sick of hovering, I walked over to where the bright red paint of a classic convertible peeked out from under the carport between the support stilts of the house.

"Holy shit. Is that a sixty-six and a half...no way," I whispered as my hand stroked over the immaculate paint job.

"It's Grayson's Mustang," Mia answered. "He barely drives it, but it's his."

"It's beautiful." Classic, strong, and old-fashioned like Grayson. Even the dent on the right front panel. Just a little damaged. "What's that from?"

"A lapse in judgment," Grayson answered from behind me.

"I'll give you guys a second," Mia winked at me where Grayson couldn't see, and skipped off.

"We're heading out." I turned, and Grayson stepped forward, effectively trapping me against the passenger door.

"Can I see you tomorrow?" he asked, his walls firmly in place.

"Do you want to?"

"I'm not a fan of staying in separate houses," he admitted with a slight raise of his lips. "I like you where I can keep an eye on you."

"I'm a big girl." He brought our lower bodies flush. A rush of heat spiraled through my stomach and I simply...wanted him. But I wanted *my* Grayson back, not the Gray I'd been watching all evening.

"You're tiny." His hands encircled my waist, his heat warming my skin through my thin sundress.

I raised an eyebrow. "You know what I mean."

"I do." His gaze dropped to my lips and they parted. If Grayson was half as good at flying as he was kissing, he was pretty much guaranteed top position on the OML.

He lowered his head, and my blood sang in my veins, vibrating at a pitch that threatened to explode. I closed my eyes as his lips grazed over mine and he whispered my name. "Samantha."

Just like that, my Grayson was back.

I smiled and leaned into him, ready for a real kiss—the kind he gave that turned me on more than sex ever had. The kind that melted every reservation at the first touch of his lips and made me hungry for the feel of his hands on my body. God, they were such delicious hands. "Grayson," I whispered as he—

"Gray?" Parker called from a few feet away. "Really? Mom and Dad are looking for you."

I ducked my head, resting my forehead against the firm muscles of his chest. I had to get him out of this shirt at some point.

"Mom! He's here!" Parker shouted over her shoulder before she walked away.

Or, I just needed to get my head out of Grayson's freaking pants. Holy shit, I'd never been this hot over a guy before.

Grayson steadied me, and then stepped back as his parents walked over. His dad was a well-built, older version of Grayson with a kind smile and a firm grip on his wife's waist. But his eyes were as hard to read as his son's.

"So this is where you've been hiding her," he teased.

Grayson's jaw flexed. "I'm not hiding Sam, just trying to keep her out of Parker's crosshairs."

"Good luck with that."

His mom smacked him lightly in the stomach with the back of her hand. "Sam, why don't you come to dinner tomorrow night? Just you and Gray? We'd love to get to know you better."

A chance to get to know Grayson's family? It might be the key to unlocking him.

"I'd love to—"

"She's on vacation, I highly doubt she'd want to."

We spoke at the same time, then locked eyes. His mouth set in a firm line as my eyebrows lowered.

"Then it's settled. We'll eat at six. It's been lovely to meet you." She smiled, but it was guarded. "Gray, the Bowdens would like a word."

"Yes, ma'am," he replied without taking his eyes off me.

They returned to what was left of the party while I glared at Grayson. "You don't want me at dinner?"

He looked away for a moment and then back to me. "Things are complicated here. I just...I'd rather be at the beach house with you."

"Right. Where you can be Rucker Grayson instead of Carolina Gray, so you can keep your two worlds neat and tidy."

"You have no idea."

I stepped to the side, then backed away from him. "Right, because you won't let me. You don't let *anyone* know both sides of you, do you? I swear, since I landed, you've given me whiplash. You know what? If you don't want me here, then I certainly don't want to be here. Give your mother my thanks and make my excuses."

"Sam."

I shook my head and turned around, walking toward the Yukon.

"Samantha!"

I sucked in my breath at the almost-desperate edge to his voice and paused only long enough to turn around and say, "I'd do just about anything for you, Grayson, but I'll never stay where you don't want me."

CHAPTER SEVENTEEN

The sun warmed my skin as the ocean breeze cooled it. I turned the next page in *The Odyssey*, lounging on the beach while Jagger and Paisley walked through the surf.

English was never my strong subject, and if I got this book read before fall term started, I'd be ahead. I had to ace those classes if I was going to get back into a university. Besides, all my chem and lab work was caught up.

"Sam!" Mia's voice rang out, and I lowered my sunglasses as she skipped down to my lounge chair in capris and a sleeveless polo.

Her smile was contagious. "What are you doing here, Mia?"

"I told Grayson I wanted to show you around, so he gave me the address."

Instead of showing me around himself. Not that he'd bothered to so much as call since I walked away from him last night. What was I supposed to expect? I'd told him to treat me like I wasn't here; I couldn't really be hurt when he did just that. Except that I was. Hurt, annoyed, missing him—he made me a kaleidoscope of mixed emotions, and I would have killed for a single, solid picture.

"Well, I'm glad to see you."

"Good. Now get dressed." She took my book out of my hand and headed back to the house, leaving no room for argument.

I changed into a flowy knee-length magenta skirt and a white halter top, loving the contrast against my sun-tanned brown skin, and found Mia in the living room, sitting opposite a smiling Will.

"It does have the best dancing in the Outer Banks," she cajoled.

"I'll definitely think about it." He grinned.

"I'd be happy to show you—"

Oh, nuh-uh. Not happening. I tapped Mia on the shoulder from behind her chair. "Your brother would be happy to show Will what the ocean floor looks like. Let's save his life and send Morgan with him, shall we?"

Mia flashed Will a killer smile. "Shame."

He flat-out laughed, which brought Morgan in from the kitchen. "What's so funny?"

"Look me up when you're about four years older, will you?" he asked Mia.

"Oh, you bet," she answered as I pulled her out of the chair.

"Or when you have a different brother," I muttered, leading her through the house until the sunshine hit my face. "Okay, where are we headed?"

She unlocked a black Jeep Liberty and motioned to the passenger seat. I got in and buckled while she did the same. "I figured I'd give you a tour, but I need to drop some stuff off to Parker first." She pointed to a purse in the back. "She's volunteering today and might want to buy lunch."

"No problem." Parker didn't exactly strike me as a candy striper. Where the heck did she volunteer? The Outer Banks House of Pain?

"I'm so glad you're here!" Mia began to chatter as we headed north toward Kitty Hawk. Two run red lights and three stories later about how her boyfriend dumped her since she was leaving for UNC in the fall anyway, we pulled into the hospital parking lot. Who the hell taught this girl to drive? "Besides, Gray needs you, and I want everyone to see what you do to him."

Well, this just got awkward. "He's different here."

She parked, killed the engine, and then grabbed Parker's purse from the back. Go figure, it was black...to match her soul. *She's probably not that bad.*

"Gray hasn't been himself since *it* happened," Mia answered. "The closest I've seen has been when he's with you."

I didn't know what to say to that, so I stayed silent.

She patted my hand like she was older and not vice versa. "How about you come in with me? I don't want to leave this at the desk, so I might need to hunt a minute or two to find her."

It was better than sitting in the hot car. "Sure."

The doors opened, and the sterile air conditioning swept over us. "Hey, Mia," the receptionist called out with a wave. *Small towns.*

"Hey there, Suzie. Have you seen Parker? She forgot her purse." She lifted it up.

"I think she's up on the eighth floor today. Who is your friend?" She sent a curious look my direction.

Mia just about glowed. "Oh! This is Sam. Grayson brought her home from Alabama for the weekend."

"That's not exactly what—"

"Isn't she gorgeous?" Mia cut me off, looping her arm around my waist and pulling me to her slight frame. "They're adorable together."

Suzie's stare became instantly appraising, and she swept up and down my figure, no doubt cataloging everything about me to recall at a later time. "Well, it is lovely to meet you."

Mia pulled me toward the elevator as I called back, "You, too!"

Mia punched the number for the eighth floor as the doors closed. "I figured we'd check out Kitty Hawk, and maybe swing by Jennette's Pier?"

"Sounds good," I answered, happy for the distraction.

The doors opened, and Mia continued to rattle off potential destinations as we walked down the sterile hallway. "Mary!" Mia called out to a nurse with flip-flop–patterned scrubs.

"Hi, Mia." She smiled, obviously busy.

"Have you seen Parker? I wanted to drop off her purse."

"I think she was with Miss Bowden." She motioned her head a few doors down.

"Thanks!"

I followed Mia to the room and waited outside while she popped her head in...without knocking. "Mia!" I hissed. What if the patient had been naked or something?

"She's not in there." She pursed her lips. "Okay, you stay here with Grace, and I'll go find her."

My stomach plummeted. "Grace?" *Bowden.*

Mia nodded, already looking down the hallway for Parker. "Yeah. She's watching *One Tree Hill*, so just go in and sit next to her. They had her watching cartoons for a while, but then I read this news story on this guy who was in a waking coma for like twelve years, and when he came out of it he was so pissed about them making him watch *Barney.* So I figured she loves *One Tree Hill*, right?"

My mouth opened and closed like a fish out of water.

"Oh, come on." She pulled me through the door, where a frail blond girl sat semi-reclined on her hospital bed. "Sam, this is Grace. Grace, this is Sam. Grayson brought her home for the weekend."

"Stop saying that," I whispered, my eyes locked onto Grace's vacant stare in the direction of the flat-screen.

"Please. Grace would love that Grayson has found someone. She wouldn't want him to live his life like he has been." Mia's hand stroked over Grace's cheek. "She doesn't have a mean bone in her body. She would want him to be happy." Then she turned to me with a wide smile. "You make him happy, Sam. Therefore, Grace would love you. I'll be right back."

She left. I froze, staring at the empty doorframe.

I should leave. I can't be here. But I couldn't just leave, either. I couldn't walk out and pretend that Grace didn't matter, even if the situation brought a whole new meaning to awkward.

Turning slowly, I tried to swallow, my throat suddenly dry from the hospital air. *Pretend she's not...you know...comatose.* The chair. Right. I could sit for a little bit.

The armchair next to her bed was surprisingly comfy, except for the lump under my butt. I reached under and pulled out a black hoodie. I didn't even have to look at it to know whose it was because it smelled like Grayson. Just like that was his backpack leaned against the wall.

I brought the hoodie to my nose and inhaled the scent a little more. Need slammed through me—the need to hold him, heal him, touch him. "I wish I could figure him out," I said to no one...to Grace, really. "He has these walls no human can climb. Or maybe I'm not the human he needs." Pain streaked from my heart, radiating through the rest of my limbs as though I'd physically been stabbed. Knowing I wasn't the one he needed was one thing, but saying it out loud was brutal, crushing. I folded the hoodie neatly and laid it across my lap before I looked over at Grace. "I think he needs you. I see that now, the way he comes here all the time."

Her mouth hung slightly slack as her head rested on the pillows. "I feel like a mess talking to you like this. You're his girlfriend, and I'm his..." I dropped my head into my hands. "God, I don't even know what I am. The girl he kisses because he can't kiss you? No. I know that's not true. He's not the kind of man to do that to someone.

"He's... He's Grayson. He doesn't only save me; he inspires me to save myself, to change. He lets me in long enough for me to start falling for him, to want this life I have no right to ask for, and then he shuts me out. And it's not like he pushes me away. He's too good a guy to do that. He disappears into himself, this little world where I can't follow. When he does that, I can see him, touch him, but part of me wonders if he's really here...with you. If he'll ever really be mine." Could I truly fall for him, knowing that I'd only have half of him, if that? There was a piece of Grayson that would always belong here, with Grace, but how big of a piece?

Was there even a way to compete? She was perfection in his memory, and I had more flaws than could be counted.

My eyes burned, and I blinked back tears. "I guess what I'm trying to say, as convoluted as it's coming out, is that I want what's best for him." I reached for her hand and took it in mine. Her fingers were long, elegant, as I knew she had been. I imagined her dancing in Grayson's arms, the perfect picture of a high-school romance turned lifetime love. They would have complimented each other, her lithe frame and his strength. Their genetics alone would have made gorgeous babies. But their fairy tale had a nightmare ending.

And then there was me, coming along after Prince Charming was broken, trying to cram my oversized foot into Cinderella's slipper, willing to cut myself to the bone to make it fit.

"I am so sorry for what's happened to you. For what's happened to both of you. Neither of you deserved any of this. From what I've heard, I know that in his life, you are the love story. And I know that I'm standing here with a second-place ribbon stuck to my heart, but he's worth it. I've never met anyone like him. He's strong, and smart, and loyal, and he... He makes me want to be the person he sees in me. And maybe I'm selfish for taking what I know isn't mine, but I'm really hoping that I can make him happy." I smiled through the lone tear that crept down my face. "You know, as happy as Grayson gets. But I'm really praying that you'd be okay with us, if you're listening. Because he needs you—I see that now. But I need him so badly."

She blinked, and I gasped. "You blinked. Oh my God. You blinked." I had to tell someone. A nurse. Right? Yes. I jumped out of my chair and nearly ran over the guy walking in.

He caught me by the shoulders, and I looked into a pair of concerned brown eyes. "What's wrong?"

"She blinked!" I squeaked.

His eyes drifted to Grace and back to me. "Yes. She does that."

Now it was my turn to blink. "Brain-dead people don't blink."

He tilted his head to the side and smiled. Wow, this guy was actually really good-looking. Maybe a little too soft, too boy-next-door for me, but good-looking nonetheless. "She's not brain dead. At least I don't think so. That's what the nurses always tell me." He stepped back and dropped his hands. "Hi, I'm Owen, a friend of Grace's. You are?"

Owen. That name should mean something, but I couldn't remember where I'd heard it. I forced a polite smile, still a little shaken. "I'm Sam. I'm a friend of Grayson's."

His eyebrows shot up. "Gray? Is he here?"

Was that panic in his eyes? "No. I mean, his stuff is, but I haven't seen him."

"Then I'll only stay a minute." His eyes swept over me. "You know, you don't look like his type."

What. The. Actual. Fuck. "Because I'm not a blond white girl?"

He startled. "No, no. You're gorgeous. You're just not..." His eyes shot over me to Grace again. "Comatose. He hasn't shown interest in anyone since Grace's accident."

Because she still owned his heart. He didn't have to say what we both already knew. I rubbed my hands down my arms, warding off the cold that was seeping into my bones with every moment I spent here, every second I realized what I'd done to my life...again. I was falling for someone who belonged to another woman, and the worst part was that I didn't know if I could stop.

I wanted Grayson so badly that having even a fraction of him was better than nothing.

"Right." Owen stepped around me and went to Grace, taking her hand in his. "So you don't think she's brain dead?" I couldn't help but ask.

He shook his head. "The doctors say so, and she wakes and sleeps and blinks. Maybe I'm an idealist. She slept the whole first year, and when she woke up, everyone was so excited, but she still wasn't *here*. They say she's in a permanent vegetative state; I choose to think she's healing. But maybe that's because I can't wrap my head around her never recovering." He sent a sympathetic smile over his shoulder at me. "But Gray's never left her. He keeps visiting, even as...hard as he's become. I hear he's different around you, though."

My eyes narrowed. "From whom?"

"Parker."

He was friends with Parker, that explained how I'd heard his name. "Ah, yeah, she's not exactly my biggest fan."

He laughed. "That's Parker. Don't let her get to you. She's holding a torch for G-squared to get back together."

"G-squared?"

He turned back to Grace, his thumb circling the back of her hand. "Grayson and Grace. You know, like Brangelina, or Bennifer?"

My mouth popped open. They had a freaking *name*? Of course they did. They were perfect. Where the hell was Mia? "You know, I think I'm going to go find Mia. She was actually looking for Parker..."

"Miranda, that's Grace's sister, she's in labor. My guess would be that's where Mia and Parker ran off to. Did you hear that, Gracie? You're about to be an aunt."

"What the hell are you doing here?" Grayson's voice boomed before he stepped fully into the room.

I stepped forward, ready to explain my shoving another

foothold into his life and apologize, but it wasn't me he was yelling at.

Owen stood from Grace's bedside and put his hands up. "Gray, I just wanted to stop by and see her. I didn't realize you were home this weekend until I saw—"

Grayson grabbed ahold of Owen and shoved him against the wall. *What the hell?* "You come here? You don't get to see her. Ever." A framed painting fell off its nail and crashed to the ground, shattering the glass. His forearm pressed against Owen's throat, and then he leaned in.

For the first time, Grayson's strength scared the shit out of me.

"I'm sorry, Gray," Owen garbled. "I've tried to tell you for years. I'm so sorry. I check in on her when I'm in town."

"You're sorry?" Grayson's voice dropped dangerously low. I'd never seen him so angry, so ruled by emotion. What the hell could this guy have done to bring down Grayson's prized control? "You're fucking sorry? Let me know when sorry wakes her up and gives her back the five years you've taken from her! From all of us!"

It clicked. *Owen.* He was the one driving that night. He was responsible for what had happened to Grace. Grayson leaned further, and Owen's color changed from a mottled red to a sickening purple.

"Grayson!" I shouted as I ran to him.

His gaze pivoted, full of so much loathing and hatred that I barely recognized him. I gasped, my hands inches from his skin.

The second he recognized me, his eyes widened and his face softened. His grip on Owen didn't. I stepped forward slowly and laid my hand on his arm. "You have to let him go. You're going to kill him."

His breath released in a rush. Without taking his eyes off mine, he released his hold on Owen, who slid to the floor among the glass shards.

"What are you doing here?"

Trespassing. Again. I flinched. "Mia brought me. She told me to wait here while she found Parker."

"They're with Miranda." His voice was flat, and I retreated, putting the physical distance between us that the mental seemed to call for.

"Owen?" I called out softly, leaving my eyes locked on Grayson. "You should probably go. Now."

He scurried to his feet, coughing, then passed me as he moved to the doorway. "Gray, I'm sorry. I know I was wrong, but I thought you were dead, and I lied. You and Grace were my best friends—"

"Were," Grayson snapped. "Never forget that."

Owen swallowed and looked at me. "I hope Parker's right, that he's different around you. Because that"—he pointed to Grayson—"unforgiving prick...is not the Gray I grew up with."

"Maybe you killed him that night, too." Grayson moved, blocking Owen from my view with his massive back. "Never speak to her again. Ever."

"Which one?" Owen's tone was challenging for a guy who'd nearly been choked to death.

Don't make him choose. I'm not ready for the answer.

Grayson stepped forward. "You've already ruined Grace's life, and if you come near Sam again, I'll finish what I started five years ago."

Both of us. *How diplomatic.*

"You going to try to hit me with your car again?"

"I won't miss, and even Parker won't be able to save you this time. Do you understand?"

"Loud and clear."

Owen's footsteps faded, and I stood entranced by Grayson's back as it rose rhythmically with his breaths. He finally turned around, pinning me with his eyes.

Everything we were and could be simmered there, just out

of reach—too far away to keep me warm, but dangerous enough to incinerate what was left of my heart.

"Grayson, I'm sorry. I didn't mean to intrude. Mia just kind of dumped me here."

His eyes flickered from mine to Grace and back again. "You...you can't be here. It's too much." He shook his head like he'd answered a question that hadn't been asked, and walked away, leaving me alone with Grace.

I blinked furiously as my eyes prickled with tears. *Suck it up. You barged in where you don't belong.* This was what I wanted, right? To know who Grayson was behind the defenses he so painstakingly maintained. I just hadn't expected the revelation to hurt so fucking much.

"See what I mean?" I asked Grace as I picked up the largest pieces of broken glass. "The man has walls you'd need a miracle to break through."

Because I wasn't her. I never would be.

CHAPTER EIGHTEEN

SAM

Grayson: *I'll be there in 15 to pick you up for dinner.*
The text message flashed across my phone as I applied the last of my makeup. "Shitty apology," I mumbled.

"He's...a little difficult to read," Paisley answered, sprawled out on my bed, flipping through a magazine.

"If there was a manual on Grayson, it would be written in a dead dialect of Aramaic and then published in Braille. He's impossible."

She smiled up at me. "You look stunning."

I rubbed my lips together to evenly distribute the gloss. I'd dressed carefully, stopping at the outlet mall and picking up a new dress with thicker straps, a fitted bodice, and a flirty yet classy skirt. "Thank you. I'm still half tempted to tell him to shove this dinner up his ass."

Paisley sat up, the scar from open-heart surgery peeking out the top of her shirt. It was a jarring reminder of how close Jagger had come to losing her. He loved her so completely that I could feel it when they were in the same room. Hell, in the same state.

"I'd use this time to snoop. If he won't let you in, then ask his family the questions you want answers to."

I narrowed my eyes at her. "Miss Southern Politeness 2015, really? You never snooped into Jagger. You wouldn't."

She chewed her bottom lip for a second. "You're right. But

Jagger and I kept too many secrets. We should have come clean early, and it would have been so much easier. Do you love him?"

What? "Love him? I wouldn't go that far. I care about him. Deeply. I love things about him, but I wouldn't rush into using that word." No. That word got me screwed, in more than the literal sense, in the past.

"Hmm."

"Hmm, what?" I strapped my wedges onto my feet.

"You remind me of someone."

"Who? Morgan?" Our outspoken natures had been compared more than once.

"Me, right around the time I started dating Jagger."

Grayson called my name before I had time to process that.

"Have fun!" Paisley called out as I headed down the steps.

Grayson waited for me at the bottom of the stairs, wearing pressed khakis and a light blue dress shirt that was unbuttoned at the top and rolled up just past his elbows.

I stopped on the second to last step, making me equal with his height, and ran my tongue across my lower lip. He looked incredible.

"Wow," he said as his eyes scanned over me and then came to rest on my mouth. He leaned forward, and I stepped back up a step.

"Oh no," I said. "You're not going to kiss me and think that gets you out of what happened today." I shook my head for emphasis.

A corner of his mouth rose. "I didn't think it would."

"Ugh. Don't do that half-smile thing. It makes me think you're back to being my Grayson and does *things* to me."

He stepped up the next step. "I'm always *your* Grayson. Now tell me more about these things."

I put my hands on his chest to stop his assault and nearly groaned at the feel of his muscles playing beneath my fingers. "No. You give me whiplash, I swear. Now take me to dinner. I'm not starting this with you again to get called out of it halfway through." Hell no. I liked sex, *loved* sex, and the need I felt for Grayson's body had me ready to rip his clothes off on the stairs. But I selfishly wanted *all* of him with me, every thought on me, every touch only for me. I didn't want to share him for a single second, and I didn't know if that was possible after seeing things go down today, or if I could separate sex from my feelings for him. They ran too deep already.

His arms slid around my sides, pulling me off the step and into his arms. "The next time I get my hands on you, Sam, I'm not stopping. So if you're not sure about this, about us...well, this is your warning."

I wound my arms around his neck as he carried me down the steps. Mad or not, I wanted him too much to not enjoy the tiny moment. "It's hard to be sure about anything when you keep me locked out."

I cringed as the wall went up behind his eyes. "We're going to be late."

The drive to his parents' house was only about ten minutes, but I enjoyed every one of them. He pointed out places that held significance to him and held my hand.

"Are we going to talk about today?" I asked, fidgeting with the hemline of my dress as we pulled into his parents' driveway.

He parked and turned to me. "Yes. I promise. Let's get through dinner, and we'll talk after."

I had to ask. "Did you really hit Owen with your car? Is that the damage on the front end?"

His jaw locked. "I hit the fence post right next to him."

"You're a different person here," I whispered as he held my face. "I don't like it."

He answered with a soft kiss. "I promise. After."

I nodded. "Okay."

He held my hand as we walked up the steps to the door but paused before we went inside. "Oh, Sam?"

"Oh, Grayson?" I smiled up at him, soaking in this one moment that he was still my Grayson.

"Can you remember not to mention anything about flight school?" His forehead puckered.

"Uh. Sure? Why would—"

He kissed me again, this time swiftly sliding his tongue along mine. I quickly forgot my name, let alone what I'd been asking.

"Ahem." Mia cleared her throat. "Maybe you should come in before Mom comes out?"

Grayson released my mouth with one more quick kiss. "After."

I nodded, and then growled as my head cleared. "Stop doing that."

"Stop doing what?" he asked with mock innocence.

"Kissing me to stop me from asking questions."

"You look very kissable while asking questions," he answered as we stepped into the house.

"Excuses." I laughed.

"Where is everyone?" Grayson asked Mia, who was grinning at us.

"Oh, Mom set up the table outside. There were too many people here for the dining room." At the look on Grayson's face, Mia clarified, "Only family, I swear."

"Good," Grayson replied as we walked toward the back of the house.

I stopped at the doorframe that led to the kitchen. "You have one!"

"What?" Grayson asked.

My fingers skimmed over the inked lines with dates and names. "Your heights. They're all marked as you grew up."

"Yeah?" Mia asked.

My cheeks warmed. "It's just really cool to see you guys grow up in this house. It's all right here. A family story." I stood, my eyes prickling, and brushed imaginary lint off my dress. "You probably think I'm silly."

Grayson tilted my chin. "Mia?"

"Yes?"

"Leave." He didn't wait for her response, instead pressed me against that doorframe and kissed me breathless, tilting his mouth over mine to get the deepest, sweetest angle.

I was dizzy and ready to strip him by the time he finished. "What was that for?" I asked, unable to tear my eyes off his mouth.

"Now it has the next chapter of my story. I'll never look at it again without thinking of the way you taste."

Excuse me while my panties evaporate. I swallowed and tried to get my reaction under control.

"Grayson Masters!" his Mom called from the back of the house.

"Coming, ma'am," he responded, but his eyes sparkled in a way I hadn't seen since before the disaster of a party. Maybe kissing him was my best weapon, the key to keeping my Grayson in the world that demanded Gray.

"Your accent isn't as strong as theirs."

"My dad's a northerner. I always tried to emulate him, so I guess mine was never as heavy."

We walked onto the deck, and my hand tightened reflexively around Grayson's. The family stood around a perfectly set beach-themed table, and Grayson led me to a set of empty chairs so I'd be sandwiched between him and Mia. He held out my chair and then pushed it in as everyone sat. His dad did the same for his mom.

Chivalry wasn't dead in North Carolina.

"Sam, you remember my dad, Constance and her fiancé, Bryan"—he skipped two empty chairs—"Mom, and Parker, of course."

"Hi." I smiled, waving to everyone, especially Parker. She

wasn't getting the best of me tonight. I needed all my strength to deal with her brother later.

"Who are we missing?" Grayson asked.

"Sorry we're late!" A couple in their mid-forties came up the porch steps behind us. The woman reminded me of a blond Gillian Anderson and the man looked like someone had permanently pinched a nerve...in his ass.

"Ian, Tess. We're glad you made it," Grayson's dad welcomed them and motioned to the empty chairs. "How is Miranda?"

"A healthy girl! Amberly Grace." Ian grinned. "We couldn't be more thrilled."

"You two should be celebrating." Connie handed down a bottle of wine.

"Well, we wouldn't miss a chance to see Gray, would we?" Tess smiled at Grayson as she accepted the bottle.

He nodded to them. "It's good to see you."

Maybe they were an aunt and uncle? Grayson took hold of my hand under the table. "Sam, these are the Bowdens. They're very close friends of my parents and own the house next door."

"As Grace's parents," Parker added with a smile, "they're family. I figured they'd want to meet you, Sam, so I asked Mom if we could invite them."

"Of course you're always invited," his mom agreed.

My stomach fell twenty feet to the patio below us. Of course Parker invited them. How better to slam it home that I wasn't wanted in his life? Like today's reminder hadn't been enough? Grace was ingrained in every single detail of his life here.

In an instant, my excitement over getting to know Grayson's family, and hopefully find out more about him, was squashed under the awkwardness of his girlfriend...wait, was she still his girlfriend?

As long as he wants you, that's all that matters. I straightened my spine, pushed my shoulders back, and gave Grayson some side-eye. I was the daughter of a Colonel in the United States

Army. I'd held my own at parties with people a lot more powerful and with harsher ulterior motives than Parker could ever dream. I could handle Parker. *Thank you, Mom.*

He brushed his lips over my ear in a delicate kiss and whispered, "I didn't know, and I'm so sorry."

I gave the tiniest nod possible and tried to remember what he'd said. *I'm always your Grayson.* But how would he hold up when everyone expected Grace's Gray?

Dinner was passed family style with grilled chicken legs, roasted potatoes, green beans, and some kind of stuffing that looked delicious. The others made small talk while I dug into the stuffing, lifting the fork to my lips.

"No!" Grayson shouted, knocking the fork out of my hand. It clattered to the table, nearly taking out my wineglass.

Well, there went the small talk.

"Gray?" his mom asked while I stared wide-eyed at him.

"That has pecans in it," he explained to me, panic in his eyes, then matter-of-factly switched our plates, since his had yet to be touched by the stuffing.

"Thank you," I said softly as his hand brushed across my cheek.

He took a deep breath like he was steadying himself. "Sam's allergic to nuts."

"Oh my, Sam, I'm incredibly sorry," his mom apologized.

"Don't be, you didn't know." Holy shit. That could have been bad. "I didn't even bring an epi pen," I said to Grayson. "It's at the beach house. What was I thinking?"

He squeezed my hand under the table. "I carry one, don't worry."

"What? Since when?"

"Since I almost fed you that banana-walnut muffin. I ordered it online," he answered with a shrug.

"Seriously?" Parker asked.

"Seriously," he shot back, his voice harsh.

We all chewed in relative silence. He carried an epi pen? For me? Well, crap if I didn't love that about him now, too.

"So, Sam, how did you and Gray meet?" Grayson's dad asked.

I swallowed my food. It had begun. "We're roommates."

"You're living with this young woman?" Ian set his knife down abruptly. *Better than picking it up, right?*

"Funny story there," Grayson cut in. "I thought she was a guy when I said yes to another roommate, and well..." The way he looked at me caught my breath. "As you can see, she's an incredibly beautiful woman."

"So you're living together. In a relationship and living together," Tess said, then took a shaky swallow of her wine. "That's nice."

"So, Sam, what are you studying in school?" Connie asked, trying to keep the peace.

"Mathematics." I gave her a thankful smile.

"You want to teach?" his mom added, and my head swiveled to the opposite end of the table.

"No, ma'am. I tutor now, but it's not my strong suit. I'm more interested in applied mathematics." I tucked my hair behind my ear, and Mrs. Bowden cleared her throat.

"Grace was going to be a teacher," Ian Bowden added. "She thought it would be a perfect fit once Grayson came home to take over the shop."

Take over the shop? He'd never even mentioned it.

Joey sat up a little taller and all but stabbed her chicken. This was definitely going down as the most awkward meal I'd ever had. What was I supposed to say to that? "I'm sure she would have been a wonderful teacher."

He looked somewhat appeased.

"Math, huh?" Parker raised her eyebrows and leaned forward to make sure I saw. "I bet that's useful while you're helping Grayson study, right?"

Crap. I should have asked him what he *did* tell his family.

Grayson tensed beside me. "Parker?"

"Oh, I'm sorry, Gray. I didn't tell you. I found your study guide today at the hospital." She threw his 5&9 cards into the middle of the table.

"What is that?" his father asked in a tone that was anything but forgiving.

I reached across Grayson and snatched them, putting them in my lap. "I'm sorry, I must have left those in Grace's room today."

"Right, because you fly helicopters." Parker laughed.

"Helicopters?" Grayson's dad shouted. "Gray?"

Grayson stared straight ahead, unfocused, so I looked to Mia, who looked devastated. "Gray?" his mom prodded.

Silence stretched. Not even silverware hit the plate. "Tell me this isn't true, Grayson. We forbade it. You agreed."

"I never agreed," Grayson said softly, finally looking up at his father. "You assumed and never asked what branch I chose after I graduated. You simply assumed it was the engineer corps because it's what you wanted."

Answering questions about my collegiate career would be less awkward at the moment, and I slept with my teacher.

"You will quit immediately. This isn't up for discussion." His father slammed the side of his fist on the table, bouncing the flatware.

"This isn't something you quit. I'm under a contract with the government." Grayson's voice was even, but it scared me more than his outburst had this morning.

"You will find a way!"

"No."

His mother gasped.

"You got your degree in maritime engineering. Masters & Son, remember? You doing a few years in the Army Corps of Engineers while we waited here at home. That was the agreement. You come home, and I agree to let you and Joey both manage the shop. You getting yourself killed playing pilot wasn't in the deal."

Wait. Was he using Joey to leverage Grayson? Joey all but slammed her glass on the table. *Yep.*

"And that hasn't changed. But I've always wanted to fly, to serve my country. I'm doing just that." If his grip hadn't intensified on my hand, I would have thought he really wasn't affected.

"What is going to happen when you crash, Gray?"

"Well, I'm banking on that not happening, Dad."

It was like watching a macabre tennis match, everyone's eyes darting between the two of them.

"And when it does? When you screw something up, read a gauge wrong? What are we going to do when you get yourself killed?"

"Then I guess you can cremate me and put me up on the mantle, where you can control everything I do. Or better yet, put me in the shop with you."

Why wasn't someone stopping this? Everyone from his mom through his sisters looked shocked, but no one did anything.

"Don't upset your mother."

"Then have a little faith in me, Dad. I'm not asking for a lot."

Mr. Masters' jaw flexed, like Grayson's did when he was ready to lose it. "How did you even get into flight school? Who the hell would let you in?"

"I'm a good pilot." Grayson's voice dropped while his father's raised.

"It was a nightmare teaching you to drive a car, and now you think you'll be capable of flying a helicopter? Respect your goddamned limits, Grayson. How good could you possibly be?"

"Language," his mother whispered, like the swearing had been the most offensive thing said.

I'd had enough. My mouth opened before my brain caught

up. "He's good enough that he finished Primary at the top of his class as the best pilot. Good enough to select the Apache, and good enough to be selected for class leader."

Grayson's grip tightened almost painfully. "Sam, don't."

"Someone has to," I hissed at him.

"So you're not moving home? I thought you'd be gone for three years after you graduated," Tess asked, her tone accusing.

"I'm contracted for six years after I graduate flight school. I'm trying to get stationed at Fort Bragg, which is only four hours away. I will still be close enough to come home on weekends"—he looked at Joey—"and I will keep my promise."

"Why not Virginia Beach?" Ian prodded. Of course Grace's dad would want him closer.

"They only have Blackhawks stationed there, and I fly Apaches. I have to go to a post that supports them."

Five months. That was all I had with him.

"Then why didn't you fly Blackhawks?" Tess's voice rose in pitch and volume.

"Because I want to fly Apaches. I worked my ass off for this."

"Language," his mom whispered.

"Mom, maybe now isn't the time," Constance said quietly.

Christmas would come, and he'd be gone, moving to North Carolina, closer to the woman he loved. While I...what? Lived in Jagger's empty house and went to community college after all my friends had moved on?

I was going to be left behind. Again.

"What about the shop?" Mr. Masters bellowed. "Everything I have done there, every boat has been for you—for our future."

Joey sucked in her breath, and Grayson's eyes snapped toward her. "I think Joey has done a great job, and she's more than capable. We hold the same degree, and she has way more experience than I do."

"I don't need you to stand up for me, Gray," she spat.

Apparently stubbornness was a family trait.

"Who is in the mood for dessert?" Mrs. Masters asked, only to be run over by Tess.

"So you're not moving back to Nags Head."

I scoped out her wineglass to see if she was drunk. Hadn't he clarified that?

"No," Grayson answered.

"You mean not yet." Mr. Masters' glare could have cut Grayson in two.

"I mean not any time in the near future, if ever. I haven't decided." My heartbeat rushing in my ears was the only sound in the silence that followed.

Every eye at the table was locked on Grayson, who nonchalantly took a bite of his potatoes. "These are really good, Mom."

Take the peace offering.

"But, but…" Parker stuttered, and I braced for impact. "But you can't *not* live here. What about Grace?"

Boom. There was not enough wine in the world to deal with this dinner.

"I think I deserve a life, too. A future." Grayson spoke each word slowly, with a kindness I couldn't have shown in the same situation. A small sliver of hope embedded in my heart, just strong enough to hold my deepest fears momentarily at bay. *A future.*

"And what did my Grace deserve?" Tess fired.

"What about your copilots, Gray?" Mr. Masters came in for the kill. "Don't you think they deserve to live? You have no right to be in the cockpit. You'll get someone killed…just like before."

My mouth dropped. His father still blamed him. It was no wonder Grayson kept his life neatly compartmentalized. He was perpetually under attack at home. His muscles coiled beneath my hand.

"That's enough!" Mrs. Masters stood, her chair falling to the ground behind her. "Gray, this is your life. We might not like your choices, but you're a grown man. Honey, get over it. Joey's been running the shop with you for years and has more than earned her place, agreement or none. Tess, Ian—I love you as family, but if you ever insinuate that Grayson was responsible for Grace's...condition, you will no longer be welcome in my home."

Grayson pushed back from the table. I followed him, since he still held my hand. In my other, I clutched the study guide that had brought this all on. "Mama," he whispered as he kissed his mother's cheek. Then he turned to the table, where everyone sat as if they'd been frozen. "We'll be leaving now."

With a hand at my lower back, he led me into the house while the table remained eerily silent behind us.

I buckled into his Mustang as he threw the car into drive and tore out of his parents' driveway. Grayson's face was a mask of harsh angles and unforgiving lines. When I reached for his hand, he moved it away.

I didn't try again.

We pulled into the rental, but he didn't kill the engine, or even look my way. His gaze was fixed ahead of us, on his past, no doubt on Grace, on everything that had been thrown in his face tonight. He was as close as my next breath and as unreachable as yesterday. I had to find a way to get through to him. "Stay with me tonight."

His hands tightened on the steering wheel, and I waited.

"Okay. I have to get my stuff from my parents' house and deal with...all that."

I cupped his stubble-rough cheek in my hand. "I'll wait. And Grayson. You're amazing and deserve to fly. If they can't see that, I'm sorry. But you do. I'll pin your wings on myself if they don't come around."

"Promise?"

"On my life." He deserved so much better. Yes, he was

leaving in five months, and yes, under that fiercely jumpable exterior lurked the hottest mess of a man I'd ever seen. But maybe, if I could put my own emotional baggage to the side for a minute, I could help him the same way he'd been helping me since I got to Alabama.

He never looked me in the eye, but he pressed a kiss to my palm in way of good-bye and drove away once I had the front door to the house open.

He was at war with the two sides of himself. I could see it as clearly as if there were literally two of him. I just didn't know which one would be coming back to me.

I was also too far gone to care. Maybe I could save both sides.

CHAPTER NINETEEN

"Come on," Morgan begged as she leaned back into the passenger side of the Yukon. "You know you want to come dancing. Grayson is as moody as they come, and this is vacation."

"It sounds like a ton of fun"—*and right up my usual alley*—"but I just can't."

"You're leaving me with *him*?" She tilted her head toward where Will waited, his arms crossed.

"Something tells me you'll be just fine." I smiled. Like I hadn't seen the sparks between those two. They were more metal-on-metal than kindling-a-fire sparks, but they were there.

Jagger took her place in the open door frame as Morgan looped arms with Paisley to head inside the bar. "Look at you, all grown up and not coming out drinking."

"Yeah, well, I'd hate for Grayson to have to pull me off another bar." *If he bothered to come looking.*

"You sure this is what you want to do?"

The dashboard clock said eleven o'clock. It had been over four hours since Grayson left me. "Yes," I answered.

"That guy has walls thicker than the Great Wall of China."

"I don't think anyone's ever really tried to break through them. He deserves someone who will show up with a bulldozer." And maybe two hundred pounds of C-4, or hell, even a nuke.

Jagger sighed. "Last year, Grayson told me, 'sometimes voicing something gives it power over you.' I used to think it was because he was incredibly wise…"

"But now?" I asked.

"After seeing him this weekend, I think he's incredibly quiet because he has so many demons dying to gain that voice. The guy is in constant survival mode, Sam. He's wired for fight or flight. Always has been, and you're a threat to whatever peace he's attained by keeping those walls."

"He's worth the bulldozer, Jagger." With every word, my conviction grew. So did my will to fight for him.

"Yeah, he is, and you are, too. Just…be careful."

I nodded, and he shut the door.

His words stayed with me as I drove to the directions of the GPS location Mia had given me when Grayson hadn't shown. I crossed the bridge to Roanoke Island and turned into Manteo. A few turns later, and I was parked along the waterfront. The sign hung on the large warehouse read MASTERS & SON.

I killed the lights and my indecision, and then stepped out of the car. I knocked first, and when no answer came, I turned the unlocked handle, walking into a small, lit office. "Grayson?"

Another door later, I walked into a giant work area, where a huge boat rested on a trailer. The only light came from the boat itself, casting eerie shadows along the floor and walls. The beginnings of other boats took up various locations, but the one in the middle was obviously the showpiece, and her back read *The Alibi*.

"Grayson?" I called out again.

Movement came from high above me on the boat. "Sam?" Grayson sat on the edge, leaning on the railing as his feet dangled over the side. "How did you…"

"Mia," I admitted. "Is it okay that I'm here?"

He studied me for a moment, and I braced. "Yeah. There's a ladder at stern, the back of the boat."

I kicked off my wedges as he came toward me, then climbed the ladder, using the handholds on the last rungs until I stood inside. "It's beautiful," I whispered, taking it in. The lines were smooth, every detail exquisitely attended to. This wasn't an ordinary sailboat, or one I could dream of affording. The polished decks gleamed in the lights, the luxury seats were the softest leather, everything was buffed, polished, and standing in the middle of it was Grayson. Beautiful, ripped, kind, and complicated Grayson.

I'll take one yacht and the deckhand, please.

"Your family built this?"

"She's Dad's pride and joy. We started the design a couple years ago, but only started building her this year. I helped out on the design, and whenever I was home. Well, when I wasn't—"

"With Grace," I finished for him, running my hand along the wheel. "You can say her name. You can talk about her, Grayson. I'm okay with it."

His hand covered mine, the contact stopping my movement and my breath. "I don't want to talk about her."

Even the dim lights couldn't soften his features. His jaw was tense, unyielding, his mouth set in a firm line. "Who are you?" I asked softly, resting my hand on his chest. "Are you the dutiful son? The one who moves home and takes over his family business? Designs sailboats?"

"Yes." His hand rested on my hip.

My heart lurched. "Are you the army pilot at the top of your class, ready to be assigned somewhere? Deployed overseas?"

"Yes."

I drew my gaze up from his chest to look in his eyes. "Are you the guy who kissed me covered in brownie batter? Or the guy who threw his ex-best friend against the wall?"

"Yes." He pulled my hips against his, and a rush of desire slammed through me.

My hand tightened on the steering wheel. "Grayson, you

can't be both. You're a whole different person here. At home, you're a little hard, but here…you're angry, and dangerous, and more than a little tortured."

His other hand released mine on the wheel so he framed my hips.

"I get it. I see how they treat you, and what they all expect. I can't fathom the guilt you feel over what happened to Grace, but I know it fuels what happens here…who you are here."

"Sam—"

"No, let me get this out." I steadied my nerves with a huge breath and stepped backward, out of his arms. "You were nothing I had planned. Not that I ever have a plan, right? But you happened. And I know you're graduating flight school in five months, and then you'll be gone. I get it. We're not permanent. But you *happened* to me. And I have no claim on you, no right to you, and I'm falling for you. That's…that's dangerous to me." His eyes, his mouth, his very being softened. "And coming here, seeing you like this—it hurts my heart. I would give anything for you to have your miracle, to have Grace back, but I can't."

"I'm not asking you to," he said softly, stepping toward me.

I retreated. "Stop. I can't think when you touch me."

A corner of his mouth lifted. "Okay." He took another step.

"It's just that when you're home at Rucker, you're mine. Maybe not…*mine*, mine. But…I know we have something. And I come here…" *Why is this so hard to get out?* "Here, you're hers. And I don't mean romantically, though I totally get that, too. Here, you're still paying penance for something you carry no blame for. I feel like the only person who has a chance of breaking past your walls is lying in a coma. Here, you're hers, not mine, and I'm *falling*, Grayson."

I put my hands out to block him, but he simply reached under them and lifted me by my hips until I was eye level with him. He was strong enough to carry me with just his arms; I didn't even need to brace my weight on his shoulders. *So damn hot.* "Grayson."

"Shh. My turn." He placed me on the captain's chair, keeping our faces a breath apart. His hands were warm as they cupped my face. "You're right, and I am all those things. Here, I'm what they need me to be. I'm my parents' son, and my sisters' brother. I serve as a link to Grace for her parents, and I take a little of their burden for caring for her. I'll shoulder their blame, even as subconscious as it may be, because I deserve it." His thumb pressed over my lips when I tried to speak. "No, it's true. I'll never forgive myself for letting Owen drive. For not taking his keys. That's going to haunt me for the rest of my life, and Grace is a living reminder of it. When I'm here, I'm still her best friend. I still pray for a miracle, because if anyone deserves a happy, full life, it's Grace."

My stomach dropped. Believing he was always going to be hers and hearing it from his lips were two different things. His thumbs stroked my cheekbones, and I fought against leaning into him, for taking any moment he was willing to give, even if I was selfishly stealing it from her.

"But, Samantha, it doesn't matter if I'm at our house at Rucker, or walking the beach here. I'm still yours. Sitting next to Grace? Yours. Studying for my next flight? Yours. Arguing with my sisters, my parents, the Bowdens...I'm still *yours*. I might not say it, but if I *happened* to you, well, you sure-as-hell more than happened to me. You challenge me, transform me every day. It doesn't matter what everyone sees, or what role I have to play, you're under my skin, and when I come here, you're along for the ride. This is not a temporary thing between us. There is no deadline. I. Am. Always. Yours."

He kissed me softly, his tongue tracing my lower lip. "So go ahead and fall. I've gotten really good at catching you."

My fingers dug into the back of his shirt at the same moment my lips molded to his. Hands on my hips, he pulled me flush against him, and that fire we'd kept carefully banked raged to life. God, I was ready to burn.

I deepened the kiss, stroking my tongue against his, and he took control, tilting my head to get a better angle. His hands shifted lower, cupping my ass, and he lifted me off the chair. I wrapped my arms around his neck and my legs around his waist, locking my ankles behind his back.

My fingers ran through his hair. Lips caressing, teeth nipping, tongues stroking, soothing—our kiss consumed each of my senses. He slipped one of his hands under my dress, and then the other, until he held me by bare skin. He lightly squeezed the backs of my thighs, his fingers achingly close to the small strip of lace that separated them. "I love your skin," he whispered against my mouth. Then he kissed down my throat, sucking the tender patch of skin that met my collarbone.

"And the way you smell..." He ran his nose along the line of my neck. "I could live here, Sam."

I tugged his hair, bringing his mouth back to mine, and sucked his tongue into my mouth where it belonged. He groaned, tightening his grip on my thighs, and then we were moving. He tore his mouth away from mine long enough to press my head to his shoulder as he carried me down the stairs to the cabin of the boat.

As soon as we cleared the ceiling, his mouth was mine, our kisses taking a harder, more desperate edge. I tugged at his shirt, but it caught on my legs. "Impatient?" he asked against my mouth.

"Get it off. You have no idea how long I've been waiting for this." My mouth watered at the idea of tracing every line of his phenomenal body with my tongue.

"I was thinking the same thing."

He carried me with one hand and opened a door behind me with the other. One more step and he lowered me to a bed, complete with the softest sheets I'd ever felt. "The bed is made?" I asked as he stepped back.

"Photo shoot this morning for the brochure. Would you like a tour?" He motioned to his back.

"Of you? Yes, please." I sat up on my knees at the edge of the bed. "Now."

He reached behind and pulled his shirt over his head. I took it off his arms and tossed it, too intent on what was in front of me to see where it landed.

Every muscle in my core clenched. Grayson was made for sex, ripped, his muscles not just defined but built, thick and strong. His skin was a beautiful light bronze and incredibly soft to my touch. My fingers worshiped the lines of his eight-pack abs. "You're… God, I don't even have words for what you are." My breath became choppy as I trailed over his pecs, and he sucked in his breath when my thumbs grazed his nipples. I leaned forward and ran my tongue over one, and he hissed, his hands weaving through my hair to hold me as I gently scraped my teeth over him, then kissed the flat disc.

Sitting back on my heels, my eyes devoured every incredible inch of him. His stomach tensed under my hands, and I looked up to be held captive by the most intense, hungry stare I'd ever been given. "What are you thinking?"

"That every single weight I've ever lifted, or mile I've run has been worth it for you to look at me like that." He caressed my cheek, then slid his hand down to the straps of my dress.

I crossed my arms in front of my stomach, a chill overpowering the heat in his gaze. "Grayson…I'm not…" I motioned to his torso.

He raised an eyebrow as his fingers toyed with the zipper under my arm. "Trust me."

I'd never been self-conscious about my body before. *Stop it. You rock your curves.* Eyes locked on each other, I raised my arms above my head. Once he finished unzipping me, I nodded my assent, and he tugged the fabric gently over my head.

Was his breath shaky on that inhale? I opened my eyes and found his all over me. My skin tingled, heated wherever he paused in appreciation, his mouth dropping as his eyes locked onto my lace-cupped breasts, my stomach, then my red lace panties.

"Samantha. Damn. You're perfect." He reached for me, then paused. "If I start—if I touch you now..." He shook his head.

We were at his threshold, and he was giving me a choice. *Like there is even one to make.* I wanted him. I needed Grayson's weight, those gloriously stacked muscles on me, his strong hands on my body. I needed him so deep that I would still taste him tomorrow—smell him on my skin. I was done waiting.

Reaching behind me, I unclasped my red lace bra and slid the straps down my arms one at a time. He never looked away, and I witnessed the moment desire for me overpowered his every other thought. I actually *ached*, more turned on by the possessive, predatory widening of his eyes than I ever had been with anyone else.

Once my bra met his discarded shirt, I leaned my breast into his outstretched hand. "Touch me. Don't worry and don't stop. I want this. I want *you*."

He snapped.

One moment he was in front of me, and the next he was over me, pinning me to the bed as he kissed the breath out of me, one elbow bracing his weight and the other palming my breast. I gasped as he rolled and lightly pinched my nipple. A devious smile lit his face, and my heart stuttered. Holy shit. He was always hot, but smiling? Grayson was beautiful.

I cried out when his mouth latched to my nipple. His tongue swirled and danced, flicking in time as his fingers gave my other breast the same attention. My eyes fluttered shut, trying to absorb the sensations as shots of lightning ran straight through my veins.

He kissed my mouth, settling between my legs. His chest crushed my breasts, abraded the sensitized skin as his hand palmed my curves, resting on my ass. I looped my leg over his hips and rocked into him, using his erection to gain some much-needed friction against my clit.

"Off," I mumbled, my foot running down his cargo shorts.

He stripped quickly to his boxer briefs, pulling a condom from his wallet and tossing it next to us on the bed. Even his thighs were hot, roped with heavy muscles. "Better?" he asked against my neck, kissing his way down between my breasts.

"Much."

He grinned, and I had an all-new definition of who *my* Grayson was. This was him—needy, happy, hungry...mine.

He kissed every inch of my stomach, sucking lightly where my stomach dipped from my rib cage. He treated me like the most important test he could study for, returning to the places that made me gasp, cataloguing what I liked, what made me writhe.

Grayson teased his way down my legs, pausing behind my knees when I sucked in my breath, then pressed his thumbs into the arches of my feet. He was turning me into a puddle of pure hedonistic desire one kiss, one touch at a time, with the patience of someone who'd planned this for a while. My hips rolled as his breath skimmed the lace of my panties.

His grin was nowhere to be found when he locked his eyes on mine and waited for me to nod, then took my panties with him as his hands slid down my legs. He massaged his way back up my legs, keeping agonizing inches away from where I desperately needed him to touch me.

I was going to combust if he didn't do something about it.

"Grayson, you're killing me." My body wouldn't stay still, needing contact, friction.

"Good. I've been dying since the morning I saw your ass on my kitchen counter." He squeezed the curves for punctuation, then rose to kiss me. I whimpered into his mouth, and he bit gently into my lower lip.

"Samantha." My name on his lips felt almost as good as his fingers parting me, sliding through my folds until he brushed against my clit.

Amazing. I arched against him. "More. Please, Grayson. More."

"Do you know how long I've planned this? How many nights I lay in bed across from your room and thought about how you'd feel under my hands? How many times you'd bend over and I'd want nothing more than to step behind and slide into you?" His fingers swept through me again, and he groaned as he circled my clit. "How wet you'd be." His breathing accelerated and his jaw locked as he slid one finger inside me. My muscles clamped down, and I couldn't control the moan that slipped free. Another finger joined, and he kissed me, his tongue thrusting at the same slow, deliberate speed his fingers were. "How tight you'd be," he whispered against my lips.

Everything in me coiled, centering in my core, winding higher with every word he spoke, every press of his fingers. He used his thumb to apply pressure to my clit as his fingers worked within me. "God, Sam. I've dreamed of this, fantasized a million different ways. Holding you. Exploring you. Having sex with you. Making love to you." He kissed me gently, and I melted a little more, despite the tension building to a breaking point within me. "Fucking you."

Leave it to Grayson to make that word the sexiest thing I'd ever heard.

His fingers sped up, curled inward, and his kiss turned carnal. I rode his hand, arching into him through every stroke, my fingers biting into the skin of his back. My eyes shut, every sense too overwhelmed with pleasure to take the overload. "Grayson…" His name became my chant as the tension built to the breaking point.

"Look at me," he demanded. "I need to see you come."

My eyes flew open as he pinched my clit and stroked my G-spot simultaneously. I cried out soundlessly as my orgasm ripped through me, sending pure bliss through every cell in my body.

His thumb circled those nerves as he brought me down, then pressed lightly, sending another jolt through me. His hand slid away, and though I'd just had the most astonishing orgasm of my life, I felt another spark ignite as he licked the pad of his middle finger. The one that had been *inside* me.

He groaned. "You taste better than I ever imagined, and believe me, I imagined it a lot." His eyes were wild, his infamous control slipping by the moment.

I did this to him. Pushed him to the brink of madness. It wasn't enough.

I wanted him absolutely fucking insane.

With one hand on his shoulder, I urged him to his back, careful to snag the condom before he rolled onto it. It was his turn to gasp as I licked my way down his chest, savoring each line, breathing in his scent mingling with mine.

I worshiped the sexy V that led to his boxer briefs, kissing the tensed muscles as his hands wove into my hair. "Sam," he groaned.

"Do you know how long I've wanted to do *this*?" I countered. "You take over my thoughts at the gym, at home, anywhere you feel the need to take your shirt off. It's like you have a direct line to my panties with each inch of skin you show." I nipped at his flesh, then kissed it. "It's not fair."

"Sam," he whispered, and I met his eyes, which had gone almost feral. "Between us? You have all the power. All the control. You always have. I'm hard for you the minute you so much as smile, or curse, or walk in the damned room."

"Show me."

I gripped his erection through the fabric of his boxer briefs, and his hips bucked as he sucked his breath in through his teeth. Emboldened, I ran my fingers along the elastic, and then under. Then I took them off, never once breaking eye contact. The intimacy of what we were doing was nearly overwhelming.

My tongue skimmed my lower lip as my hand unerringly found him. Of course he was huge. Was there anything about Grayson that wasn't built like a Greek god? He groaned, his fingers tightening against my scalp.

He was hot in my hands, smooth and rigid, soft at the tip when I ran my thumb over him, wiping away the small bead that had formed. Then I gave in to the need to know how he tasted and ran my tongue along the underside of his shaft until I circled the head. My hand gripped his base as I took him inside my mouth, humming with pleasure as he called my name. "Samantha. Fuck. Yes… No. God, you can't. I'll come." His legs trembled beneath me.

"So?" I whispered, then swirled my tongue over him. "Come."

"I need to be inside you," he growled, leaning up on his elbows.

I ripped open the foil wrapper and rolled the condom onto him. "Okay."

He didn't need to be told twice, and flipped me to my back. This wasn't the patient, controlled man who'd just brought me to orgasm. Grayson was hanging on to his control by a thread. I could tell by the tension in his muscles, the firm set of his mouth.

That thread needed to be cut.

He knelt between my thighs, and I raised my knees as he nudged my entrance. "Grayson," I urged when he paused.

He searched my face for an excruciating moment before shaking his head. "No."

What? Was he seriously going to stop?

His mouth found mine, thrusting his tongue at the same moment his fingers worked his magic against my hypersensitive clit. "Fuck you feel so good," he whispered as my body responded, flaring to life. "I can't wait to be inside you, Sam. I'm going to ride you until you come screaming my name. You're never going to look at me again without thinking of how many ways I can think of to get you off, and believe me, I'm very imaginative."

His words pushed me higher. "You have a surprisingly dirty mouth, you know that?" I sucked his lower lip into my mouth as my hips rocked against him, needing more than the external stimulation. I needed him inside me.

"I have a dirty mind. I'm just letting you see inside it."

My heart stopped for a breath of a second. I had his walls down, open for me.

"Sam?" He paused.

I shed every reservation, every inhibition, and kissed him like my life depended on our mingled breaths. I gave myself over to the sensations his fingers brought and then his lips at my breasts until I couldn't stop the motion of my hips.

Sweat beaded on Grayson's forehead. "Grayson, please. *Please.*" How much more did he expect me to take?

He positioned himself over me, resting his weight on his elbows as I almost drowned in the depths of his eyes. "Anything you want, Samantha. It's yours. I'm yours. All of me."

Inch by slow inch, he entered me. There was a slight burn where he stretched me, but it was nothing compared to the exquisite way he fit. "Oh my God," I moaned as he slid home.

His eyes widened. "You. Feel..." His forehead dropped to mine. "Better than perfect." He kissed me sweetly, and my eyes pricked. "My Samantha."

I rolled my hips, and we both groaned. Then he raised one knee toward my chest and slid even deeper, hitting a spot that had me crying out, then keening as he began to thrust powerfully in perfect time.

Each stroke lifted me higher, wound my muscles tighter. I met him with each push of his hips until sweat dripped off us both. Between our thrusts, hands, and tongues, I lost track of where I ended and he began.

"Grayson..." I whispered as my muscles seized, locked. I was so close, hovering on the precipice. He shifted his angle so he rubbed against my clit with his next thrusts, and I went spinning off into the void, holding onto him as my only solid ground.

He called out my name as he came, tensing above me, his eyes unguarded as he pulsed within me. In that moment, he felt like what he proclaimed—mine.

Grayson collapsed next to me, peppering my shoulder with kisses. "That was... I don't even have words for that."

I found the strength to smile. "Me, either. I say we rest before you talk me into round number two."

He laughed. "You'll like it, I promise."

I leaned on my elbow above him and kissed him, savoring, trying to commit every second of this moment to memory. "Any time. Any place."

He stroked his thumb across my lower lip, his eyes lighting with a fire I thought would be extinguished. "I'll hold you to that. But I'll let you sleep...for a few hours."

He cleaned up, and then pulled the covers over us, drawing me into the hollow of his body. Of course we fit together perfectly. The heat from his body and steady heartbeat lulled me to sleep within minutes.

Joey calling Grayson's name woke me up just as quickly. "You'd better not be in there, Grayson Masters! I found Sam's shoes, so I know you're not alone!" Sunlight streamed in the small porthole.

Oh. My. God.

"Shit!" Grayson shouted, sitting straight up and covering me with the sheet. "Do not come any closer, Josephine!"

"God damn it, Gray! The photographer is going to be here in a half hour!" she yelled from inside the cabin.

"That was yesterday," he replied.

"We moved it to today." She was close enough that I heard her sigh. "Okay, I'm going to leave Sam's shoes out here. Just... For God's sake change the sheets. There's an extra set in the closet."

She retreated and Grayson kissed me. "Good morning. Perhaps we should move quickly?"

"You think?" I nearly shouted. I'd never gotten dressed or changed sheets that fast in my life. I held my shoes in one hand as Grayson helped me down the ladder, and then strapped my wedges on.

He led me out the side door, where Joey stood in jeans and polo. "Seriously, you two?"

Grayson lifted my hand to his mouth and kissed the palm. "Yeah."

She rolled her eyes. "What am I going to do with a boat that smells like sex?"

Grayson shrugged. "Make it part of the package?" When he turned to me, his playful smirk grew into a full-blown smile. The morning sun shone, lighting the silver flecks in his eyes, and kill-me-now, a dimple appeared. *A fucking dimple.* He radiated simple...joy.

My heart warmed to almost burning. *Oh, no.*

He kissed my mouth soundly. "I need to grab my wallet from the boat, meet me at the car?"

I nodded, unable to say anything.

Joey's mouth dropped open in the way mine would have if I hadn't been defenseless. "Wow." She crossed the distance between us and hugged me, holding me like I was something precious and sacred. "Sam. Wow. Thank you. That's really Gray... and I haven't seen *him* in years. I knew I liked you for a reason."

"Get off Sam, Joey," Grayson called over from the door, wallet in hand. She let me go and hugged him before she ran inside.

"You okay?" he asked, his smile wider after another kiss, and my chest tightened in a way I couldn't deny...or allow.

I nodded and forced a smile to match his as we walked toward the car.

This was not okay. Not even close. Taking down his walls had shattered mine.

I'd fallen in love with Grayson Masters.

CHAPTER TWENTY

GRAYSON

"You look good with a baby," Miranda said from the corner armchair in Grace's room.

"Maybe one day." I pulled the little pink-and-blue striped hat up a little more so it didn't get in the baby's eyes. *Amberly Grace.* It was fitting for her somehow. What would it be like to have a daughter? Would she get my stubbornness? Her mother's spark? My gray eyes, or her mother's hazel-green ones? God help me if she wore her skirts as short. No skirts. Ever. No boys, either. Yeah. And I'd need a better gun. Or I could park the Apache in the front yard. That would scare the fuckers off.

Right. I was pretty well screwed if I had a girl, because if my daughter was anything like her mother, even a loaded AH-64 parked on the front lawn with Hellfires pointed at them wouldn't keep the boys away.

Kids with Sam?

Holy shit, my mind ran amok.

"Hey, earth to Grayson," Miranda called out with a faint smile. Her hair was pulled into a messy bun, but despite the circles under her eyes, she looked beautiful. Exhausted, but beautiful.

"You're supposed to be in bed," I lectured. "She's less than a day old."

"I wanted Amberly to meet her aunt," she said through a yawn.

I swayed with Amberly, trying to focus more on the new life in front of me than the one comatose next to me. "Did you know that Owen visits her?"

Her eyes fell away. She knew he'd been here to see Grace. "He did his time, Gray. I know he lied, and you weren't racing, but he was eighteen, reckless, and he made a mistake."

"An unforgivable mistake." I snapped each word.

Miranda tilted her head, just like Grace used to, but the similarity between the two wasn't as painful anymore. "Is anything really unforgivable, Gray?"

I didn't take the fucking keys. "Yes."

"I don't think Grace would see it that way, no matter what our parents say. She would tell you to stop suffering more than you have to. She would tell you that moving on is okay. It's healthy, and you need it. She would tell you that your new life, flight school, this new girlfriend of yours...they all look really good on you."

Girlfriend? Yes, Sam was my girlfriend. Is that what I had done? Moved on?

"Where is she anyway? Sam?" she asked.

"How do you know—"

"Mom and Dad. They filled me in on the epicness of dinner last night." Her eyes started to droop, and I crossed to her, handing over an extra blanket.

"Ahh. Yeah, that was fun. She's actually with my mom right now. She wanted to have lunch with Sam since we're leaving tomorrow." I checked my watch. "If she's survived, she should actually be getting here pretty soon."

Miranda didn't respond. When I looked back, she'd fallen asleep, her head propped on the back of the chair.

"Well, more time for you two ladies," I whispered to Amber.

I gently sat on the bed, facing Grace, who had been turned onto her side. Then I snuggled Amber in face to face with her. "Grace, meet Amber. Amber, meet your aunt Grace."

I held my arm against Amber's back so she didn't slip down the slight incline of the bed and let them get acquainted. If I had been a romantic, I would have said that Grace focused on her niece, her eyes locked onto Amber's. *But you're not a romantic, and you know that you just set her in Grace's eye line.*

"What would you say, Gracie? About that girl yesterday?" I pumped some lotion into my hand and pulled some gymnastics to rub it into Grace's dry hand while keeping Amber safe. Babies were tricky.

I took in everything about Grace in that moment. Her slight frame, her vacant eyes. There was still love there for her, I knew it. I felt it. But it wasn't the same as what I felt for Sam. Grace had been steady, soft, and went with the flow, always content for me to follow my path because she would choose whatever I did. And while I knew I missed her, my best friend, the ache had softened.

"What would you tell me to do?" My heart burned because I already knew the answer. I stroked my thumb across her pale cheek. "You would tell me to be happy. You would tell me not to waste love...if that's even what this is with Sam. It doesn't feel the same as when I loved you, Grace. She's fire, but the kind that burns me just right. She doesn't take my crap, and she's a giant pain in my ass. But when I kiss her...I can breathe. I don't know if this makes me an asshole or not, but when I'm with Sam, everything fades away. The hurt, the loneliness, the indecision." I rubbed a piece of her hair between my thumb and forefinger. "Even the guilt slips to the back. It's like she's the midday sun, and my shadows don't just hide...they shrink. They disappear."

And the sex... Sam wiped away every single conscious thought when we touched. It wasn't just a five-year dry spell. I remembered sex *really* well, and Sam transcended the very meaning of the word. It wasn't like I hadn't been offered more than my fair share, even at the Citadel where the guy-to-girl ratio was definitely in favor of the fairer sex. But Sam was the first woman I could look past Grace to really...see.

And Sam saw me, too, got me on a level that no one else had even come close to.

Closer than even you, Grace. I was such an asshole for even thinking it.

Amber grunted, and then let out a shrill cry. "I've got her," Miranda said, blinking awake. I placed the tiny baby into her arms. "I need to get back to my room anyway. James is bringing me dinner. Hospital food sucks."

"It was good to see you, Miranda."

She placed Amber in the clear, rolling bassinet, and then squeezed my arm. "You, too. Gray...maybe you should think about living your life for a while? Take a few months before you come back. Focus on flight school. Fly your badass helicopter. You deserve to find out what's really out there for you when you're not drowning yourself here."

"But Grace—"

She quirked an eyebrow. "Isn't going anywhere. And she would want you to."

Spend a few months away? Stay at Rucker and study? Stay at home with Sam?

Miranda sighed, and then punched my shoulder. "Wake up. You're not choosing one girl over the other. You're not leaving Grace for Sam. Grace left on her own a long time ago. So choose you. Choose to live. Choose to step outside the storm you've been given and soak up your sun."

I blinked. "You were listening."

She smiled and gave a pat to the shoulder she'd hit. "I've been worried about you for so long. Always here, drowning. But now? I'm not. You're going to be okay. Be happy. Be with Sam. You deserve this." She'd almost pushed Amber to the hallway before she turned back to me. "I've known you since you were born, which means I have a pretty good grip on who you are, and your next argument is going to be that it's not fair to Sam, right? That she deserves someone whose heart isn't split?"

I opened my mouth, and then closed it. She was right.

"You're not split, Gray. Listen to what you just told Grace. You loved her."

My eyes narrowed. "Right. I've loved her since we were kids."

"True, but you're not *in* love with her anymore." She glanced back at Grace with a sad smile, then back to me. "You used the past tense when you told Grace just now, and I bet you don't even realize it, but your subconscious does. She's your past, and she always will be. Sam is your future for as long as you're capable of holding on to her with that broody Heathcliff thing you have going on."

Broody? "Thanks, Miranda."

"I don't want to see you until October, Gray." Her face twisted, and I laughed. "What?"

"You've been a mom less than twenty-four hours and you've already mastered *the look*." I smiled, and it felt...good.

"I'm only letting you get away with that because I haven't heard you laugh in years. October, Grayson Masters. I'm serious."

She left, and I pulled out my cell phone.

Grayson: *Where are you?*

Samantha: *Miss me already?*

Grayson: *The minute I left you.*

Samantha: *Wow. Think you're getting lucky again or something?*

Grayson: *I KNOW I am.*

Samantha: *LOL. You're probably right. Mia just dropped me off.*

I took the elevator and headed to the lobby, where Sam was coming in, biting into a chocolate chip cookie. Her smile was instant, and mine came easily.

She made everything easier.

"Hey, flyboy." She came up on her toes and kissed me. I licked the stray chocolate off her lower lip and then forced myself to let her mouth go. Pretty sure she didn't want me pulling her into the first empty exam room. I could've shut the door, pulled down those shorts that barely covered her anyway, and put my tongue on her like I'd been fantasizing about for months. I'd skipped that last night, too desperate to finally be inside her. *Get a grip, you're in the middle of the hospital.*

Damn. I thought having sex might slake that fire for her, but instead it fueled it. Now I wasn't guessing how she felt—I knew, and she was better than I'd ever dreamed.

Shit, we needed to get out of here. "You ready to go?" I asked.

"Ready to see the sights! Your mom said there's a great lighthouse nearby."

"I'm sorry, I didn't want to leave you alone with her, but she was pretty adamant."

"She was fine, I swear. Mostly asked questions, didn't really divulge your sordid past." She poked me. "I did get a peek at your yearbook…"

I groaned, and it wasn't because we'd walked out into the afternoon sun.

"You were cute!" She giggled, dropping her sunglasses over her eyes.

"Are you seriously laughing at me?" I grabbed for her, but she darted ahead.

"I almost didn't recognize you," she said as she walked backward.

"Well, I weighed about a hundred-and-sixty pounds soaking wet."

"Like I said, you were cute." She backed into the hood of the Mustang and braced her hands on either side of her.

I swallowed, my throat thick at the picture in front of me. Sam's legs stretched out in front of her, impossibly long under shorts that begged my fingers to explore the hem...and under. She wore a grin I couldn't wait to kiss off, and her button-up shirt had come undone enough to hint at the curves I knew lay beneath. Leaned up against my car, she was the hottest girl I'd ever seen. *Holy shit, I get to touch her.*

She must have seen the change in my mood, because her smile disappeared and her lips parted as I cupped her face in one hand and her ass in the other. "Still cute?"

"Maybe. I'll let you know when the verdict is in." She pushed her sunglasses to the top of her head.

Damn. The girl had to push my buttons. She wet her bottom lip with the tip of a very pink tongue, and I pounced. Within a few strokes of that tongue, she made me forget we were in the middle of the parking lot. Hell, she made me forget my name.

I kissed her until she whimpered, which nearly broke me, sending images through my head of bending her over the hood, or having her straddle me in the driver's seat.

"I'm going to fuck you in the parking lot if we don't stop," I growled against her mouth. "Your shorts are sexy as hell."

She laughed in response. "What happened to that legendary self-control you're so famous for?"

"Overrated."

"Well, I really don't think getting arrested for indecent exposure would help your career, so maybe we should skip the sights and get back to the beach house."

I kissed her once more before I let her go, just because I could. "Now look who has the self-control."

The last button on my shirt slid home, and I rolled the sleeves past my elbow. A pair of cargo shorts, and I was good to go. The sun was setting, which meant the fireworks would start soon.

Sam had already gotten dressed, if the discarded shorts and shirt on the floor were any clue. I picked them up and tossed them into the laundry bag, shaking my head. It wasn't like I could be mad. I'd learned a long time ago that people didn't really change. You either accepted them complete with their faults, or you had to let them go.

Sam was messy. If that was her biggest fault, I was pretty damn lucky.

I headed down the stairs and passed the second floor before I heard his voice, and Sam's escalating response. "If he wants me to know something, he's going to tell me himself, and you can't assume because he had one tragic car accident that he's going to fail at being a pilot."

Shit. Why couldn't Dad butt the hell out? He always had in the past.

"And if you care anything about his life, you'll listen to me. He's dangerous up there." Dad's voice boomed from the living room.

I upped my pace, jumping the last step.

"I've flown with Grayson for the last year, and he's anything but dangerous. His reflexes are unparalleled, and he aces every test. He works his ass off, which is something you should be proud of."

Great, now Jagger was defending me. How long until Dad opened his mouth?

"Written or oral?" Dad tossed back.

"Both," I answered before he could fuck my career. I came up behind Sam to wrap my arms around her waist. She sagged against me, and I nodded to Parker, who stood with her arms crossed next to Dad. "And you're done harassing my girlfriend."

Sam stiffened.

"Girlfriend?" Parker choked out.

"Girlfriend," I assured her.

She shook her head. "Whatever. Look, we're only here because you didn't show up at the Bowdens' for the barbecue and you weren't answering texts."

My eyes narrowed. "I was in the shower, my phone is upstairs, and we're not going."

"But it's tradition." She looked at me like I'd grown two heads.

"How about I take everyone down to the beach for the fireworks," Jagger offered, giving me a hard pat on the back. "Family can be a bitch," he added quietly.

"You would know," I replied.

Sam turned in my arms. "I'm going to head down with them. Unless you need me?" Her voice was laced with concern.

"No, I've got this. I'll meet you in a few." I kissed the soft skin of her forehead, inhaling sanity and relief that she was escaping. She didn't deserve the fight I knew was coming. She gave me a reassuring smile and squeezed my hands as she took off after Jagger.

A few moments later, the door shut and the house was ours for the yelling. My stare wavered between Parker and Dad, unsure of who I wanted to start with.

"Girlfriend?" Parker threw the first volley.

"Yes, Parker. I have a girlfriend. She's Sam, and I'm happy for the first time in years. Is that so awful? Are you so against me being happy?"

Her mouth opened and closed. "But Grace—"

"What about Grace?" I shouted. "I loved Grace. A part of me will probably always love Grace, but she's not coming back, Parker, and she wouldn't want me to spend my life in that hospital room with her body when her soul is already gone. If I can finally accept that, you can, too."

"That's not true!" she fired back. "She's imp—"

"Enough." Dad didn't have to yell. "Parker, Gray has been

through enough. He deserves to be happy. He deserves to be loved. I'm pretty sure that staying faithful to Grace for the last five years earns him sainthood. You do not get to encroach on his character, or the character of that lovely young woman because you have some idealistic fantasy in your head."

Holy shit, it was nice to see my dad again.

"Dad," Parker pleaded, and my head drifted to the side.

"Why is this so important to you, Parker?" I asked, struggling to keep level.

She blinked back tears, and my heart sank. "It's always been you two, you know? Growing up, getting through school. Grayson and Grace. You two made me believe in the idea of soul mates and...love. And then that night happened..."

Grace's screams, the impact, the utter horror seeing her underwater when I came to—it all flooded me. I closed my eyes and took a shaky breath. *Sam.* I held on to her green eyes, the feel of her in my arms, the way she set me on fire and filled me with peace all at the same time. Then I opened my eyes.

"It was tragic, losing Grace. But, do you want me to die with her?"

She looked away. "No."

"Then you have to let me live. And Sam, whether or not you like her, makes me feel more alive than I ever have. I love you, Parker. I do. But I can't let you sabotage the best thing that has ever happened to me."

"So you're not coming tonight?"

"Give it up, Parker, and go wait for me in the car," Dad instructed.

She hugged me, and I held onto her for a second longer than normal. "Don't give up on Grace. Be happy, be with Sam, but don't give up."

"I won't ever give up on Grace, and I'll still be here when I'm needed." She nodded and headed for the door. "Parker."

"Yeah?"

"I won't give up on you, either. No matter what."

She nodded and shut the door behind her.

"I'm not going to be as easy to get rid of," Dad started in.

"Yes, you are. You have absolutely no right to mess around with my career. None, Dad. I have earned everything I've accomplished, and proven myself. I'm a damn good pilot."

"You can't do this. I won't allow it."

"I'm not five anymore."

"You are still my son!" he shouted. "God, Grayson. I love you. Is that so hard to understand? I want you safe, and you're intent on killing yourself."

"Is that what you think? That I want to die?"

"Whether or not you want to, you're going to. If you can't respect your own limits, how can you respect that helicopter?" He crossed his arms.

The set of his jaw, the flex of his arms as he held himself in check—he was me. I was him. And there was no winning this argument. "We're going to have to agree to disagree. I'm currently the top pilot in my class, which isn't exactly a small feat. You can choose to trust me for once in my life, or you cannot. I didn't tell you for a reason. You will not convince me to hand in my wings before I even get them."

Battle lines drawn.

In the contest of wills, this was a dead heat. He passed me on his way to the door but clamped down on my shoulder with a firm grasp. "I love you, Gray. Anything I've ever done has been because I love you."

"I know, Dad. I love you, too. Come to graduation. See me fly. I'll change your mind."

His lips pressed together, biting back what he wanted to say. "I'll see you soon, Gray." He left, and I walked out onto the deck, breathing in the comforting smell of the ocean. It was nearly dark, but I still made out the crashing waves.

This was home, and yet it wasn't. Sam was right—I was one

person at Rucker and one here. She waved to me as she walked up the wooden bridge to the beach that crossed the dunes. I may have been two different versions of myself, but they both belonged to her.

"Everything okay?" she asked, leaning against the railing next to me.

"It is now." Having her near me settled my soul in a way I wouldn't examine.

"So, girlfriend?"

"Girlfriend."

"So we're labeling this." She looked away, and I gently tilted her chin up until she met my eyes.

"Did I manage to scare Samantha Fitzgerald?" Her hair was soft as I brushed it off her cheek. She turned into my palm and leaned. It was such a simple gesture, but her trust in me deepened my feelings for her. I wasn't sure how much deeper I could go before using words I wasn't sure I was capable of.

"Labels...I just..." She closed her eyes and took a deep breath. "You're graduating in five months, Grayson. If I use that label—if I start to depend on you and then you go—"

"Sam." She opened her eyes, and I nearly lost it at the fear I saw there. I wasn't the only one risking something here. She trusted me. "We'll figure it out. All of it." I wasn't letting her go, she just wasn't ready to hear that yet.

"It doesn't scare you?"

"Everything about you scares me, but calling you my girlfriend is the least of it. That doesn't change what you are to me, or define us except for the convenience of other people." My thumb ghosted across her lower lip. "You're my Samantha. I'm your Grayson. That means a hell of a lot more to me than saying you're my girlfriend like we're back in high school."

"But I'm your girlfriend."

"Would you like my letterman's jacket as proof?" I kept a

straight face. "I can probably run back to my parents' house and get it."

"You choose now to start cracking jokes?" Panic crept into her eyes.

"You. Are. My. Girlfriend." I punctuated each word with a kiss. "My. Samantha."

"And what about everything here? Everyone...here?" Her voice dropped on that last word. "Please don't offer me something you can't give. I can't go through that again."

My hand flexed with the need to beat the shit out of the professor that had taken advantage of her, nearly broken her. "Since I left for college, I've always left one foot here, straddling both worlds. Tomorrow morning, we're flying back to Alabama. Everything and everyone is staying here. For the first time, all of me is leaving and going home with you."

She surged up and brought her mouth to mine. I pulled her against me, savoring the complete perfection of Sam as the first fireworks shot off the pier, lighting the sky with a kaleidoscope of colors.

Then I carried her upstairs so I could see the fireworks explode behind her eyes while I was deep inside her.

CHAPTER TWENTY-ONE

"Banana, strawberry, protein powder, and kale." I handed Grayson his protein-packed smoothie as he walked into the kitchen, sweaty from his morning run. I didn't dwell on where that sweat was dripping, otherwise I'd follow him into the shower and be late for class...again.

"Mmm," he hummed against my neck as I tried to pour my coffee into a travel mug. "What if I'd rather have you for breakfast?"

I doctored it with honey and creamer and sealed the cup before turning around. "Oh, no, you will not. You had me for dessert and midnight snack last night. I have my summer final in twenty minutes." I set my hands to his chest, barely covered by his running tank, and suppressed a groan. I'd had so much sex the last month that I should be unable to walk.

Instead, I was only hungrier for him.

"Fine, go work on those chem skills." He stripped off his shirt, and my mouth went dry.

"You..." I pointed my finger at him. "You do not play fair, Grayson."

He shrugged with a smile, and that dimple came out. "Guess I'll go shower."

I reached up on tiptoes, my flip-flops not exactly helping in the height department, and kissed him quickly. "How did I live so long without seeing that smile?"

He flashed it again, and my insides turned to a puddle of goo. God, I loved him so much. Now if I could only work up the courage to tell him. But what were we supposed to do with love? He was still leaving in four months. After the last two rejection letters I'd received, both from North Carolina schools, I wasn't any closer to getting into another college. *Hit a professor, and you'll never be accepted to another university again.*

Grayson's lips grazed my hairline. "The same way I don't know how I survived before I met you." He kissed my forehead and walked off, calling back, "Have a good day at school, dear."

"You, too," I replied, trying to keep my voice level. When he said things like that to me, it almost made me believe.

"Where's my smoothie?" Josh asked as I passed him on my way to the door.

"Very funny," I tossed back, sticking out my tongue. "When do I finally get to see my best friend again?"

He grinned. "This weekend. I swear, I knew it was going to suck going a month without seeing each other during that anthropology thing she went on, but it's too long." He grabbed his flight suit top off the back of the couch and put it on.

"Sometimes I forget," I said quietly.

"Forget the anthropology dig?" he asked.

I motioned to his uniform. "That this isn't *normal* army. That one day you guys are going to have a hell of a lot more than a month to get through." Mom had only been home a little over a month, but we already knew she'd be headed back over next year.

"You, too, from what I see with Masters."

My hand paused mid-reach to my messenger bag. "I'm not sure what the long-term plans are…or if he even…" I shook my head. "You know, I should probably be talking to him about this, right?"

He put his hand on my shoulder. Funny, a couple of years

ago that would have probably sent me into a tizzy, having high-school hockey hottie Josh Walker touch me. But now he was just my best friend's guy, and, well, he might still be hot, but Grayson blew him out of the park.

"Sam, you've made that guy human, which wasn't exactly an easy task. He's wild about you, so I don't think you have much to worry about."

"You guys are graduating in four months." My stomach sank like it did every time I thought it.

"Pretty sure peace between warring nations has been nego-tiated in less time than that. You and Grayson can figure it out."

"And you and Ember?"

He flinched. "Yeah, well she wants to stay in Nashville and go to Grad school, and I—"

"Want to go to Fort Bliss so you're closer to home, she told me."

"You think it's a bad idea?"

"I'm dating Grayson, who's killing himself to be top of the OML so he can get his first duty station selection and be closer to his comatose girlfriend. I'm really not sure I'm the one to pass judgment. But you guys will figure it out."

My cell phone alarm blared. "Shit, I'm going to be late!" I ran out the door and called back, "There are smoothies for you and Jagger on the counter!"

"Thanks, Mom!" Josh yelled back as the door shut.

I tossed my bag into the backseat and was almost into the driver's seat when Grayson ran out in flight-suit bottoms and a tan T-shirt that stretched beautifully across his chest. Was my heart ever not going to pound when he was around?

"Babe?" I asked.

He lifted my chem notebook and jogged over. "You left it on the nightstand."

"That would have sucked," I said, taking it from him. "Thank you."

"I actually like seeing your stuff all over my room, but I figured you'd need it for class."

"Hey, I confine it to my side of the bed."

"Uh huh." He gave me an ultra-intense look and then kissed me, pulling me into his body like he had all the time in the world. His skin was still damp from his shower.

Once he released me, I wavered. "What was that for?"

"I've never been this happy, and I think I like it." He kissed me again, and I melted into it, uncaring that my book dropped to the ground. "Get to class," he whispered against my mouth, and then left me standing there, all sorts of turned on. Damn that man.

I smiled. He was happy because of me. "I love you," I whispered to his back as he closed the door to the house.

I was late to class, but I smiled as I took my seat.

Turns out I'd never been that happy, either.

"Are you *still* studying?" I asked Grayson three weeks later as I leaned into his doorframe. His note cards were spread out on the bed, and he sat in the center, selecting random questions to answer. His light blue tee draped over him in a way I couldn't wait to, and his dark blue board shorts left his legs bare.

"Yep."

Ooh, work-mode Grayson was in effect. "You've been at it since I left this morning, and it's after eight."

"Yep." He flipped another card.

"Have you even eaten?"

"Yep."

"So all day you've only studied, eaten, and worked out?" I'd seen him a few hours earlier at the gym. Well, more like salivated over him lifting while I pretended to work.

"Yep."

"Can you give me more than a one-word answer?"

"Yep."

I snorted, which earned me a smile.

"I'm fine, babe, just need to get this down. We have a test on Tuesday."

"It's Thursday, and a four-day weekend. You're going to seriously burn out if you go at it like this all weekend."

He sent me a look so hot my thighs clenched. "Don't worry, I'll still have time to study you, too. I'm almost done, I promise."

"Okay." I walked back into my room and shut the door, stripping off my work clothes. A shower later, I felt ready to tackle the challenge of Grayson in study mode. It wasn't that I wanted to distract him, but damn, the man's brain was going to explode. He seriously had five modes—work mode, study mode, workout mode, sex mode, and sleep mode.

I could at least get him through the last two.

Ten minutes later, I was ready. Thank God we had central air, because there was no way I could have pulled this off in late August without it.

"You about ready?" I asked, peeking my head around his doorframe.

He barely looked up from the cards. "Yeah. Just a couple more minutes. We've been in the bag all week, and that stress isn't doing me any favors."

I sat on the edge of his giant bed, careful not to disturb the cards. "You doing okay?" Flying was his strong suit. If there was an issue there, his rank would slip, and Jagger was hot on his heels.

He looked up, his beautiful gray eyes a little dim with exhaustion. "Yeah. It's tough, flying with the cockpit blacked out, but I'm adjusting to the scope. It gives me a pretty bad headache, though, which is killing my study time. Plus we lost Pritchards this week. They pulled him out this morning."

"I'm sorry. I know you did all you could to help him. Will they transition him to another aircraft?" This was the second pilot his class had lost, and as class leader he took it personally, like he'd failed them.

He raked his fingers over his hair. "I don't know. I really thought giving him the extra hours would help him."

"This isn't your fault, Grayson." He looked back at the cards. "How about I help you study?"

"Want to quiz me?" His eyebrows shot up like he'd asked if he could have ice cream.

A slow smile spread across my face. "That's exactly what I had in mind." I scooped up the cards and then stood at the foot of the bed. "Lean back against the headboard."

"What?" His forehead puckered. "And why are you in a sweat suit? It's like ninety-seven degrees out there."

"You heard me. Lean back against the headboard. I will be happy to quiz you, but you are not allowed to so much as breathe in my direction until you've earned it." I used my most authoritative voice.

"Okay." He sat back with a playful smirk on his face. Despite what he said, I knew with Grayson I was only in control when he allowed it.

"Good boy." I grinned and then went for the first card. "Dual engine failure/Low Airspeed and Cruise."

He lost the smirk, all business. "Autorotate. Chop button—reset only if an engine chop warning message is present. Reset may be accomplished by either crew member. Wing stores jettison—as appropriate."

"One point for Grayson." His lips parted as I unzipped my University of Colorado hoodie and tossed it to the ground, leaving me in a tank top and bra underneath.

Understanding lit his eyes, and he leaned forward. "Are you—"

I waggled my finger at him. "Sit back. I'm asking the

questions here."

He did, but every line in his body tensed. I knew that look all too well. He was ready to pounce.

"Autorotation. Both Engines Fail."

"The cyclic should be adjusted as necessary to attain and maintain the desired airspeed of 77 to 107 KTAS. In autorotation, as airspeed increases above 70-80 KTAS, the rate of descent and glide distance increase significantly. Below 70 KTAS the rate of descent will also increase but glide distance decreases."

Damn, he really was that good. "Another point for Grayson." I kicked off my shoes.

"Seriously? Shoes? How is that fair? That answer was worth way more than the shoes."

My head tilted to the side. "Oh, but I thought you needed more study time?"

His eyes narrowed. "In this case, less is more."

I quirked an eyebrow but removed my socks, throwing them near my discarded hoodie. "That's all you get, flyboy."

"Give me another question."

Holy shit, the way he looked at me was hot enough to melt my panties. "Ng Limits."

"105.1 Maximum, Greater than 105.1 Red. 102.3 to 105.1 Transient 12 second limit, Yellow. 63.1 to 102.2 Normal Operation, Green. 63 Minimum engine out warning annunciated—less than 63.0 red with box."

I slid my fleece pants down my legs and kicked them away.

"That's cheating!" he shouted, pointing at my bike shorts.

I shrugged. "My game, my rules."

"Damn it. Give me another one." He shifted on the bed but didn't attack.

"Airspeed."

"Maximum airspeed with symmetrically loaded external fuel tanks (2 or 4) installed is 130 KTAS to prevent structural damage to the airframe."

I made damn sure he was watching as I wiggled my hips, tugging the spandex shorts off my legs. That hiss of indrawn breath coming from the bed said he'd definitely noticed. "Next," he barked.

"APU Operations Limitations Caution."

"Avoid prolonged operation at 94 to 96% Nr with the APU running. The APU clutch will oscillate from engaged to disengaged. This creates high loads on the clutch and shall be avoided."

I crossed my arms and pulled my tank top up over my head.

"Damn, honey." His gazed raked me from head to toe, taking in my matching silver lingerie I'd bought because it reminded me of his eyes. I licked my lips as he rearranged himself in his shorts.

I may have started this to distract him, but my engine was now roaring at two hundred miles per hour. Two more questions. "Autorotation Airspeeds."

His eyes hadn't stopped traveling the path from my toes to my hair and back down.

"Grayson."

His attention snapped back. "What?"

"Autorotation Airspeeds."

"How is this fair? You strip down and all I can think about is untying those little bows on your hips and licking you until you scream my name."

The mouth on that man was unbelievable, and hot as hell. As if his tongue had actually touched me, my nerves jumped to life, and the ache was instantly excruciating. I managed to pick up my tank top. "Autorotation Airspeeds." That even sounded breathless to my ears. When he still didn't respond, I moved to put it back on.

"Max 145 KTAS. Min rate of descent 77 KTAS. Max glide distance 107 KTAS."

The tank hit the ground again, and then I unsnapped my shiny bra. We locked eyes as I took it off, and then dropped it on the floor. Between the air and his feral appraisal, my nipples hardened.

I selected one last card, and then crawled across the bed until I straddled him. "The way your brain works is unbelievably sexy."

His hands grasped my hips, pulling me forward until I rubbed against his erection. "Coming from the smartest woman I know, that's a fantastic compliment." His fingers tangled in the straps of my panties. "Give me the last question, Samantha."

I glanced down at the card. "Maneuver Limits."

He sat up, bringing his chest flush against my breasts, and the contact sent a jolt of need spiraling through me. His lips grazed my neck, and chills raced down my arms. "Maximum reward/sideward flight speed," he said against my neck. "Is 45 KTAS"—he continued at my jawline—"for all gross weights."

He didn't wait for me to tell him he was right. He took my mouth, undoing the ties at my hips with deft fingers and then winding his fingers through my hair as he consumed me like he needed to claim me, mark me.

I was already his. Every part of me had fallen in love with Grayson. From the way he fought so hard to keep at the top of the OML to the way he battled his demons all while taking care of me, he was pretty perfect. Even the way he brooded, sexy and distant, only made me want to snuggle up closer to him, dig through whatever blocked him from me. He was a delicious puzzle that I somehow had the answer to.

Love.

I just had to be brave enough to tell him.

I tugged at his shoulders, and he broke the kiss long enough to remove his shirt. As soon as his skin touched mine, I was gone, logical thought stripped clean like the panties he'd tossed to the floor.

His hands drifted down my body to cup my breasts, massaging and rolling just how I liked, and I gasped against his lips. "I believe I had something on my mind," he whispered as his fingers dipped lower, stroking over my folds.

I sucked in my breath, every thought concentrated on his fingers slowly driving me mad. Then he stopped suddenly, gripped under my thighs, and lifted me as he slid down the bed. "On your knees," he demanded as his shoulders passed under me.

My knees landed on either side of his head. "Hands on the headboard."

I braced my hands on the dark wood, and my pulse hammered a spastic beat in anticipation. "Grayson."

He locked eyes with me as his tongue swept across me... into me. I cried out, my fingers biting into the headboard. "I love the way you taste," he said before working me over with his mouth.

He licked, kissed, and stroked me until my thighs began to shake. It was too much, overwhelming. When I jerked, he banded his hands around my thighs, holding me still while he took his time. He sucked my clit into his mouth, and I screamed.

Then he used his tongue to press on that bundle of nerves and flicked.

I came apart while he watched.

Grayson slid out from under my thighs while I caught my breath, laying my head on my hands. His clothing landed on the floor, and I heard the condom wrapper tear open before he was at my back.

He pulled me against him, his chest to my back, and his erection slid between my thighs. His grip was tender as he turned my head to the side and kissed my mouth, then whispered in my ear, "I love watching you come, Sam. It's my favorite part of making love to you."

"Do you want to know mine?" I asked.

"God, yes."

"That first moment you sink inside me, when I have you. All of you. All of your attention, your body, your trust...you." I rocked my hips back into him.

He nudged my entrance. "Like this?" And he eased into me inch by inch.

I moaned, my head falling back against his shoulder. "Yes."

"You always have all of me, Sam. Every second I'm breathing, I'm yours." Then he thrust home, burying himself completely.

I called out his name, and he kissed me again, stroking his tongue against mine in the same rhythm he kept as he thrust into me. "Headboard," he whispered, and I complied, leaning away from him to grasp the frame.

"So damn sexy. I love seeing you like this." His fingers dug into my hips, leaving what I was sure would be bruises, but I didn't care. He started a rhythm that had me keening as he hit a spot. This angle was almost too much.

"More!" I cried out, pushing back to meet him with each thrust. *So good. So, so good.* My muscles tensed, locked. "Grayson...I need...I need..."

He growled and pushed into me one more time before pulling completely out. I almost cried at the loss. He flipped me to my back like my weight was nothing, lifted my legs over his shoulders, and kissed me as he slid back inside.

"I need to see you," he panted against my lips. "Fuck, Sam. I love the way you feel around me." He began a punishing rhythm, steady and hard. I kept one hand on his shoulders and the other braced against the headboard for leverage.

He cupped my cheek, dragging his thumb across my lower lip. "You were made for me."

His declaration cut free the last of the ties holding me back. He consumed everything about me, my body, my mind, my heart. His eyes caressed me, tearing through the last of my defenses to reach my very soul. He was over me, inside me, around me until there was nothing but Grayson and the overwhelming love that burned like the most addictive drug. A love that demanded to be known and was strong enough not to need reciprocity.

I gasped, holding his stare. "I love you, Grayson. I'm in love with you."

He paused, his chest heaving, a myriad of emotions I couldn't name passing over his face as he searched my eyes. "Sam—"

"Don't," I whispered, smiling through the tears that slipped free. "Just let me love you. I don't need anything else." *Don't ruin this.*

He kissed me deep, sweetly, but with enough heat to burn the house down around us, and then changed his rhythm as he made love to me.

Slowly, powerfully, he stroked us both to completion, taking his time to build the sweetest pressure I'd ever felt. I cried out his name, and he kissed me as I came, riding me through my orgasm until it kicked back in aftershocks that jolted me.

Then he joined me, shuddering over me as I held him. My fingers played between his shoulder blades, dipping into the hollow. When he regained his breath, he kissed me, then left to clean up.

I should have been worried, right? I'd laid my soul bare and then instructed him not to do the same. I should have been horrified that my love most likely wasn't returned, that I still wore a second-place ribbon, but I wasn't. I was too full of love for him, joy that I'd found the courage to tell him, to worry about spoiling it.

He came back to bed and pulled me into him, wrapping himself around me. "Sam. You...you're everything."

My heart warmed, expanded even more to love him even harder.

I fell asleep in his arms and woke up draped across him like a blanket.

"Morning, sleepy." He grinned, trailing his fingers down my

spine and back up. "I love sleeping next to you. I think it should be a permanent arrangement. No more of this going back and forth between rooms."

Yes. Wait... "Is this because of what I—"

He pressed his lips to mine. "No. It's because I want you with me, even when we're sleeping."

"Your room or mine?"

His eyes narrowed as he thought. "Mine. It's bigger."

"I would make your room a mess."

He nodded. "Yes. I'm willing to chance tripping over your clothes if that means I know you're sleeping here."

"Are you sure?" We already lived in the same house, but moving into the same room felt like...well, moving in together.

"Certain." He grinned and playfully smacked my butt. "Now go get ready so we can hit the farmer's market. I'm thinking osso buco for dinner."

"Ooh, that sounds like a plan!" I gave him a smacking kiss and ran to the shower.

Once I was clean and wrapped in a fluffy towel, I wiped the steam from the bathroom mirror and began my skin routine. How different this was from the first shower I'd taken here, from when I'd been scared to encroach too much on his space. Now every space on my body was deliciously sore from Grayson.

Pretty fitting.

"All yours, flyboy," I called as I went into my room and got ready. Grayson's phone rang, and then went to voicemail. The shower started up again as I dressed in a flowy skirt that hit beneath my knees and a cute halter top.

Grayson's phone rang, and rang again. The shower turned off, and I crossed into his...our...bedroom, and picked it up off the dresser as it rang yet again. Three missed calls from Parker.

Something had to be wrong.

"Grayson." I knocked on the bathroom door. "Parker's calling, and it looks important."

The door opened and steam wafted out as he stepped into the hallway, taking the phone. "Wonder what she's pissed about now."

He squeezed my hand and went into his room to call her while I searched for a set of matching shoes in the pile of insanity I called a closet. Two Grecian sandals later, I knocked on his door. "Grayson?"

"Come in." His voice was tense, curt.

"Everything okay?" I asked as I stepped inside. "What?" He had a bag on the bed and was furiously packing, throwing clothes in haphazardly.

"Thank you, that will work," he said into the phone, and then hung up.

"Where are you going?" I asked, my voice small.

"Home. I just booked a flight." He wasn't looking at me, too busy throwing underwear in the bag.

He zipped the bag and slung it over his shoulder. As he walked toward me, he looked right through me, dazed. "Grayson," I called out, catching him by the hand as he passed me into the hallway. He turned, then looked down at his hand, surprised that I held it.

"What's going on?" I stroked the rough skin of his unshaven cheek. "Do you need me? Can I help you?"

He shook his head and stepped back, dropping my hand. "That was Parker."

"Yes?"

He looked back up, his face contorted in shock, and joy, and something indescribable as he backed away. "I have to go, she's asking for me."

A sense of foreboding came over me, depleting the room of oxygen and gravity. "Who? Parker?"

"No, Grace. She's awake."

He was gone before I could find air to pull back into my lungs.

CHAPTER TWENTY-TWO

GRAYSON

I parked my rental car in the hospital lot. Parker had offered to pick me up at the airport, but I had this inexplicable need for solitude.

The salt in the air tasted like a memory. Dozens of times I'd stood outside this hospital—the morning Mia was born, the day I broke my arm, when Mom had her gallbladder taken out…the night I lost Grace, but I'd never felt this numb.

Or this afraid.

Because I'd been here before, taking the call that she'd woken up. Getting special dispensation to leave the Citadel for the weekend. Rushing to her side to realize that while she'd opened her eyes, she was still comatose.

That was the last time I ever gave a thought to the hope that Grace would return to me.

I took a shuddering breath and entered the lobby, waving at the desk clerk. The elevator dinged, and I stepped inside, and then waited the torturous hours to reach the eighth floor. The doors opened, and I prepped myself to hear that this was a mistake. She wasn't awake, they'd misinterpreted a blink.

Or hell, maybe I'd wake the fuck up.

"Gray!" Parker ran toward me, her arms outstretched.

I caught her easily, but her show of affection only cemented that I was in a dream. This wasn't real. "Hey, Parker."

She grinned, lighting her face in a way I hadn't seen in years. "It's a miracle. Just…a miracle."

"Right," I answered.

They were all gathered outside her hospital room—Constance, Joey, Mom, Dad, the Bowdens. Everyone was smiling, slapping me on the back as I walked through the crowd like I'd scored a touchdown at the homecoming game. They all spoke, but only certain words registered.

"Trial program."

"Stem cells."

"Miracle."

"Are you okay?" Mia broke through the haze, standing directly between Grace's door and me.

"Sure." Because this wasn't real.

"Gray." She snapped her fingers in front of my face, and I looked down at her.

"What?"

"Listen. She's awake, for now. She's been sleeping a lot, but the doctors say it's part of the progress. So if she falls asleep on you, don't panic."

"She's been sleeping a lot… But I got the call eight hours ago, Mia. How do they know what is normal?" The fog in my brain started to lift. She'd been awake long enough to establish a normal.

"She wanted us to wait until she was strong enough to see you."

My eyes narrowed. "How long has she been awake?"

Mia swallowed. "I didn't want to keep it from you, but Parker said—"

I wanted the numbness back. Anything was better than the volcano of rage building in my stomach warring for control with the nausea that warned this was too good to be true, which had its own fight with the tiny sliver of hope that this was real. Yeah, numb was a hell of a lot better. "How long?" I shouted.

She flinched.

"Almost three weeks," Mrs. Bowden answered.

I turned to face the crowd, whose smiles had all disappeared. They weren't here to see Grace, they were here to watch *me* see Grace. They all knew. They knew and had only gathered here to witness this moment like we were some circus show.

The door creaked behind me as Mia pushed it open.

"Three weeks," I growled.

"It was what she wanted," Parker whispered. "To be strong when she saw you for the first time."

I looked each of them in the eye. One by one their gazes dropped.

I'd fantasized this moment so many times that I'd lost count. Picturing the joy, the wonder, the amazement of her waking, calling my name. But to have them all know, and keep it from me?

This was some fucked-up dream.

"Gray?" Her voice rang out behind me, punching me in the stomach and nearly dropping me to my knees. My breath left in a rush. Five years I'd been dreaming of that voice, clear as a bell, sweet as honey, everything that defined Grace.

I turned slowly, not ready for the dream to end.

Mia patted me on the shoulder, and I stepped into the room, shutting the door behind me. I cleared the four feet of hall and she came into view.

Grace sat up in her hospital bed, her blond hair falling in perfect waves around her. Her hands fidgeted, her nervous tell. Her mouth formed a shaky smile, and her eyes... *Holy shit.* Her eyes weren't just open, but bright and focused...on me.

"Hey, Port," she near-whispered.

"Hey, Starboard," I answered automatically. We'd never told anyone about those nicknames. Ever. So this was either one hell of a dream...or she was real.

In the time it took me to cross the room to her, every memory crashed through me. Building sand castles as kids, laughing on the beach, learning to sail. Our first kiss, our first I love yous. The fight. The crash. The blue tinge to her skin when I pulled her out of the water. The sound of her parents screaming at the doctors for suggesting organ donation. My broken voice begging her to come back to me. Making promises to her to take it all back and make it right, to God, to anyone who had the power to bring her soul back to her body. Five years of agony erupted as I fell to the chair next to her bed.

"You're really here," I whispered, taking her hand. She squeezed it back, and I cracked, my soul bleeding.

"I'm really here."

My best friend hadn't lost her southern accent.

I collapsed forward, my head landing in her lap, and she ran her fingers through my hair like she hadn't been gone the last five years. I was six, and ten, and eighteen, and twenty-three years old all in one moment.

"I'm really here," she repeated softly.

I let it overpower me, the gift I'd been given. She was back. She would live.

Nothing else mattered.

"Explain," I said to the crowd of family in the waiting room a few hours later, once she'd fallen back to sleep. Watching her eyes close, surrender to sleep, scared the shit out of me. It was too close to what she'd looked like before.

"Why don't we do this in private, Gray?" Mrs. Bowden suggested.

Miranda handed the baby to her husband and came with us into an empty room. It was set up like Grace's, and I started pacing between the wall and the foot of the bed. "Explain," I repeated.

"The stem cells from Amberly," Miranda offered. "We'd contacted the trial program at the University of Texas at the beginning of the pregnancy, and when Amberly's cells were a match, they agreed to let Grace into the clinical trial. She's their first success."

"And you didn't think to tell me?" God, I needed a run, or a punching bag, or something, anything to let this energy out. I felt like a caged tiger, desperate to rip something to shreds, confined to a barred cage.

"We didn't want to get your hopes up," Mrs. Bowden answered.

"Okay, I'll give you that. But when she woke up? You didn't think I had a right to know about that? Three weeks!" They both stepped back as I pointed at them.

Miranda's gaze flickered to her mom before coming back to me. "Her waking has been gradual," she explained. "At first it was only a half hour at a time, if that. She didn't speak right away, either. That took nearly a week. She still barely gets through sentences."

"I noticed." She'd had to carefully think through everything she said before she said it. It was almost a perfect parallel to when I'd learned to read, and she'd sat patiently by my side. Now it was my turn.

"She's still working on basic tasks. She can't walk, or even stand for more than a few seconds." Miranda started to fidget with her hands. Family trait.

"And what the hell does this have to do with keeping me in the dark?"

"We didn't know the extent of her damage, if she'd remember anything, or if she'd be mentally sound, Gray. We didn't want to get your hopes up until we knew something, and the minute she started speaking..." She glanced back at her mom.

"What?" I shouted.

They both flinched. "She wanted us to wait. She said that

she needed more time before she could see you. She didn't want you to see her that weak."

"Weak? I held her in my arms, half *dead* until they could get to us. I have rotated her for bedsores, changed out her catheter bag, checked IV fluids and feeding tubes for five years! I deserved to be told, and you know it!"

Miranda nodded, but it didn't soothe the ticking time bomb approaching detonation in my chest. "Three weeks. I've never gone more than three weeks without seeing her..." Everything in me went deadly still, and my eyes locked onto Miranda's. "You knew. When you told me to live my life, to soak in my sunshine, to not come until October. You knew this was the plan."

"Yes," she admitted softly, and had the sense to look away. "We didn't know the trial would do anything. She's really and truly a miracle, Gray. Our Hail Mary."

"Full of Grace," I whispered to myself.

Mrs. Bowden stepped in. "The team came here from the University, and they've been kind enough to let us stay here. We'll go to Texas in a month for tests, of course, but their doctors are constantly flitting around."

"How long will she be in the hospital?"

"That's up to the doctors."

I nodded, trying to process everything without losing my shit.

"How long can you stay?" Miranda asked.

Reality split again. I'd spent so long praying for her to wake up, I'd never considered what would happen after she did. "I'm on a four-day."

"Did you happen to bring Samantha with you?" Mrs. Bowden asked.

My head snapped toward her. *Sam.* I closed my eyes for a second and let the thought of her rush through me, calming everything just enough to breathe.

The consequences of the miracle in front of me unfurled, hitting me harder than the fake-terrorist during SERE school. Sam. My Samantha.

Grace needs you.

Suddenly there wasn't enough oxygen in the room, or the world.

"Gray?" Mrs. Bowden prodded.

"No, I didn't bring her." She was at home, with my study guides, my helicopter, my friends...my heart. And Grace was here. *Fuck.* I tried to silence the screaming in my head long enough to form a coherent sentence. "Does Grace know? About Sam?"

Miranda's eyes filled with sympathy. "No. None of us have breathed a word of it to her."

Mrs. Bowden touched my arm lightly. "We thought it best to let her be happy. We don't know how she'll react, what the stress might do to her. She knows that you're here every chance that you get, but that's all. We'd...we'd like you to let her heal before, well, anything."

"You'd like me to lie? Or you'd like me to conveniently forget that I have a girlfriend at home in Alabama?" I growled, nausea rolling in my stomach.

"No," Miranda shook her head at her mother. "No, Gray, we don't. We just need to figure out what she assumes about now—what she needs. Telling her about Sam, that's your choice. What you choose to do now that she's awake—well, that's your choice, too."

I nodded once, then pushed past them to the door and through it. I ignored my name being called from the waiting room, from the hall behind me, from the person standing in the hall. The door swung open in front of me as I entered the stairwell and then hammered my way down the eight flights.

Sam. Grace.

My future. My past?

Everything I'd ever wanted had suddenly appeared, but I couldn't have it all. I had to choose between the Grayson I was five years ago, the one who'd loved Grace with every heartbeat, and the one I was now, who'd fallen for Sam so completely that she was as crucial as oxygen.

Even now, as I rounded the staircase to the ground floor, every cell in my body screamed out for Sam, to hear her voice, her laugh, feel her heartbeat under the palm of my hand. But eight floors up, Grace was awake, the answer to every prayer, blissfully unaware that I'd fallen in love with another woman while she'd been unable to put up a fight. Grace, who'd been my best friend since we could walk. Grace, who'd always been my future until that night. Grace, who needed me.

I burst through the doors on the ground floor and didn't stop until I was outside the hospital. The air hit my face, and I took gulping breaths to calm my racing heart. Saliva filled my mouth, and my stomach rebelled. I made it to the bushes before I vomited, bringing up everything I'd eaten and then heaving nothingness.

"Oh, Gray." Mom's hands patted my back like I was eleven with the stomach flu.

I took the bottle of water she held out for me, swished out the sour taste of bile, and spit. She took my arm and led me to the bench that rested inside the gazebo, where we sat side-by-side in silence until I was ready to speak.

"Grace is awake."

"Yes." She squeezed my hand.

"I'm in love with Sam." The words, spoken aloud, sent a bittersweet feeling through me that radiated from my heart to my limbs until I swore my fingers tingled. I thought the first time I said them would be freeing.

I thought the first time I said them would be to Samantha.

"I know."

"I haven't told her. I was scared that if I said something, let myself really love her, plan a life with her, something would happen. I'd lose her...like I lost Grace. I've been paying for that night for five years, and Sam is the first really good thing to happen to me. But maybe she's the price?" My stomach rolled again, and I leaned over, resting my forehead on my fists. "Maybe God, fate, irony, whatever...maybe it needed this last ounce of pain it could wring from me, and I deserve it. I do. But Sam doesn't. Grace doesn't."

"Look at me." Her voice was sharp, and I raised my eyes to her. "You did not deserve this. You were not responsible for what happened to Grace. You saved her life. You were not responsible for Owen driving that night. None of what's happening is your fault. You cannot carry the burdens of this world on your shoulders. Even you are not that strong."

But it had been my fault. I knew he was too drunk to drive. I hadn't taken the keys. "What am I going to do? No matter what I choose, someone gets hurt."

"You're going to let some of this blame go, Gray. You're going to spend this weekend with Grace, and you're going to go home to Sam. And then you're going to figure out what you want your life to look like now that Grace is in it again. Oh, and you're going to come home with me while Grace is sleeping. I need your help rearranging some furniture."

I knew she made that up to distract me, get me out of the hospital for long enough to clear my head. "Furniture, huh?"

She gave me a mock-innocent face. "I pay in brownies."

"Deal."

"Thank you for this," Grace whispered, her head resting on my shoulder as we looked out over the ocean from the front seat of my Mustang. If you'd asked me about five-and-a-half years ago where I'd see myself now...well, this was it.

"You get five more minutes before we have to head back. They'll notice you're missing and send the cavalry to find you."

She wound her fingers through mine. "And you have a plane to catch."

"Yes." I looked down to our intertwined fingers. What was once effortless felt a fraction off, like a puzzle piece that had warped in water.

"Are you happy there? In Alabama?"

My chest tightened, picturing Sam's smile, the feel of her wrapped around me in the morning because she didn't understand that it was possible to share the bed without acting as a blanket. "Yes."

"I'm scared. Five years, Gray. What am I supposed to do with myself? The whole world kept spinning while I was paused."

I leaned my head to rest on hers, the familiarity too easy to sink into. "You don't have to be scared, Grace. We're all still here."

"But you're not. They said you came all the time." She took a breath, and I waited, knowing it took supreme effort to form the sentences. "You kind of put your life on pause, too, but you live eight-hundred miles from here." She shivered, and I pulled the hospital blanket up higher to cover her shoulders.

"I'm always only a phone call away."

She nodded. "It's just...different. Tell me something. Anything. Maybe about flying?"

The waves crashed in front of us as I told her about flight school. I told her about beating out both Carter and Jagger for top of the OML during Primary, and being class leader now. "I'm fighting like hell to graduate at the top of my class. I should get my choice of duty stations, and then I can get Fort Bragg. I'd be close."

"Is it safe? You know...for you to fly? Do you struggle?"

Of course she would ask that. "I'm safe. My reflexes make up for any extra time it takes me on the gauges. So far I haven't had a problem."

"Is it hard?"

"Sometimes. I spend a lot of time studying." Sam flashed in front of my eyes, straddling me, asking that last 5&9 question before she'd let me touch her. "I have help."

"And you have...friends there?" She pulled back and looked up at me, her eyes large and so open, honest.

I swallowed. "I have friends." Sam's name was on the tip of my tongue. It wasn't fair for Grace not to know, but maybe her mom was right. She needed to heal. I wouldn't lie if she outright asked me, but I knew Grace, and if she hadn't asked, it was because she didn't want to know.

She nodded and tucked her head back onto my shoulder with a jaw-cracking yawn. "You should probably take me back. Mom will have a cow if she notices I'm gone."

I took us back to the hospital and lifted her into my arms as I snuck in the back entrance. "When did this happen?" She motioned to my torso as we rode the elevator. "I'm not complaining, but you're...you're kind of massive."

"It started after the first year you were...yeah. When they thought you woke up the first time, I had all this rage, so I channeled it."

"Did I miss the purple shorts?" She blinked up at me, and the elevator dinged.

It took me a second before I caught on. "I'm not the Incredible Hulk."

"Hmmm." She gave me that knowing look, and the last five years faded.

"There you are!" Parker exclaimed after the doors opened on our floor. Her joy at this situation was a ten on the what-the-fuck scale, like someone had taken my angry-spikey sister and dipped her in Care Bear fluff.

"I wanted to see the water," Grace said with a smile.

"Of course! Gray, can I see you before you head out?"

"No problem." I carried Grace to her room and got her settled.

"When will you be back?" she grasped my hand after I pulled the covers around her.

My throat closed. "I'm not sure. I wasn't planning until October, but I'll see if I can make it sooner."

Her face fell. *Shit.* "Right. Of course. But I can call?" She picked up her iPhone 6 that her dad gave her this morning. "I mean, it's not all that different from the 3, right?"

A corner of my mouth lifted. "Right. You have my contact in there, so call, text, whatever you need. I'm here for you."

She nodded. "I'll miss you."

I leaned over and kissed the top of her head, inhaling her lavender shampoo. "I've missed you for five years, Grace. God, I'm glad you're back."

She forced a smile that didn't reach her eyes, and I squeezed her hand. "I'll see you soon, Gray."

"Okay. See you." I picked up my backpack on the way out and slung it over my shoulder.

"So?" Parker nudged me in the ribs.

"So what, Parker?" I hit the button for the elevator.

"G-squared, back in force! It's perfect! You get a fairytale ending! I want to bask in that happiness for a bit."

I got on the elevator as the door opened and turned back to Parker looking too damn chipper in that candy-striper uniform. "I have to get home, Parker. To Sam. You may have forgotten that I have a life in Alabama, but I haven't."

Her mouth dropped, and she thrust her hand into the closing elevator doors to keep them open. "You can't be serious. Grace is a miracle, Gray. *Your* miracle. Fuck your other life and come home. We need you. Grace needs you."

Every muscle in my body tensed. "I have to go."

"Yeah, as always. You go. Run away. Leave us here. Leave Grace here. It's what you're good at, right?"

"At least you're acting more like yourself."

"Well, you've been handed the fucking glass slipper and you're still acting like an asshole." She moved her hands, and the doors shut.

The house was pitch-black when I unlocked the front door. Then again, at two a.m. I didn't expect any different.

I climbed the stairs, my heart pounding, my hands aching to fill themselves with Sam, to soak up the peace only she brought to me. She was going to be pissed. I hadn't even called, but what was I supposed to say to her? *Hey, sorry, I'm trying to walk this fine line of pretending you don't exist and flat-out lying to my best friend.*

I crept into our room, quietly undressing so I didn't disturb her. I slid into bed, only to find it empty. *What the fuck?* She hadn't moved in. *Of course she didn't. You left her standing in the middle of the hallway while you ran home to your non-comatose girlfriend. Ex-girlfriend. Whatever.*

In only my boxer-briefs, I crept across the hall, opened her door, and dodged every landmine of clothes on the floor as I made my way to her bed. The moonlight shone in through the window, illuminating her curves as they dipped along the mattress. Her lips were slightly parted as she slept, one hand grazing her cheek. My breath caught at how fucking beautiful she was, what a gift I'd been given when she fell into my arms.

I needed her. Now. Needed to be inside her, connected to her so deep that she'd never get me out.

I pulled back her covers and then carefully brought her into my arms. "Mmmm," she hummed, her lips at my throat. "Grayson?"

"I'm here." I flipped off the hallway light and kicked our door shut gently as I brought her into what was now our bed. *Where she'd stay, damn it.*

Hovered over her, I kissed the lines of her collarbone until I pulled down the thin strap of her tank top. Her eyes blinked open, sleep-hazed. "Grayson, what are you doing?"

"I know you're pissed, and you should be. And I'll explain, I swear. But right now... God, I need you." My voice broke.

Her hands cupped my face, gently pulling me from her chest so she could look into my eyes.

"Sam?"

A gamut of emotion ran across her face while I waited for her verdict. Anger and defiance softened in those green eyes as her hands ran down my cheeks. "Are you okay?" she asked with more concern than I had any right to.

"I just need you, Sam. Connect me. Ground me. Love me." *Pull me back from the edge of something that could destroy us both.*

Our eyes spoke more than words could ever manage. Hers widened in almost panic as her fingers slipped to my hair. "You still want *me*," she said as if she didn't think it was a remote possibility.

"I will always want you."

Her eyes watered, but she nodded and kissed me gently, slowly. "I love you," she whispered against my mouth, and I was lost. I made love to her slowly, carefully, cherishing each line of her body and savoring each gasp, each moan. Once she was writhing, I entered her slowly, pushing deep until I was surrounded, enveloped by heat. *Home.* Our tongues and breaths mingled as we rocked together, and I caught her every exhale when she came apart in my arms and gasped my name. I followed soon after.

I pulled her into my side and stroked the soft-as-petals skin of her back as she drifted off to sleep, warm and content. I couldn't live without this—without her.

What the fuck was I going to do?

Grace needed me.

I needed Sam.

CHAPTER TWENTY-THREE

Sunlight streamed in the window, and I buried my face deeper into the pillow, denying the existence of morning. Grayson's scent filled my head, and I forced my eyes open. I was in his room, in his empty bed. Well, our bed.

Or was it our bed? Was there an "ours"? An "us"?

I'd half thought it was a dream when he came for me last night after three and a half days of silence, but the delicious soreness between my thighs said either he was home, or I'd had some wicked real dreams.

The clock read seven thirty. No classes today, but I only had a couple hours before work. I fought the urge to go back to sleep. I'd slept like shit this weekend, no thanks to Mr. No-call, but I wasn't going to be in here asleep when he got back.

Or quite as complacent in his assholery as I'd been last night. *You pretty much let him get off one more time before he breaks your heart.*

Or maybe I'd been saying good-bye for myself, preparing for the inevitable nights where he wouldn't be in my bed... my life. But the look in his eyes when he'd said he needed me, begged for me like I was the only person who could right his world...I was powerless against him. Well, that shit had to stop. Especially now that Grace was awake.

I found my pajamas and underwear, got dressed, and

headed downstairs.

"Coffee?" Ember asked and nodded toward the seat across from her at the table, where my favorite mug waited. "Peppermint creamer and honey, just the way you like it."

I dropped onto the chair and brought the steaming mug to my lips, inhaling the aroma before I took my first sip. "Thank you. I'm glad you're here, even if it's just for the week."

She propped her feet on the chair next to me and leaned back, waiting.

"Do you remember prom when we were seniors?" I asked.

"Sure," she said. "I went with Riley, and we had that big party at Strawberry Fields. Where are you going with this one?"

"Do you remember who I went with?"

Her forehead puckered. "Dustin McClair? Right? That was right after…"

"Right after Corey broke up with me the week before. I was so scared of being alone, of missing out on my senior prom, that I went with Dustin, who I had absolutely no interest in, who ruined my dress when he spilled beer in the limo, and who reeked of garlic all night. Oh, and then he got really pissed when I wouldn't sleep with him."

"That was definitely a night to remember." She leaned forward. "Sam?"

"Do you remember what you said to me when I told you I was going with him?"

"Not exactly. Something along the lines of, 'are you sure…'"

"You said, 'you've never been one to settle for second choice.'"

She took a sip and nodded. "Well, you never have been."

"Right. And that's the thing. Grayson? I'm so in love with him that I can't imagine a future where I don't wake up to him. There's no one on this earth who makes me feel like he does, who brings out the very best in me. He's complicated, and smart, and has an incredible heart. Add in that he's gorgeous and I can barely keep up in bed with him…well, he's my first choice."

"Yes."

"But I'm his second choice. And first place just hopped back on the track, and she's so far ahead of me that she's almost got me lapped."

"Sam, Grayson loves you. I've seen the way he looks at you, the way he talks to you, or about you."

"He cares a lot about me, Ember, but love… I don't know how you can love someone if you never get your heart back from the person who took it in the first place. He loves Grace. He's always loved Grace. It was one thing to compete against a ghost, to make peace with that, but the real flesh-and-blood Grace? This was over before it began."

"You're not giving yourself enough credit. Or him." She stood to make another cup of coffee. Our shared caffeine addiction was as strong as our friendship. "What happened when he came home last night?"

Warmth rushed to my cheeks. "We didn't exactly talk. I… slept with him and woke up in his bed this morning."

She leaned back against the counter as the machine hissed out another dose of energy. "So he came home off the late flight, and the first thing he did was move you to his room, his bed, and make you come."

I almost spit out my coffee. "Holy shit, Josh is rubbing off on you."

She shrugged. "I'm just saying that doesn't sound like a guy who thinks you've been lapped by another girl."

"He didn't so much as call."

"Okay, well, that doesn't really help his case, true. But give the guy a break; I'm sure he was in a little shock."

"What if he slept with her?" The agony that ripped through my chest at the thought was nearly paralyzing.

She tilted her head at me. "The girl was in a coma for five years. I hardly think she woke up like, 'let me get some of that.'"

"But what if he wanted to?" I hated this, the insecurities

that had reared their ugly head and were currently choking the hope out of my soul. "Last night was different. It felt like he was saying good-bye." My face twisted, and I rubbed my hand over my forehead. "I'm going to have to let him go, aren't I?"

The front door opened, and I sucked in my breath, composing myself as Jagger and Josh came into the kitchen, both sweating like pigs. Attractive pigs, but yeah.

"What? No smoothie?" Josh teased me and then kissed Ember lightly. "Good morning."

Jagger grabbed two bottles of water from the fridge and tossed one at Josh.

"Where's Grayson?" I asked, trying and failing to keep nonchalant. I didn't miss the look that passed between the guys.

"He's on the phone," Jagger said and then drained his bottle.

I took a deep swallow of coffee, wishing I'd poured liquor into it.

"Yeah, that sounds good," Grayson's voice reached me at the same moment the door shut. "I know, I do, too, but I can't. Looking at the schedule, we won't have another four-day until the middle of October." There was a pause, and everyone in the kitchen looked anywhere but at me. "I know," his voice softened in a way I thought was only reserved for me, and I *knew*. He was talking to her. "It doesn't work like that, and I can't miss days, or they'll set me back a class. I'll try in a few weeks, but I can't promise anything. Why don't you have Miranda set you up with Skype and I can see you later?"

My heart crumpled, and it felt like a sucking wound, a black hole pulling everything in around it. This hurt so fucking much. Worse than being left behind when my friends went to college. Worse than being left when Ember took off for Nashville. Worse than Mom leaving for Afghanistan. Worse than Harrison walking away after I discovered his wedding ring.

Grayson might be here, but he'd already left, too.

Somehow I'd done it again—become the other woman, the

one left behind and forgotten.

I felt it happen—the bricks of my defenses started to click back into place. It was like a tiny army invaded my heart and tried to slow the hemorrhage by shutting off every feeling.

"I'm so sorry I'll miss it, Starboard, but I can't leave."

Holy shit. She had a fucking nickname. Ultra-serious, calls-me-Samantha Grayson called her by a nickname. *Click. Click. Click.* That tiny little heart army mortared the last brick into place.

Anger conquered hurt in the wrestling match to control my emotions.

Grayson came into view as he cleared the half wall between the living room and kitchen. Why did he have to be so beautiful? His eyes met mine, and my stomach sank. "Okay. I'll talk to you later. Bye."

He said it to her, but it felt like it was meant for me.

"You headed home again?" Jagger asked.

"No. At least not for a couple weeks, if that."

He said that one straight to me.

"Sounds like you're needed," I choked out.

"It's a ridiculous news story that Parker leaked. I'm not joining that circus or acting the part she's assigned." He walked around the counter and caught the bottle Jagger threw at him. "I'm not even sure why the news is interested."

"Beautiful miracle girl awakens from five-year coma to the gorgeous, dutiful boyfriend who never left her side. Pretty sure that has Lifetime movie written all over it." I faked a smile, and his eyes narrowed.

"Sam." He did the little headshake thing that meant he wanted to say something more but wouldn't.

But I sure as hell would. I wasn't getting left this time. Hell no. I was getting ahead of this bull before it ran me the hell over. "It's okay, really. You have everything you've dreamed of, and even got in a farewell fuck last night."

His head snapped back like I'd hit him.

"And that, people, is our cue to leave," Josh said. The room cleared while Grayson stared me down. I didn't flinch, despite the energy crackling between us.

"Samantha." He stepped toward me, and I thrust my hands out as I stood.

"Don't bother."

"You can come upstairs with me while we have a civil conversation, or I can carry you there, but either way, you don't get the last word. We're going to talk."

Tense moments passed until I sighed. "Fine." My feet carried me to his room without being told to, and Grayson shut the door behind him. He pressed me up against the back of his door before I could mutter a protest. One of his hands held both of mine captive above my head, and he pressed his weight against me, connecting us from breast to thigh.

My traitorous body melted. *That bitch.* Why was there such a fine line between angry and turned on? He glanced from my eyes to my lips and they parted.

Grayson kissed me, claiming every recess, every line of my mouth. His free hand cupped my neck, angling me for a deeper kiss, and I responded, pressing against him, giving back everything he was putting into it. If this was our last kiss, I wanted to brand his soul so that he'd never kiss again without thinking of this—of me. He wedged one of his massive thighs between mine, and applied subtle pressure. My body positively hummed, and it took all of my control not to rub back against his thigh.

I whimpered, and he retreated. He'd wanted my surrender, and damn it, I gave it.

When I opened my eyes, he was almost nose-to-nose with me, his eyes boring into mine. "First of all, I didn't fuck you last night, Samantha. I made love to you, and there's a huge difference. Second, even when we're fucking—hot, sweaty, skin slipping against each other, and my only thought is craving that little keening sound you make when you come—I am still making love to you. I never touch you with anything less than my soul. Don't ever cheapen what we do. Third, why the hell haven't you moved into this room? I want you in my bed. Sleeping, not sleeping, that's your choice. And fourth, last night was not a good-bye. I'm not saying good-bye."

Move in? "Are you on drugs? There's no chance I'm moving in with you after what just happened. You have a girlfriend, Grayson."

"Yes, and I'm looking at her right now."

"You didn't call. You left, and went to her, and you didn't call."

His eyes closed like he was in pain, and he rested his forehead against mine. "I am an asshole, and I'm sorry. My head was not the best place. But I swear, not calling you didn't mean that I wasn't thinking about you. I didn't know what to say to you. I didn't know what to say to myself."

"Or you were thinking how to break it off with me."

He kissed me again, this time tender. "I'm not breaking it off with you. I'm not leaving."

"Yet. You're not leaving *yet*. But you will." It was simply inevitable. My eyes prickled. "Why won't you do it now and save us both a lot of pain?"

Grayson released my hands and then brushed my cheeks with his thumbs. "Save us pain? Like splitting now wouldn't hurt? Fuck, Sam. I…" He swallowed. "I'm not sure I could survive losing you, and maybe that's selfish. I know I'm graduating. We still have to figure out what *we* are going to do in December. But I'm not leaving you."

"Even for her?"

He didn't look away, but I felt, more than saw, the war raging beneath the surface. It was in his rigid posture, the ticking in his jaw, the tender way he stroked my skin absentmindedly.

"I'm with *you*."

"For how long? Until we get to North Carolina? Until you realize that I'm a hot mess who's barely pulling herself together and can't hold a candle to the resident paragon of the Outer Banks? What happens then, Grayson? What happens the first time I see the look in your eyes that you made the wrong choice? Or the first time you realize that if we'd stayed away from each other, you wouldn't be in this situation? A few months. You made it five years staying faithful to her, and I ruined you in just a few months."

"You didn't ruin me. You brought me back to life. Why are you so sure I would leave you? Why can't you have a little faith in me?"

We stared at each other, the silence charged with so much tension it should have come with its own weather forecast. Maybe he was right, and I needed to show a little faith. Maybe I was being horrendously unfair to the man I was in love with. Maybe there was a chance he would be the exception, and not leave. "What did she say when you told her about us?"

He paled, and his hands fell away from my face. My little army of defense-building minions couldn't help me this time. "You didn't tell her," I whispered.

"Damn it." His hands raked over his face. "I wanted to, but her family asked that I wait and give her time to adjust. Her whole life is in upheaval, and I couldn't bear to add to it. I've loved her all my life. She's my best friend."

Loved her all my life. She hadn't just lapped me; she'd left the track with the flowers already—victorious.

I pushed on his chest lightly, and he stepped back. "And I'm just the girl who sleeps in your bed." How much pain could one person handle? How many ways could a heart be shredded before it shriveled and died? I wanted it to die. At least then the feelings would go with it.

"Samantha, please." He reached for me, but I sidestepped.

"Let. Me. Go." I meant it in more than one way, and given the way he started to shake his head, he knew it. "I love you, Grayson. But you are the last person I want to see right now." He moved enough for me to open the door.

"We're not done talking about this," he called after me as I slammed my bedroom door.

"You look like death warmed over," Avery said as she walked into the gym. Her sweet little southern accent didn't soften the insult. She wore her gym polo over a pressed pair of capris, her blond hair in a messy knot at the back of her head.

"Nice to see you, too, cupcake," I replied from my spot behind the desk.

She came into the raised office area and dropped her book bag on the ground. "Seriously. And I'm pretty sure you're wearing two different shoes."

I scoffed and looked down. "I most certainly do n—" *Well, shit.* "They're the same color, it's an easy mistake."

"Except one's Adidas and the other's Saucony." She pulled out her books and put them on the desk next to the phone.

"Rough morning," I said, tucking my feet under the desk.

"Trouble with the flyboy?" She opened her trig book and her notebook. When I didn't answer, she swung her head my direction and blinked. "Whoa. Really?"

"Nothing you need to worry about, Avery. How is your homework?" I peeked over her shoulder.

"Confusing. It probably didn't help that I spent most of class making moon eyes at Grady Alexander. But in my defense? This stuff doesn't make any sense, and I zoned my teacher out."

"Bet you wished you'd paid as much attention to your teacher as you did Grady, huh?"

"Ha-ha. Very funny. Homecoming is in like a month, and I don't have a date. That is way more important than trig." She tapped her eraser on the blank sheet of paper.

At twenty-one, I knew that wasn't true. Then again, here I was deciding my collegiate future on where my boyfriend planned on moving so that he could be closer to his other girlfriend. I was four years older than Avery and still a fucking mess.

Not to mention, I remembered what it was like to be seventeen. "Why don't you ask him? Grady?"

She looked at me like I'd grown six heads. "Yeah, okay. No. I'm not one of the girls he goes for, trust me. The most communication we have is when he asks me for a pencil. Every day, he asks me for a pencil. Like, what am I? A pencil-supply store? But if he brought his own pencil, then I wouldn't have a reason to even talk to him."

"It's kind of cute. You have something he needs, and he asks you every day because he knows that you'll take care of him." Ugh. Now I was analyzing high-school crushes.

But what does Grayson need? What are your pencils? Faith. The one thing no one else had. He needed me to have faith in him. *At what cost to yourself?*

Avery shook her head. "Computers are easier for me than boys. Give me good internet connection, and I can change my grades. Give me a homecoming dance, and I can't change my fate. I'm so pathetic."

I looped my arm around her slight shoulder. "No, you're not. Is he coming in today?"

She shrugged. "It's Tuesday, so he might come in to lift after football practice."

"Then you'd better get your homework done now, because I have a feeling your little moon-eyes will be back."

"Will you help me?" she asked quietly.

I rolled my chair closer to her. "Let's do this." I spent an hour explaining the differences between cosign and tangent, using the walls and equipment as visual aids. Avery worked best with imagery, not rote memory.

"Name one time I'll actually have to use this when I grow up."

"I'm going to use it all the time," I answered.

"Yeah, well I have no intention of majoring in math, or anything of the sort. You'd better get your homework done, too, since you started classes last week." Her eyes flicked to the clock. "Almost five."

I'd finished summer term with two A's. Now it was time to bring home four more before term ended in December. "Grady might be here soon," I said with a smile.

"Flyboy might be here soon," she answered with her own.

We both sighed.

"Mail is here!" Maggie called, bringing a stack of envelopes in the door. "I ran into our carrier, so I brought it on in."

"Hi, Mom."

Maggie kissed her daughter soundly on the cheek. "How's your homework?"

"Done!" she replied enthusiastically.

Maggie's eyebrows rose. "Good job!" Then she came up behind me. "Thank you," she whispered as she sorted the mail.

I smiled at her and answered the phone and my tenth question that day about our hours.

"Maggie Norman, Advantage University? What the..." She flipped the envelope over, and I snagged it out of her hand.

"Yeah, actually that one is for me. Sorry." I slipped it into my lap.

"Oh really? What are you up to?"

"I wanted to see my transcript from my college in Colorado. I'm trying to apply for places in the spring, and I wasn't sure what was on it." I gave a bright smile. If I finally gave in and read the exact wording of the disciplinary report, I could write an effective application essay that might give me a shot at a

North Carolina school.

Just in case.

"Well, it's good that you're prepared. Avery, did you want me to carry you home before I headed over to the bar?"

Carry, take, whatever. I was never going to get used to the small southern terms.

She shook her head. "No, I was going to stay with Sam and help out cleaning the equipment, if that's okay. She said she'd take me."

I plastered the smile on my face like we'd planned it the whole time.

"Sounds good. Thanks, Sam." She kissed Avery on the cheek again and headed out.

I smacked Avery's shoulder with the back of my hand. "How about a little warning."

"Sorry," she said, biting her lower lip. Then she looked over my shoulder and her whole expression changed. Her eyes went wide and she started to fidget, suddenly occupied with the paper clips in front of her.

"Hey, Avery, how are you?" Grady asked as he signed in.

She took a minute to answer, but he waited, never looking away. "I'm just fine, thank you." Her voice was a whisper, but her eyes flicked up at him once.

"Glad to hear it." He smiled and then headed into the locker room, a black backpack hanging off one shoulder.

"You could, you know, speak to him," I chastised her.

"He makes me so nervous," she answered.

"Go clean something, then you can ogle a little less obviously." I motioned to the gym floor. She giggled and chose something near the desk, no doubt waiting to see where he'd start.

The door opened and Grayson walked in, gym bag in hand. He took off his cover and signed in, but I kept my eyes on the desk. "Samantha."

I shook my head. There was zero chance of us getting into it here.

He sighed and went to the locker room.

"You could, you know, speak to him," Avery called out.

"Do you want me to slip a pack of pencils into Grady's backpack?" I answered quietly enough that only Avery heard me.

Her mouth flopped open.

"I thought not."

She stuck out her tongue, and then moved on to the next machine a little further away.

I ripped open the envelope as soon as she was out of sight and unfolded my transcript.

What. The. Fuck. My grades freshman year were fine, all normal, but the transcript showed me failing classes in my sophomore year, when I knew for a fact I'd pulled straight A's until fall of my junior year. Not that all were F's. Some were D's, or incompletes. These were wrong.

No wonder I wasn't getting in.

I flipped the page to see the attachment I'd dreaded. My stomach dropped, and my cheeks burned like everyone in the gym knew what I'd done.

Disciplinary Report: Samantha Fitzgerald.
One count of assault against a teacher, November 2014
One count of misconduct regarding an academic grade,
November 2014
One count of plagiarism, September 2014
One count of cheating on a final exam, May 2014.

I blinked. It had been doctored. Altered on purpose.

Roaring filled my ears, and embarrassment was no longer the issue. Oh no, I was going to rip apart the person who did this to me. Harrison. That cheating asswipe. He'd have access to the system to change my grades. He'd told me I'd never be rid of him.

I hopped on the computer and booted up my email, going straight to the spam file. There were four more suspicious emails. All with the subject lines of universities I'd applied to. The first three called me a whore, told me I'd never be rid of the shame of what I'd done.

"Yeah, tell me something I don't know," I muttered and opened the last one.

LITTLE WHORE—

HAVEN'T YOU FIGURED IT OUT YET? THERE'S NO HOPE, AND THE HARDER YOU PRESS, THE MORE JOY I HAVE RUINING YOUR FUTURE THE WAY YOU RUINED MY LIFE. WHY DIDN'T YOU STAY HERE, WHERE I COULD WATCH OVER YOU? IN CASE YOU REALLY ARE AS STUPID AS I FIGURE, I'LL MAKE IT CLEAR. FOR EVERY APPLICATION YOU SEND IN, YOUR PAST BECOMES A BETTER REFLECTION OF YOU. ONE LITTLE F AT A TIME.

STOP TRYING.

"Asshole," I whispered, and closed out the email.

Grayson walked out of the locker room and shot me a longing look before heading to the weights.

For a split second, I debated telling him.

If anything, he'd kill Harrison, end up in prison, and I'd be to blame for ruining his life, too. *Put that in your miracle-coma-girl movie.*

No. I could do this myself. I couldn't lie down anymore and pray my grades from here would outweigh what was clearly becoming an unusable transcript. I didn't even have a way to dispute the grades.

I tried the online system to pull my old report cards, but I'd been locked out, which didn't surprise me. I closed out the program and rolled back in my chair.

My eyes automatically drifted to where Grayson was lifting.

The muscles in his arms bulged with every rep, and my mouth went dry thinking of all the times he'd lifted me like I weighed nothing. All the times he'd held me against a wall while he worked my body into frenzy. I looked at the mirror so I could see his face in the reflection, and my lips parted. He was staring right at me, and his eyes said he'd seen me watching, and he liked it. The single arch of an eyebrow told me all I had to do was say the word and I'd be up against the lockers.

But I wasn't right for him. I couldn't even keep my bedroom clean, and I knew that was his pet peeve. Hell, if I were as organized as Grayson, I'd have hard copies of my report card in order of date-received all filed away.

Like my mother.

I pulled out my cell phone and dialed.

"Hi, baby girl."

"Hey, Mom. I'm at work, so I can't chat, but I have a quick question for you."

"Fire away." Her curt tone told me she was still at work.

"Do you have hard copies of my report cards from UCCS?" I held my breath.

"Of course. Do you need them?"

Thank you, God. "Yes. Do you think you could scan them for me?"

"I'll get it done tonight. Love you."

"Thank you, Mom. I love you, too."

We hung up, and I spied Avery wiping down the same piece of equipment she had been for the last ten minutes, staring at Grady as he used the leg machines.

"Avery?" I called out gently, and cringed when she fell forward, distracted. She caught herself before she hit the ground, but her face flushed scarlet.

"What's up?" she asked at the counter.

"How good at computers are you really?"

She smiled slowly.

CHAPTER TWENTY-FOUR

SAM

I shifted in my seat as my English teacher droned on. Maybe it was that I hated literature? Not reading it, but analyzing it. Math was easy. A problem, a solution, bingo, done.

"I think it's about staying faithful," a deep southern drawl to my left answered the question I hadn't heard.

"And what's the overall lesson learned?" the professor prodded.

"That you're rewarded for staying true," a girl answered behind me.

"Until your husband is killed and you're married off like Penelope," I muttered.

"Good point, Ms. Fitzgerald. So if staying true isn't the lesson, what is?" He raised his clichéd glasses up his nose.

I shook my head. "I don't know. Maybe not to piss off the gods. Not to make choices that bring you more suffering than fate has doled out, because then they just keep it coming."

And then they fuck with your transcript.

"And what happens when you obey the gods? Is there still suffering?"

They wake up your boyfriend's comatose girlfriend just to watch the drama.

"There's always suffering," a guy answered ahead of me. "But it's how you deal with it that matters."

"Interesting point."

The discussion droned on until the professor dismissed us. I gathered my books and exited with the crowd. The sun stung my eyes as I made my way into the parking lot.

"Sam."

I pivoted to see Grayson leaned up against one of the support pillars, looking good enough to eat in that uniform. "What are you doing here?"

He brought his hand from behind his back and handed me a small bouquet of flowers. "Grayson." I sighed and took his offering. I brought them to my nose and then lightly stroked the blue and white petals. "How did you get Rocky Mountain Columbine?"

"State flower of Colorado, right?" he asked.

I nodded. "I love these."

"Yeah, I remembered." He gave me a shy smile that shattered my walls.

"Thank you, but shouldn't you be flying?" It was already ten a.m.

"Yeah. We're in academics right now."

What? He was skipping academics?

"Then you'd better go! You're going to be in a ton of trouble."

"I don't care. I'm going to prove to you that I'm not leaving. If that means meeting you out here every day after class to show you that, I'll do it. I probably can't afford to overnight the flowers every day, but I can be creative."

My fingers tightened on the delicate stems. "You can't. You'll lose your spot on the OML, get set back a class, or kicked out of flight school if you miss too much. You know that. You won't get North Carolina." Everything he'd been working for would be thrown away.

His jaw flexed twice, and then he shook his head. "I don't care. I want to be where you are, and if you can't believe me, then I'll have to prove it to you. I'm not leaving you, Sam."

"What about Grace?" I whispered.

He looked away and back to me. "I don't know. I'll tell her about us the next time I see her. I'm being as honest as I can with you, and I don't know what's going to happen. I've lived without Grace for five years, and I'm thrilled to have her back. She's my best friend. But I don't think I could live without you for five days. Hell, it's been like twenty-four hours and I'm already on my knees here."

A smile spread across my face. This was Grayson, who'd pulled me out of my self-destruction and stayed with me after he knew my darkest secrets. He had faith in me, wasn't it only fair that I return it?

"Okay." I nodded.

"Okay, you'll trust me? Or okay, I'd like to see you out here every morning?"

I knew it was against the rules, but I leaned up on tiptoes and pressed my lips to his, nearly knocking his cover off his head. "Okay, I'll believe in us."

He lifted me off the ground and kissed me with far more tongue than he should have in uniform. I was definitely not complaining. "Get your butt to class, now, Grayson."

"I'll see you at home?" There was still something shaky in his voice.

"I'll be there, I promise."

He stole another quick kiss with a smile that could have dropped any of the panties on campus, because it was certainly about to drop mine. "Go!" I lightly pushed him, and he backed away grinning before turning to sprint to his truck.

Gods, fate, suffering be damned, I loved that man.

"Hey honey, would you take the potatoes out of the oven for me?" Grayson called from the backyard as he flipped the steaks.

"Sure thing, sugar-lips!" Jagger called back, and Paisley smacked his chest with the back of her hand.

"I think he meant me." I laughed and opened the oven. Sunday night family dinners were my favorite part of the week. I only wish Ember lived closer so she could be here.

"Hey, don't ever doubt our bromance, Sam. We've come a long way in the last year. He even speaks in multiple-syllable sentences now." He saluted me with his open beer as I pulled the potatoes out and set them to rest on the stovetop.

"No more grunting, either," Josh added, offering me a beer.

I shook my head, not wanting to stress out Grayson. We'd been back to our state of normal for a week and a half, and it was glorious. I hadn't moved into his room yet, but I slept in his bed every night. Our bed.

Other than the random phone calls and texts, which I did my best to maturely swallow, we were just...us. It was this beautiful bubble that I couldn't help but feel was about to pop. Once a pessimist, always a pessimist.

"I think we're ready," Grayson said, putting the steaks on the table to rest. Josh brought over the salad, and I popped the potatoes onto a serving plate. I was midway to the table when Grayson's phone *dinged* with another text message. My stomach clenched, but I ignored it. Or at least tried to.

His brow furrowed as he typed back.

"What's up?" I didn't really want to know, but I had my best supportive-girlfriend hat on.

"It's Grace, she was just asking what I'm up to."

"Do you have a drink?" I asked, skipping right over the part where I daydreamed I took his phone and crushed it into a million tiny pieces.

"Do we have sweet tea?" he asked, not looking up.

"Coming up." I poured us two glasses and set them at the table.

"Do we *what*?" Grayson said aloud.

"Hmmm?"

"Grace wants to know if we have two extra seats for Sunday night dinner?"

Everyone's head snapped to Grayson, and then to the door when the bell rang. *No way. No fucking way.* Grayson met my eyes with a panicked look, and as my stomach fell to the floor, I felt myself systematically shutting down.

Maybe there were more responses than just flight or fight. Maybe shut-down-and-deny was a viable option. "You'd better get that," I said.

He nodded and left the room.

I sat on the side next to Grayson's seat, while Jagger and Paisley took up the side to our left. His hand took mine from where they were playing with the silverware and gave it a soft squeeze. If Jagger wasn't even being sarcastic, we were headed for a hell of an evening.

"Holy shit, you're standing!" I heard Grayson exclaim.

"Not for long," a sweet voice responded.

"Help her out, Gray," another voice snapped, and my hand gripped Jagger's.

"Parker?" Paisley asked softly. I nodded, and she sighed. "I suppose I should grab the extinguisher in case you accidentally set her on fire. I'll also provide the lighter."

Jagger snorted and kissed her on the cheek.

Grayson's head popped over the half wall, and everything inside me turned ice cold, froze, and shattered. In his arms, with her dainty hands wrapped around his neck, was Grace. She wore a white sundress, and with her hair twisted and braided up like that, their goofy smiles, and the way he carried her... *I now present to you, Mr. and Mrs. Grayson Masters.* Holy shit, I was going to be sick.

"Breathe," Jagger whispered under his breath.

I'd seen the possibility of her beauty while she lay comatose, but Grace awake was far more than I could have imagined. Her tiny feet kicked lightly and her smile was infectious and full of such joy that I knew I was totally screwed.

I couldn't even bring myself to hate the woman who would steal away the man I loved.

"Hi," Grace said, looking us all in the eye. When she reached me, her eyes widened for a split second before she spoke. "Thank you for letting us barge in on you like this."

"It's no trouble. I'm Paisley, and you must be Grace," Paisley responded, southern manners to the rescue. "Grayson, why don't you settle her at the table?" Her chair creaked on the floor as she pushed back and headed to the cabinet.

"Where do you want this?" Parker asked, pointing to a small suitcase. "Mia said you have a thing for this peppermint-mocha coffee creamer she made us bring."

Grayson smiled. "That's for Sam, actually."

"I'll take it. Thank you, Parker." I wound my way around the table to take the suitcase from her.

"Wow, I didn't realize you were still living here, Sam."

Oh, her claws were out. "Parker," Grayson growled as he settled Grace into the seat closest to his on the corner.

"Not for long," Parker whispered in my ear, and then skipped over to Grayson and gave him a hug. "I've missed you, Gray!"

"You are tougher than this, and that man worships everything about you, Sam," Paisley said, squeezing my hand as I put the creamers into the freezer.

I nodded, unable to say anything.

"So let me guess who is who?" Grace asked as Paisley set places in front of her and Parker. "You must be Jagger, and you're Josh." She turned, sending me a kind and curious smile. "So you must be Sam? Grayson's other roommate?"

Paisley was wrong. I was so not tougher than this.

"Actually, Grace," Grayson started, sending me a smile, but I shook my head. I wasn't going to destroy this girl at the dinner table. That was a private conversation for them to have. His face fell, and I dropped my eyes, skimming past him to take my seat.

"What?" Grace asked.

"You know he thought she was a guy when she first moved in," Josh supplied. "He didn't realize she was a girl until he met her."

Grace's mouth popped open in a perfect *O*. "What happened?"

I gave my first genuine smile. "He basically implied that I was sleeping with these two"—I pointed to Josh and Jagger—"and then I slipped off the counter and fell."

"She'd been standing on it to reach the coffee," Grayson explained, dishing food onto her plate. "I've since moved the coffee lower, of course."

"You weren't hurt, were you?" she asked.

"No," I said softly as he took my hand under the table. "Grayson caught me."

She turned a soft smile on him. "Good. He's got good reflexes."

Even though it was my hand he was stroking, the smile he gave her made me feel like I was intruding on an intimate moment. I didn't see a cheese-grater, but it felt like one was shaving down my heart a little more with each passing second.

"It's so good to see you guys side-by-side," Parker cooed. "It's like high school all over again!"

Grayson stroked his thumb along my palm and dropped my hand to put food on his plate. "Yeah, except that it's not, Parker."

She cut into her steak with quick, angry motions.

"Sam?" Grayson asked. "Did you want some steak?" He held out the plate.

"What's wrong, did you lose your appetite?" Parker asked so sweetly she would have given a dentist cavities.

I took a piece just to spite her.

"So this was a long drive for you ladies to make on the fly," Josh said, breaking the silence.

"We flew, actually," Grace offered. "I wanted to see Gray and his new life, and Parker was kind enough to bring me. We cleared everything with the doctors, of course."

"So you've planned this for a while?" Jagger asked.

Grace looked from Parker to Grayson. "For about a week now. Parker said you'd like the surprise, Gray. She said you'd been down lately."

"I'm always glad to see you, Grace," he answered.

"Good, because you've got us for three whole days!" Parker finished.

Kill me now. Right now. Lightning strike me dead.

"I figured I could take the couch, and Grace could bunk with you?" Parker flashed Grayson a smile.

I sputtered mid-sip of my tea, and Grayson took it from me while I coughed. "Are you okay, Sam?"

I nodded, still hacking. "Wrong pipe," I managed.

Paisley's hand peeked above the table, brandishing the blue bic Grayson used to light the grill. She shrugged when I laughed softly.

"Parker is kidding. We wouldn't dream of putting y'all out. We saw a hotel down the road. We can stay there."

Crap, I really liked Grace.

"No. You're barely standing. I'll take the couch, you and Parker take my room."

Crap, I hated my boyfriend.

After the most awkward dinner ever, I helped Grayson change the sheets on his bed. "I'm so sorry about this," he said after we fluffed the comforter.

"Don't be."

"I'll tell her tonight," he said, taking both my hands in his.

"Well, that might ruin your chances of keeping her." The joke fell flat.

"I want you," he promised.

I didn't doubt that, but it wasn't just about wanting me.

"There's no part of you that wants her? Because watching you two, I can't believe that's true. And I'm not mad. Jealous, maybe...okay, definitely, but I get it." *Please tell me now before I fall any harder.* He'd loved her all his life, he said so, but never once had he uttered those words in regards to me.

"There's no part of me that doesn't want you," he answered, tipping my chin toward his to kiss me gently. "Have a little faith, remember?"

"Seriously?" Parker hissed from the door and brought in two small suitcases. "What if I'd been Grace? Can't you two just not...ugh."

Grayson turned to face her. "First, this is my house, and we're not in North Carolina. You want to invade my life, fine, but you're not going to tell me how to live it. Second, Grace can't walk up the stairs. Third, so what? She deserves to know that I'm with Sam. I'm not lying to her, not so you can live out this insane fantasy."

Parker blanched. "You can't tell her. We don't know what her health will do. She's so fragile, Gray, and you're what she's holding on to. You can't abandon her."

"She's smart enough to know that things change in five years, and she's strong enough to adapt."

"And what if she's not? You haven't been around, as usual. You haven't seen how hard this is on her, knowing everyone kept living while she...didn't. If you tell her that you moved on, that there's no chance for the two of you to be together, you will be the tipping point for her."

"Parker, that's not fair," I said, "and you don't get to come in here and lay blame on Grayson for something that was never his fault. This is our home."

She side-eyed me, and got up in Grayson's face. "You owe her this much. You knew how drunk Owen was. You knew the minute he threw that punch when you asked for his keys. What did you do? Told him to 'fuck off' and walked away. You owe Grace at least enough time to get on her feet before you shred her."

I placed my hand between his shoulder blades, wishing I could take the sting out of her words, or just plain shut her up. It took everything in my willpower to bite my tongue and remember that this was Grayson's sister. "She's wrong, Grayson. It wasn't your fault."

"It was," he answered, not even turning around. "If I'd stood my ground, none of this would have happened."

"Exactly," Parker agreed. "If it had never happened, you'd be happy. Both of you."

"That's crossing the line." Grayson's voice dropped.

"Maybe. But I'm right. You know I'm right, too, don't you, Sam?"

My stomach dropped like I'd gone off the rails on a high-speed roller coaster.

If none of it had happened, he would have gone to UNC with Grace. They'd have gotten married after graduation and made perfect, G-named babies and raised them on the beaches of the Outer Banks. But his perfect life had come unraveled.

Grayson would never absolve himself of the guilt, and Grace would always hold that string.

He would never be entirely mine.

"Don't tell her." My voice sounded flat, like it belonged to someone else.

Grayson spun around and took me by the shoulders. "What?"

"Parker's right." The words tasted like acid, but I had to lessen some of the guilt that was suffocating him. "You don't know what it will do to her. Her doctors aren't here. She's eight hundred miles away from home, and you might very well break her heart. She doesn't deserve that."

"Neither do you."

He put me on equal footing with Grace, and even though I didn't deserve it, I loved him all the more for it. "I'm strong enough to handle a few days of ambiguity. Just...keep your hands...you know."

His face was stoic but his eyes, they spoke volumes. "My hands only want to be on you."

I forced a smile. "See, nothing to worry about." Parker's smug face was a blur as I passed her, damn-near tripping over my feet to get out of that room. His room. Our room. Where she would sleep. In his bed. Our bed.

While he set everyone up, I studied in my room.

"Sam?" Parker knocked and entered in the same motion.

"What can I do for you, Parker?" I asked, putting my book down.

She looked at the general chaos of my room and forced a smile as she sat on my bed. "I know we don't really get along."

"That's a gross understatement." I tiptoed the line between handing Parker her ass and remembering that she was important to Grayson.

"It's not that I don't like you—"

"Oh, you don't like me, but there's no legitimate reason. You see, I don't like you because you treat Grayson like crap. You won't forgive him for something that happened five years ago, when he was basically a kid. Something that wasn't ever his fault, though you won't let it go because you love Grace so much that you needed someone to blame."

She picked up the pencil off my notebook and twirled it. "Yes."

"So you take it out on Grayson, which is why I don't like you. Valid. But you don't like me because I have the audacity to love your brother."

"I watched him pray for a miracle. For years, at her bedside, he begged. Now he has his miracle. She's here, and he's throwing it away…for you. You're the instrument of his ruin, and if you really loved him, you'd be unselfish and let him go. But you won't, will you? You'll make him suffer, torn between the two of you so that you can hold onto him a little longer."

Selfish. She hit the nail on the head with an accuracy that exposed every one of my nerves. "He wants to be with me."

My soul ached, all my deepest insecurities laid bare in front of the last person I would ever want to display them for.

She looked at me, all traces of menace and snark gone. "Just do me a favor. While she's here, watch them. See how they fit together, complement each other. Really pay attention to them, and when you do, you'll see it."

"What?" I asked, my voice cracking.

"His future. Their future. He wants to be with you, yes. But he loves her. It's his happiness in your hands, Sam. Let him go." She patted my knee like I was a dog, and left me alone with a heart that was slowly ripping itself in two.

In the middle of the night, Grayson came into my bed, sneaking like we were teenagers. My laughter didn't last past the first kiss. He made love to me like we had forever, lingering, savoring, promising me things with his body that I wasn't sure his heart was capable of.

God, I wanted so badly to believe it.

We fell asleep in a tangle of limbs, and when the sun rose, he kissed me gently and snuck back downstairs to the couch as quietly as possible.

Like we'd done something wrong. Dirty.

I scrubbed myself clean in the shower, and as I came out into the hallway in my bathrobe, I startled and stepped back so Grayson could pass with Grace in his arms.

He shot me a longing look, but that was it.

"Good morning, Sam!" Grace called back over his shoulder as they headed toward the stairs. Her hair was perfectly mussed, and her eyes joyful as Grayson jumped the last two steps to the landing. They both laughed.

She makes him laugh.

Dazed, I walked back into my bedroom and stared at my bed. The extra pillow still smelled like him, and I held it to me for a few moments. Then I ripped every piece of linen off the bed and threw it in a pile by the door for the laundry.

What had I done? I'd moved to Alabama. Gotten a job. Gotten into a college, even as small as it was. I thought I'd grown, changed, evolved, but I hadn't. I'd made over everything about my life except the most important part: me.

It had almost been a year, and I was still in the same place I'd been in Colorado, in a sideline relationship with another woman's man.

And for the first time, I felt every bit the whore those emails called me.

CHAPTER TWENTY-FIVE

A pencil smacked me on the back of the head. "Pay attention," Jagger hissed.

Holy shit, I'd been lost in my own thoughts for the better part of ten minutes. I scrolled furiously through the notes, trying to catch up to where the instructor was now. How the hell had I let myself get so distracted? Oh, yeah, because I had three women at my house right now. One who thought I was still dating her, one who was pretending I wasn't, and one I generally wanted to stick on the fastest plane out of here.

And I loved them all.

We were starting night training on Monday, it wasn't like I could slack off now. I blocked out every thought except the academics in front of me and paid attention. Helicopters, I understood. They were machines that did what you told them to, excluding external variables.

It was the external variables that fucked you up.

I somehow made it through class without dazing off again. "Earth to Grayson, you with me?" Jagger asked as we headed to the parking lot.

"I'm here."

"Good, because I need your help," he said as he climbed into the passenger side of my truck. Why didn't we drive separately? I could have stopped into the gym and seen Sam. Grace left tonight, and I was so fucking sick of sneaking around. I loved Sam, and I shouldn't have to hide it.

But she'd told me to. What a fucked-up situation.

I went to text her and swore when I saw my phone was dead.

"Masters!" Jagger waved his hand.

"Sorry, I'm a little distracted."

"You think? Do you want me to drive?" he asked as I pulled onto the road.

"No."

"Okay, because I'd really hate to die before I got the chance to ask Paisley to move in."

"That's right," I said, driving home carefully as Jagger went into extreme details on proposal planning. If I didn't know better, I'd think he was carrying around the latest issue of *Alabama Bride* in his pubs bag.

"So do you think you can help?" he asked as I pulled into the driveway.

"Absolutely." He was the closest thing I had to a brother, of course I was going to help.

"Sweet," he said, swinging to the ground and shutting the door. "I'm off to her house, so wish me luck!"

"Good luck!" I saluted, and headed inside.

"Hi, Port," Grace called from the couch. Her eyes were half open.

"Hey, Starboard. Were you napping?" I shut the door softly behind me.

"Kind of. Parker went out somewhere after she packed us to leave. Feel like reading to me?" She looked so damn hopeful.

"Sure, just give me a second." I went upstairs and changed into cargo shorts, a T-shirt, and a zip-up hoodie, then came back down, my copy of *The Odyssey* in hand.

When I took a seat on the couch, she wiggled over, lying across my lap like we hadn't skipped over the last five years, and assumed the Grayson's-reading-to-me position we'd used since we were seven.

"Does it still help you to read?" she asked.

"Yeah. As long as I'm reading every day it seems to be easier."

I started reading at the beginning. Tripping over the first passages as usual. Her forehead puckered. "Skip to the part you haven't read yet."

What? "Okay." I skipped to book nine and began to read. When Grace shivered, I unzipped my hoodie and helped her into it. "Better?" I asked as I zipped it up.

"Much, thank you," she replied. "I missed this, listening to you read to me."

I brushed her hair back with my empty hand. "What do you remember?"

"While I was…out?"

"No, from before the accident." She bit her lip. "No pressure. I'm just trying to figure out where your memory leaves off. Where your gaps are." I ran my fingers across her forehead, and she relaxed. Some things never changed.

"I…I remember sailing. You, me, and Owen."

"That was the day before. Is that where it cuts off for you?" I asked. She didn't remember the fight…or what followed. God, I was going to have to experience it all over again, because she had to know.

She shook her head. "No, I remember being mad at you because you wanted to turn down the Citadel. You thought it was your responsibility to be with me at UNC."

"Yes. You told me that if we loved each other, four years wouldn't matter."

"Did five years matter?" She leaned against my chest.

"Grace, these last five years weren't normal years. They changed me in ways you wouldn't have liked. In ways I still don't like."

"Don't say things like that. I like you just fine." Her eyes were level with mine as she sat up in my lap. "I'm so sorry for what happened. For what you've been through, but from what I've seen, you've come out on the other side stronger, more focused. Maybe a little less goofy, and you don't laugh as much, but you're still my Gray, my Port. And I'm still your Starboard."

"It's not that easy."

She wound her hands through my hair. "It can be if we let it."

I knew where this was leading and couldn't stomach it going any further. She was much too close, and not in a good way. In a way that sent me back five, hell, six years, to when I loved her without concept of what that really meant. Where I'd dated my best friend because it seemed the most logical step. With one touch, she took me back to a time where I'd confused infatuation and love with being *in* love.

And now, I knew better. Now I had Sam.

Grace was an anachronism in my life, and as much as I'd missed her, as easy as it was to remember how I felt, she wasn't what I needed, because I wasn't the same guy who'd loved her in high school.

I cupped her cheek in my hand and prepared to shatter her. Again.

"It's been five years, and I know this is hard to explain, but my feelings for you…" I took a breath and prepared for the worst. "Grace, I'm in love—" *With Sam.*

"I knew it." She kissed me before I could get it out. A faint clicking sound resonated in my brain.

I froze. Her lips on mine were familiar and foreign at the same time, the wrong texture, the wrong pressure, the wrong taste. Because she was the wrong woman.

I jerked back to break the kiss.

"Grace, we can't."

"Oh, please, don't stop on our account," Josh said from behind me, his voice dead and even. *That clicking had been the door opening.*

I turned slowly, my hand falling away from Grace's cheek.

Sam stood next to Josh, her eyes wide, her lower lip trembling. He stepped in front of her and used his arm to guide her around his back as he murdered me with his eyes. He was protecting her? From me. Because Grace was in my lap, with her hands in my hair, wearing my sweatshirt, and Sam had walked in to see my hand holding Grace's face as she kissed me.

Fuck. My. Life.

This was the shit that happened in movies, not real life.

"Sam, this isn't—"

"Shut the fuck up. Now." Josh enunciated each word more than clearly. Then he turned so I couldn't see Sam, and took her upstairs, guiding her under his arm.

I all but dumped Grace onto the couch and ran. "Sam!"

Josh stood in her doorway. "No. Turn your ass around and go back downstairs."

He may have had a couple inches on me, but I had at least thirty pounds of muscle on him. "Move. I need to talk to her."

"I love you like a brother, but I'm two seconds away from beating the shit out of you," Josh fired back.

I stepped toward him. "No offense, but we both know how that fight would end, and I'll finish you if it means I get to Sam. Grace kissed me. I didn't kiss her back. You walked in at pretty much the worst possible second."

"I don't give a fuck if she tripped into your clothes and landed on your mouth, Masters. Sam was my friend long before you were." He crossed his arms.

"Let him in, Josh," Sam said quietly from inside her room.

"Can I hit him first?"

My eyes narrowed, but he looked unapologetic.

"No," she responded. "Just let him in. I'll be fine."

"I'll be downstairs," he said to her, looking straight at me.

"I'm the guy who turned himself in with you for that fucking polar bear, Walker. You really think I'd hurt her like this on purpose?"

"I don't care about the why, only that you did." He stepped to the side, and I headed into her room.

She'd pulled down a suitcase and two large duffels onto the bed and was stuffing them with her clothes.

"Where are you going?"

"Away from you," she answered, pulling another stack of clothes from the closet and shoving them into the suitcase, hangers and all.

"That was not what it looked like, and yes, I know how cliché that sounds."

"You're right, it is cliché. Then again so was walking in on you and your girlfriend. God, I'm so fucking stupid. I knew. I knew! And I still let it happen."

"Stop, Samantha. Talk to me."

She spun, the streaming tears only making the green of her eyes brighter. Misery was etched on every line of her face. "What is the point?"

"You can't leave. Not like this."

"Then how? Maybe the next time when I walk in to see your girlfriend wearing your sweater? Then your boxers? Your *mouth*?"

"She kissed me. I stopped it!"

She clapped. "Bravo. Extra points for stopping it after you obviously let her onto your lap and into your arms."

Shit. She's right. "You're right. God, Sam. You're right. I should have stopped her when she laid across my lap while I read to her. I should have told her about us right then."

"I shouldn't have asked you to wait," she said, then pressed her lips together as more tears fell.

"We both made mistakes, and we handled this all wrong. Let me get her back to North Carolina, and we'll figure this out between us."

She shook her head. "There's no us. We're done."

My breath rushed like I'd been punched. It hurt. Fuck, did it hurt. I blinked, half expecting to see Sam holding my ripped-out heart in her hand.

"I didn't kiss her!"

"I believe you."

My mouth opened and closed a couple times, unable to find the words. "Then what the hell are you doing?"

"Just because you didn't kiss her today doesn't mean it won't happen. I've sat here for three days and watched you with her. You guys touch each other without noticing. Yesterday at dinner, she drank your sweet tea when hers was gone. You didn't blink, just took a sip and put it back next to her plate!"

I tried to breathe. "I guess I fell into old habits."

"And how long until you fall back into the habit of sleeping with her? You've loved her your whole life, you told me so."

"I wouldn't sleep with her. That would never happen." I reached for Sam, and she stepped back, bumping into her dresser.

"Well, this morning I would have said that you'd never kiss her, either. And last week, I would have said that she wouldn't be sleeping in your bed. Do you not see the progression? How naive do I have to be to stay and watch this happen? Do I need to wait until you *accidentally* put a ring on her finger?" She let loose a self-deprecating laugh that I instantly loathed. "Then again, with my track record, a ring probably wouldn't stop me. I'd still let you fuck me while your wife slept across the hall and you snuck out at sunrise."

"Sam..."

"Because that's what you do to me. How passionate I am for you—how much I love you. I would sacrifice everything about myself to have those moments with you. I know because I'm already doing it. And I'm worth so much more than that!" She sobbed the last sentence, and I died a little more.

"You are worth everything."

She shook her head. "But you can't give me everything. There will always be a part of you that belongs to her."

"That's not true. You have me." If anything, the last few days had only made that clearer.

"Oh my God, look at your life! Everything you've done has been for her. The constant flights home. This driving need you have to be top of the OML so you get your first-choice duty station. Fighting for North Carolina so you can be closer to her. I grew up in the army, Grayson, and I know that there's not that many people requesting North Carolina, but you're killing yourself on the off-chance you have to beat someone out. All. For. Her. There's no room for me."

"How can there be room, when you have one foot out the door at all times?" I fired back.

"Would you stay? Just waiting to be broken down little by little? Watch your heart shrivel and die when you see phone calls, and text messages, and accidental kisses?"

"For you, I would endure hell." Fire. Damnation. All of it. Without question.

"Grayson, I love you too much to ever ask you to, and therein lies the difference."

My hands ripped over my hair, desperate for a grip on anything at this point. "Do not do this. Do not leave me. I will get on my knees if that's what you need, but don't give up on us."

"Give me one good reason."

"Because I fucking love you!" The words carried through the room, the hallway, the house, my whole soul. "I'm in love with you, Samantha. You own me, body, heart, mind, soul, whatever there is to give, it's yours."

Her shoulders sagged, but instead of looking relieved at my confession, she looked defeated. "I waited so long for that," she whispered.

"I should have told you sooner." I gambled and stepped closer, bringing my hand to her soft, wet cheek, and used my thumb to brush away a new trail of tears.

"Sooner? How long have you known?"

"Since you stood up and yelled at my family that night at my parents'." I smiled at the memory. "I've never had anyone defend me."

"Why did you wait so long?" Her eyes lit with a sliver of hope.

"At first because I didn't recognize the emotion. It was so much stronger than anything I'd ever felt, and it scared me. But then Grace woke up...and I knew I couldn't say those words to you without having my shit straight. You deserved someone who had everything together in his head, who knew his path." The hope in her eyes died. "What? What did I say?"

"You didn't know who you would choose. Grace...or me." She pulled back, and I lost my hold on her.

"I never said that."

"You didn't have to, and I don't blame you. I don't blame you for any of this, Grayson. You are amazing. Strong, tender, smart, kind, and just enough of an ass to dish back my crap at me. You are everything I needed, and you saved me when I was pretty sure I wasn't salvageable. I won't stand between you and your miracle."

"What?"

"I know you love her. I know what losing her the first time did to you, and I won't be the person responsible for it happening twice. You kissing her may have been an accident, but crap like that doesn't happen without underlying emotions. And you saying you love me minutes after I find her in your arms? Love doesn't work like that."

"Sam, don't do this."

"It's already done, Grayson. I fell in love with you, and your lost love came back to life in this honest *miracle*. How could I possibly say that I love you and not do what's clearly best for you?"

"It's not already done, your stuff is all still here. I'm here. You're here."

"Grayson!" Parker yelled up. "It's time to leave for the airport!"

"Have Josh take you!" I shouted.

"Seriously?" she said from the doorway. "You're not going to take us yourself?" She took in the scene and backed up. "Whoa. I guess you finally saw it, didn't you? His future?" she asked the question softly, without the usual Parker bite.

"Get the hell out, Parker."

"Just take them," Sam pled.

"I'll wait downstairs," Parker said as she retreated. "This conversation isn't done."

We stood in stalemate, and Sam swatted away her tears. "It's better this way. You're graduating in December, going to North Carolina. I'm not. What's the point of suffering like this for a few more months when we both know it's coming to an end, anyway. Isn't this better? Make a clean break now, and you can have Grace. You can be happy."

I took her face in my hands again. "I don't want Grace. I want you."

"I already waited too long. I can't afford to fall apart any more than I already have."

Panic took hold, threatening to close my throat. "I told you I will always catch you."

"But you didn't. Not this time." Another tear slipped unnoticed down her cheek.

"We're not at the bottom yet, Samantha. Have a little faith." I kissed her, putting every ounce of love I had in me into it, drinking in the perfection of her mouth against mine. "You were made for me. This, right here? This is everything." She parted her lips, and I slipped inside, melding us together in the only way I could. Our bodies had always communicated better, so I let them. She melted into me, and I almost fist-pumped. Instead, I kissed her harder, deeper, committing myself to her whether or not she wanted me to, and she gave back everything I knew she was, sweetness, passion, completion.

I broke away first, and then kissed her one last time because she looked too damn kissable. "Stop packing. We'll figure this out when I get home."

She shook her head. "I love you, Grayson Masters."

As she stepped back, the distance between us suddenly felt like a canyon. "I'll always love you, Sam." She needed the reassurance, I got that.

"I know. But can you honestly tell me that you'll never love her again? Can you know that?"

I blinked, and my mouth wouldn't work. I knew the right answer, but it wouldn't come out. Love Grace again? I'd never stopped, but it wasn't the same as what I felt for Sam. The two couldn't be compared. "That's not fair."

"Because you can't say no, and I can't blame you." Sam's posture drooped.

"Grayson!" Parker yelled.

"But I can't stay. Second place isn't good enough, not anymore."

My throat threatened to close. "Wait, and we'll talk when I'm back. Just wait."

She flattened her lips and nodded. "It's not like I can pack out of here in an hour, anyway."

"Stop packing and wait. I'll be back as soon as I can." I moved forward quickly, pressed a kiss to her forehead, and whispered, "I'm in love with you, just trust me." She didn't answer, and I didn't wait.

Grace and Parker were both silent all the way to the airport, but I didn't care much. My head was too full of Sam, of what I could say or do to bring us to solid ground. At least the door was open.

I lifted Grace into her wheelchair, got them checked in, and then brought them to security at the small airport.

"You good to go?" I asked.

Parker nodded and then stood to the side so I could say good-bye to Grace. "I love seeing you, but I might need some time."

"You're in love with her. Sam?" Tears filled her eyes.

"Yes. And I'm sorry it hurts you. For the last five years, I've been waiting, and I thought it was for you to wake up, to finally be together, but the more I think about it, I was always waiting for her to wake *me* up. I can't live without her."

She nodded and gave me a watery smile. "I understand. I only want you to be happy, Gray. That's all I've ever wanted."

I crouched down to her eye level. "I know. You're my starboard, my right hand. But she's my squall, this storm that I never saw coming. I can't let her go. I have to buckle up, hold on, and steer where she's headed, because nothing else could compare after loving her."

She squeezed my hand. "She's lucky. You both are. I'll always be your friend, and I'll always be here. Bye, Gray."

"Bye, Grace."

I left them at the airport and raced home, breaking every speed limit from Dothan to Enterprise. We were in the open, everything behind us. We could make this work. I pulled into the driveway and barely had the engine killed before I was out and running for the front door. It swung open before me, and I raced up the stairs. "Sam, I'm home!" I called out and knocked on her closed door.

"Sam?" I knocked again, and then opened it slowly.

Fuck. No. No. No.

I lost the ability to breathe, my lungs searching for air that simply wasn't there.

Her room was empty, furniture and all. I laced my fingers on my head and walked a small circle in the room. I'd only been gone two-and-a-half hours. That was it. But she'd erased herself completely, like she'd never been here at all.

But my pulverized heart wore the scars that proved she had been.

She'd given up. Left. Didn't trust me to love her.

How the hell could I fight for someone who had no faith in me?

CHAPTER TWENTY-SIX

"There you are, you vampire," Avery said as I walked into the gym.

"Hey, yourself," I replied, and plopped my bag on the desk.

It was a fitting description really, since I felt like the living dead. In the three days since I'd left Grayson, Maggie had been nice enough to move my shift to nights, when I knew from Jagger that Grayson was flying.

So what if my schedule revolved around his? At least it meant that I had no chance of running into him, which was exactly what I needed. It also helped that Paisley hadn't told him that I'd taken over her room and now lived with Morgan. Not that he'd asked. Or texted. Or called. Or...anything.

"What brings you out during daylight hours? Connor is on shift right now." She didn't bother taking her eyes off Grady as he worked on his lats.

"Your mom needed help with the schedule." Of course I'd said yes, then waited until after six thirty p.m. to come in.

"Mmmm," she replied.

"How's your homework?" I waited for her to respond, then bopped her on the head with a pencil when it became obvious that she wasn't going to. "Avery. Homework."

"Ow!" She rubbed her head and finally looked over at me. "Whoa. You look...um."

I raised an eyebrow at her.

"Swollen?" she answered with a smile.

That's what happens when you can't quit crying for three days. "Rough few days. Enough about me, what's going on with homecoming?"

Her eyes flew toward the machines again. "Nothing."

"Does he have a date yet?"

She shook her head, tucking her hair behind her ear. "I don't know why I'm holding out hope, really. I'm just like...his office supply store."

"You don't know that," I said. "You're beautiful and smart. Grady would be lucky to have you as a date."

"Sure, if he liked dating the bottom of the social food chain." She tapped her pencil on her trig book and sighed.

I couldn't hide my smile.

"What? You think this is funny? This is my *life*." Her forehead hit the book.

Oh, to be seventeen. "One, stop being so dramatic. I was thinking that you remind me of my best friend. She had this thing for this ultra-popular hockey player when she was a sophomore. He was a senior so she thought she didn't have a chance. She didn't do anything about it, and he went off to college."

She rotated so her cheek lay against the book. "That's the most depressing story *ever*, but thank you."

"Not really. Turns out he'd had a thing for her all along."

She sat up and leaned in. "Really? What happened?"

"They met up again when they were in college, and they're madly in love. Like off-the-charts kind of love. They've been together over a year now."

Her gaze flickered toward Grady.

"See, it's possible, so don't be so hard on yourself. Stop letting where you think you rank, or anyone's opinion define you. You'll be a hell of a lot happier once you do." I sorted the mail and started to work on the next week's schedule.

"What, like you're happy?" she fired back, working on the next problem.

"With who I am? Not yet, but I'm realizing that I might not ever be. I am a glorious work in progress, Avery. Stand back, I may spontaneously combust at any moment." I winked at her.

"And the tears?"

I took a deep breath and let it out slowly. "Yeah, well... sometimes love is just...complicated."

She glanced at Grady and let out a dramatic sigh. "Yeah, I know what you mean."

I hid my smile a little better as I turned on the computer to fire up Excel. "Hey, have you had any luck on our computer problem?"

Her eyes lit up. "They're all looped, each one responsible for the other, so I just need to find the one origin email that began the chain. But I can tell you that they all originated in Colorado."

Fucking Harrison. "Thanks, Avery. I really appreciate it."

She shrugged with an impish grin. "I like doing it."

A weight clanged to the ground, and Grady bounced on one foot. "You okay?" I called out.

"Grady, you all right?" Avery said at the same moment.

He turned scarlet and picked up the small dumbbell. "Yeah, all good."

I didn't miss the way his eyes dropped away from Avery when he picked up the weight. *Interesting.* He quickly retreated to the locker room.

I finished the next month's schedule quickly and printed it as Grady walked out of the locker room, his black backpack slung over his shoulder. "Is that the same backpack he uses for school?"

"Yep," she popped the P. "He brings it to every class."

"Okay, well, I'm done here. You good with your homework?"

I stood in a hurry.

"Yeah, I think I'm getting it."

"Sounds good!" I said and nearly ran to the front entrance, throwing open the glass door with more energy than I'd had in the last four days.

Grady stood two cars over, digging through his backpack, muttering about his car keys. Perfect. I snuck over, quiet as I could be, until I was only a foot away from his back.

"Hiya, Grady!" I squeaked.

He jumped, losing the grip on his backpack. It hit the pavement, spilling open. Dozens of pencils rolled under the car.

"Oh, I'm so sorry! Let me help you with these." I picked up all the pencils but pocketed one without him noticing. "You like pencils, huh?"

"No problem, Miss Samantha. And...uh...yeah." He stood, his face flushed, and damn-near raced to get in his car.

Once he had peeled out of the parking lot, I skipped back into the gym. "What are you doing back?" Avery asked.

I leaned over the front of the counter and grabbed the fine-tip permanent marker. A few seconds later, I'd scribed the word *Homecoming?* along the shaft. "Give this to him when he asks for a pencil tomorrow."

She took the pencil and scoffed. "Yeah, right."

"Woman to woman, trust me. You're not his office supply store."

A faint hope sparked in her eyes, and I smiled. First love was so freeing, like the first wing beats of a baby bird on its fall from the nest.

It was the messy, quasi-adult kind of love that plucked your feathers until you fell from the sky.

I headed out, this time grabbing my keys, and nearly ran into Josh as he opened the door. "Hey!"

"Hey, Sam." He assessed me, no doubt looking for the tell-tale signs of heartache like puffy eyes, dark circles, generally unkempt hair. I was rocking all three. "You been okay?"

I nodded. *No.* "Yeah, of course. Morgan is actually a ton of fun. Thank you for getting me out of there so quickly the other day. I didn't know you could move furniture that fast."

"I'm a man of many talents."

"So I've heard." I smacked myself in the forehead. "That was so wildly inappropriate. I'm sorry."

He laughed. "I'll be sure to tell Ember." His smile fell. "Seriously though. You're okay?"

My smile fell. "How is he?"

"He's got a wall up."

"Go figure. It's not like I expected him to break out the ice cream and pour his heart out to you guys."

"Yeah, I don't see that happening. Ever."

"He hasn't guessed I'm at Paisley's, so there's that. Not that I'm hiding from him, but I don't think I could handle seeing him. Not yet."

Josh rubbed his hand along my arm. "Sam, he knows. Jagger told him. It was in the same conversation that he called him an idiot, stubborn, stupid, and an asshole."

"Oh. He knows? But he hasn't..." *Tried to see me.*

Josh swallowed. "Yeah. He said something about no fight without faith, and then went for a run. A ten-mile run. In the rain."

I forced a smile to keep from crying. "Well, I guess that settles that."

"Sam—"

I stepped around him, craving the solitude of my car. "Don't worry, Josh. It's what I wanted. What I asked for." *It just feels like shit.* "I'll catch you later."

I didn't break down until I was behind the wheel.

Have a little faith in me. That hurt. How could he think I didn't?

I had ultimate faith in him. That was the problem. He'd

commit to me, and mean it. He'd stay by my side with unwavering loyalty...while his heart died a slow, painful death pining for his miracle.

I'd never stand by and watch that happen.

He deserved better. So did I.

The ocean breeze ruffled the spiral curls I'd worn my hair in today as I leaned against my car, staring at the pier I needed to be on in exactly ten minutes.

He said yes! I held onto that last text Avery sent me yesterday as my happy thought. Now I just needed some fairy dust, and maybe a new heart. Yeah, that might help.

"You going to be okay?" Ember asked as she leaned next to me.

"Yeah. I mean, we're here for Jagger, right? This isn't about me." *Or my stupid broken heart.*

She looped her arm around my shoulder and rested her head against mine. "I think you're really amazing, do you know that?"

"You're my best friend. You're morally obligated to say crap like that." But it still felt good to hear.

"No, I'm not. Have you seen him yet?"

I shook my head. It had been two weeks, two days, and—I checked my watch—twenty-three hours. Eleven weeks until he would graduate. "I feel numb inside. Do you think that's going to go away?"

"Yes," she answered as we watched Josh carry the last of the giant boxes up onto the pier. "And I think when it does, you'll want it back."

"I miss everything about him."

"He misses you. I've seen him, Sam. He's the most stoic train wreck ever. Like...a statue of a train wreck? It's really sad to watch."

"It's really sad to live. When you pushed Josh away, I thought you were quite possibly the most clueless girl I've ever known. He so obviously loved you, and you him. Am I being clueless? Should I have stayed?"

She sighed. "I don't know. Our situations are completely different. If Josh had loved someone like that before me, and then she came back into his life?"

"I'd cut her down for you," I promised.

Ember laughed. "I can do the same. I haven't met this piece of perfection yet. I'm still allowed to hate her."

Grace's face came to mind, her open smile, easy laugh... and the way she'd looked like an extension of Grayson in his arms. "I can't even hate her, Ember. She's lovely, and sweet, and did nothing to deserve any of this."

"Neither did you." Ember lifted her head and turned to face me. "Sam, you didn't do anything to deserve this pain. This isn't because of what happened with Harrison. It's not some wild fated retribution. What you're suffering is far beyond anything Karma could give you."

"I'm not so sure about that," I said quietly.

"Well, I am, so I can believe it enough for both of us until you do, too."

Josh jogged toward us, and I pulled my shit together. "Is he here yet?"

"No. He had an errand to run or something. You going to be okay?" he asked, pulling Ember into his side. They couldn't be in the same airspace without touching.

"Yeah, of course. We're here for Jagger, so let's rock this." I shoved the pain back deep into the box I'd kept it in for the last couple of weeks. It was safe there, contained.

We made our way up to the pier and took our designated spots behind the railing. Each of us had one of the large crates to open when signaled. I studied mine, determined not to screw this up.

"It's this lever here," a lanky girl with enormous sunglasses said, sitting beside me. "Twist there, and pull."

"Thanks," I answered with a smile. There was something about the shape of the girl's face that reminded me of someone.

"Hi, I'm Anna Mansfield...Bateman...it's complicated." She flashed me a closed-lip smile and thrust her hand out to be shaken.

"Oh wow!" I said, shaking her hand. "You're Jagger's sister, right? I'm Sam Fitzgerald. I've known him for a few years, since we used to live next door in Colorado. I have to admit, I've been so curious to meet you."

She studied me from behind the glasses. "Well, I'm Jagger's twin, and I'm only here as a weekend pass from rehab. I'm a big fan of drugs, but they are not such a fan of me, it turns out." She sighed. "Sorry, it's easier to say it than have people whisper your dirty little secrets, you know?"

I didn't bat an eye. "I slept with my professor, found out he was married, clocked him in front of a crowd, and was expelled from my university."

"Did it feel good to hit him?"

"Yes."

She laughed. "I like you."

"Likewise," I answered.

"They're here!" Josh stage-whispered and we all hit the deck, leaning our backs against the railing.

"Ember, Mrs. Donovan, you're on the banner, right?"

"Joshua Walker, we've gone over this fifteen times. I know when to release it. Mrs. Donovan knows when to release it. I swear, you'd think you were the one proposing." She pursed her lips at him.

"Was that an invitation? Because I'd marry you so hard." He smiled at her, and she laughed.

"Pay attention to your birds," she chastised, but flashed him a grin.

I looked at the lever in front of me. "Lift and pull," I

repeated, fingering the latch.

"It's this one here. Slide it over, then lift up and pull it out." His voice washed over me, and my chest burned, trying to keep a lid on that damned box of feelings.

Slowly, I raised my eyes past his light-blue board shorts and tight white tee with MASTERS & SON emblazoned on the front until I reached his eyes. My breath abandoned me.

"Can you do it?" he asked softly, despite the hardest expression I'd ever seen on his face. It was like he'd been carved out of stone, each line stiff, unyielding. But his eyes locked on to mine, and he was there, my Grayson. Lightning arced between us as if he'd touched me. God, I needed him to touch me. Kiss me. Remind me why love was worth the gamble even when the outcome had already been determined. My lips parted, and his gazed dropped to them and then lifted to my eyes. Raw hunger radiated from him, the kind that used to end with me pushed against the nearest flat surface.

My pulse jumped, remembering his hands on me, his tongue worshiping me. The way he gasped my name when I ran my lips down his stomach. My body hummed.

"The birds," he whispered. "Do you have the lever?"

How the hell was he speaking? I nodded my head wordlessly, and he gave me a curt nod of his own before moving down the line.

"Holy shit, I may need a cigarette after all that eye sex," Anna said, fanning herself. "You two always like that?"

"Yeah," I sighed.

"Is the sex that hot, too?"

"Hotter." I tried, but my eyes followed him without permission, thirsty for the sight of him.

"Any hotter and the pier would have caught fire," she murmured.

"Ready?" Josh signaled. "Banner!"

Ember and Mrs. Donovan unfurled the banner, and then

we all stood. Jagger and Paisley were in the water beneath us, and my heart almost exploded from the love, the perfection of this moment for them.

"She said yes!" Jagger shouted, and we erupted in cheers. I turned to the box. *Slide. Lift. Pull.* The doors flew open and my birds took to the sky, joining the rest of the enormous flock. The sky turned white, and I laughed, unable to suppress the sheer joy of it.

We all walked down the pier to meet them on the beach, and my footsteps felt light, easy. The breeze kicked up my skirt, and I used both hands to hold down the soft green eyelet fabric.

Jagger carried Paisley from the water, and as soon as her feet touched the sand, she ran to her parents. They held on to her like she was their most precious possession, and then grabbed Jagger into the hug. Jagger reached for Anna and brought her in.

I'd never seen anything as beautiful. My smile was so big that it almost hurt my cheeks, and tears pricked at my eyes as the moment overwhelmed me. This was the ultimate depiction of love in its most beautiful state.

Pure. Raw. All-encompassing.

I flicked away a tear as Jagger moved, and my eyes locked on Grayson.

He stared at me, the love I'd so sorely needed pouring from his eyes, saying everything we couldn't. *This could have been us. This could still be us.*

Have a little faith in me.

The craving to speak to him overruled logic, but General Donovan was already talking to him by the time I made it over.

"So you turned in your duty station requests last week, right?"

I paused behind Paisley's dad, waiting for Grayson's response.

"Yes, sir."

"Well, Jagger tells me you're up at the top of the OML, so it shouldn't be that hard to get your first choice if you stay there."

"No, sir."

"Where were your three choices?"

I held my breath. *At least one of them, Grayson. Just one.*

"Well, Fort Bragg, North Carolina, sir. That's my top choice."

I pushed past the ache in my chest for that one. It wasn't unexpected.

"Good post. You have ties to the area?"

"That's home for me, sir. My loved ones are there."

My ears roared, the sound louder than the ocean.

"And your other two choices?"

"Fort Campbell, Kentucky, and Fort Stewart, Georgia, sir."

That tiny swell of hope that had sprung up watching the proposal died a slow, agonizing death, bleeding out at my feet in a heap of regret.

"Well, if you can't get North Carolina, I guess those are the closest for you…"

General Donovan's voice faded as I walked away, my heart protesting each step as I made my way across the beach. Grayson knew I wanted to go to Colorado, and out of his three choices, none of them were even close.

I was so fucking done with this.

"Sam!" he called out from behind me, but I didn't stop. Stopping would mean surrendering to him, and I couldn't do that anymore.

"Please say something." It was the plea in his voice that broke me.

I turned and looked up at him, his frame so large he almost blocked out the whole sunset. What could I possibly say to him at this point? "I miss you," I admitted. "Every time I take a breath, my chest hurts because I miss you so much, and it *hurts*, Grayson. Everything hurts, all the time."

"Sam," he whispered, but I moved before he could touch me.

"Don't. You touch me, and I'm lost." I slid into the small opening of my car door, and he recognized it for the escape maneuver it was.

"You know I had to pick North Carolina. I had no choice," he argued.

"I know, but you left me with none, either. Just cut our losses, Grayson."

I shoved the lid on the feelings box and got the hell out of there.

CHAPTER TWENTY-SEVEN

SAM

"Ice cream?" Morgan asked, sliding a pint over the counter island before taking spoons out of the drawer.

"Why not, after all, no one will be seeing this ass for a while." I shrugged and popped the top on the chocolate-chip cookie dough. That little beach trip two days ago was definitely the last of bikini season.

"We could always head out for a drink if you need something stronger," she offered. "Tornado watch be damned."

A year ago I would have jumped that offer so hard I would have bounced. But using alcohol to cope meant I'd wake up in the morning hungover and still heartbroken. *No thank you.* "This is perfect, thanks."

"Well, ice cream is the only real action I've been getting, so I've become quite the connoisseur." She dug out a bite.

My phone buzzed.

Avery: *Hey, I have news for you. Want to meet me at the gym?*

As if on cue, a branch from the hydrangea bush outside the kitchen window slapped the glass. The sky was dark for six o'clock at night, and the wind was moving with the approaching thunderstorm. "Looks like we're in for an evening, anyway," Morgan said, securing the latch on the window. "Guess I'll go take off the bra. Want to marathon some Netflix?"

"Sounds good. Anything but *One Tree Hill*," I answered automatically, pretty sure I'd never see it again without thinking of sitting in Grace's hospital room.

I texted Avery back.

Sam: *We're under tornado watch. Why don't we meet up tomorrow?*

My curiosity would have to wait. I didn't want her out in this.

"You and Grace." Morgan laughed.

"What?" My head snapped up.

She waved her spoon. "Oh, you know. The *One Tree Hill* comment. I went over to the house with Paisley one day when you were at school, and when I asked her if she wanted to watch TV she said the exact same thing."

Huh. Odd. "Weird. Mia said it was her favorite show."

"Not sure." Morgan shrugged. "She said something about hating the last season, and it being overplayed? Anyway, I'm seriously getting in my pajamas. Meet you at the couch?"

I couldn't even escape Grace in my own kitchen. She was everywhere.

My cell phone buzzed, and I nodded at Morgan. Jammies weren't a bad idea, and definitely more comfortable than my jeans.

Avery: *I'm actually here already.*

The wind picked up, and a weather alert sounded on my phone.

Tornado Warning, Coffee County, AL until 9 p.m. Seek shelter immediately.
Trained weather spotters reported a funnel cloud near Kinston. A tornado may develop at any time. Doppler radar showed this dangerous storm moving Northeast at 45 mph. Locations of impact include...Enterprise... Fort Rucker...Take cover immediately.

Crap. Looked like we'd be watching television from the cozy confines of the downstairs bathroom.

Sam: *Hey, there's a tornado warning.*

Avery: *I saw. Mom already shut the gym down.*

Sam: *Good. Get home, okay?*

I took a bite of ice cream and savored the chill on my tongue. Since the proposal, I'd been numb. No tears, no pain...nothing. Even this tornado warning? Meh.

Maybe I'd exhausted every possible emotion in my body, wrung myself dry until all that was left was an overdose of lidocaine that made me bite my tongue more than anything else.

But maybe that was good. Maybe it would be easier to move on now.

Avery: *Grady dropped me off here. Mom is in Dothan.*

My stomach fell.

Sam: *You're there alone?*

Avery: *Yeah. No worries. Mom will be here in an hour or so. I'll bunker down in the sauna or something.*

Alone? No way.

I pulled up the weather map. She didn't have an hour if that turned into a tornado. I looked out the window. Weren't the skies supposed to turn green? Mom had raced us to the shelter in Kansas, it wasn't like I'd actually seen anything.

A few clicks and I had the television tuned to a local channel, where the six o'clock news had been commandeered by the meteorologist.

"...away from windows or flying debris. Again, a tornado has been spotted traveling northeast at what looks to be about thirty miles an hour. If you are in the city of Enterprise, take cover. Folks, this one is coming right at you."

The remote fell from my hand.

"Morgan!" I ran to the entry hall, where I'd dropped my shoes, and put them on.

"What's wrong?" she asked, coming down the steps in

flannel pajama pants.

"Tornado headed for us." I threw on my hoodie and raced back to the kitchen, where I'd left my cell phone on the counter.

"Confirmed on the ground?"

"Yeah. You need to get in the bathroom." My fingers flew over the text screen.

Sam: *I'm coming. Keep the door unlocked and get away from the windows.*

"Well so do you." She grabbed the emergency pack from the hallway.

"I have to get Avery. She's all alone at the gym." Where the hell were my keys? The entry table? My purse? The coffee table. Right.

"You can't go out there if there's a tornado on the ground."

"They said it's moving thirty miles per hour, it's currently estimated to be twelve miles away, giving us twenty-four minutes. I can get to the gym in five minutes. I'll be back before it comes close."

"I'll go with you."

"No. My car only has one seat empty. The back seat is full of boxes. Just stay here, stay safe."

"Then take this." She threw the bag to me. "And be careful."

"I will." Once the rain hit my face, the full consequences of what I was doing slammed into me. A tornado nearly destroyed this town almost a decade ago. It would be foolish to assume that it couldn't happen again.

I threw the bag in my passenger seat and fired up my car. I had already hit Rucker Boulevard when my phone synced to the car. "Call Avery," I said clearly as rain pelted my windshield.

"He-hello?" her little voice came through my car speakers.

"I'm on my way, okay? Stay away from the windows, and when you see my car, come out."

"I don't want you out in this, but I'm scared."

Tree branches danced above me as I halted at the stoplight,

their movements creaking, cracking their trunks. "Me, too."

Lightning split the sky.

"Avery, do you have the radio on?" I leaned over my dash, getting a better view of the sky. Was it getting lighter? That wasn't right.

"Yes. They're saying to take cover."

"I'm coming, I promise."

Green light. Go. I gunned the gas, passing the other lone car out here. Call-waiting beeped, and I glanced at the screen long enough to see Grayson's name.

He would know what to do. He always did. But I couldn't hang up on Avery. Not when she was alone.

"The sky is yellow," I said softly.

"That's not good!" She panicked.

Shit, I should not have said that out loud. "It's okay, Avery. You're going to be okay."

Now if I only believed that.

"Shit!" I shouted, slamming on the brakes as a branch crashed in front of me.

Oxygen filled my lungs in great, heaping breaths. I couldn't panic. I wouldn't.

"Sam?" her voice pitched high, terrified.

"I'm okay." I backed up and detoured around the limb. A few blocks later I breezed through the biggest intersection and got a view of the funnel cloud.

"Holy. Shit. Avery? We need to shelter there. I don't think we're going to make it back to my house in time."

"Okay." Her breath came in rapid, short spurts.

Lightning flashed again, and the power died around me, killing the stoplights and storefronts. "Sam?"

"I know. I'm almost there." I'd never been more aware of how little protection my soft top offered.

One hand on the wheel, I unzipped the bag next to me, finding the flashlight, and tucked it into one of the front pockets of my hoodie.

Grayson beeped in again: *I'm okay. I want you. Where are you? Are you safe? Please be safe.* My finger itched to click over, but I couldn't do that to Avery.

"Thirty seconds," I said to Avery. I pulled into the parking lot and slammed on the brakes before hitting the curb and killed the engine. The emergency brake cut into my stomach as I leaned over, grabbing the duffel bag. "I'm here!"

"I see you!"

I hung up the phone and shoved it in my back pocket as I tripped out of the car, hitting the pavement on my knees. The sound of metal crunching blended with Avery's screams. Glass busted above me as a tree limb was thrust through my window, narrowly missing me. *You're okay. This is okay.*

The roar was deafening, but the sound of shattering glass and metal crashing were far worse.

"Sam!" Avery's shrill cry propelled me to my feet, and I stumbled to the open door where she waited, grabbing her by the arm to pull her in behind me.

"What's the centermost room?" I asked her. Rocket Man sounded from my pocket. Avery crashed into my back and the ringing stopped as I assessed the gym. All this equipment would be one hell of an arsenal of flying projectiles.

"The storage room." She raced ahead of me, and I followed as a glass panel behind us exploded, flinging glass through the gym. My arm stung, and I shifted the duffel to the other side as Avery opened the storage room door. Once we were inside, she closed the door, and I flicked on the flashlight from my pocket.

"Are you okay?" I asked.

"You're bleeding!"

"Avery, are you okay?" I asked louder, shining the light toward her face.

"Yes," she answered.

I blanched. Behind her were shelves loaded with free

weights and equipment parts. "Oh, hell no!" Was this a fucking horror movie? We'd be slaughtered in here.

I jerked the door open and pulled Avery behind me, running for the locker rooms. They were internal. "We need to get to the locker room! The showers!" I yelled to be heard above the all-encompassing roar that I knew was about to slam into us.

We cleared the door and I slammed it shut, throwing the deadbolt. Avery rounded the corner to the showers just ahead of me and slipped, crashing to the ground. The roar was louder, if that was even possible.

"Avery!"

Please, God. She's so young. I'm so young. Grayson, I love him. He has to be okay. They have to be okay.

I dropped the duffel bag and reached for her, stepping over her to help her up.

"Sam! Look out!"

I covered her head with my arms as I looked behind me.

Oh. God. The lockers. They were—

CHAPTER TWENTY-EIGHT

GRAYSON

"Sam!" Her name tore from my throat as the phone went dead. I was already out of the front door, keys in hand. She didn't realize she'd answered the phone.

I'd heard everything.

The funnel cloud headed northeast. It had missed us by what I guessed was less than a mile. The wind almost blew me backward before I caught my balance, and then I raced toward my truck. It was still standing. Undamaged.

Thank you, God, for small miracles—what the fuck is that?

A huge piece of debris plummeted from the sky to the left of me, decimating the sports car two houses down. Holy shit. It was a car. On top of a car. Two cars.

Get a grip. Once I climbed into my truck and pulled out on to the bypass, I calmed, taking deep breaths. My phone hooked up to the wireless Bluetooth. "Call Sam."

It rang. And rang. And rang.

"Hi, you've reached Sam. Leave me a message, and I might call you back...if I like you. Bye!" *Beep!*

"I don't know if you'll get this, but I know you're at the gym. I heard it all. Everything. I'm on my way, Sam. I'm coming. I love you so damned much. Just hold on. You're tougher than this. You're a fucking squall, nothing is taking you down, so you hold on."

The longest fifteen minutes of my life passed as I made my way to the gym. I cut across half a dozen yards, and got out at one point to move a fallen tree with three other guys.

Fire trucks passed, sirens blaring.

The devastation was… *Damn.* There were no words. Roofs were ripped from houses, trees downed, people stood aimlessly in their yards, surveying what was left. I flipped the 4X4 switch and crept over the debris that lay scattered into the road, and then threw it into park when I reached the remains of the gym. There could be people under there. Sam could be in that mess.

The windows of the gym were all blown out, and the roof was gone. It was a bare-bones structure, only the support beams remaining intact. I saw more than one treadmill attached to the trees that surrounded the gym.

"Avery!" Maggie screamed behind me.

She'd parked her car behind the truck. "She's with Sam," I answered.

"Oh, thank God. Where are they?"

I shook my head at the pile of rubble in front of us. "They're in there. They made it to the locker room before it collapsed."

She bent over at the waist, gasping for breath.

"Wait here, Maggie." I wanted to comfort her, but I didn't have anything to give.

My eyes scanned the debris field as I climbed over it, making my way slowly to the gym. Water sprayed from somewhere in the corner. The showers. I picked my way over equipment, careful to watch where I put my hands.

She was here. She was alive. She had to be.

There was simply no other option.

I forced the terror further back in my mind. It would do her no good right now. My foot fell through a hole in the rubble, and I hissed as the wood scraped my shin. Oh yeah, that was bleeding. I pulled my leg free and wiped the blood away. Just a scrape.

Another couple minutes and I stood at the frame for the locker room. The handle twisted in my hand, but the door wouldn't budge. She must have used the deadbolt. Smart girl.

Using my hand, I dug through the wood and mangled metal until I got to the floor so I could open the door. I had to be able to get her out. "Sam! Avery!"

"Here!" the muffled sound came, and I nearly collapsed in relief.

"Avery, I'm coming! Is Sam okay?"

"I...I don't know. She's not moving, and there's blood. A lot of blood."

I had to get in there *now*. What could I use to break the window?

Where was it? The fucking window breaker tool she keeps? Where is it? The water was creeping in, and she still wasn't breathing.

I blinked and banished that memory. Sam wasn't Grace. Sam was stronger, tougher, less likely to take the shit fate handed out lying down. She was a fighter. She was alive, damn it.

I looked up to see rebar sticking out of the framed wall. Crouching low, I jumped, and grasped the metal in my hands. It protested, but held my weight as I pulled up and then swung my leg over the top of the wall. I landed in a shower, careful to absorb the impact.

"Avery? It's Grayson."

"Here!" The sound came from the left, so I walked that way and saw a stream of light shining from under a pile of concrete.

She's alive. Just dig. She's there.

I startled as my phone rang, then pulled it out of my pocket. Jagger.

"What?" I snapped.

"Are you okay? Jesus, this place is destroyed. Not the house. We're okay. Paisley, Josh, we're good. But Grayson...we can't reach Sam."

My throat closed as I started pulling the concrete cinder blocks from the top of the pile, wedging the phone between my ear and shoulder. "I know. I'm digging her out now."

"Fuck. Is she…"

"I don't know. It's bad. Jagger, I don't care if you have to get your fucking father on the phone, you need to get an ambulance here. We're at the gym. Please. Do this for me. Do this and I'll never ask you another thing. I'll fail the next test and give you the OML spot. I don't care, just help me." My fingers were already scraped and raw as I lifted brick after brick off the pile. Off the girls.

"I'll do my best to get an ambulance, but this town is blown to shit." He swallowed. "I love Sam like a sister, Grayson. We'll get someone there. I'm with Josh, and we're already at the intersection of Rucker Boulevard and Eighty-four. We'll be there in a couple minutes. Let me make some calls."

I hung up without waiting for him to finish. He needed to get a fucking ambulance here, not baby me. "Avery?"

"Yeah?" she asked in a shaky voice.

"I need you to tell me if you start feeling more pressure, okay? If I do anything that squeezes you?" I flipped another brick.

"Okay."

"What's on top of you? Is it hard? Heavy? I need an idea of what's pinning you."

She was quiet.

"Avery?" I pushed the bricks faster.

"Sam."

"What?" I paused.

"It's Sam. She's on top of me. She covered me when the lockers fell."

My eyes closed as pain tore through my chest, at war with the overwhelming pride I felt in her. "Of course she did," I said. "She loves you, Avery."

"I know." She squeaked the last part.

I dug and dug until I was joined by other hands. Josh and Jagger.

"Fuck. Grayson, look at your hands," Jagger said, pulling at my arms.

My fingers were raw, dripping blood. "I can't feel it. I don't care."

"Let us take over," he urged while Josh started pulling the support beams off and away from the pile.

"If it was Paisley?"

Fear lanced through his eyes, and he clamped down on my shoulder. "We're going to get her out."

We dug, soon joined by other people, some in uniforms, some not. Finally we reached the blue metal lockers. "She's directly under these," I said so they didn't fuck up and hurt her.

Six of them gripped the sides of the wall unit and then lifted slowly while I crouched next to the floor. As it rose, I saw her fingers dangling. "Stop! She's wedged in one of the lockers!" I couldn't pull Avery out, not without knowing if she had neck trauma. "Step three feet toward the showers."

The group did so, and I crawled under, then rolled until I was directly beneath where Sam hung in a macabre suspension, her eyes closed. *Don't think about it. Don't you dare.* Her arm was twisted in an unnatural angle that sent saliva into my mouth. *Livable.* The other had a gash that was steadily dripping blood, but not pulsing. *Cosmetic.* It was the blood that ran in a steady stream from her hairline, down her cheek, and dripped off her chin that worried me.

I carefully dislodged her hips from where they held her pinned, and then worked her shoulders out one by one. I was slow, exceptionally careful not to jar anything that could break her spine. If it wasn't already broken. *Shut the fuck up.* There was never a complaint from the crew that held up the heavy locker system.

Freeing the last inch of her shoulder, she dropped the twelve inches to me, landing heavily on my chest. "She's free!" Slowly I lifted my hands to test her pulse.

Steady. Strong. *Thank you, God.*

Her nose lay in the hollow of my throat, her forehead resting under my chin. I felt every breath she released, and kept rhythm with my own breathing, like I could do the work for her. Slowly the lockers moved until all I saw above me was blue sky.

The storm was already gone.

"Is she okay?" Avery asked, lying next to me.

"Don't move. There are paramedics ready to take you, but don't move in case you injured your back or your neck."

"Is she okay?" she repeated.

"I don't know. Did she wake up at all while you were under there?" *Please.*

"No."

My eyes squeezed shut against the panic that crept up my spine, infecting every nerve with the need to fight, to do something. Anything.

The paramedics came for Sam first, laying the backboard on top of her and then maneuvering the straps between our bodies until she was tight. They kept asking if I was okay. Was I hurt? Was I uncomfortable?

What did any of it matter?

She wasn't awake.

She was warm but lifeless. Nothing would wake her, nothing would bring her back. I pushed her long blonde hair out of her eyes and prayed. We'd made it out of the car, the water, but this I couldn't pull her out of. I was powerless.

Fuck. Sam wasn't Grace. I couldn't compare the two, but that was all my brain wanted to do.

I followed the paramedics out, passing Maggie, who was being held back by a first responder. "Avery's okay," I told her.

They lifted Sam into the ambulance, and I climbed in

with her. "Sir…"

"Where she goes, I go."

I stared him down until he nodded his head and let me in.

"I heard somewhere that this helps with the nausea," Jagger said as he handed me a ginger ale and sank into the empty waiting room chair next to me.

"Yeah, and what asshole told you that?" I took it and popped the top. The taste put me back in another hospital. Another waiting room where I'd sat alone, waiting for news. Waiting for them to release Owen from the small line of fucking stitches he'd needed, to give me news on Grace.

"This guy who'd lived through a hell of a lot more than I had and somehow came out the other side." He leaned back against the waiting room chair. "I called Ember. She's on a flight with Sam's mom. Josh is headed to Montgomery to pick them up."

"Good. That's good." I braced my elbows on my knees and leaned over, trying to force air into my lungs.

"You need to get your hands checked out."

"Yeah." At some point. Right now? Not high on my priority list.

I fucking hated hospitals, and yet here I was again. This time was a little different. The waiting room at Southeast Medical Center was full. All the hospitals were, with Enterprise out of commission. The wounded poured in, and the families did all they could…waited.

The other waiting room in Nags Head had been nearly empty except for the family who told me I wasn't to blame, but the looks they'd given me sure as hell said differently. Especially Parker, once she'd shown up, hissing at me that I should have taken his keys, should have never let him drive.

Yeah, the waiting room was different, but everything else

felt very much the same, right down to the unparalleled fear rushing through my veins.

I should have been with Sam. I never should have let Grace sit on my lap, no matter how harmless it seemed at the time, never let her kiss me. I should have told Sam sooner, made her see how much I loved her. If she'd known, she wouldn't have moved in with Morgan. She would have been with me.

She wouldn't have ended up under a pile of rubble.

"She's going to be okay, Grayson. I've never met anyone with as much grit as Sam. She's a fighter, she'll be okay."

My spine snapped straight and my eyes narrowed at him. "You don't know that."

"She's—"

"She's been through a tornado, crushed, and hasn't woken up in the four hours that we've been here. Her pupils were uneven and dilated. You. Don't. Know. Anything." My shoulders sagged. "None of us do."

"You're right, I don't. I know that you've been through hell already, and lost one woman that you love, only to have her come back while you lose the other. Emotionally, of course. Fuck, I didn't mean like...*lose her*, lose her. I don't know what to say." He raked his hands over his Red Sox hat, curving the bill. "To be honest, you're usually the one who says...the thing."

"The thing?"

Jagger shrugged. "You know. *The thing.* You always know what to say. I don't, and I really wish I did. Especially now."

I watched another doctor come in to talk to a different family. "Yeah, well, that's probably because there's nothing to say. Not this time."

Because this may have seemed a lot like a repeat of what happened five years ago, but this was so much worse. This was Samantha. My Samantha.

Jagger slowly nodded. "Okay. Then how about I just sit

here with you?"

But this time I wasn't alone.

"Yeah. That'd be good."

Her arm was fractured in three places. One broken rib. One laceration on her arm. One dislocated shoulder. Multiple contusions. A definite concussion.

"And you are her next of kin?" the doctor asked us three hours later as we stood outside the ICU.

"Yes," Jagger answered. "I have her medical power of attorney."

"You what?" I snapped, not caring that the doctor flinched.

"Sam has a lot of foresight, Grayson. She had it done before she ever agreed to move down here. Well, her mother did. With deployments and no grandparents, we're the only family she has, at least until her mom gets here," he said to the doctor.

Inexplicable rage festered in my chest. If anyone was going to make decisions about Sam's health, it was going to be me. Period.

"She has a concussion, and we're monitoring for any swelling in her brain. We've started a course of drugs to help, and we're oxygenating her. Right now she's responding well."

"And if her brain swells?" I asked, trying not to panic.

"If that happens, we'll have a couple options. First, we can do surgery to help remove the pressure, or we can put her into a medically-induced coma to let her brain rest, or shut down if you will."

"No!" My voice echoed down the hallway. I grabbed Jagger's arm. "I don't care if you're one of my best friends. You put her in a fucking coma and I'll put you in a grave."

I wasn't letting Sam go where I couldn't follow her.

Jagger's hand covered mine with a pat. "Okay." He turned

back to the doctor.

"We're nowhere near that yet," the doctor interjected.

"When will we know how it's going?"

He looked sideways at me but answered. "We're continuously monitoring her, but she looks promising."

"When can we see her?" I asked. I needed to feel her warmth, her pulse.

"Once we have her stabilized." He excused himself and went back through the glass doors that separated me from her.

I took two steps back, bumped into the wall, and slid down it until I hit the ground with my arms on my raised knees.

"I need to check on Paisley, man. You okay for a minute?"

I nodded. "And Avery. Check Avery."

"You got it." Jagger left.

My phone rang and I answered with a mumbled, "Hello?"

"Are you okay?" Grace asked.

I stumbled through the story, glad to have her voice of reason with me.

"You don't deserve this," she said after I'd finished.

"Karma? Sure, I do. What I did to you—"

"Stop. Gray, you weren't to blame for that. Owen was. If anyone on the planet should be able to absolve you of that guilt, it's me."

My head landed against the wall. "Sam is the one who didn't deserve this. You were an innocent party. Wrong place, wrong time. But Sam? She was there to help Avery. She literally ran toward a damn tornado."

"She's brave," Grace said softly.

"Yes. And funny, and complicated, and sexy, and smart. But, God, it's that heart of hers I don't think I can live without. I don't know what life looks like without her in it. I keep thinking back to when it was you in there, while we were waiting to hear about your brain function."

"How does this compare?" she asked.

"Honestly?"

"Of course. You might not be my boyfriend, but you're still my best friend. I know that might not be the same for you, that you've adapted to life without me, but I want to be here for you. So yes, honestly."

I swallowed and let myself feel it for a second, the all-encompassing fear that threatened to kill my ability to think, to breathe. To imagine Sam lying there the way Grace had. Or worse, burying her. "It doesn't compare."

"I'm so sorry I did that to you," she said softly.

"No, I mean, this is a million times worse. I loved you. I thought you were my future, if not as my eventual partner, then always my best friend. But Sam? She's this wrecking ball who tears down my defenses and makes me feel, forces me to live. My need for her is about the same as my need for oxygen."

"I'm so sorry this is happening to you, to Sam. She's truly remarkable, Grayson." Her tone was honest, without sarcasm or malice, as she always had been.

"She is." And I'd been a damn fool not to show up on her doorstep every morning for the last few weeks and demand she come home, back to me. A bigger fool for not requesting Colorado when I knew that was what she wanted. The greatest fool for letting Dad's ultimatum rule my future.

I hung up with her as Jagger appeared, thrusting a cup of coffee into my hands. "It's two a.m. It's either time for sleep or caffeine."

I took the cup and a sip, wishing it burned more, hurt more, made me feel something.

"Holy shit, is that Vivica Fox?" Jagger asked, his eyes wide as he stared down the hall.

I leaned forward to see a beautiful, no-nonsense woman strutting down the hallway, Ember, Josh, and Paisley all struggling to keep up with her. The way she held her head high reminded me all too much of someone else. "That's Sam's mom. Has to be."

She walked up to me, dropped to my level, eyed the blood covering my shirt, and took my hands. "You're Grayson." Her eyes, the same color as Sam's, locked onto mine.

"Yes, ma'am." I steeled myself for the attack, the blame I knew I should shoulder.

Instead, she cupped my cheek and pressed her lips together, her eyes shiny with tears. "She loves you."

"I love her."

She nodded. "Thank you. If you hadn't gone after her, dug her out, I think this conversation would be under much different circumstances." She squeezed my hands and then stood, entering the ICU with quick, sure steps.

"How was the drive?" Jagger asked Josh.

"Good, but the weather is going to turn to shit. A new front is pushing this way, and they're calling for another outbreak of tornados tomorrow."

"Shit," Jagger muttered, and kissed Paisley's head.

They all took seats next to me, lining the hall outside the ICU. "You know there's a waiting room," I said.

"We're good," Josh replied.

An eternity later, Colonel Fitzgerald walked out, her face stern. I jumped to my feet. "Well?"

"Her shoulder's been put back in. They're waiting for the swelling to go down in her arm before they reset the bones. Her laceration has been stitched."

"Her brain?" I asked, and held my breath.

She took a deep breath. "They've kept the swelling down. We won't be able to tell the damage until she's conscious."

Where have I heard that one before?

"Can I see her?"

She shook her head. "Not yet. They barely let me in."

I cursed as my cell phone rang. I'd forgotten I even had it in my back pocket. "Hello?" I asked.

"Lieutenant Masters?"

Fuck. A two a.m. phone call that started like that couldn't be good.

"I am," I answered.

"This is Major Davidson. I'm sorry to call you so late, but we have an emergency." His voice was clipped.

"Yes, sir?" If one of the guys in our class had gotten a DUI, I would kick his ass.

"We have another weather front pushing in, calling for tornadoes. We were lucky to suffer no damage to the aircraft during this tragedy, but we need to evac them all."

"Yes, sir." My stomach clenched.

"We've exhausted most of our experienced pilots today and don't have enough instructor pilots to move out all the aircraft. I asked the instructors for their best pilots, and your name came up."

"Yes, sir," I repeated.

"You're leaving at first light, which is in about five hours, so I suggest you get some sleep. You'll be front-seating Mr. Stewmon, your usual instructor. Risk assessment has been completed, and we're good to go. We need to move these aircraft out. Oh, and I'll need Bateman, too."

I couldn't leave. Not now. Not with Sam in the ICU.

"Sir, I'm at the hospital right now. My girlfriend"—*ex-girlfriend*, my brain clarified—"was injured today, and they're monitoring her. I more than respect and appreciate the offer, but maybe there's another pilot better qualified?"

"I'm sorry to hear that, Lieutenant Masters. She's not your wife?" he asked.

"No, sir." *Not yet.*

"Then I'm sorry to say that that wasn't an offer, that was an order. We need you. I expect you at Cairns by seven a.m. Get some rest." He hung up before I could even argue.

"What's up?" Jagger asked.

"We've been ordered to report to Cairns by seven a.m. They need the 64s moved out to the evacuation zone for the new storms coming in."

"Damn, they're letting you two fly long-distance? I'm impressed," Josh added.

This was one instance where I was anything but thrilled to be at the top of my class, or hell, in the army. I turned to Sam's mom. "I tried to get out of it. I don't want to leave her, but we have to go."

Sam wasn't my wife. She had no legal standing or claim to me in the eyes of the army, which meant I didn't qualify for any special consideration to stay by her side. And I'd signed a goddamned contract where I'd basically traded my autonomy for a commission in the United States Army. It was go, or be charged absent without leave.

She threw her hands up. "Not my chain of command. I can't do anything to help you with that. Orders are orders. But maybe I can help you here. Follow me."

The door swished open and we walked into the ICU. The nurse at the desk cocked her head to the side. "Can I help you?"

"This young man has just been called away on military duty. He needs to see his fiancée before he goes." She saw my wide eyes and whispered, "You do intend to marry my daughter, do you not?"

Hell yes, I do. "Absolutely."

"He didn't mention that they were engaged before." The nurse looked up at me skeptically.

"It's so new that they both haven't really had time to process it." Colonel Fitzgerald smiled, and I stood stock-still, knowing better than to try to lie.

I sucked at lying.

The nurse looked up at the clock and then sighed. "Fine, but you have to be quick."

I didn't need to be told twice, I'd already memorized her

room number from the white board behind the nurse's station.

"I'll be outside," Colonel Fitzgerald said as I opened the door.

"Thank you, ma'am. For everything."

The steady beeping of the monitor greeted me as I pushed back the curtain that shielded Sam from the door. Her left arm was in a sling, she was attached to an IV, and obscene monitors attached to her head at equidistant intervals.

I pulled the chair closer to her bed and sat, taking her right hand in mine and pressing a kiss to her palm.

"I love you. I have to leave for a few days, but I'll be back once this storm cell passes. Then you'll be awake, and we can figure out what the hell we're going to do, because if this has taught me anything, it's that I can't exist without you. You broke down every defense and made me feel, so you'd better be around to help me figure out what to do with all these feelings. We have to find a way, Samantha. We just do."

I sat with her, watching her chest rise and fall with each breath. She would wake up. She was stronger than Grace, and if I repeated that to myself enough, I could get through this. She was going to wake up.

"Hey." Colonel Fitzgerald lightly shook my shoulder, and my eyes snapped open. "It's two thirty. You fell asleep. Probably a sign that you need to get some rest before you fly."

My thumb stroked across the smooth skin of the back of Sam's hand. "I don't want to leave her."

A soft, sorrowful smile came over her mom's face. "I never want to. It's the hardest part of my job, leaving her, especially when she doesn't have anyone else, really. But if there's anyone who understands duty and military orders, it's Sam. This is the only life she's ever known, Grayson. She was brought up in it, and something tells me she'll marry into it. She'll understand."

"She shouldn't have to. I should be here. We haven't spoken..." My throat closed.

"I know. She told me. You two are the right people at the wrong time. Odds are stacked against you, I logically know that, and with that math-freakish brain of hers, so does Sam. But she's never been one to back down from a challenge or to take the easy route."

"She must get that from her mother."

She laughed. "Stop sucking up and get out of here. I'll stay with Sam. She won't be alone."

With every cell in my body protesting, screaming to stay by her side, I leaned over Sam's bed and brushed my lips against her cheek. "I love you, Samantha. Fight like hell. I'll be home soon. Please forgive me."

I physically walked out of the door, but my heart stayed in that bed.

CHAPTER TWENTY-NINE

Everything hurt.

I pried my eyes open, and the world came into focus. I was in a hospital. Where? Why? The tornado.

I moved my head slowly and saw Mom sitting in a chair, reading on her tablet. "Mom," I croaked.

Her eyes flew wide, and she smiled just as big, dropping the tablet to the bedside table and pressing the nurse call button. "Hey, Sam. Relax. You've had a rough day."

"Water?" My mouth tasted like a fuzzy animal had died in there. Where was Grayson? Was he okay? Was the house hit?

She lifted the clear cup to my lips, and I took a few swallows. "Better. Thank you."

"What do you remember?" she asked.

My face scrunched. "We made it to the locker room, and then the wall came down. I think. Oh God, how's Avery?"

"She's fine, only broke her pinky finger, and she's been sitting in the waiting room all morning. You did a damn fine job of protecting her, and I'm incredibly proud of you." She sat on the edge of my bed.

"Good. I'm glad she's okay. What day is it?"

"Tuesday. You were only out overnight. They were worried about brain swelling, and you have a beautiful concussion."

"And the sling?" I tried to move my arm and gasped at the

pain that coursed through me. "Fuck that hurts."

She quirked an eyebrow but didn't chastise me for my language. "Don't move it. You fractured it in three places and dislocated your shoulder. They'll remove the splint and cast it later today now that the swelling has gone down."

I dragged my tongue across my incredibly dry lips. "Grayson?" I asked softly.

"That boy loves you, Samantha." She squeezed my hand.

"Where is he? Is he okay?" I should have answered the phone when he called, if only to hear his voice.

"He's fine, other than some very pulverized fingers." At my face, she smiled. "He's the one who found you, who dug you out. You're very lucky. Turns out he was on the phone. You must have inadvertently answered it. He heard you say 'locker room,' so he knew where to dig. The gym is a total loss. A few square blocks of the town is actually. They called it an EF-3."

He'd come for me. Found me. "Where is he?"

Her face fell. "You know the military. The best and brightest get hit the hardest. They needed spare pilots to evac the aircraft. He was ordered to go. I swear to you, that boy was broken up over it. He did not want to leave you."

I nodded and swallowed back my twinge of resentment. "Duty and country, right, Mom? I mean, I shouldn't be surprised. I've always known he's army, but it's easy to forget when you're at a training base. Of course he went."

"Sam." She reached, and I moved my head.

"No. It's better this way. He's graduating in two-and-a-half months and moving to North Carolina. Nothing has changed."

"You still love him," she urged. "Maybe this is something worth exploring, even with the Grace mess."

"I can't be the other woman, Mom. Not again." The pain in my heart was ten times worse than my body, but that morphine drip they had me on wasn't going to touch it. "Not like..." I couldn't finish.

"Not like I was? I know how that feels, more than anyone. I have a life of regrets, Samantha, that I chose the wrong path, that I fell in love with the one person I couldn't ever have. But the one thing in this world I don't regret is you. You are the love of my life, my baby girl. And I can't stand to see you hurting."

"Then support me in this. I don't want to see him. I can't. You needed a clean break when we moved that first time, and I need one now. Give me that."

"I saw his face, watched him kiss you good-bye. That boy needs you."

"No. He just thinks he does. I was his crutch, Mom. I woke him up, and got him through. I love him. God, I love everything about him. And he waited five years for her, with that damned honor he has. If I asked him to sacrifice that for me, he wouldn't be the same, and I can't do that to him. I'm not blind, I know he loves me, but she's..." I struggled for the words. "They call each other Port and Starboard. They're two halves of the same whole. And she's...Mom, she's amazing. Kind, and beautiful, and so damn nice. I can't even hate her, I like her too much. She's a fucking unicorn, and Grayson deserves that kind of perfection. I'm not exactly up to that standard."

The doctor cut off any reply she could have made, introducing herself and then checking me over. "I think you're ready to get that cast, now."

Broken bones. Broken heart. Yeah. It was time to get everything set so I could heal.

"I'm just glad you're okay. Is your brain...you know...normal?" Avery asked, sitting next to my bed a few hours later.

"Yeah. A concussion, but the swelling is already down. Plus, my cast is pink. Who doesn't like that?"

She smiled. "I'm so sorry."

"Hey." I took her hand. "This was not your fault, and I would do it all again."

She shook her head. "I didn't think the weather was going to get that bad, I swear. Even when she called to tell us to close the gym, you know? She keeps apologizing for not being there."

"This isn't her fault, either. She had a manager on duty, and she didn't know you were going there until you'd already been left."

"Yeah. I just really wanted to show you what I found, and instead I showed you the inside of a locker." She looked away.

"Well, in your defense, I didn't actually see the inside of the locker. I woke up here." I lifted my good arm and smiled.

She laughed. *Mission accomplished.*

"Okay, tell me what you found out."

"Really?" She grimaced. "Right now? While you're here?"

"I can't think of a better time, or a more needed distraction. Plus, this room has been a revolving door of visitors. You staying with me a little longer gives me a reason to avoid the other stalkers."

"Okay." Her eyes lit up as her techno-speak kicked in. I caught a word here and there, but for the most part she lost me.

"Bottom line?"

"Oh, right. Okay, so bottom line is that your cyber bully is actually pretty lazy. She started one of the original accounts from her work email at the University of Colorado at Colorado Springs."

"Wait. She?" It wasn't Harrison?

"She is most definitely a she." Avery pulled a piece of paper from her back pocket. "Michelle Proctor."

Oh my God. Of course. His whole damn family worked for the CU system. "She works in the registrar's office," I whispered as everything fell into place.

"Yeah! How did you know?" She handed me the paper.

"Because I hurt her very badly without even knowing it."

The paper felt soft in my hands. Frail.

"Hurting someone doesn't excuse what she's been doing to you. Nothing does. You need to call the University and tell them. You need to stop her."

"Maybe I deserve it."

Avery's eyes narrowed. "Okay, now that's bullshit. You have to do something, Sam."

I shook my head. "You don't know what you're asking me to do. I'd have to go back to Colorado—"

"Which you've wanted to do anyway," she interrupted.

"Right, but not like this. I'd have to face a disciplinary hearing, and everyone would know the thing I'm most ashamed of. Could you imagine that? Walking into your school and telling them the most embarrassing thing you've ever done?"

"You mean like handing the hottest football player in school a pencil that asked him to homecoming?" She arched an eyebrow.

"This is different. This is putting my most private shame on a public stage."

"Which has got to suck. I'm not saying it doesn't. But what about the others?"

My chest tightened. "What others?"

"There's at least five other email addresses that she's sent similar emails to. I bet she's done the same thing to their transcripts, too. And I also bet that they don't have the slightest clue she's the one doing it. If you won't stand up to this girl for yourself, then stand up for them."

Other girls? I wasn't the first. "When was the last email sent?"

"She started attacking another girl about two months ago."

I wasn't the last, either.

"I'm just saying that I know this girl, and she's amazing. A great tutor, and an even better friend. She ran into a tornado to save me. A tornado! If she could do that, she could do this.

Maybe you should ask her." Her eyes bored into me in an open challenge.

Five other girls were going through the same thing I was. Five girls who couldn't get into colleges, or move on with their lives. Five girls who had their futures stolen all because they made the same mistake and slept with the wrong man.

I had to go back to Colorado.

"Do you mind if I say hello?" Grace asked from the doorway. "W-what are you doing here?" I asked, then shook my head. "I'm sorry, that was incredibly rude. I blame the pain meds."

She gave me a soft smile and then claimed the chair next to my bed. "We were driving to Texas for testing, and Gray asked if I would swing by and check on you."

"You went hundreds of miles out of your way?"

"He's my best friend, no matter what's happened, and the woman he loves won't take his phone calls. So yeah, that's worth a few hours to me. And I wanted a moment with you that wasn't an awkward phone call."

"So awkward drop-in visits are better?"

"Jury's still out," she said with a laugh. "So, you're feeling better?"

"It's been a few days, and I'm out of ICU. No brain swelling, so they think I might be able to go home tomorrow."

The phone in my room rang, and I ignored it. "Did you want me to get that?" Grace asked.

"No."

"Oh, okay." We sat in silence until it stopped ringing.

"So Texas?" I asked, trying to move conversation along.

She nodded. "Yeah, they need to poke me like a lab rat."

"You are the miracle," I said with a smile. Maybe it was a

little forced.

"Not really." Her smile fell. "The treatment made it possible for me to wake up, that's true...but..."

"But you were always aware," I finished.

Her eyes snapped to mine. "Yes. How did you know?"

"You told Morgan that *One Tree Hill* had been played out and the last season ruined it."

She blinked at me.

"The last season of that show came out while you were in your coma. Mia had them play it for you after she read about that guy who'd woken up after a twenty-year coma or something, and he'd been forced to watch *Barney*."

"Oh. No cartoons, those were awful."

"How long were you aware for?" I asked.

"I'm not sure. It was gradual, and time started to jump a lot. I think about two years in, maybe? I was trapped in my own body. When Gray came, begging me to wake up, it was the worst. I loved his visits and I dreaded them because I couldn't talk to him, or help him with what he was going through."

"Losing you was hell for him."

A nurse knocked on the door. "Ms. Fitzgerald? There's a Grayson Masters on the phone for you."

I swallowed and avoided Grace's eyes. *Awkward.* "Could you tell him that I'm sleeping?"

"Sure thing," she said, and left.

"He's freaking out. Maybe you could call him?"

I shook my head. "No. I need a clean break. He's better off with you, no matter what he's thinking right now. You're his miracle. His Grace. If I see him, talk to him...I just can't."

"You love him."

"Deeply," I answered, and then studied my blanket. "This has got to be the most awkward conversation ever."

She laughed. "No. Try having constant one-sided conversations for years, and then we can chat awkwardness."

"True. Wait. If you were aware all that time, you met me. You knew about us, and you still kissed him." I took my hand back.

She swallowed and looked away for a moment. "Yes. People do things they're not proud of when they're scared. I woke up and everything was different. The whole world had moved on while I'd stayed stagnant. Gray was the one stable thing I'd always had. I should never have kissed him, or even come to Alabama. It wasn't fair to you, or him, and I am truly sorry. I hope you can forgive me." Her voice faded to a whisper.

"Grace, he belongs with you. I'm doing everything I can to walk away from him for his own good, and for yours. Please don't make it harder for me."

"Well, I'm trying to do the same. Especially now. He's changed so much. He's harder, more distant, not as quick to laugh. He didn't used to be like that. Oh, and he used to love raspberries! I put them on his cheesecake at dinner with my folks after the beach, and he didn't even eat them."

"The seeds get stuck in his teeth," I explained.

She nodded. "Right. What I'm saying is that I'm the same Grace, for the most part, but he's not the same Gray. And as much as I love him, as my best friend, I don't think we'll ever be more. I want him to be happy, and that goes for you, too."

"There's too much history between you. You have nicknames for each other, and you know him on a level I never can." And that hurt more than anything, knowing there were pieces of Grayson I'd never have when he owned every inch of me.

"He calls you 'squall,' you just don't know it," she said.

"What?"

"Squall. Like a sudden storm that comes out of nowhere, shakes up the ocean, overturns everything. You did that to him. You were the only thing to pull him out of himself and get him to live, and I watched that transformation from the first time he told me about you a couple weeks after you met."

He was a storm in my life, too.

"I have to go back to Colorado. There are things I have to do there...on my own. The odds are stacked too high against us. He made up his mind and chose North Carolina."

"Then make him change it." The ferocity in her voice brought my eyes to hers.

"Would you? Force him to choose between love and his family? Or make him wait while I get the rest of my life sorted out? He waited five years for you to wake up. I can't ask him for that."

"I would choose love."

How simple she made it seem, instead of the shaky Jenga tower we'd built ourselves, pulling the blocks out one by one until we crumbled.

"Yeah, well, I choose Grayson's happiness, and the two don't go hand-in-hand at the moment."

There was no answer.

CHAPTER THIRTY

GRAYSON

"Where the hell is she?"

Morgan flinched in her doorway. "I told you. Yesterday the movers arrived and took her stuff. I don't know where."

I was ready to rip my fucking hair out. "No forwarding address? Nothing?"

Morgan shook her head. "No. Nothing. I'm so sorry, Grayson."

"Yeah. Me, too." I made it back to my truck in a daze and climbed behind the wheel. A week. I'd been gone a week, and in that time she'd checked out of the hospital, cancelled her cell phone, and moved out of her apartment.

How the hell was I supposed to find her when she didn't want me to?

My phone rang, and I hit the button on the wheel to answer it. "Hey, Mom."

"Grayson."

"Oh, hey, Dad. Sorry, I saw the number and assumed Mom."

"No, she's out shopping. I wanted to call and tell you that she told me about your long-distance flight."

"Oh, yeah? It was crap timing, but I did really well." *Hint being—get off my ass.*

"It was foolish."

"I had orders." Like he was ever going to understand. We

could go rounds and rounds, and we'd still end up at the same place.

"I waited for you to see the light, son. To be safe."

"Yeah, well I'm a chronic disappointment there, Dad."

"I need you to know that I love you. That everything I've done is out of a place of love, and needing to protect you."

"Dad, I'm twenty-three years old. I don't need you to protect me."

"Yeah. You do. God, I love you, Gray."

"I love you, too, Dad."

He hung up, and I blinked. Was he apologizing for being such a dick while I was home? Probably not. It wasn't in his nature, and he wasn't exactly approving.

Thirty-seconds and two blocks later, my phone rang again.

"Lieutenant Masters?"

"Major Davidson?" *Please don't send me anywhere else. I have to see Sam.*

"Son, I'm going to need you to come in and see me."

My chest clenched. "Okay, sir. When do you need me?"

"Right now. I know you just landed a couple of hours ago, but I need you to come to my office."

"Yes, sir. I can be there in ten minutes." There was an audible *click*. Good thing I hadn't changed out of uniform.

Had I fucked up something on the flight?

I went through every detail of the flight as I pulled onto post, trying to find where I could have made an error. I'd had Mr. Stewmon with me, who would have blasted me if I had, that was for sure.

I parked next to Jagger's Defender and headed inside. At least none of us had moved a thousand-pound polar bear in the last week. I couldn't shake the sense of foreboding, like what waited was a hell of a lot worse.

Jagger sat in the hallway with Mr. Stewmon on his left.

"Any clue what this is about?" Jagger asked.

"Not unless I made a mistake during the flight?" I looked to Mr. Stewmon, who shook his head.

"Lieutenant Masters," Major Davidson called from his office.

"Sir," I said, stepping inside. It had been a year since I'd been here last, and he still hadn't decorated.

"Have a seat."

I did so, but didn't lean back. He tapped his fingers on his desk, thumbing through a file. My medical records. *Shit.*

"I received a call today that made some very serious allegations about your health history, Lieutenant Masters. Allegations that, if true, would end your place in the flight school program."

My fucking father. "Sir?"

"Are you dyslexic?"

Funny thing about ripping off a Band-Aid—it still hurts like hell. "Not that I'm aware of, sir."

He sighed. "That's what he said you'd say."

"My father." The words tasted sour.

"Your father." He nodded. "Would you care to explain?"

"I can't explain what there's no factual base for, sir. I have not now, nor ever been diagnosed as a dyslexic. I was slow to learn to read in school, yes, but by high school graduated in the top two percent of my class, as well as at the Citadel. Neither location found a reason to believe I would be dyslexic."

"Why would your father say this?"

"Because he thinks I'll kill someone while flying." *Be brutally honest, it's the only way they know you're not lying.* "The night of my eighteenth birthday party, I was involved in a car accident where the other party was drunk. I didn't react fast enough. My girlfriend spent five years comatose. My father believes it was my fault. He's never accepted my decision to become a pilot."

Major Davidson nodded slowly. "Can you prove that you're

not dyslexic?"

"Sir, can you prove that I am? I take tests slowly, yes. I read slowly, yes. But take a look at the Order of Merit list for Primary, where I finished in the number one position, and the Apache course, and I can guarantee I'm in the top five percent. Five percent because I'm in the class with the walking 5&9 book of Jagger Bateman."

"True."

"Sir, there is no record of any concern of dyslexia. Not since I began my education, or before. These accusations are unfounded."

He studied me, and I stared back, unflinching.

"Send in Mr. Stewmon as well as Lieutenant Bateman, and wait in the hallway."

"Yes, sir." I gripped my cover so hard I thought I might rip it, and walked into the hallway. "He'd like to see you both."

"Everything okay?" Jagger asked me.

"Family is a bitch."

He clapped me on the shoulder and looked me straight in the eyes. "Until you find your own, right?"

"Right."

He nodded and then went into the office, shutting the door behind him. I'd take a polar bear over this shit any day. At least I'd done it, moved the fucking bear.

I tapped my foot while waiting, watching the minute hand pass fourteen times until the door opened. "Come on in," Mr. Stewmon said, holding the door for me.

I took the empty seat while he stood behind us. Major Davidson was on the phone in the corner with his back to us. More than likely ending my flight school career because my father couldn't trust me. Ever.

"Did you move Sgt. Ted E. Bear?" Jagger whispered.

"Not the fucking time."

"Oh, come on. Like you weren't thinking it."

"Since the moment I walked in."

Major Davidson hung up the phone and turned. "There's no record of the word 'dyslexia' appearing in your records from the Citadel or high school."

"Sir, I will say it again. I have never, in my life, been tested for, or diagnosed with dyslexia. I think my scores and grades speak for themselves."

"I concur," Mr. Stewmon agreed. "Lieutenant Masters shows exemplary knowledge base, as well as reflexes that make him a superior pilot. He has excellent spatial reasoning, communication, and judgment. I can count on one hand the number of times he's answered a question wrong, and I'll be the first to say that I ask a shitload of questions. Bateman is wrong more often than Masters."

My eyebrows shot up. Jagger shrugged in my peripheral vision.

Major Davidson looked between all three of us, settling on me. "Are you aware that dyslexia automatically disqualifies you from this program?"

"Yes, sir. As does poor vision, epilepsy, and being hard-headed, though they're still developing a test for that last one."

Now Jagger raised his eyebrows.

"Your attitude is far better suited to Lieutenant Bateman."

"He's rubbing off on me."

"Do you have dyslexia?"

Blunt honesty. "My doctor says no, and he's a hell of a lot better educated for making such a statement."

"If Lieutenant Masters were to have dyslexia, I'm comfortable saying that it has had zero impact on his ability to fly, or to not only maintain, but dominate academics as well as fulfill his duties as class leader," Mr. Stewmon finished.

"If he were to have it," Major Davidson added.

"Then he would in every way qualify for a waiver."

"If there were a condition to waive, which you're saying

there isn't." Major Davidson leaned across his desk.

"It's impossible to waiver something that's never been diagnosed or even suspected," Mr. Stewmon pushed back.

Major Davidson rubbed the skin between his eyes. "You two are killing me. You know that? Masters... You, Bateman, Walker, and Carter. You are my eternal damn headache."

I hovered, one foot on each side of the scales, waiting to see which way he was going to tip me.

"This matter is closed. You have given me no reason to think there's an issue, and we'll let this go. You're dismissed."

The air rushed out of my lungs. "Thank you, sir."

We filed out one by one, but before I could exit, Major Davidson stopped me. "Lieutenant Masters."

I turned slowly. "Sir."

"I have a great deal of respect for you, and even a dose of admiration for what you've accomplished." He held out his hand, and I shook it.

"Thank you, sir." I couldn't get out of there fast enough.

"Go ahead, Bateman, he'll catch up," Mr. Stewmon said as we walked toward the parking lot. Jagger gave me the sucks-to-be-you face, and basically ran.

"Thank you, Chief."

"My son has dyslexia. Did you know that?" he asked.

I swallowed. "No, sir."

"When he takes a test, he reads every question twice, taking a deep breath in between the reads." His eyes bored into mine.

I nodded.

He sighed. "What I'm saying, is that I knew the first day, from that first test. But I also knew that you graduated top of your Primary class, which meant you worked your ass off and didn't let it hold you back. If at any point I thought you were a danger to myself, or to your fellow officers, I would have turned you in myself. You have never given me a reason to, and I will always champion you. But, I knew. I know."

"Know what, Chief?" I asked, deadpan.

He slapped me on the shoulder. "Exactly."

"I think today deserves a beer," Jagger said, heading to the fridge.

"Get me one," I answered, which earned me two turned heads.

"Seriously?" Josh asked.

"I was accused of dyslexia by my father, nearly getting me kicked out of the program, the woman I love has disappeared, while the woman I used to love is catching up on the last five years of everything. Give. Me. A. Beer."

Jagger popped the top on a Fat Tire and handed it to me. I'd barely gotten it past my lips when there was a knock at the door.

"I'll get it," I said, heading for the door. My beer nearly dropped out of my hand when I saw who was behind it. "I thought you left."

Sam's gorgeous hazel-green eyes popped when she noticed the beer. "Is this a bad time?"

I shook my head. "I managed to not get kicked out of flight school for being dyslexic, so it seems like a pretty good time, I guess." The one-color vibe she had going with her black capri pants and halter top was broken up by the hot pink of the cast peeking out above her black sling. She still looked phenomenal.

"You're dyslexic?" Her eyebrows drew together in concern, not judgment, and I sagged a little with relief.

"Not according to the army."

"But you are." She shook her head. "It all makes perfect sense now. The studying, needing to know the answer to a question when only the first few words had been asked. Are the gauges dangerous for you?"

I shook my head. "I've never had a problem when flying, or

driving. Only written tests, and that's only when I'm overloaded."

"How did they find out?"

"My father called and voiced his concern."

Her mouth dropped open. I wanted to suck that bottom lip into my mouth, to close the unforgivable distance between us. "I can't believe he would do that. I mean, I know he doesn't want you flying, but to sabotage you like that?"

"He's sure my...difficulties caused the accident with Grace. Sure, he acknowledges that Owen may have had something to do with it, but if I'd been a better driver, I would have been able to avoid going over. Owen didn't exactly help and said he'd been way ahead of us when he entered our lane, instead of less than a couple car-lengths."

"It wasn't your fault."

"I'm beginning to leave room for that possibility."

She smiled, and my heart ceased functioning.

"I've missed you," I whispered.

Her smile faded.

"Are you going to invite her in, or just stand in the doorframe all night?" Jagger asked.

"Hi, Jagger. Thanks for not donating my brain to medical science while I was unconscious," Sam replied.

"Only because they didn't offer me enough money," he teased.

"Come on in," I offered, stepping back. "It's your home, too, you know."

She stepped inside but shook her head. "Not anymore."

What hope I had dwindled as I shut the door. Jagger and Josh were still leaned up against the kitchen counter. "Want to talk in my bedroom?" *Our bedroom.*

An awareness passed between us as she looked at me. "I think the couch is safer."

"Only to those with no imagination," I replied softly.

She closed her eyes. "Don't. This is hard enough already."

Shit. That wasn't the line of a woman who came to make up. "Let's sit."

She took the loveseat and I took the couch. "We're going to…" Josh started.

"Go somewhere a little less awkward than here," Jagger finished.

"Nice," Sam replied. They both came around the loveseat and took turns hugging her.

"You got the keys?" Jagger asked.

"I'm all set. Thank you again," she said with a soft smile. Was she moving back in after we moved post-graduation? Just waiting for me to leave?

"I keep it for a reason. I'm just glad it'll be of use. Text when you get there, and soak up that Colorado sunshine." He hugged her again and left us alone.

"You're leaving." My voice came out a hell of a lot mellower than I felt.

"So are you," she answered.

"Not for two more months. You're running away. From what? Me? Us?" I leaned forward to where our knees almost touched.

"It's actually the opposite. Harrison? My ex? Turns out I'm not the only student he slept with. I have an enemy in the registrar's office, and she's been altering my transcript every time I apply to a new school. Given the harassing emails she's sent me, my guess would be she's done the same to the other girls."

"Damn. Why didn't you tell me?"

She sagged. "Because I thought I deserved it? If getting into college with an assault on my discipline report is my penance, then fine. I deserve it. But when she started adding cheating, and plagiarism, and failing grades? That's where I draw the line. I shouldn't be held accountable for things I didn't do."

"You shouldn't have to suffer. Not for any of this."

"Well, that's where I set this right. I have to go back to Colorado. I have to help those other girls, and myself. I deserve a future. And so do they."

Pride swelled in my chest. She wouldn't fight for herself, but she'd don battle armor and face down her biggest fears if someone else was being bullied. "You deserve the best future." *With me.* "What about classes here?"

"With the damage to campus, they're allowing a full refund of tuition, but my English prof said I could finish by correspondence. There are good things about the age of Skype."

I grasped. "Like long-distance relationships?"

Sam avoided my eyes. "You chose North Carolina."

The weight of responsibility was getting so damn heavy. "My family is there. My dad's boatworks, my sisters, my mother. Parker is a damn mess, and I struck a deal with my dad that Joey could take over the shop as long as I did, too. I can't break that promise. She'd be devastated."

"I know." Her eyes met mine, and what I saw there threatened to cripple me. Love shone through, as tangible as anything I'd ever run my fingers through. Love, acceptance, and regret all in one soulful gaze. "One of the things I love about you is your loyalty, your sense of duty."

"It took me away from you after you'd been hurt."

"Yeah, it did. I'm not new to this lifestyle, Grayson. It's all I've ever known. Mom left a lot. I had babysitters, nannies, random friends that I lived with for a year or so during deployments. It wasn't until I met Ember that I had another family unit to latch on to. It sucked as a kid, but I never doubted that my mother was made of magical, incredible things to be able to dedicate herself like that to an ideal. I resented a lot about our life, but never her. And I didn't resent you when I woke up and you weren't there."

"I resented it."

She leaned forward and set her hand on my knee. "I know.

You have that same loyalty in you that my mom does. That same unwavering dedication. To the military, to your family. That's why I understand that you need to go back to North Carolina while you can, because you don't know where you'll be stationed next. I get it, and if I tried to change that about you, then you wouldn't be...you. I would never ask you to be someone you're not."

My hand covered hers, regret washing away every other emotion. "If I'd chosen Colorado?"

Her eyes widened. "But you didn't, and it's too late to change it now. Everything is in North Carolina for you. And now that Grace is awake..."

"She has nothing to do with this. I swear it to you. Yes, she's my best friend, and that's probably not going to change, but I am in love with you, Sam. Not Grace."

She shook her head slowly and blinked back tears. "She has everything to do with this, Grayson. She's in everything about you. You prayed for a miracle. I'm doing my best to give you that. Go back to North Carolina. See how things happen with Grace, or *if* they happen at all. I need to go back to Colorado and 'pull my shit together,' as this great guy once told me. We want different things." Her voice broke and took me with it.

I slid to my knees and reached for her, bringing her to the floor with me and into my arms. "There has to be another way. I don't accept this." She curled into me, sobs softly racking her tiny frame as I adjusted her on my lap, careful not to injure her broken arm or tear the stitches on the other one.

"I just want you to be happy," she whispered against my neck in between tears. Chills raced down my skin, and I held her a little tighter, but it didn't stop her body from shaking.

"I've never been as happy as I am with you."

"Me, either."

I drew back, cupping her face in my hands, memorizing each line, every flicker of emotion. "Tell me why we can't make this work. Because these excuses are all bullshit. Tell me why two adults who love each other can't find a way to be together. I fucking love you, Sam. I'm not willing to let that go."

I thumbed away another tear as it slipped down her face.

"I love you, too, so much that it hurts to breathe. Right now, here in Alabama, we're in a bubble of time. That bubble is popping, and you and I want two very different things. I want to graduate from the college I worked my ass off in. You want to be close to your family. I love you, but…but I'm choosing *me*."

"I understand."

"Do you?"

"I can't be mad at you for wanting the same thing that I did. I fought for the Citadel, and despite my parents being extremely upset with my choice to leave after the accident, I went. I chose me. I chose not to wither there as Grace wasted away. So yes, I understand."

She ran her fingers down my cheek. "I have to take accountability for my actions and face my demons, or I never will."

I kissed her, pressing our lips together in a soft promise that I understood. "I'm so damn proud of you. I just wish I could help you do it."

She laughed through her tears. "I think that would be cheating."

"Your mom told me, 'right people, wrong time,' when you were in the hospital. I was so scared you wouldn't wake up, that I'd be sitting next to your bed for the next five years."

"Grayson, I would never ask you to do that."

"But I would, and it wouldn't be out of guilt, like a lot of Grace was. It would be because there's no woman like you on this planet. No one else that can piss me off and make me laugh all in the same breath. No one else pushes me to the brink of every known emotion and then reels me back in the way you do."

"Right people. Wrong time," she repeated, this time kissing me, sucking on my lower lip gently.

"What about when it's the right time?" I asked.

"What?"

I nodded, more to myself than anything. *Yes. This can work.* "We aren't the fish and the bird, Sam. One day you'll finish college, and as soon as I can get Dad to let Joey take over without me, I'll be clear. You're my right person. My only person. I'll wait for you."

She lunged, kissing me like this was the last possible time she'd ever be able to. Our tongues met in a fury of open mouths and soft moans. God, I'd missed the taste of her. She ran her fingers through my hair, and I slanted my mouth over hers again and again, unwilling to stop, because I knew our bubble was popping.

Finally, she pulled back, gasping for breath. "I love you, Grayson. You spent five years waiting, and I won't ask you to do that for me. I won't let you." She pushed back, stumbling to her feet, and then ran out the door. The slamming sound echoed in my heart, shattering everything I'd held on to.

When I finally found the strength to stand, I made my way to the door, like she'd still be standing there. Instead, I found it, the ace of hearts, her last card, lying on the entry hall table.

"I'm incredibly selfish but foolishly selfless only when it comes to you. I won't let you put your life on pause for one more day. Not on account of me." The words were scrawled in permanent marker.

She'd written them before she came, because she knew what I would do, even when I didn't. I grasped my forgotten beer from the coffee table and downed the bottle. Five months with her, around her, and the girl knew me better than I knew myself.

But she couldn't stop me from waiting on her any more than she could stop me loving her.

There were some things even Samantha Fitzgerald couldn't boss around.

CHAPTER THIRTY-ONE

SAM

Six of us stared at each other as we sat around the coffee table, sipping steaming mochas at Montague's coffee shop in Colorado Springs.

We were all different in some respect. We were blond, brunette, even the lone redhead. We were tall, short, thin, curvy, heads of the class, and...not. Hell, the only thing we all had in common was that we'd all been played by Harrison Proctor.

Well, that and we were all being victimized for it.

"We're due to see the Dean in an hour. Are you all ready for this?" I asked, and laid my binder-clipped stack of emails on the table with my good arm. Two more weeks and this thing was off. "Everyone is going to know what we did."

Carrie, a wide-eyed brunette, put her emails next to mine. "He needs to pay."

There was some mumbled assent.

"No." I shook my head. "This isn't about Harrison. What he did to us was wrong, but come on, ladies. Did any of us not know that he was a professor? Were any of us led to think something else?"

They dropped their eyes as I looked around the table.

"This is about Michelle, and what *she*'s doing to us. If we go in there acting like some spoiled school girls bent on revenge because the guy we were screwing lied to us, we'll fail."

"What he did was wrong," the redhead, Lesley, added.

"Yeah, it was. But we were wrong, too. All of us. If we want our lives, our transcripts, our futures back, we're going to have to own up to that. Our dirty little secret is about to be exposed to everyone. If you're not okay with that, it's time to duck out. We're stronger together, but I'm not going to ask anyone to wade through their personal hell for me if they're not willing."

Thwack. Thwack. One by one, packages of emails landed on the table until all six of us had laid our nightmares bare.

An hour later, we stood outside the Dean of Student's office, all dressed in varying degrees of business attire. Okay, so maybe Lisa looked a little *Legally Blonde*, but I think we presented an adult and united front.

We weren't children to be taken advantage of.

His secretary, a darling silver-haired woman with cat-eye spectacles, assessed us as we waited by her desk. "And you're all here to see him?' she asked.

"We are."

"Okay, then," she answered with a sweet, tolerant smile and disappeared into Dean Miller's office.

"Last chance," I said softly, looking at the girls gathered around me.

They formed a line and stepped forward. When the time came, we walked into Dean Miller's office with shaking smiles and clutched papers. I took front and center while the girls fanned out behind me.

The Dean sat behind a large mahogany desk framed by a stunning view of the Front Range behind him. "Miss Fitzgerald, I didn't realize you'd be bringing an army with you," he said with a furrowed forehead.

"I'm sorry, Dean Miller, but I wasn't sure who would want to come forward when I made the appointment."

"When you made the appointment, I thought you'd want to discuss your assault on Professor Proctor last year." His eyes darted to the other five females. "Now I'm not so sure."

My face heated, and I took a huge breath. *Here we go.* "What I did was wrong, and I am willing to answer whatever disciplinary action you require of me in order to finish my degree here."

"I'm glad to hear that, Miss Fitzgerald." His smile was tight.

"However, that's not why we're here today." I stepped forward and placed my clipped collection of emails, my original report cards, and the newest transcript on his desk.

"What are these?" he asked as he started to thumb through.

"For the last ten months, I have tried to apply to other schools. I was too embarrassed to come back here after my behavior toward Professor Proctor. No matter what led up to it, I never should have struck him. However, what you have in front of you is evidence of the way I have been systematically bullied and harassed since last year. These include taunting emails as well as my transcript being altered by the registrar's office."

His eyebrows drew together as he scanned the pages.

I barreled ahead, needing the momentum to push me through. "If you flip through to the end, my technical investigator printed out the evidence that these email addresses are owned by a member of the UCCS staff in the registrar's office."

"Michelle?" He shook his head. "She's not the kind of woman who would do this, even for hitting Professor Proctor."

One of the girls placed her hand on my back, and it gave me the little boost I desperately needed. My stomach nearly rebelled, but the truth crept up my throat until I knew it would no longer stay there. "Not because I hit him, but *why* I hit him. It wasn't a bad grade."

"Okay?"

"I was sleeping with him."

He froze but showed no other outward emotion.

"I didn't know he was married. That's why I hit him. I'd just found his wedding ring. None of us knew." Why was my throat so dry? I couldn't move past the lump growing there.

Dean Miller looked at each girl in turn as they stepped forward to hand him their own packets of damning proof, laying a collegiate sex scandal on his desk.

"Michelle Proctor is bullying us because we all slept with her husband."

His hand shook a barely discernable fraction as he hit his intercom. Was he going to throw us out? Label us whores?

"Mary? I'm going to need you to cancel the rest of my day. Oh, and I'll need about four more chairs in here so these ladies can sit. Thank you."

My chin dropped to my chest, and my shoulders shook once, twice, before I sucked in a breath and got control of my overwhelming emotions. He was going to listen. And at that second, I wanted nothing more than Grayson waiting outside the doors to hold me, to tell me he was proud of me. But I'd said I needed to do this on my own, and I would.

The chairs were brought in by a couple older classmen I recognized, and by the looks on their faces, it was mutual. I raised my chin and smiled. *No more making assumptions about me.*

"Please have a seat, ladies," Dean Miller said once they'd left. He cleared his throat. "I assume you'd like to keep this investigation private and behind closed doors?"

"Oh no," Carrie said, gripping the arms of her chair next to me. "We'd like it out in the open."

"But given the delicate nature of the situation..." he urged.

"We've all spoken," I said, confirming with a few looks to the girls beside me, "and our pride and that of the University, which I assume you're trying to protect, isn't as important as identifying other potential victims. We want it out there, so if another girl is enduring the same hellhole we have been, she'll have the strength to come forward."

He sighed as he shuffled through our papers. "We still have

to follow some legal policies…involve the Title IX office. This isn't going to be easy for you girls."

I sat up a little straighter and thought of Grayson, his dyslexia, his determination to stand by Grace, even if in friendship only, and still maintaining that number one spot.

"Nothing that's right ever is."

CHAPTER THIRTY-TWO

GRAYSON

"Nothing like Thanksgiving dinner at the hospital," Grace said with a tired smile from her bed. "They promised this was the last round of testing, but at least they let me stay here for it."

"Actually"—I placed the plate Mom had made for her on the rolling table—"this would be the sixth Thanksgiving dinner I've brought to you while in a hospital bed, so I like to think of it as tradition."

"How about we not repeat it next year, or ever. I've had enough of hospitals for the next three lifetimes."

My eyes narrowed as I spotted my book on her dresser. "Is that my *Odyssey*?"

"Yeah. You left it after your last visit. I've been reading, I hope you don't mind."

When I came home after the tornado. Images flashed through my mind, laying under Sam, catching her limp body as I dislodged it from the lockers, praying I wasn't doing further damage. "No, go ahead."

"So..." She glanced sideways at me a few times, her telltale sign for working up the courage to say something unpleasant.

"Are you about to harp on me about Sam?" I asked. "It's been all of twenty-four hours since your last lecture."

She blinked. "No, actually, but while the subject is open..."

"Ugh." I leaned my head on the back of the chair. "Nothing's changed. She wants to finish school in Colorado, and see that all through."

"Go be with her," she urged.

"And if by some army miracle, I find a loophole and move out there? Not that one even exists, but let's say I do, and she still wants nothing to do with me? Keeps insisting that she's second choice? What then?" *I'd be crushed.*

"Take a chance. Call her, send a carrier pigeon, or use Morse code. I don't know, but do something besides mope. I lay here for five years, and life just kind of kept going, except for you. Sure, you went to college, joined the army, went to be all bad-boy pilot, but you still had one foot stuck here. I know it was because of me, and I'm cutting that tether. Go. Move. Live."

"It's not that easy." I closed my eyes, wishing it was.

"Why? I know you feel like you need to protect me, but you don't. Gray, I was aware of what was going on for most of the last three years of that coma."

My eyes jerked to hers. "You what?"

Her cheeks flushed crimson. "I didn't tell you because I didn't want you to feel guilty, or think about me being aware, trapped here."

"You were? How did—? How much do you remember?" An edge of desperation crept into my tone, and her smile was sad. *Shit.*

"A lot. Enough that I knew who Sam was when Mia left her in here. She talked to me, and I instantly knew she was it for you. I mean, I honestly knew the first, well, maybe the second time you talked about her."

"And before that?"

Her forehead puckered. "Umm. I think I remember right around your junior year at The Citadel? When that physics class was giving you a hard time?"

My eyes widened. "You do remember."

She nodded and tears welled in her eyes. "And that's not all. A couple weeks ago I started to remember everything...before."

The hairs on my neck tingled. "How much of before?"

"You mean, do I remember enough to know that we broke up before your birthday party? That we were fighting when we went off the bridge?"

The air was sucked from my chest. "Grace, I'm so sorry."

"Stop. Stop now. I have heard *enough*." Her hands slammed onto the table, and her plate jumped. "We broke up, Gray, for very good reasons."

"We wanted different things. Ironic, right? That's why Sam won't try."

"I wanted you to go out and discover your dreams, and maybe I wanted that for me, too. We'd been best friends since we could walk, and loved each other all through high school, and when I looked around, my entire life wasn't just built around you, it was built *on* you. I had no idea who I really was unless it was in relation to you. Breaking up was the right move to make, despite that love we felt. You and I both know it wasn't the kind of love we crave—the kind of love we both need."

"That's not true. I loved you."

"I know, but you staying here all these years? There was love, but there was way more guilt than you needed to bear. You were driving. We argued. Owen's truck came up on our left side. I remember...seeing him flip us off with a grin, his finger pressed up against the window, but you were too busy concentrating on the road. He cut us off, hit the guardrail. We... went over."

"Do you remember anything after?" I cringed. *Please don't.*

She stared off into space for a second. "No. We hit the water. Then I woke up here...and then they took me home, but I'd be back here pretty often. Knowing that despite your right to walk away, you never even told anyone we'd broken up."

"It seemed wrong. Like I'd be using your accident as some

kind of excuse, and I couldn't abandon you like that. Owen was going to jail, and there was just me."

"Humor me. How do you love Sam?"

My eyes narrowed. "Really? You want to go there?"

She crossed her arms in front of her chest. "Really. I was your best friend long before we started throwing the boyfriend/girlfriend thing in the mix. Now, talk."

I raked my hands over my hair, but gave in.

"She frustrates the shit out of me, pushes me past my comfort zone. She breaks down every wall I have with no permission or apologies. She turns me wild just to get my hands on her, and when I do..." I closed my eyes. "She owns me. It's not that I'm not capable of being me without her, but I'm better with her. Because of her. She's the only possible future I see for myself, and that's what scares the shit out of me."

My eyes closed, and I swallowed back the fear I'd lived with since the moment I saw Grace awake. The moment I knew Sam would walk away.

And if the roles were reversed? I would have kicked, clawed, beat the shit out of anyone to keep by her side, to prove I was the better choice.

But Sam never thought she was in the running, and I'd fucked up, chosen North Carolina and confirmed her worst fears—that I'd never be able to put her first.

"That's the kind of love you deserve, Gray. We all do." She sighed. "There was no part of that accident that you're at fault for. You saved me. This moving back to North Carolina so you can be close to family? Save Joey's place? That's you continuing to pay penance for a sin you didn't commit. That's you suffering by choice, and it has to stop. I know it. Sam knows it. You want her, then you have to admit that you're not fighting to be here for your family, or even for me, but because you can't bear to forgive yourself. You're Odysseus, Gray, winning your sorrow beyond what is given, blaming fate, blaming the accident, blaming everything but your own inability to let go. Fate handed you Sam by literally shoving her into your arms. She wants to live in Colorado? Live there. It doesn't affect your career, so go. Stop clinging to your notion of penance, because you're ruining your only chance at happiness."

She let that sink in for a second. "Don't let her get away. She's your match in every way."

"I don't know how to keep her." My voice was strangled.

"Prove to her that she's your first choice. Take all your other priorities and give them the second-place ribbon for once."

She was right, and I knew just where to start.

"And you're sure this is what you want to do?" Mom asked as I packed my bags the next morning.

"It's what I want to try. I don't know how she'll feel about it, but I have to try." I zipped my suitcase and lifted it off the bed.

"You need to stop by the shop and say good-bye to your dad and your sisters," she said, following me down the stairs.

"I will."

"Your father loves you, Grayson," she said once we'd stopped on the porch.

"Love has never been the issue, Mom. Trust? That's the issue. He nearly ended my flight career before it even started. I don't know how to forgive him for that."

"We do strange things when we fear for the ones we love. It makes him human."

I kissed her cheek. "I love you, and I'll see you at graduation?"

"I wouldn't miss it. Here, take my car and have Mia bring it home."

"Thank you, Mom. For everything."

"You're still not getting the brownie recipe." She laughed.

I shrugged. "One day…"

"Maybe when you grow up and realize what's good for you," she teased. "Go, get out of here." With a smacking kiss on my cheek, she shoved me out the door.

"Hey, Joey," I said to my sister as I walked in the front door of the shop.

"Gray!" Her smile was contagious. "What are you doing here?"

"I just stopped in to say good-bye. I'm headed back to Alabama a little early." I leaned over the counter and looked through the glass. "Is she ready for Miami?"

"Go take a look. The boat show is in two-and-a-half months, but I think after the navigation system upgrade is installed she'll be ready. Then we might have a shot at the Pineapple Cup if the design goes over well and we can find a crew to race her."

"I think I will." The workroom was cool but not too cold as I closed the door behind me. *The Alibi* sat on her trailer, ready to be taken to water.

I put my foot on the first rung, and my memory flashed with Sam standing on the captain's chair. The second rung, and I felt her mouth on mine, opening, trusting. The third and she was beneath me, writhing as I ran my tongue over her nipple. By the fourth rung I was inside her, losing every shred of control with her gasps, the way she said my name. My phone was in my hand by the time I hit the deck, my finger grazing over her contact. I hesitated for a second before I typed out a message.

Grayson: *Standing on The Alibi and thinking about you.*
Grayson: *Not that I'm not always thinking about you.*
Grayson: *Because I am.*
Grayson: *And now I'm texting like a stalker.*

Parker's laugh caught my attention as I stood on the deck. She laughed so little lately, and I missed that easy attitude she used to have before she morphed into my personal grief-giver.

She was sitting up on one of the workbenches, flirting with the new hand. Dad was going to kill her if another one quit on him.

But something about the way he tilted his head, tilted his baseball hat up to see her better...

"Son of a bitch!" I jumped off the boat, not bothering with the ladder, my knees screaming about landing on the concrete floor below.

"Gray!" Parker yelped.

"What the hell do you think you're doing here?" I shouted at Owen as he turned around with his hands up.

"Your dad hired me. No one else would, not with the criminal record."

I had him pinned against the wall by his shoulders before my sister could so much as squeak. "You're lying, as usual. No one in this family would hire you after what you've done."

"Gray!" Dad shouted, flying out of the back room. "Let him go, son."

"Name one good reason."

"He's not lying. I hired him." Dad's hand landed on my shoulder.

I shrugged him off and backed away, my chest heaving. "Why the hell would you do that?"

"Because he was a kid who made a mistake. Grace is awake, pulling her life together, and he served his time for what he did. There comes a point where the punishment isn't necessary."

I didn't stop until I was ten feet away, far enough that I couldn't kill him easily. "So it's okay to call me out to my commanding officer, but you'll hand over a job to Owen. He nearly killed us!"

"The risks you take every time you climb into that cockpit aren't the same. You knowingly risk lives on a daily basis. Owen's been one of your best friends since you were little, a part of this family. His mistake was in the past. You continue to make yours every day."

"You are unbelievable. What do I have to do to prove it to you? I've been in one car accident. One, because he nearly drove me off the road"—I pointed my finger toward Owen—"and don't you dare lie. I was there, and so you can spin your story, but between the two of us, we know what happened. Unless you were too drunk to remember it."

"That's not fair," Dad fired back. "You have to learn to accept your mistakes, Gray."

"And you have to learn to trust me! I'm the number one pilot in my class, Dad. I work my ass off to the point that even if I do have dyslexia, they would waiver me because it doesn't affect how I fly. What do you say to that?"

"Maybe I should have let the doctors test you! Maybe I shouldn't have let you deal with it on your own, so that no one laughed at you. Maybe I should have put you with all the specialists and the labels so this never happened in the first place."

"Well, you didn't. You couldn't have your perfect boy not-so-perfect, could you? If I was marred, unable to accurately read calculations, your dreams of Masters & Son were doomed. Well guess what, Dad, all you did was push me so far that I'll never come back here. I hope Joey grows a penis, or you learn to accept that she's better for this business than I ever will be."

"Gray—" Joey protested, standing in the office doorway.

"Don't, Joey. I only came to say good-bye. I'm going back to Fort Rucker to endanger some more lives in that helicopter I love so much." I headed toward Joey.

"You're leaving?" Parker asked.

"Yes, and it seems like it's about damn time."

"You can't walk out on this family, Grayson," Dad yelled.

"Walk out? Fuck, Dad!"

"Language!" Parker shouted, which we all ignored.

"You're shoving me out by inviting him in!"

"He's not continuously making asinine decisions!" Dad responded. "That one car accident you were in could have been avoided if not for your...confusion!"

"Fuck. You. I have had it with you blaming me for something I had no control over on that bridge. You weren't there! You want to blame me for something? Fine, blame me for not fighting him harder for his keys, but you taking this asshole's word over mine is the last straw."

"Grayson!" Dad shouted at the top of his lungs as I made it to Joey.

"Stop! He's right!" Parker shrieked. "All of you, stop! Dad, Grayson couldn't have prevented what happened."

"How would you even know, Parker?" I fired back, turning around. She chose now to stand up for me?

"Because..." She took gulping breaths. "Because I was there. We lost control and cut them off so close I thought we'd take out his bumper. If Gray hadn't swerved, Owen's truck bed would have gone right through Grace's windshield. They would have died instantly. I...I was in the truck."

My eyes narrowed, and I stepped toward her.

"No, you weren't," Joey said. "I'm the one who called you to tell you about the accident. I picked you up that night from Gray's party."

"I walked back after the accident," she mumbled. "I lied to you."

"I told her to go," Owen added. "She was so young. I didn't want her caught up in it. The minute the car went over...I thought you guys were dead, Gray, and I was too drunk to do anything about it. I will never forgive myself. And I never would have told that ridiculous racing lie if I'd realized you were going to live."

I didn't even bother looking at Owen. My eyes locked onto Parker, and the way she'd huddled in on herself, rocking on the bench. *I remember…seeing him flip us off with a grin, his finger pressed up against the window.* Grace's words roared in my ears.

"You drove drunk with my little girl in the car?" Dad asked.

"Sir, there's no excuse for what happened that night," Owen recited that fucking line, the one he'd always used.

"You drove drunk with my little girl in the car!" Dad roared.

"No, he didn't. He wasn't driving," I said softly, but everyone stopped and looked my way. I kept my gaze on Parker. "You were, weren't you, Parker? You drove. Otherwise Grace couldn't have seen Owen against the passenger-side window as you passed us."

"Gray—" she pled.

I shook my head. "I'm right, aren't I? That's why you've been on my ass about Grace, about me not moving on. Why you constantly harp on me about moving home? Why you showed up in Alabama and did everything in your power to make Sam run."

"I was trying to fix what I broke," she whispered. "You belong with Grace."

"It had nothing to do with Grace! It was your own guilt! Maybe I ruined my relationship with Sam, but you sure as hell put the crack there and then exploited it. It wasn't enough to run us off the road, you had to ruin the woman I love now?"

"I was trying to make it right! I didn't go away to college, I stayed here while Owen was in jail. I took care of Grace when I could. When she woke up, I embraced the miracle, and thought you would, too. You are perfect together."

"As friends. I'm in love with Samantha."

"Y-you were driving?" Dad stuttered.

Parker nodded her head. "You wouldn't let me get my license."

"You were reckless," Dad answered.

"Owen was drunk, and I knew he couldn't drive, so I talked him into letting me drive."

"I tried that," I countered.

"Yeah, well, you don't have boobs."

I stepped closer to Owen who threw his arms up. "I've never touched your sister, I swear to God."

"You went to jail for her?" Joey asked, coming up beside me. "You could have told the truth and not spent four years in prison."

"Parker was like my little sister. I couldn't turn her in. Not when she'd only been driving because I was drunk."

"It was an accident, Gray. I was going too fast. Just an accident."

Owen looked at me. "You have always been a brother to me, and you know I love Grace. For every second you've spent cursing the moment you didn't wrestle me to the ground and take my keys that night, I've spent two wishing I had let you. I live with that every day."

Too much. It was too much to absorb. To feel. To take in.

"You know what?" I threw my hands on my head and backed away. "I'm done. Everyone keeps telling me to get my shit together. But you guys take the cake. I'm done with every. Single. One of you." I pointed to Owen, Parker, and Dad, kissed Joey's cheek, and walked into the parking lot.

I grabbed my phone to check in for my flight, and I had three missed texts.

My Samantha: *I think about you every time I breathe.*

My Samantha: *Doesn't change anything, though, but I wish it did.*

My Samantha: *I don't mind psycho stalker-texts as long as they're from you.*

My Samantha: *Colorado is really pretty this time of year.*
Grayson: *So is North Carolina.*

My Samantha: *That, I don't doubt, especially if you're there.*

Less than a month to graduation. I had way too much to do to waste another moment on hesitation.

Or North Carolina.

CHAPTER THIRTY-THREE

GRAYSON

The rip of packing tape echoed in my steadily emptying room. Another box down, and only a few more to go.

"You ready?" Jagger asked, leaning on my doorframe. "Are you seriously packing? In dress blues?"

I put down the tape gun. "Yeah, well, I figured I had a minute. You guys ready?"

"Yeah, the girls are finally ready to go. Bummer about Grace."

I adjusted my suspenders over the white dress shirt before pulling on my dress blue jacket. "She said she'll make it in for graduation tomorrow. I honestly thought about skipping this thing."

"You can't skip the graduation ball. You're the fucking class leader."

"So I've been told." Damn, I didn't want to sit there while they told Jagger he was the distinguished honor graduate, first in the class. Not that he didn't deserve it, I just...wanted it. Wanted to wave it in front of my dad and tell him to fuck right off.

I'd worked my ass off, my every second consumed with studying, the gym, flying, or thinking about Sam. Planning a point-by-point plan to get her back, to force her to see that she was it for me.

Once my jacket was buttoned, we headed downstairs. "Your parents are coming?" Jagger asked.

"Mom's here with Mia. Parker and I are still working things out, and both Joey and Connie are needed at home. You?"

Jagger snorted as we hit the first floor. "Yeah, so he can hold a press conference and I can smile like a puppet? No thanks."

"Agreed."

"I am a lucky man," Jagger said as he wrapped his arm around Paisley, who was wearing a long green dress. "Not that Josh isn't, too," he said to Ember as she came out of the bathroom in a long black one.

"Yeah, yeah," Ember waved him off and stuck her arm out for Josh to help her with a bracelet.

"Everybody to the car!" Jagger called out, then stopped once the three others were already out. "Crap, I forgot Paisley's wings. Masters, will you wait here?"

"Sure." I leaned back against the wall and listened to him curse from the next room.

"Fuck!" A drawer slammed.

"Can't find them?" I asked.

"Apparently not!"

I swallowed the lump that gathered in my throat. "You can give her the set I bought." *For Sam.*

His head popped out of the doorframe. "No, man, I know those were supposed to be hers. I couldn't ask you for that."

"Paisley's feelings will be butchered because you're negligent, and I'm not going to let that happen," I said, heading up the stairs. They were in my nightstand, where they'd been ever since I bought them. I flicked open the velvet box. The dainty, platinum aviation wings hung from a platinum chain, slight but strong. Just like Sam. They should have been hers, hung in that perfect spot under her collarbone, but I'd never worked up the damn courage to ask her to come back for this. Or to pin me like she'd promised so long ago.

She was happy in Colorado, finding her footing.

I was headed to North Carolina next week before Christmas.

Turns out that whole "set your love free and it will come back?" Yeah, that's all bullshit. My eyes closed as I took a deep breath, then snapped the box shut and left my room.

"Here," I said, thrusting the box into Jagger's hands at the bottom of the steps.

"I can't—"

"You can. Shut up and get in the car. You're making us late." I walked past him and into the cold December air. It had a bite to it, but was still pretty damn mellow.

"There's room!" Paisley called out from the passenger side of Jagger's Defender.

The fifth wheel.

"I think I'll drive, but thank you, Paisley." I didn't wait for her reaction, or to listen to them tell me it was *okay* to ride with them. That it was *okay* to miss her. *Okay* to spend time with my best friend. If one more person told me everything was *okay*, I was going postal.

Everything was not fucking okay.

I drove to the Landing, where our ball was being held, and parked a little ways away. All the guys with dates needed the closer spots and it wasn't like I had to make the hike in heels.

"Thank you for saving my ass," Jagger said as I met him in the lobby.

I nodded my head. At least if someone was going to wear Sam's wings, it was Paisley.

"I think they have us sitting by class. We found our nameplates, but Josh and Carter are across the floor."

"Who did Carter bring?" I asked, not really caring.

"Morgan." Jagger grinned. "As friends, of course."

"Right," I drawled.

The ballroom was packed as we descended the steps, every seat filled with ball gowns and dress blues. We made our way to our table where Paisley, Patterson, and Wallace from our class, and their wives waited.

Grace's setting was still there. "I forgot to tell them she wasn't coming," I muttered.

Jagger threw Paisley a nervous glance as he sat on her other side. What the hell did the guy have to be nervous about? The other pilots introduced us to their wives, and I nodded politely.

"Honey, this is Masters. He's the lucky bastard that got Fort Bragg," Patterson said.

"Oh, that's where my family is," his wife said. "You'll love it."

The pit in my stomach formed like it did every time I thought about it. But I'd made my choice, and I'd report after the New Year.

"You'll love Colorado," Jagger offered. "I went to college there, and it's gorgeous."

Paisley shot me a look that told me that's where I should have chosen. *No shit.* But there was nothing I could do about it.

"And you guys are headed for Fort Campbell, right?" Wallace asked.

"We are," Paisley replied as Jagger kissed the back of her hand.

As the waitress took our drink orders, I motioned to the setting next to me. "Actually we won't be needing—"

"Oh, but we will," Paisley said with a smile to the waitress, who then moved on.

"You want to explain?"

She full-on grinned. "I may have called in a favor with a friend when I knew Grace couldn't make it."

My jaw clenched. *God love well-intentioned Southern ladies.* "I'm not sure tonight was really the night to set me up on a blind date, Paisley, though I'm sure your friend is lovely."

"Oh, hell yeah, she is," Jagger said, looking over my shoulder.

My muscles tensed one by one. This was bad enough without Grace, but a stranger?

"She came a long way, Grayson, so play nice." Paisley gave me her serious face, and then tilted her chin to motion toward the door behind me.

I turned in my seat slowly to see her walking down the stairs.

My breath rushed from my lungs, and my jaw dropped more than the self-respecting amount. Her hair was up off her neck, and her strapless blue dress hugged every curve, accentuating her tiny waist before it fell to the floor. She was so damn beautiful. *My Samantha.*

I'd damn-near sprinted to her before I realized I'd even gotten out of my chair. She paused halfway down the staircase with a wide smile but wary eyes. *She's afraid you don't want her here.*

By standing a few steps beneath her, we were almost equal in height. "Samantha."

"Stop." She put her hand out. "This is a Cinderella thing."

One of my eyebrows drifted higher. "As in you came in a pumpkin, or you'll be losing a shoe? Because either way, I can deal."

The smile that spread across her face cracked open my chest, and my heart started to pound. "As in I'm only here until tomorrow afternoon. I have to leave after graduation."

"You're here for graduation?" Holy shit, I sounded like a five-year-old who just found his Christmas presents.

Her fingers swept down my cheek. "I promised I'd pin you, right?"

My mouth dropped open again. She remembered.

"I mean, if you made other plans, I totally understand—"

Not giving a fuck about her lipstick, I surged forward, took her face in my hands and kissed her. *In public. In public. In public.* My brain chanted to remind me to keep my tongue in my mouth and my hands on the outside of her incredible dress. "You're perfect," I managed to say.

"No sex."

I froze. "You're seeing someone?"

She shook her head. "Of course not. I just need you to promise me."

"Can I kiss you? Was that okay?" She'd been in the same room for less than five minutes, and I'd already mauled her when I had zero rights to her body.

"Hell yes. Kiss me all you want, but that's as far as it goes."

Fear streaked across her eyes, and I nodded slowly. "No sex."

"No matter how loudly I beg," she whispered.

Holy shit, I was about to embarrass myself in the middle of this ballroom if I didn't get my dick under control.

"Grayson, swear it. On your honor, or I walk out this door."

"I want you for more than your body, Sam. I don't care if we play Scrabble all night. Not having sex is fine." It fucking sucked, but if that was the price for having her with me, I'd be celibate for the rest of my life.

"I never said I was spending the night with you," she rebuked, but her grin was back. "I'm staying at Morgan's house."

"I will sleep on the damn doorstep if that's as close as I can get to you." We both paused, words from an earlier vow running through our heads. *I'd sleep on the floor to get closer to you.* Six months, and nothing had changed.

Everything had changed.

Dinner was signaled, and I led her to our seats. The meal was a blur, and honestly, all I could think about was getting my mouth back on Sam. She kept her hand in mine while we ate, only breaking apart to cut our food. I couldn't stop touching her.

"If I can have your attention?" Major Davidson called from the podium.

We all turned in our seats to where he spoke from across the empty dance floor. "We're very lucky to have General Donovan with us tonight. He has some special interest in this class, and he'd like to address you before we announce the distinguished honor graduates."

Paisley's father took the podium. His remarks on loyalty, bravery, and accomplishment were short, and I heard next to none of them over the steady pounding in my heart. It didn't matter. First in my class or not, I'd gotten my duty station. The actual class ranking shouldn't matter to me.

Except it did.

Major Davidson announced the Chinook class first, and we all clapped. Then the Blackhawk class.

"It's cool Josh is graduating with you guys," Sam whispered.

"Yeah, they should have been done a while ago, but they needed the aircraft during the tornado relief and it set them back long enough to coincide with us. I'm not complaining." There was a sense of poetry to going out together.

"Distinguished honor graduate from Blackhawk class 1509 is Second Lieutenant William Carter."

I clapped a little harder and toasted my water charger when he smiled over at me. *Not second-choice Carter anymore.* Maybe Sam had made me soft, but even that ass had grown on me.

Sam took hold of my hand and wove her fingers through mine until they fit in that perfect space of familiarity. *Here we go.*

"Distinguished honor graduate from Apache class 1506 is Second Lieutenant"—*Jagger Bateman*—"Grayson Masters."

My breath stalled.

Sam kissed my cheek as the crowd applauded again. "You did it. I'm so proud of you!"

Jagger clapped me on the back. "Congratulations, man!"

"It should have been you."

He shook his head. "You kept up with me test for test academically. Trust me, I paid attention. And in the cockpit, you're a better pilot. Take the fucking accolade, Grayson. You earned it."

I pulled Sam under my arm and kissed her forehead and then her lips, putting all my joy, incredulousness, and hope into it. This moment was perfect.

"Now, soon-to-be aviators. We all know that you didn't get here alone. In Army Aviation, we have a tradition. You ladies put up with late nights, early mornings, absent spouses, irritated, worried, over-stressed spouses, and I'd bet that more than a few of you know the 5&9s as well as they do." Laughter rolled over the small crowd. "So, gentlemen, invite your ladies to stand, and pin them. They've earned it."

Fuck. What was I going—My velvet box appeared in front of me. "You didn't think I'd actually lose Paisley's wings, did you?"

"You knew. Asshole." I was too relieved to have her wings to actually be angry.

He had the audacity to wink as we stood. I offered my hand to Sam, and she stood slowly, unsure of herself. "I'm not your wife."

"Not yet." I grinned at the way her jaw dropped. My fingers fumbled with the chain, finally working the tiny clasp and securing it around her neck. The wings rested exactly where I knew they would, in gorgeous contrast to her perfect skin. "I wouldn't have made it through without you."

She laughed. "That's not true. If anything I was a deterrent when I was here, and I've been gone over two months. This one is all you."

"First, you became my motivation." I bent down to her ear. "Second, you play a mean game of strip 5&9," I whispered and kissed the delicate shell. She shivered, and I tried to remind my dick that we'd agreed to no sex. Her lips parted as I kissed her gently. "And just because you weren't here doesn't mean you weren't with me every day."

Applause sounded in the room, and we were dismissed to begin dancing as the music came to life through the speakers.

Couples headed out to the floor, but I didn't care. I was too busy kissing the woman I was completely and utterly in love with.

"Gray." Dad's voice met us as we walked up the sidewalk to the house after the ball.

I stopped mid-step, Sam tucked under my arm, wrapped in my dress blues jacket to keep her warm.

"What the hell are you doing here?"

His gaze flickered to my friends, and he shoved his hands in his pockets.

Paisley spoke up. "How about we all head inside where it's warm?" The group mumbled assent, and Sam looked up at me.

"Do you need me?" she whispered.

"More than you'll ever know, but I can handle this. Want to go wait in our room?" *Our*. Yes, I said it on purpose.

"Okay." She kissed my cheek and turned back to my dad. "It was nice to see you again, Mr. Masters."

He gave a genuine smile. "I am relieved to find you here, Sam."

I waited until she'd shut the door before I spoke to him. "Well?"

"You graduate tomorrow."

"I am aware."

He pinched the bridge of his nose. "Why do you make everything so hard?"

"I get it from my father."

"Just because I don't approve of what you're doing doesn't mean that I don't love you, that I'm not"—his throat worked—"incredibly proud of you, and what you've accomplished. My worry doesn't diminish that."

"You almost ended my career."

"For which I am incredibly sorry." The apology was enough

to stun me. "Look, Gray. I should have believed after the accident. I should have believed you when you told me you could handle flying. I should have trusted you, and I didn't. I was so busy trying to protect you that I didn't realize I was suffocating you. Did I want you to come home and work at the shop? Of course. Do I realize that Joey will probably surpass us both in boat design? Absolutely."

"Then let her have the shop." The wind bit through the thin material of my dress shirt.

"Grayson."

"You want my forgiveness? Prove you've changed, that you won't hold her rightful place hostage."

"It's still your place, too."

"It hasn't been in years. Sure, I helped a little with *The Alibi's* design, but it was mostly Joey, and you know it. You may want me, but you need her. Let her prove it to you if you don't think she has already."

"How?"

"Give her the reins at the Miami show. Let her hire a crew and race the Pineapple Cup."

"She's softer than you think, Gray. It would crush her to lose."

"Joey won't let you down. She doesn't know how to fail."

He crossed his arms in front of his chest and looked off in the distance, a pose I knew meant he was deliberating. "Okay."

And just like that, I was free, the last tether chaining me to North Carolina cut. "Okay."

Dad cleared his throat. "Anyway, I just wanted to tell you that I'm here, and I'll be there tomorrow if you want me. There's nothing in this world that could stop me from loving you. Whether you graduate first or last, I don't care as long as you're happy. I'll...trust you to be safe."

It was all I'd ever wanted, but I still couldn't stop thinking that Sam was upstairs. Time to make her my first priority.

"I'm glad you're here. I really have to go spend time with Sam, Dad. I only have her for a few hours." I was sorry, but I wasn't.

"I understand."

I walked past him, but turned once my hand was on the handle. "Dad?"

"Yeah?"

"I want you there tomorrow. And I didn't finish last. I'm first in my class." I watched that sink in.

He simply nodded his head. "I'm not surprised. I'll see you tomorrow."

I watched him get into a rental car parked across the street and drive off, probably to the hotel Mom and Mia were at. Then I took the stairs two at a time until I got into my room.

Heaven. Sam stood with her back to me, tugging at the zipper. She glanced over her shoulder. "Oh, do you mind? I'm borrowing a shirt and some boxers."

A surge of possessiveness overwhelmed me at the thought of her in my clothes. "Not at all."

"Good." She laughed. "Then get over here and unzip me."

I rubbed my hands together to warm my fingers and then pinched the small zipper between them. When it wouldn't budge, I slipped the back of my hand inside her dress to get a better grasp, and the zipper gave.

My dick hardened with every inch of exposed skin, and I groaned when the dress parted to the top of her ass, revealing the tiny bow at the back of a blue thong. "You're. Good. All unzipped."

I ran my fingers up her spine and relished in her gasp. "Thank you."

My own clothes felt foreign as I handed her the shirt and boxers she'd pulled from my dresser and turned my back. Every muscle in my body clenched when fabric rustled to the floor. I crossed the distance to my dresser and pulled out a pair of sweatpants, quickly stripping to my underwear and pulling them on.

"So you leave your clothes on the floor now?" Sam asked, already sitting on my bed.

Stop thinking about how naked she is under those clothes. What the hell? She was always naked under her clothes. Everyone was. I rubbed my forehead. "Yeah, well, maybe I'm just anxious to join you."

"No sex," she reminded me, sitting up on her knees.

"Even if you beg," I reminded her as I slipped under the covers, and then pulled her against me. She tucked under my chin perfectly and gasped when our hips meshed. "It doesn't exactly stop me from wanting you, Sam."

She kissed the underside of my jaw. "Yeah, me, either."

Fuck, I wanted her. It had been so damn long, and now she was here, dressed in my clothes, pressed up against me in my bed. But if she needed to realize I wanted her for more than sex, I could make that happen.

I just might be a corpse before morning.

"Tell me about Colorado," I said. She sighed, intertwined her smooth legs with mine, and then started to talk. She told me about the upcoming hearing, the other girls who had come forward, and that her transcripts had already been corrected.

"Once the news got ahold of it, I had a hard time. They tried to keep our faces out of the story, but they haven't exactly been successful."

"I'm proud of you." I rubbed lazy circles along her back. "I know it wasn't easy to come forward."

"We're stronger together, the other girls and I. We have a stronger case, and I think I have a chance of getting back into classes after the hearing in January, even though I hit him."

My palms itched to do the same. "I want you in my life." The words were out before I could stop them, and then it was like a stream of vomit I couldn't contain. "I love you. This right here, holding you, tells me everything I need to know about my future, because this is where I want to be. I don't care if I'm in Colorado, or you're in North Carolina, or if we move to North Dakota." I pulled back so I could look into those green eyes that I prayed would show up on our future daughters. "I know you can't stay, and I can't go. So I don't know how, but we have to figure something out. I swear I can't breathe when you're gone."

Her lips found mine, and she gently stroked my lower lip with her tongue. "I know, and I feel the same. But I can't walk out on what I'm doing right now. And as much as I miss you, and need you, I have to see this through on my own. The hearing will be over in January, but no college is going to take me until everything is cleared up. Maybe it's selfish, but I want to graduate there."

"Look at you, all accountable." I kissed her, but kept it quick. "Tell me what to do, and I'll do it. Just don't walk out that door again without giving us a way. I almost didn't survive last time."

Her fingers ran through my hair, and I arched into her touch. "Me, either," she whispered. "We've been apart for months with almost no contact, and I still love you. I crave you every moment. I don't see that changing while we work through all of this."

The tiny spark of hope that flared to life when I saw her at the ball caught fire, and I burned with need for everything she was. "Long distance? I can do it."

She laughed. "Yeah, you've proven yourself there. Grace?" Her expression fell. "I can't help but feel like I ruined your miracle."

I shook my head. "You're all I see, all I want. No one else has this effect on me." I dipped my head and kissed her, running my tongue along the seam of her lips until she let me in. The kiss was slow but full of so much love that I couldn't help but sigh. "Sam, you're right. I got my miracle, but it wasn't Grace. It was you. You kick-started my heart and brought me to life the minute you opened your mouth and dished my own shit back at me. You gave me something to fight for, a reason to see beyond the shit hand fate had given me, and start to imagine a future. And when I think about my life, you're all I see. You're it. You are my miracle."

Her eyes shined, and her lips trembled as she kissed me lightly. "Okay. We'll figure this out. I don't know how, but we will." Her eyes lit in a way I hadn't seen since before Grace woke up, and her smile was enough to bring me to my knees, if they weren't already tangled with hers. "Oh, and I brought you a present."

"You did?"

"I figured graduation was a brownie kind of moment." She rolled out of my reach and brought a box between us, then handed me the chocolate square. "So I baked while I was at Morgan's. Hopefully I got it right."

I bit into it and closed my eyes in ultimate surrender. They were perfect, with that special hint of something I could never define. My eyes popped open. "These are my mom's. I've been after this recipe for *years*."

She shrugged. "She taught me that day she invited me over."

"She swore she would never give it to me until..." *When you grow up and realize what's good for you.*

Sam squeaked when I knocked the box to the floor and pulled her underneath me, chocolate still smearing her lips. "Kissing is fair game, right?" I asked, grinning.

She nodded slowly, her eyes darting to my lips.

I looked to the clock. "We have to be at graduation in seven hours. I'm going to kiss you every single minute of it."

By the time we showed up at graduation, our lips were swollen, and her neck was irritated from my now-shaved scruff.

Samantha pinned my wings to my chest with a silver set she'd had engraved with my initials. My dad even smiled. Pictures were taken, lunch eaten, and I took her to the airport.

"You're mine?" I asked, my arms wound around her waist at security.

"As much as you're mine," she answered, her fingers locked behind my neck.

"We'll find a way."

She leaned up on her toes and kissed me. "We'll find a way."

I watched her until she'd gone through security and waved.

Then I went back to finish packing. I would find a damned way. I was done leaving my life up to fate, done waiting for things to work out, and done waiting to be with Sam. I'd find the way, or I'd fucking make one.

CHAPTER THIRTY-FOUR

SAM

My footsteps were sure as I walked toward the administration building, never faltering despite the ice beneath me. I made it to my seat in front of the disciplinary board, passing by Harrison and his wife, a slender woman with a beautiful face and a bitter mouth. They'd already been fired. He was here as my accuser, and she was pending trial for criminal charges for what she'd done to us, but her only purpose today was to see what my punishment would be for hitting her husband.

My phone buzzed, and I took it out of my pocket.

Grayson: *Thinking about you. I hear the weather is gorgeous today for a verdict.*

My heart swelled to the size of the Colorado sky.

Sam: *I'll call you after. And blue skies would be perfect for flying, just saying.*

Grayson: *You make Colorado perfect. I'm so proud of you.*

Missing him had become the status quo the last month, but it struck even harder right now. I got out one last text before the board walked in.

Sam: *I know I said I needed to do this alone, and I did. But I really wish you were here right now.*

I slipped my phone into my purse as they took their seats. This would be my only opportunity to speak...to any of them. If I could keep lunch in my stomach, it just might work.

Dean Miller, flanked by equal parts faculty and student disciplinary committee, cleared his throat before speaking. "Ms. Fitzgerald, we've spoken at length both about your offense and what you have suffered since. Is there anything you'd like to say before we discuss your future?"

I nodded my head and stood, holding on to the corner of the table with my fingertips. *Don't puke.* "What I did that day was inexcusable. I'm not asking for consideration for the circumstances. I struck a member of the faculty, and I'll accept whatever punishment you decide. Colorado is the only home I've ever really known. I came to UCCS so I could stay here, in what I love as my hometown. I'm just asking that you allow me to finish my degree here."

My stomach tightened, regret washing over me with the force of an unbreakable tidal wave as I turned to face the back of the room where the Proctors sat. Michelle raised her chin, hatred evident in the set of her eyes. "I'm truly sorry for the pain I caused you," I said to her, ignoring Harrison. "I never knew he was married, and if I could take it back, or take some of the pain away from you, I would. You don't deserve what happened to you."

She tore her gaze from mine, blinking back tears. What she'd done to me was reprehensible, but there was a small part of me that understood, and an even bigger part that already forgave her.

I turned back to the committee and remained standing.

Dean Miller gathered himself with a deep breath. "Ms. Fitzgerald, we do find that you struck a member of the University faculty. While there are extenuating circumstances, we feel that were we not to impose a punishment, it would be a detriment not only to you but to the university itself. However, we are not willing to lose a student like you. So we ask that you provide twenty hours of community service to the University, preferably by tutoring the lower sections of freshman math, while you finish your degree here at the University of Colorado."

My eyes burned, and my throat closed. I managed a nod of my head and a broken "Thank you," before the committee filed out.

It was over. I was free. I would graduate from CU.

The chair caught my weight as I collapsed, braced my elbows on the table, and let my head fall into my hands while I sucked in deep, gulping breaths. Then I folded my hands and sent up a heartfelt prayer of thanks for my second chance.

By the time I pulled myself together, the room had emptied completely. I slipped my arms into my coat, grabbed my purse, and closed the door on my way out. The sound was crisp, like the sound a book made as you shut it after the last page.

The sunshine welcomed me as I stepped out onto the walkway. The air tasted cleaner, my soul felt lighter. I started down the path and pulled out my cell phone.

Sam: *I'm in. I have to tutor, but they let me back in!*

Grayson: *I knew they would. No one's foolish enough to let you go.*

With the burden of the hearing behind me, and my future open, the full weight of missing Grayson hit me. It was two fifteen p.m. on a Friday. If I went straight to the airport, I could make it to him by tonight and spend almost a week with him before classes started.

Yes. That's what I'd do. Screw packing new clothes, I'd just wear his all week. I opened my internet browser to search for flights. It would eat up a chunk of my savings, but it was worth it. This month had been entirely too long.

Grayson: *You seem pensive. What are you thinking?*

Sam: *That I miss you, and I'd do anything to sleep curled in your arms tonight.*

A giddy smile took hold at the thought of surprising him. I walked a little faster.

Grayson: *Funny. I was thinking the same thing.*

Sam: *Oh yeah? Just sleeping?*

Grayson: *Well, I'd love to slide my hands up that red skirt, but someone said no sex.*

Sam: *Maybe I could rethink the no sex thing...*

I hit send, and then paused mid-step. *Red skirt?* Slowly, and so scared to be wrong, I lifted my eyes from the fabric of my skirt, skimming along the path until it converged with the one that led to the parking lot.

My eyes landed on a pair of black Doc Martins, then ran up a set of muscular legs encased in a pair of jeans that made my mouth water. He slid his cell phone into the front pocket of his black ski coat, and I made my way to his face, to the slow smile that lit up the darkest corners of my heart and chased the shadows into oblivion.

Grayson.

The thirty feet that separated us was all at once exquisitely painful, and I broke into a dead run, ice and all. I slipped the last couple of feet, but he lifted me into his arms before my balance could even register the danger.

My arms looped around his neck as he held me eye level. "You're here?"

"I'm here."

My eyes skimmed over his features, needing to memorize every single detail of this moment and file it away for the nights we were apart. This was why I loved him, this overwhelming feeling that defied all logic. There was just no way this much emotion could live within me.

"Why?"

His eyes looked almost silver in the sunlight, lighter than I'd ever seen them. "On the off chance you sent a text that you needed me. I knew today would be tough."

"I love you," I said before I kissed him. His lips were cold, but his tongue warm as he swept it into my mouth. He tasted like home, and as my pulse skipped, he banded one arm under my ass and used his other hand to wind his fingers through my hair until he held me to him.

"Can I take you somewhere?" he asked against my mouth.

"Anywhere," I answered.

He set me back on my feet and held my hand as we walked toward the parking lot. "Will your car be okay?"

"Yeah, we can leave it here," I said, gesturing to where it sat parked a few spaces down from his truck. "You drove? All the way from North Carolina?"

He squeezed my hand. "I did."

"Let me grab my charger out of my car?" I asked.

"No problem. I'll start the truck."

I yanked the charger from the port, anxious to be alone with Grayson and yet more relaxed than I had been since Alabama.

"Sam."

The back of my head met my doorframe. "Shit!" I grabbed the offended area and turned. "You're not supposed to be speaking to me, Professor Proctor."

"Since when did that ever keep us apart?" he asked, devil-may-care grin in place as he swatted an errant brown curl like I hadn't been through hell to get back into this school.

I looked over my shoulder, but Grayson couldn't see us from here, and Harrison was blocking my exit. "I'm not kidding, Professor Proctor, this is inappropriate."

He took ahold of my arm. Even through the layers of down that separated us, his touch felt tainted. I shook him off. "Don't touch me."

His grin fell away. "Sam, I'm not a professor anymore. You left without a word, without letting me explain. You at least owe me that much."

"I owe you nothing."

"Please, give me a chance."

"Just...stop. What could you possibly hope to get out of talking to me?"

He did his dramatic sigh that I used to think was incredibly romantic. Yeah, that had nothing on the quiet intensity of Grayson simply looking at me, which basically melted my panties right off.

"I miss you."

"I don't miss you." I shrugged, uncaring that another student gawked as she passed. I had nothing to hide this time.

"There was a time you loved me, and I know you could again. I'm thinking of leaving Michelle."

"I don't care, Professor. You two, quite frankly, deserve each other. I'm only asking that you stop hurting other people."

"I'm so sorry I ruined your life. That was never my intention, or any of this humiliation."

Laughter bubbled up, taking with it the last vestiges of shame or embarrassment as I thought about the envelope I kept securely tucked away in my purse. "You think my life is ruined? How self-centered can you be? Sure, I slept with the wrong man, trusted you, but I'm done paying for that. You knew you were married. I didn't. I'm going to finish college and be with the man I love. You're not a factor in my future, but I doubt you can say the same about me. Every time you apply to teach, this will follow you. Every time you look at your wife, this will be between you. What you've done will haunt you...not me."

I shut my door, but Harrison wouldn't let me pass. Every step I took, he matched. "You haunt me now."

"Let. Me. Go."

"No, not until you listen." I sidestepped his reach again.

Grayson stepped behind Harrison, and the tension drained from me. "Please, give me a fucking reason to end you. Do it. Put your hand on her again."

Harrison turned to look up, and up at Grayson. Then he moved to the side as Grayson reached for my hand. I took it and left everything about my past behind as he tucked me under his arm and walked me to his truck.

• • •

"Is this really necessary?" I asked, fumbling for the door handle forty-five minutes later. The damn blindfold on my eyes wasn't helping matters. I heard the door open, and a gust of cold air hit my face.

"Be patient," Grayson said softly. He undid my seatbelt, then easily lifted me into a bridal carry.

We paused, and I heard another door open, then close as warmth surrounded us. "Well, at least we're inside," I teased. There was a faint echo. Where the hell were we? I could feel his heartbeat jump through our coats. "Are you nervous? Because your heart is racing, and I know you're not tired from carrying me. Hell, I bet you could carry me for an hour and still not get tired."

He stayed silent, which was enough to almost make me rip off the blindfold. Whatever we were doing was obviously way outside his comfort zone.

"We're here," he said as he gently set me on my feet. "I'm going to take off your shoes."

He dropped, leaving my hands on his shoulders for balance. Then he slipped off my boots one by one. The floor was cool and hard under my socks.

"We might need to work on your foreplay."

He laughed softly, and the tension dissipated from his shoulders. He stood, and right after I heard a squeaking sound, I felt a soft pressure at the top of my head, and the distinct scent of...magic marker?

He kissed my lips with a reverence that had me aching for more as he pulled back and turned me around. The blindfold slipped free. "Okay, take a look."

I blinked several times, letting my eyes adjust. A door stood open in front of me with a black line etched into a spot on the left panel that read "Samantha." Farther left was another line marked "Grayson," with today's date written between them.

"You got me a door?" It was the sweetest gift I could imagine.

"A place to mark your height," he said from behind me. "To start our story."

I turned to face him, and then got distracted by the rest of my surroundings. There was so much light, so many white walls. "An empty house?" I asked, taking in as much as I could. The front door had a glass panel and a tile entry, then a nice-sized living room. Looking to the right, I saw a den, and a kitchen that had raw maple cabinets but no counters.

"There's a window seat." Grayson pointed to the den. "Like you wanted."

"W-w-what?"

"Hardwood in the kitchen. You said that was important, and there's a small porch out front. I put the swing up last week. I know you wanted granite counters, but that's kind of personal, and the granite guys said they could be here to install next week if we pick everything out in the next few days."

"Grayson."

He swallowed. "It has a good-sized backyard that's kind of flat. Do you know how hard it is to get a flat backyard on this side of town? Or how expensive this school district is? It's ludicrous."

"Grayson."

"And if there's something you don't like, I can remodel it. I bought it, so it's not like we have to ask permission or anything. But we will have to buy furniture."

Holy shit. He bought a house. In Colorado. For me.

"Grayson!"

His eyes flew to mine, a state of subdued panic rolling through them. "Samantha."

"Why would you buy a house here?"

His eyebrows rose. "Because you're here."

"But you live in North Carolina."

A slow smile spread across his face. "I found a loophole, and asked another flight student to trade me at the last minute.

I live here. I'm assigned to Fort Carson."

I sucked in a breath. "But your family…" Tears pricked at my eyes, welling so fast that he blurred in front of me.

His thumbs wiped away the tears that fell. "You are my family, and you're here. I don't work without you, Samantha."

I reached into my purse and pulled out the letter I'd been saving. "But I got into UNC. Just in case."

"Do you want to go to school in North Carolina?"

I shook my head. "I want to be here."

"Then I do, too. Burn the letter."

I still couldn't grasp that he was really in Colorado. "How long have you been here?"

"A few weeks—just long enough to buy the house. You said you needed to tackle that stuff on your own, and I wasn't going to take that away from you."

"You've been waiting for me? In the same city? For weeks? It must have been hell." There was no way I could have been that close to him and not have called, reached out, touched him. God, standing here without stripping him down was taking every ounce of restraint I had.

"I would wait forever for you."

We both snapped, reaching for each other in a fury of open mouths and searching hands. My jacket hit the floor, followed shortly by his. We made our first official mess as we ripped clothes off in a haphazard trail up the stairs.

Something told me it wouldn't be the last time I left my bra in the upstairs hallway.

CHAPTER THIRTY-FIVE

His hands were everywhere, stroking my breasts, rolling my nipples, gripping my waist. He pushed me back against the wall, and I barely registered him hitting his knees until he held my folds apart and put his mouth on me.

I screamed his name.

It had been so long, and my body was starved for him. His touch ignited an instant fire that consumed every nerve ending and left me frantic.

His fingers dipped inside me, and as I whimpered, he caressed my inner walls until he found my G-spot and then relentlessly rubbed it, curling his fingers inward as he drew my clit into his mouth and sucked.

My knees shook, and then my whole body trembled as I fell apart. He caught me before I fell to the ground.

"Condom," I whispered, aching and desperate to have him inside me.

"We're done with the no sex?" he half teased. Once I ran my hand over his length and pumped twice, he wasn't teasing anymore. "Condom," he agreed, finding a package somewhere near his pants and rolling it over his erection.

He gripped behind my upper thighs and lifted me in one small motion.

"That's so fucking sexy," I said against his jawline as I

wrapped my legs around his hips, lining us up perfectly. He carried me toward the bed. "I always wondered if you could hold me upright while we did this."

He stopped and arched an eyebrow. "Lock your ankles."

Those words alone had me throbbing again, my muscles clenching with stark need. He kissed me with sweeping strokes of his tongue, and I gasped at the taste of us mingled together. Capturing me with a fierce gaze, our open mouths barely an inch apart, he lowered me until, inch by inch, he slid inside me.

Thank you, God. I couldn't hold back the moan that ripped free as he finally thrust home. I buried my face in his neck and felt the fine tremor that rolled through him as my body adjusted to him.

"Fuck, I missed you, Sam." He said as he began to move slowly. "Every part of you. Every inch of your skin, every sarcastic comment from your mouth, every touch of your fingers. All. Of. You." He punctuated each of the last words with a thrust.

"I love you." My brain lost its ability to think, but I knew I wanted more. "Harder," I ordered.

He tried to laugh. "I'm doing my best to go soft here."

"Soft later. Hard now." He could make love to me all night long. *He'd better.* But now, I needed everything he had without holding back.

"I love you," he echoed. "Now hold on." He started a deep, pounding rhythm that demanded I do just that. My arms looped around his neck and held tight as he drove into me over and over again, the muscles in his arms bulging as he lifted me up and slammed me back down.

He shifted his hands to my ass, and tension spiraled in me again, tighter with every thrust. The man was a machine. Our eyes locked, our breaths mingled, and it was hotter than him sliding in and out of me. I was pretty sure Grayson could bring me to orgasm with a look if he tried hard enough.

He backed up until he hit the edge of the bed and then sat, grasping each of my ankles and bringing my knees flush along his hips. "I can fuck you like that all day long, but I think this might be better for you."

I let loose a wicked grin, rose up and slid back down, watching the change in his eyes. I felt powerful, desirable, and *his*.

Grayson's fingers slipped between us to massage my clit as I rode him, and any of my previous thoughts fled. There were only our bodies, and the rhythm that drove us higher, brought us closer together.

"Grayson," I cried as my muscles locked.

"I've got you," he growled, pressing on those nerves just right, and I flew. My orgasm set his off, and we clung together as we came back down.

His lips were soft as he kissed me.

"Whoa," I said, raking my nails gently over his scalp.

"Yeah, my thoughts exactly," he commented, and rolled us so we lay side by side.

I couldn't stop looking at him, or running my fingers along the back of his neck. "I missed you so much."

"You don't have to miss me anymore." His slight smile would have collapsed my knees if I'd been standing.

"And you're sure that you're okay here?" I had to ask. He'd given up so much for me. For us.

He smiled, and my heart faltered. "It was selfish of me to ask you to give up what you worked your ass off for. I'm here. I'm not leaving you until the army says we have to move, and then I'm kind of hoping you'll come with me. We should have at least a couple years here, long enough to finish your degree. But I promise we'll keep this house. Our kids will mark their heights on that door."

I arched up and kissed him. "I love the door. I love the house. I love you, and I'll go wherever I have to so I can be with you. I used to think that home was a place. Walls, and windows, and home-baked brownies, but it's not, Grayson. That's just a house. You are my home. So where you go, I'll go."

His mouth met mine in the sweetest kiss we'd ever shared. "I promise I'll always put the coffee on the bottom shelf."

"That, or you always have to be around to catch me when I slip off the granite."

His smile was brighter than the sunlight streaming through the windows. "I told you once—I'll always catch you."

I lifted an eyebrow and ran my hands down his naked back.

"You are pretty good with your hands."

He scoffed. "Pretty good? We've been apart for what, four months, and now I'm only *pretty* good?"

I brought my leg up to hitch around his hips. "I guess I could use a reminder."

"Oh, I'll remind you."

"I might forget pretty often." I gave him my best wide-eyed stare.

"I'll remind you every fucking day, Samantha."

Yes. Every day. He was my future, my home, my universe, this phenomenal man who'd altered my world and claimed it for his own. "Promise?"

"Promise."

EPILOGUE

SEVEN YEARS LATER

T he hangar doors opened on Butts Army Airfield and the crowd roared above the music of the army band playing. They marched in, all one-hundred-and-twenty-five of them, filling the empty floor with row after row of camo.

My eyes swept the front of the line until I found him, and my heart started to race. He was here. Finally. After the longest nine months of my life, he was finally home. No, this hadn't been our first deployment, but it had been the hardest.

Then again, after three of them, it always seemed to feel that way.

He faced forward, standing at attention at the head of his company while the General took the podium, but I could see Grayson's eyes scanning the bleachers looking for me. For us.

"Daddy's here!" I said to Delaney as I adjusted all forty pounds of her on my hip.

"Daddy!" she shrieked, breaking the silence to the laughter of those around us.

Who could blame a four-year-old?

I tucked one of her long, caramel spiral-curls back over her ear. "We have to wait a minute, baby."

When I looked back to the formation, Grayson's eyes had locked on to me. My stomach clenched. Five years of marriage, and he still had the power to knock me to my knees with just that look.

I wouldn't trade it for the world.

The general dismissed the troops, and the crowd rushed from the stands in a tidal wave of joy, until the hangar floor became a sea of welcome-homes. Careful in heels with Delaney in my arms, I picked my way down the bleachers until we reached the last row, where Grayson had just arrived.

"Daddy!" Delaney cried and lunged. He caught her tiny frame easily and crushed her to him, his eyes closed in bliss for all of two seconds before he yanked me into his chest with his free arm.

God, he smelled like tangy metal from the aircraft and freshly applied deodorant. Nothing had ever been more of an aphrodisiac. I held on as tightly as possible, savoring the feel of him, the steady beat of his heart beneath my ear.

Contentment overpowered every other emotion.

I met his mouth in a crushing kiss, and just like that, the taste of him flooded me, consumed me. Our lips lingered, but we pulled back reluctantly and gave our attention to the gorgeous green-eyed spitfire who was already chatting Grayson's ear off.

"And we made you signs, and they have glitter. Lots of glitter. Mommy said that you wouldn't mind, even though you're a boy, you like the sparkly signs."

"Daddy loves sparkles, Delaney-bug." Grayson smiled and kissed her cheek, gathering us all tightly together. "Oh, my girls. I missed you."

"I missed you, Daddy. Can we go home?" She yawned into his neck.

"It's an hour past her bed time," I explained, rubbing her back.

"Let's get her to bed," Grayson said, then leaned to my ear and whispered, "so I can get you to bed."

Oh yeah, we needed to find his bag *now*. He located the one labeled CPT MASTERS, and we headed to the car. I offered to carry Delaney, but he wouldn't hear of it.

He hefted the huge duffel over his shoulder and cradled our daughter in his other arm, careful not to crush the tulle of her skirt.

My hormones went into overdrive. There was never anything as sexy as watching Grayson being so careful with our little girl.

I buckled her into her car seat while he loaded his bag and then shut the hatch. As I passed by on the way to my side of the car, he caught me, and pressed my back against the hatch of my SUV. The August breeze lifted my skirt slightly, and he slipped his hand discreetly up the back of my thigh before he kissed me.

This kiss left me raw and wanting in two seconds flat. He took possession of my mouth, his other hand tangled in my hair and slanted over me, finding the best angle. Our mouths joined perfectly, like they hadn't spent the last nine months apart. Within a minute, I was ready to climb him in the parking lot.

"Take me home," I whispered against his mouth, and arched my hips against his raging erection.

"Yes, ma'am," he replied with another kiss. "God, I missed you, Samantha."

"Good, because I missed the hell out of you, Grayson."

We made it home in fifteen minutes. Delaney jumped out of the car and raced inside. We were slower, holding hands as we made our way down the hallway. She came back with a black sharpie. "Mommy said we had to wait until you were here."

"So she did," Grayson said, taking her hand and letting her tug him around the corner to the pantry door.

He opened it and waited for her to slip off her little ballet flats. He tickled her toes, and Delaney's laughter echoed through our home. Then he leaned her up against the door and marked a line over her head, and dated it.

"Whoa! You grew a ton while I was gone!" he exclaimed, swinging her into his arms. "What have you been eating?"

"A lot of tacos," she said with a very serious face that looked way too much like her father's. "Can you cook tomorrow?" she whispered very loudly.

"Hey!" I joked. "It's time for you to get to bed, young lady."

"Can Daddy take me?"

I nodded, and Grayson kissed my cheek before running up the steps with our daughter. She was a perfect balance of us both, with Grayson's reflexes, my sarcasm, and a stubbornness that rivaled us both.

I turned back to the door and smiled as I heard them giggle upstairs in her room. The door had come with us to Fort Rucker, then for a stint at Fort Bragg, and now was hanging again here at home in Colorado. On it were etched the tiny lines of Delaney's life, and our story.

Grayson's arms wrapped around me, and I jumped. "That was quick."

He shook his head. "You've been zoned out for about ten minutes. Where are you?"

I turned in his arms. "Here. With you."

"Good, because I need you." He swept me into his arms and carried me up the stairs to our bedroom. We waited until the door was closed and locked before our clothes hit the ground.

I damn near shredded his uniform to get him out of it, and I know I heard more than a few rips in the fabric of my dress as he took it off.

His body was even more cut, defined, and my mouth watered. "You look amazing." I sighed, running my fingertips along his abs.

"I pretty much worked out every time I wanted to jump my wife through the webcam. Hence, I worked out a *lot*. You're the sexiest woman I've ever put eyes on, Samantha Masters."

He picked me up, and words were forgotten in a flurry of hands, mouths, moans, and sighs. When we were finished, we got in the shower, and then started again. After we'd worn ourselves to the bone, and the sun began to warm the sky, I snuggled into his side. "Welcome home, baby."

He pressed a kiss to my forehead. "I'm so damn glad to be here."

I smiled and let my eyes drift shut for the hour or two of sleep we could manage before Delaney knocked on the door, content for the first time since he'd left nine months ago.

And though he'd been the one halfway around the world, in his arms I felt like I'd finally come home, too.

ACKNOWLEDGMENTS

First and foremost, thank you so much to my Heavenly Father, who gives me strength when I have none, and heaps upon me the blessings I don't deserve.

Thank you to my husband, Jason, who inspires delicious book boyfriends because he's the kind of man fictional characters have a hard time living up to. Oh, and he makes me go to bed at two a.m. on deadline. Thank you to our children, who fuel me with kisses and hugs (while Dad fetches coffee), and make me believe in a better tomorrow. Thank you to my parents, who never doubted this crazy little path I chose. To my sister, Kate, who reads everything I write with no complaint and never hesitates to pick up the phone. My brothers, Doug, Matt, and Chris, who wouldn't think twice to bury an unknown object if I needed them to.

Thank you to my editor, Karen, for knowing my voice better than I do and allowing me to send back funny, sleep-deprived notes in the margins. There's not enough words to describe how much I freaking love you. Thank you to Jamie Bodnar Drowley, for your dedication to the Flight & Glory series, and opening that door for me! Thank you to the fabulous team at Entangled—Liz, Heather H., Heather R., Debbie, and Brittany, you ladies are simply phenomenal. Thank you to my amazing publicity team at SSFAB—Melissa, Sharon, Linda, and Jesey. You guys keep me sane, and my life wouldn't function without you. Thank you to my incredible agent, Louise Fury—I couldn't imagine a better copilot on this publishing journey.

Emily, 19 years, and you're still my best friend. Let's keep that going—it seems to work for us. Christina, Outer. Banks. Beach. House. Thank you to Lizzy Charles and Molly Lee. You girls. You're everything and you know it. Babies, boys, and books, you two are my lifelines. Linda, my squirrel-chaser extraordinaire, thank you for keeping me grounded and as organized as you possibly can. I swear, I meant to do whatever it is I forgot. But mostly, thank you for your friendship! Mindy, Fiona, Katrina, Rachel, Cindy, Melissa, thank you for your inspiration and always spot-on advice. Corinne, Rose, Mia, Christine, Kristy, Laurelin, Claire, Lauren, EK, Whitney, Pepper, Aleatha, and Alessandre, thank you for giving me a safe place to figure out this whole writing gig. My Backspace Survivors, stop trying to make the Korean food happen. It's not going to happen. Thank you to the bloggers who take their insanely valuable time to read, review, and share your friendship: Wolfel, Jillian, Allison, Alexis, Nadine, Lisa, Aesta, Vilma, Natasha, Mint, Marianne, Elbe, Book Baristas, and the countless others who are promoting authors: you astound me. My fabulous Epics, you guys rock my socks, and you know it. And the readers, you guys PM'ing me at eleven p.m. in tears over Ember, or laughing at something in the book group, you guys are what keeps me hunched over the keyboard. Thank you.

And lastly to my husband, again, because you know he only reads the first and last. You are my one constant, my anchor, my north star. Thank you for loving me.

Beyond What Is Given is an intense romance with a happy ending for Sam and Grayson. However, the story includes elements that might not be suitable for all readers. Sexual harassment, blackmail, drowning, car accidents, hospitalizations, medical treatment and procedures, paralysis, military service and deployment, and depictions of severe weather and disasters are all shown on the page or in flashbacks. Readers who may be sensitive to these elements, please take note.

*Don't miss the exciting new books
Entangled has to offer.*

Follow us!

 @EntangledPublishing

 @Entangled_Publishing

 @EntangledPub

 @EntangledPub

AMARA

an imprint of Entangled Publishing LLC